P9-CSB-311

Cat with an Emerald Eye

By Carole Nelson Douglas from Tom Doherty Associates:

MYSTERY

IRENE ADLER ADVENTURES:
Good Night, Mr. Holmes
Good Morning, Irene
Irene at Large
Irene's Last Waltz

MIDNIGHT LOUIE MYSTERIES:
Catnap
Pussyfoot
Cat on a Blue Monday
Cat in a Crimson Haze
Cat in a Diamond Dazzle
Cat with an Emerald Eye

HISTORICAL ROMANCE
Amberleigh*
Lady Rogue*
Fair Wind, Fiery Star

SCIENCE FICTION
Probe*
Counterprobe*

FANTASY

TALISWOMAN:
Cup of Clay
Seed upon the Wind

SWORD AND CIRCLET:
Keepers of Edanvant
Heir of Rengarth
Seven of Swords

*also mystery

Cat with an Emerald Eye

A MIDNIGHT LOUIE MYSTERY

Carole Nelson Douglas

A Tom Doherty Associates Book
New York

CAT WITH AN EMERALD EYE

Copyright © 1996 by Carole Nelson Douglas

This book is printed on acid-free paper.

A Forge Book
Published by Tom Doherty Associates, Inc.
175 Fifth Avenue
New York, NY 10010

Forge® is a registered trademark of Tom Doherty Associates, Inc.

Library of Congress Cataloging-in-Publication Data

Douglas, Carole Nelson.
    Cat with an emerald eye : a Midnight Louie mystery / by Carole Nelson Douglas —
1st ed.
        p.   cm.
    "A Tom Doherty Associates book."
    ISBN 0–312–86228–8 (alk. paper)
    1. Midnight Louie (Fictitious character)—Fiction.   2. Barr, Temple (Fictitious
character)—Fiction.   3. Women detectives—Nevada—Las Vegas—Fiction.
4. Cats—Nevada—Las Vegas—Fiction.   5. Las Vegas (Nev.)—Fiction.   I. Title.
PS3554.O8237C29   1996
813'.54—dc20
                                                                                    96–18277
                                                                                    CIP

First Edition: October 1996

Printed in the United States of America

0   9   8   7   6   5   4   3   2   1

For the real and original Midnight Louie:
nine lives were not enough,
as anyone who reads this book will see.

"I discovered at the age of six that almost everything in this world was phony, was done with mirrors. Since then, I've always wanted to be a magician."

—Orson Welles, 1943

Contents

8 • Contents

Cat with an Emerald Eye

A Higher Calling

I am told that most people would be happy to receive personal advice from on high.

However, I am not most people. I am not even a person.

And right now I am preparing for my annual autumn slump. This, I believe, is a universal condition. When that first October evening turns nippy, something primitive in the cells of every red-blooded critter stops dead for a moment, looks around and turns into a couch potato, or maybe a pumpkin.

Call it a genetic disposition to hibernate. Call it a seasonal disaffective disorder. Call it Ishmael. Whatever, it is one of nature's most powerful urges, and I did not get the enviable reputation I have as the primo progenitor in this town by ignoring nature's most powerful urges.

It does not matter that my hometown is Las Vegas, where virtually year-round it is hotter than the scales on the back of a skink. Of course, my closest acquaintance with a scale is in the piano bar of the Crystal Phoenix, since I came fresh from the factory with a luxuriant coat of jet-black fur. Still, there is bone and muscle under all this velvet plush, and I am old enough that a chill can creep past my barrier fuzz and into my skeleton. Come September, the nights dwindle down to a precious few degrees, like forty or fifty. Then October, November, December kick in and it really gets cold when the daylight goes on down time.

So in late October I long to dine diligently, drink deeply and then curl up someplace off the ground, where I bury my nose in my external muffler, flatten my ears to the slap-happy, insomniac uproar of Las Vegas doing business as usual and hope for a long winter's nap. Maybe I will not even blink my peepers ajar until, say, March and the IRS is threatening. (Though I am exempt from personal taxes, and that is another story.)

As far as I am concerned, from this moment on, Miss Temple can deliver meals to my feet. She can even tent a few newspapers over my head and forget about me until the cobwebs start looking like macrame plant hangers . . . and the resident spider is big enough to go to med school.

But then, as I lie there, gently napping, suddenly there comes a twitching, as of someone gently switching a tail a-dust with itching . . . powder.

Urgh! How can I describe this unnatural, burrowing feeling that comes stealing over my contented, drowsing form? Like a fly walking tippy-toe over an emery board. Like taking a sitz bath in rock salt, or getting a grain of sand between your two hardest-to-reach toes . . .

Oh, it is awful! One of my eyelids snaps open like a runaway shade letting in a fistful of daylight. I am a peaceful, twilight kind of guy. Why else would they call me Midnight Louie?

And right now I am all a-pant for shorter days and longer nights. That way my serial naps can stretch out into one long snooze. But it is not to be, not with the kind of neighbors up with which I have to put.

And I do mean up. I can feel the intangible itching powder drifting down two floors from directly above me. My left ear does the Jerk. Then my right. A buzzing as of something nasty scuzzing about the edges of my consciousness makes my right leg try to get up and walk . . . without me.

And I am having such a splendid dream, adrift with the Divine Yvette on the river Nile as it snakes through the lobby of the huge new Oasis Hotel past a cast-chrome Sphinx with Bette Davis eyes, cruising under a canopy of tall date trees . . . that are dropping co-conuts on my head, my consciousness . . . bullets and bulletins from another, less imaginative and more wakeful intelligence.

Rats! (If it only were.)

I come cold awake with a start, my patented night vision instantly focusing on the shadows of Miss Temple's living room furniture. I am tempted to waddle into the kitchen and see what there is to eat, but another nugget of unwanted knowledge crashes onto my cranium with full force.

Louie! Come here, I need you.

You and the cast of *CATS!,* I think sourly.

Do not be grumpy, I am admonished in the privacy of my own head. *You know what you must do.*

Au contraire. I know what I will not *like* to do. So, sighing in the hopes that Miss Temple will awaken in the adjoining bedroom and rush out to take me captive (dim chance), I struggle out of my contented curl on the sofa, rise, leap down to the (ugh) cold parquet, then stretch my legs and arms in turn.

("How many arms does a cat like you have?" I can hear some yahoo asking with a sneer. Two, up front, like everybody else, and two legs out back. Anyone who wishes to consider my two front limbs mere legs has not seen me open a French door lever.)

Anyway, I stretch all four of my extremities and head for the guest bathroom, which is seldom used. Even I almost never disturb the dust in the litter box Miss Temple Barr keeps under the sink. Now I leap upon that sink (yieee, cold porcelain on my delicate pads!), loft to the sill of the long, high window and wriggle through its open slit.

The night air is compress-cold and slaps my kisser back and forth a few times, especially when I take a few drags of its frosty breath and then exhale a visible stream of icy air. Ick. All my body heat is escaping into the wild black yonder of this night in the lone-some October. I jump down to the patio, up to the railing and then up again to the arching palm tree that is my private bridge between domestic coziness and urban scuzziness, between uptown bliss and downtown danger.

Now that I am roused and on the move, the battering of my brain has ceased. I pause, my built-in pitons digging into palm bark, and gaze up, toward the moon. Nearly full, its ruddy face leers down on us all like a Peeping Tom. Or like a Peeping Pumpkin, rather, given the season so soon upon us.

I shiver, or perhaps I shudder. My kind has never liked this time of year for reasons that have to do with comfort of a kind other than physical. While I thus muse, I suddenly realize that the nighttime silhouette of the Circle Ritz, which I know so well from similar evening jaunts, has developed a startling new feature.

I stare as if seeing will make it disappear, but no such luck. Something pale and wan gleams atop the railing of Miss Electra Lark's penthouse patio against the leering dark forms of topiary trees turned into nightmare grotesques. Perhaps Miss Electra has imported an albino pumpkin to her patio, and not yet carved a face into it.

Alas, no. Though the object is round enough to be a vegetable-in-waiting for a bit of seasonal surgery, it displays a trait quite alarming in a vegetable. It walks along the rail to better see the moon.

I fear that my long winter's nap is over before it has barely begun. The reclusive creature known as Karma has never seen the light of day. Anything that has pried her from sanctuary to commune with the moon like a mere dog . . . is something that I wish to know nothing about.

Louie! Do not dawdle.

Oh, my aching inner ears! To hear is to obey, but not to like it. I run along the bowed palm trunk, leap to an upper balcony and zigzag my way up the building's slick exterior. One poorly timed pounce, and I will be road kill.

Chapter 1

Magic Acts

Temple awoke, sitting up in bed.

She patted the coverlet, hunting for the warm, furry bulk of Midnight Louie.

He was gone.

She wasn't surprised.

In her dream, the big black cat had also disappeared. But the dream cat had been a massive animal, a panther sprung to life from an Art Deco design—angular, with industrial-strength musculature.

She shut her eyes, visualizing the dreamscape again.

She was the magician's assistant for Siegfried and Roy, pinioned on stage in the glare of the spotlight, while huge white lions and tigers and one black panther cavorted around her. The Big Cats posed, paws raised, on a pyramid of perches painted to resemble the tops of New York City skyscrapers. At the highest point, atop the Chrysler Building's silvery pinnacle, sat the sole black panther gleaming as if carved from Whitby jet. All the Big Cats sparkled in the light, like giant rhinestone brooches. The white tigers' stripes were aurora borealis rainbows. These bejeweled animals even out-shone Siegfried and Roy's most glitzy jumpsuits. Both magicians sported long, Elvis-thick sideburns, Siegfried's golden and Roy's panther-black.

Temple couldn't see her own outfit, since she was the dreamer, but she knew she wore the Midnight Louie Austrian-crystal shoes, and the audience was applauding her. Them.

And though everything was viewed through the bright and gleaming telescope of Dream, Temple remembered an odd ominous sense of the darkness beyond the stage lights. Feral eyes gleamed where the audience should be, untamed Big Cats waiting to pounce and take back the stage.

Then one animal on stage leaped: the black panther balanced on the Chrysler Building (which had somehow become an Art Deco step pyramid) soared through the thin, spotlit air into the den-sity of the darkness beyond.

Oh, Temple had cried in the dream. That wasn't in the script. Then the darkness coalesced into a pride of black panthers and they all crowded onto the stage, devouring the light.

A dark magician stood atop the highest perch, a man in matte black without a face. Just before the last light went out, before the only thing Temple could sense was a smothering sound of purring, she saw him wave one arm. . . .

The dream ended. She was awake, and knew it. She wished she had photographs of the gorgeous bejeweled cats, of Siegfried and Roy in Elvis sideburns. She probably should get up and write this one down, but then she could search for Freudian symbolism and that would ruin the effect.

Temple shivered. She wished Midnight Louie weren't gone. He was warm and fairly friendly and reassuringly portable. She wished she hadn't dreamed about the dark magician. She knew she wouldn't have to look too far or too Freudian to assign the real Max Kinsella an even-more-mythic role in this dream: Death.

Chapter 2

Bad Vibrissae

"Nice night," I greet Karma.

"Not really." She turns toward me, the moonlight silvering her turquoise-blue eyes in passing.

I admit that my salutation was not original, but that is no reason to turn contrary. However, I am well aware that Contrary is Miss Karma's middle moniker. I have no idea what her last name is; certainly it is not "Lark."

"I thought you did not take the night air," I go on.

"Evil intentions frisk through the dark like dust motes," she notes lugubriously.

"Yeah, the night is made for felony. Lucky for me, or I would not have a mission in life."

"And at this time of the year, evil turns blacker."

"Oh, come now! I happen to wear that much-libeled color."

"So?"

"So *I* am not so bad."

Karma is silent.

"At least you come when called," she says at last.

Before I can resent that comment, she turns tail on me—a long, bushy tail that rearranges my whiskers and tickles my nose—and plummets to the patio stones. I am expected to follow, so I do.

The French door is ajar. Once there, she gives me the flounder eye over her shoulder. Talk about cold fish! I am facing piranha on ice here.

"You will have to be silent within, and no clumsiness, Louie. I do not want Madame Electra awakened."

"Ninja is my middle name."

"Not in my address book." In she pads on her dainty white mittens and spats.

I eel through after her, only the door seems to have swung shut again, because my midsection forces it further ajar. As I pass through, the hinge gives a screech that would disconcert an owl.

"Sssst!" my guide hisses, pausing to slip a Dainty White under the French door and pull it shut.

I am sorry to report that she manages to close it without making a sound.

Not much light squeezes through the miniblinds drooping shut on every window. Even the French doors have shirred drapes over their glassed sections. You would think Miss Electra Lark was practicing something illegal up here, given the blackout curtains.

"It is I," Karma whispers suddenly.

"I already know that, and then some!"

"I mean that it is for my sake that the mistress darkens the windows and doors. I am too sensitive."

Oh, Bast! (I should not take in vain the name of my kind's most ancient goddess, but I hate these dames that act as if they are made of mother-of-pearl and you are sandpaper.)

"Louie, please! Your negative emotions and Neanderthal attitudes rub my delicate psychic vibrissae the wrong way. You did not like it when my tail ruffled your whiskers. Please consider my spectral extensions, and contain your worst intentions, even mentally."

"Huh? You are saying that you got ghost whiskers?"

I see her fangy little smirk even in the dark.

"A primitive way of putting it, but then what else could I expect from one of your background and temperament? Yes, Louie, my vibrissae are sensitive to more than the mere corporeal."

More than the mere corporeal. . . . It only takes me a minute to figure that out.

"You say you have a private line to dead things? Cannot do much for your appetite."

"My appetite has always been dainty."

That is a laugh. This babe is a long-fendered, cream-colored limo of a lady, even if her car radio is always tuned to the Spirit Channel.

"I think better without too much food," she adds. "You could do worse than to follow my example."

"No, thanks. Heretofore, I have had no wish to communicate with the hereafter, and I do not foresee that changing. So what does a highfalutin' High Priestess of Hocus-pocus want with a streetwise dude like me? Am I not simply too down-to-earth for the likes of you?"

"Indeed." She sighs. "But I cannot subject myself to outer infelicities, particularly at this hazardous time of year. I need an emissary."

"You need your furry little forehead examined! You think this is a hazardous time of year for *you?* How would you like to walk in my pads, wearing my—albeit handsome—risky catsuit every day? Popular as black cats are in holiday decorations, on the street they are bait for every sadistic kid and the occasional deranged Satanist. You should go out in *my* place these days, not vice versa."

"That lamentable bias against black may be real, Louie, but you have survived the dangers of the season for several years, though you have never confronted dangers of the spiritual sort before."

"Say you! You should know, my good feline, that I have seen the ghost of Jersey Joe Jackson on more than one occasion."

"Oh, pooh! So have some humans who are barely psychic. A kitten could spot that tired old revenant at the age of two weeks with its eyes closed! I am not speaking of benign and paltry spirits, but of those too terrible to name. I am talking of an unholy conjunction of means, motive and opportunity. I am seeing death in the cards."

"Death? Or . . . murder?"

"All death is the murder of hopes."

"All death is not against the law, not the law of this state anyway. People do it religiously every day. So all this staring at the moon and mooning about the penthouse in the dark is to say you think someone will be murdered? You could predict that every day in Las Vegas and be right."

"This will be a most . . . unnatural death."

"Are not they all? At least in my book."

"I see someone near to you involved."

"Miss Temple Barr? Another easy prediction. She has been up to her kneecaps in murder ever since I hid behind the corpse at the American Booksellers Association convention and helped her find her first body. Our association has been the same old same-old since then."

"Have you ever wondered why, Louie?"

"Why we formed our association? I got Miss Temple eating out of the palm of my pad, that is why. I saw a soft touch and I went for it. Call me manipulative, but it is a tradition with our kind."

"I know why you have come to reside at the Circle Ritz. You needed shelter." Before I can object to this humiliating review of the con job of the century, the sublime Karma goes on. "No, Louie. I was asking another question: do you know why your mistress encounters so many instances of murder?"

"For one thing, Vegas is not exactly known for a nonviolent lifestyle, at least on and around the Strip. Then, I guess that Miss Temple, being a publicist whose job it is to make clients look good, has no liking for untidy situations that attract bad publicity. Murder certainly qualifies as that. Miss Temple cannot help herself. She is a compulsive fixer-upper."

"No. The reason is you, Louie."

"Me? What do I have to do with it, other than saving Miss Temple's Bandolinos every so often, and solving the murder without ever getting any credit for my intrepid investigations? Call me the Deep Throat of catdom."

"You have always been a big eater, but it was not until you came in contact with someone whose job took her into the city's dark

heart that crime became an avocation. You are the Jinx personified, the unlucky element that brings your mistress to the razor's
edge of danger time and time again."

"Me?" I am shocked. I have always seen myself as a debonair,
happy-go-lucky charming kind of dude. Now I am told that I am no
more than an unlucky charm.

"You have an obligation to counter your unlucky influence."

"I do my own investigations, do I not?"

"Yes, but that is after the crime. Now I am asking you to antici-
pate a crime, a terrible miscarriage of justice."

"And what do I get for it?"

This relevant question the Sublime Karma ignores.

"The crime will not be obvious." Karma cocks her head and
dark-tipped ears as if listening to someone . . . someone who is not
present in the penthouse. Or, at least, someone who is not visible.

I follow the direction of her azure glance and see only the shy
dance of stray light off reflective surfaces in Miss Electra Lark's
eclectically furnished living room. There is the dull gray gleam of
the picture tube on her blond fifties television console. A more lurid
spark lights the huge green glass ball that sits atop a base formed
from some brass elephants with hemorrhoids doing the lambada.
On second thought, I am glad that I do not "see" anything. What is
said to be invisible, I think, often has good reason for that condition.

Karma is strangely silent.

Well, Karma is always strange, so I should say that now she is
more unlike herself, or anybody else for that matter. Still she
freezes in that uncanny listening position, as if someone uncanny
were nearby to do the talking.

I am getting that itchy-twitchy feeling all over again. Like all over
my toes and ears and tail.

"Okay, Karma! You got it. I am your most obedient servant. Just
cut out communing with the out-of-normal-range and tell me where
to go and what to do, and I will be out of here."

Something I said got through to her Birman brain, for she
abruptly snaps her attention back to me.

"Are you still here? Tell you where to go and what to do? That is nothing that I can help you with. You must find out these things for yourself."

Time for the *Twilight Zone* music, could I sing. Alas, I cannot, although I do hum up quite a storm on occasion.

So, bidding an unfond farewell to the resident High Priestess of this strange exotic land on the highest plateaus of the Circle Ritz, we prepare to plunge back down the black marble mountain to less rarefied spheres, knowing little more than when we came. At least it is evident that the Grand High Karma is on another plane.

Given that, I am glad that I rarely fly, but instead depend on my feet to do the stalking.

Chapter 3

Séance, MacDuff!

Temple gazed from one impassive face of the Crystal Phoenix hotel and casino to the other, searching for signs of a joke.

"I don't think my job description includes working nights. Especially to attend a . . . a high-tech haunting."

Neither Van von Rhine nor her husband, Nicky Fontana, looked as if they were kidding; as the Phoenix's manager and owner, respectively, they almost always meant business.

"You don't *have* a job description," Van noted, her smile quick and mechanical. "But I know how you feel. No one could compel me to dabble with the . . . occult, for love or money."

"I've got both," her dark-haired husband riposted, his smile both intimate and challenging.

Van von Rhine's blond satin head shook. "I can't believe that managing a hotel could come to this, but then again, I never imagined myself managing a hotel in Las Vegas. You have a right to walk out on us, Temple, or to tell us to walk off a cliff—"

"Oh, I'm not scared," Temple said. "It's just that I don't see why you'd want me to participate in this, this—"

"Hell-o-ween Haunted Homestead," Nicky supplied with a dazzling display of even, white teeth.

"Hell-o-ween Haunted Homestead," Temple repeated, hardly able to keep from gagging on the hideously unpromotable title.

"It's for charity," Van put in halfheartedly.

"And for the Phoenix, too," Nicky said, selling hard. "The Hollywood tech people who volunteer their time setting up the attraction might be perfect for our subterranean theme park. You did say you envisioned state-of-the-art effects."

"Yeah, but . . . you want me to participate in a séance on Halloween Night? To hold hands with the seriously psychic and wait for holographic hobgoblins to appear? Isn't that a bit flaky?"

Nicky sat forward on the upholstered chrome chair beside Van's crystal-topped desk. "Sure, but that's the great angle. That's why the Phoenix is sponsoring the Crystal Ball for all the haunted-house sponsors and beneficiaries afterward. High-profile hocus-pocus, Temple. The usual Las Vegas animal act with Homo sapiens in pet suits. The, uh, séance will be set smack-dab in the middle of the haunted house. Everyone who goes through can peek in."

"Oh, goody two-shoes, I'm to be a centerpiece as well as a chump."

"It's a socko publicity shtick. All the colorful psychic types between here and Hollywood getting together to do a Halloween séance to end all séances: they're going to try to bring Harry Houdini back from the dead."

"So what's new?" Temple asked. "People have been trying to do that since ought-seven or something."

"Nineteen twenty-six," Van corrected meticulously, smoothing her already slick French twist. "He was a rabbi's son, born in Budapest, did you know that?"

Temple shook her head. She did know that Van had grown up in a suite of four-star European hostelries managed by her German-born father after her American mother died.

"He really made his reputation in Europe and is still revered there," Van went on, "so I learned all about him when I was young. Shortly after Harry Houdini was born Erik Weisz in the Pest part of Budapest, the family emigrated to Appleton, Wisconsin, of all places, where Houdini grew up as Ehrich Weiss before taking his stage name. But he died in nineteen twenty-six, and quite tragically, I remember."

Nicky slid closer to the chair's seat-rim. "Yeah, but he died with a code under lock and key so that if anyone claimed he had come back from the dead, there would be a way to prove it. Think of it! The greatest escape artist of all time escaping Death itself."

Nicky's voice had become a baritone vibrato of excitement. He could have sold pickled herring to a vegetarian with that face, that voice, that air of eager certitude. Temple admired the effect, as did a riveted Van across the desk, but she knew too much to fall for sizzle when steak could be had.

"Houdini was a great escape artist, yes," Temple conceded to Nicky's salesmanship, "but that doesn't give him any special qualifications for surviving death. Escaping is an art, a technique, that requires practice, showmanship, physical agility and an audience willing to believe. I'd worry more about somebody nobody *wanted* to come back actually doing it, someone spiritually spooky like . . . oh, Rasputin, say."

"Rasputin doesn't sell in Las Vegas," Nicky said quickly. "Houdini does. Besides, if you know there's not a ghost of a chance that the dead dude would actually show up, all the better, huh? Just go along for the ride, take mental notes, watch the weird effects and let us know what you think of the people who put it together. You said you wanted the Jersey Joe Jackson Mine attraction to be a little scary. Here's a little scary in our own backyard. It should be a scream. Hey, I wish I could do it, but I've got to escort some bigwigs around here before the shindig tonight."

Temple nodded. The Crystal Ball had been her idea. Las Vegas always loved a chance to outglitz itself, and she had always felt Halloween lacked a certain élan as a holiday. Great costumes and effects, but no place really elegant to show them off except everybody's front porch.

She had designed the Crystal Ball as an adult Halloween fantasy, combining the elegant decadence of Mardi Gras with the homespun dress-up of Halloween. The hotel's Crystal ballrooms—the Lalique, Baccarat, Orrefors, Steuben and Hawkes—had been draped in a diamond dazzle of cellophane cobwebbing and spinning crystal balls, of wands and weirdery, until the rooms were a bright, interconnecting Wonderland of the fantastic and ghostly. White Witchcraft, Van had called it on first viewing the interconnected suitescape earlier that day. Temple considered ensnaring the notoriously superstitious hotel manager with a supernaturally themed event one of her biggest PR triumphs.

She was beginning to love planning events on a P. T. Barnum scale (especially with the Crystal Phoenix's money). So how could she refuse Nicky and Van's wanting her to sit in on some publicity-mongering séance that was likely to be as genuine as a sawed-in-half lady?

"All right. I usually need my beauty sleep, so participating in something that doesn't start until midnight isn't terribly thrilling, but at least I'll be awake for the big ball right after."

"Good." Van sounded relieved. "By the way, the Glory Hole boys are working as consultants at the haunted house, since their ghost-town attraction gives them a certain expertise. So you won't be friendless at the haunted house. Oh, and will your new Midnight Louie shoes arrive in time for the ball?"

"Yes, godmother."

Van smiled, not at all mechanically this time. "I'm so eager to see them! I can't imagine how anyone could get *all* of Louie on a size-five high heel."

"It isn't really Midnight Louie," Nicky explained, unnecessarily. "Just a generic black cat."

"Perfect for a Crystal Ball." Van smiled conspiratorially at Temple as she rose from her desk. "I can't wait to see what you're wearing to go with them."

"Or *who's* going with *you*," Nicky muttered to his Armani tie as he bent to pull Temple's heavy chair away from the desktop's thick blue crystal edge.

Temple flashed him a stern look while trying not to flush as red as her hair. More people in Las Vegas were speculating on her love life these days than played the dollar slots at the Goliath.

The Storm cleared its throat for a moment when she turned the ignition key in the Phoenix parking lot. Though the sun was baking down at a steady sixty-five degrees, night temperatures were growing considerably colder and Temple's bright-aqua car was getting a tad paler and a lot older. She patted the dashboard encouragingly as the engine revved, then wove through the parking-lot aisles onto the moving sheet-metal lava flow of the Las Vegas Strip.

Visions of sugar pumpkins danced in her head. Hell-o-ween Haunted Homestead. *That* wasn't her idea. Still, the haunted house had been a particularly well-run Las Vegas staple in recent years. Adding a hokey midnight séance to the attraction didn't seem like such a hot idea to her, but if Nicky and Van wanted her to play along, play along she would. Yawn. She would have had to stay up for the Crystal Ball, anyway, but now what she wore would be a concern. She couldn't wear party clothes to a séance in a house streaked with fake blood.

Nicky hadn't thought of that; men never did. And Van so disliked the séance topic that she hadn't tumbled that asking Temple to be on duty, like Cinderella, up until the very hour of the big ball ("from one to whenever A.M." was her own line in the promotion), meant she'd need more than a fairy godmother to get in ballgown gear. Maybe she could wear something over her ball outfit at the séance, like a pup tent. Except she'd probably be suspected of transporting concealed apparitions across haunted thresholds.

Temple shook her head as she drove. The situations public relations people got into! But a séance might be intriguing . . . and what was she going to wear to her very own Crystal Ball, anyway? Something that wouldn't obscure the Midnight Louie shoes yet would look a little like Good Witch Glinda. . . .

Temple was almost at the Circle Ritz when the UFO appeared in her rearview mirror at three o'clock low. Big and silver, it hovered behind her as if planning to land.

Yikes! A vampire already, and still three days to Halloween. She'd never seen the Hesketh Vampire from the front like this. The motorcycle was streamlined Mercury on wheels, its windscreen swept sharply back, its helmeted driver—rider, get with it! she admonished herself—an anonymous face behind a curve of smoked acrylic.

Max.

Max was back. Why wouldn't he take his favorite 'cycle for a spin? *Spin that I'm in . . .* Where did that line come from? "That Ol' Black Magic." Well, she was getting into the Halloween spirit anyway. Was silver magic as potent as black?

Keeping her eyes more on the rearview mirror than the familiar street, Temple steered the Storm into its regular parking spot. She let her key ring clank deep into her tote bag and wriggled out of the front seat.

The classic motorcycle had paused nearby, purring like a brushed-aluminum tiger, kept upright only by the ball of its rider's foot on the ground. Riding motorcycles was a balancing act that always made Temple uneasy, like watching a wirewalker.

The rider, who wore a navy nylon windbreaker and chinos, pushed the smoked visor upward. Temple braced herself for having words with Max.

But it wasn't Max, and for a moment that fact so disoriented her that she couldn't tell who it was, especially with the shiny pumpkin of silver helmet reducing the face to a wedge of obscured features. Not Electra's, of course, but she'd already deduced that.

The men who had attacked her in the parking garage sprang to mind with the sudden palpitation of her heartbeat. Maybe they knew Max was back and wanted to pound out another message. . . .

"What's the matter?" the rider asked.

"Matt! You scared me."

"Sorry. I guess this helmet looks a little sinister."

"What are you doing on that thing?"

The helmeted head shook. "That's what I wanted to know, but Electra insisted on dragging me over to the Our Lady of Guadalupe playground for lessons. Says I need wheels and she hardly uses these." He eyed her for a moment. "You thought I was him."

"Well, there was a fifty-fifty possibility."

"I told Electra that I didn't like the idea."

"That wouldn't change Electra's mind."

"And she said the last thing Max would want now was to be seen on anything as high-profile as this."

"True."

He turned one handle, revving the powerful motor to a faint whine protesting its inaction. "If the parishioners at Saint Rose of Lima could see me now—they always gave the parish priest a slightly used Volvo."

Temple's unease teetered on a fit of giggles. "Very practical. This isn't."

"I really feel silly."

"So would I."

"Maybe I'll get into it." He shrugged. "I could use a way of getting around, and beggars can't be choosy."

"Just lock it up good if you park it anywhere. It's a collector's item."

Matt shook his head again. "I'm not used to having things that anybody else wants."

This time the pause allowed the larger implications of that remark to cruise above their heads like buzzards. Max was there, the unseen dead body the buzzards circled, gone but not unnoticed all the same. Where was he really, anyway?

Electra's pink Probe turned into the parking area. She stuck an arm out the driver's window as she passed them, thumb up.

"All right!" she shouted.

"Solo flight," Matt explained to Temple modestly before putt-putting slowly to the shed behind the oleanders.

Adorable! Temple shook her head. Women would be taking him under their wings and giving him motorcycle lessons and . . . and dancing lessons and anything his little towheaded heart might desire from now until doomsday. So why did she resent the fact?

Electra caught up to her inside by the elevators.

"What do you think?

Temple eyed her landlady's ever-changing hair, but found nothing radically different. "About what?"

Electra shrugged and looked over her shoulder. "Letting Matt use the Vampire."

"Does he have a license?"

"He will. Quick pupil. Besides, I hate to think of the poor man making that long walk back from ConTact at three every morning now that the nights are taking a plunge."

Temple laughed.

"What? What's so funny? I'm never amusing unless I mean to be."

"Yes you are. *You* are! Electra, it's gotta be a heck of a lot colder racing home on that windjamming machine than simply walking."

"Not with the proper gear, like black leather."

"You may get Matt Devine on a motorcycle, but if you get him into black leather, I'll take you to dinner at the Hard Rock Cafe."

"Done!" Electra blinked as the elevator doors opened and they stepped in. "What makes you think he'll be so resistant to black leather?"

Temple shrugged. "Black looks harsh on blond men."

"Rules are made to be broken."

"But not by Matt. Besides, I think he's had enough black in his life."

"What's that supposed to mean?"

"That I don't have any concrete reason for thinking your Hell's Angel fantasies about Matt are doomed. Just an instinct," Temple finished with an exaggerated simper.

"You don't have instincts, you have ideas and inside information. I'll find out, you know."

"Great, let me know if you do."

Temple whisked out of the opening elevator doors on her floor.

action could be deemed polite) a stream of tobacco juice to the ground, where it added a new indignity to Crawford Buchanan's beautifully besmirched features.

"I like your aim," Temple noted. "And 'roped' is the right word."

"Bunch of hocus-smokus, if you were to ask me, which no one has so far. Me an' some of the other boys are here as consultants, but so far nobody wants any consultin'." He stood aside as Temple went through the door into the dark beyond. "These are high-tech whiz kids. Know everything. All we know is a *real* ghost town."

"Can you give me a tour?"

"Sure, but you should really do it at night to get the full effect."

"I think I will. Tomorrow." She bent to pat Three O'clock Louie's head. "What's he doing here?"

"Migrating local color," Wild Blue said dryly. "You can't exactly count on a cat to perform on schedule."

"Tell me about it."

Wild Blue led her through the usual spook-house terrain, a Frankenstein monster's birth canal of twisting corridors draped with spray-on cobwebs. There was the usual Unexpected Sudden Step Down, guaranteed to make one's stomach defy gravity. There were the traditional Concealed Mirrors to Hell, which would reflect not only whoever walked by, but the unseen grisly figure towering *behind* the unsuspecting stroller.

"It's all in the angles," Wild Blue said.

"So I've heard." Temple ducked a dangling web. When someone her height had to duck, that meant the spider-soft network would caress most people in the face. Wild Blue Pike ducked too, being a wiry, compact man, like most old-time pilots.

He led her through a tangletown of corridors, the kind of classic maze setup where the confused visitor trudges for what seems like forever, but has actually corkscrewed through a surprisingly short distance, if seen from a raven's-eye view.

Looking up, Temple noticed that the black-painted high ceilings had vanished, and that the black above them seemed seriously remote.

Chapter 4

Haunted House

Haunted-house attractions had never scared Temple. They looked too much like carnival midway sideshows. There was the usual luridly painted, cutout flat up front, with a dingy, boxy building cringing behind it.

No matter what terrifying effects were unleashed inside, Temple could never overlook the hokey outside. She felt the same way about Tunnels of Love. All those painted pastel hearts couldn't camouflage what was basically a trench of fetid water snaking through a darkened warehouse.

And this particular site, on an overgrown lot marked to spawn some massive theme hotel in the next year, looked discouragingly true to form. Old Las Vegas had been too rough and ready, and New Las Vegas too trendy, to grow a genuine haunted house naturally.

The city had no established streets now falling into disuse and lined with creepy, crumbling Victorian mansions that rambled for room after room. Temple had never heard of a ghost in Vegas except for Jersey Joe Jackson, and even his haunted hotel suite was barely fifty years old. How much evil could accrue in a mere half century? Not enough to raise goosebumps on a public used to slasher movies and horror novels that left no stage of death and decay to the imagination.

She finally dropped her key ring inside her tote bag and minced over the urban litter that drifted down the Las Vegas Strip like the autumn leaves the city so seldom saw, given the climate's year-round vegetation.

A crude wooden sign near the sidewalk announced a schedule of "hauntings" beginning ten days before Halloween. By now the "helliday" itself was only forty-eight hours away, but the busted-flat lot looked as if no one had trespassed on it in weeks.

That was the setup's spookiest part, Temple thought: seeing an essentially empty Strip lot at a time when the Good Ship Las Vegas tossed on a feverish ocean of construction, expansion and upgrade. Temple looked back through the cyclone fencing that surrounded the open space. Cabs cruised the Strip like barges plying some latter-day asphalt Nile. The monorail between Bally's and the MGM Grand whooshed by above street level like a silver bullet, or a French supertrain.

But here, inside the diamond-patterned steel wire, all was quieter than the eye of a storm. Not that it would be quiet, Temple reminded herself, when folks lined up for a tour, as they would tonight, on the hour from six P.M. until the stroke of midnight.

A dry, scraping sound at her feet made Temple jump. Looking down, she watched a dirty page of the *Las Vegas Scoop* skitter by. Crawford Buchanan's column happened to land facing up, and his face in the accompanying photo had been nicely wrinkled. Temple added to its troubles by clamping a foot down on the trash in mid-tumble. Her high heel put Buchanan's nose out of joint: a little higher and to the right. She bent to grab the page for disposal, but the gust wrenched it away. She watched it drift toward the lurid haunted-house façade, where a pile of orphaned papers huddled against the painted stone foundation.

Temple moved on, hearing her soles scrape on sandy, rock-

strewn soil. If the Midnight Louie shoes were already in her possession, she certainly wouldn't wear them over this blasted sand that could buff the sheen off indusrial steel.

Close up, the attraction façade looked like a mismating between the house-on-the-hill from *Psycho* and a funeral parlor with pretensions of Poe.

The real horror was the architectural styles blended willy-nilly. Grinning gargoyles rubbed stone shoulders with wooden Victorian gingerbread shaped into spiderwebs. Bats flew out of a silhouetted belfry covered in gray shingles, while the entrance was flanked by classical pillars, Southern-style, draped in shrouds of Spanish moss.

At this distance the quick rough strokes of the painting looked singularly unbelievable, but Temple detected a glimmer of some light-reflecting surface. A circle of ground-level spotlights were aimed at the cheesy artwork like howitzers.

No doubt by night the whole thing would light up in a lurid swirl of glow-in-the-dark colors. Everything in Las Vegas was built to shine at night.

The sound of a demented hinge squealing open made Temple gawk at the front door.

Though painted to resemble ancient wood and wide enough to admit an elephant, the airy ease of its opening belied the whole effect. Within the broadening frame lurked a figure more likely to amaze than afright.

Certainly Temple's jaw dropped.

It dropped even further when a big black cat threaded through the elderly man's slightly bowed legs.

"Howdy, Miss Barr," he said, further startling her. "You don't remember me, I bet. Wild Blue Pike from Three O'Clock Louie's out on the lake. You remember this ole black devil, though, right?"

"Three O'Clock Louie." The cat lifted its head as she greeted it. Temple saw the white hairs dusting the muzzle. Older, and maybe wiser, than her Midnight Louie.

"I'm here to see the layout before I join the Halloween séance party Thursday night."

"You git roped into that deal?" Wild Bill politely spit (if any such

"I guess you Glory Hole guys aren't overimpressed by the special effects around here," she commented.

"Nope. But the centerpiece is a corker, I'll give 'em that."

He made his comment just as they arrived at the complex web's heart. Temple's own heart paused a beat to give due honor.

She and Wild Blue gazed into the convoluted heart of darkness: a vast dim chamber the size of a Hollywood sound studio, plumbed by veins of metal scaffolding. Most of the trestles twisted like pretzels, but a core before them rose up like the shaft of a mine, perhaps forty or fifty feet.

All the scaffolding reminded Temple of the Eiffel Tower's deceptively lacy look, but the real phenomenon was what lay directly before them.

She gazed into a large room through glass windows that faintly reflected their own shapes on the opposite windows. A pale tracery suggesting spectral wallpaper overlaid the glass, so Temple had the sensation of peering through a solid wall made transparent.

The room was furnished in a style that Temple called Olde English Manor Eerie. It had served the classic black-and-white horror movies of the thirties and was revived in Hammer Films's more lurid Technicolor terrors in the sixties. Yards of glum brocade upholstered elaborately carved chairs fresh from Torquemada's Gothic torture chamber. A massive hearth large enough for a man to stand in, or perhaps to decorate a turning spit in, was surmounted by a mock-stone mantel bristling with grotesque faces and figures. Medieval weapons—battle-axes, maces and other appliances far nastier than mere dagger and sword—hung surrealistically before the window-walls.

"The whole setup is three stories," Wild Blue boasted with a pilot's love of even ground-bound height.

"We didn't go up or down."

"No, but *that* does." He pointed to the empty room. "If you kept on the right path, you'd go down, too. No stairs, except for the odd heart-stopping six-inch drop. The so-called ground-level slants up . . . and down. So you don't know how high or low you really are at any given time. But in the open middle, the roof is three stories up. And that there room goes up and down, bringing different ghosties past depending on what level you're on. And that's where the séance will be held."

"So it's a moveable feast?" Temple couldn't resist asking.

"Feast, hah! More like a famine, if you're planning on it making do for dinner. The house schedules regular shenanigans in the room, but Halloween night all you hand-holders will be going up and down like a yo-yo, but slower, so everybody gets to eavesdrop, and see the action as well."

"Oh, my queasy stomach! Talk about your mobile local color. We'll be nothing but a traveling carnival of the weird. I suppose this method makes it harder for any hanky-panky to go on."

Wild Blue shot her a slitty look through his famous Lake Mead–azure eyes. "Or easier, Miss Barr. You know what happens when the magician keeps one hand moving."

"Do I ever," she muttered.

Wild Blue Pike knew nothing of her ex-private life with the Mystifying Max, so he continued unperturbed, scratching at his shock of bleach-white hair like Will Rogers delivering a particularly down-home line. "Waal, it's a chance for the other hand to pull some pretty tricky stuff."

"Are you saying that the séance Thursday night will be rigged to provide a successful materialization?"

Wild Blue frowned and shrugged simultaneously. "Not that nobody tells us, but then they don't tell us nothin'."

Temple waited for the herd of double negatives to thunder through her head, leaving her none the wiser as to his answer.

"Just tell me yes, or no," she suggested.

"It ain't that easy. We're jest 'consultants,' here to make sure none of the works tangles up. When you're in that room, jest expect to be gawked at plenty, and keep your feet on the floor."

"That's what my mother told me when I went to my first prom."

Wild Blue's laugh was an eerie echo bouncing along the huge glass-sided room before them. "Good advice for here, too. If it gets too spooky, and that Houdini feller ambles in with his head upon a hors d'oovers tray, remember that there are a bunch of folks out back here pulling all kinds of strings and don't take it too serious like."

"Gotcha!"

Despite his own sensible advice, Wild Blue jumped.

By six that evening, Temple was standing in front of Electra Lark's penthouse door, her forefinger nailing the doorbell button to the backplate.

One invariably had to wait a geological age or so for Electra to answer her door. That made Temple, always imaginative, speculate about secret admirers being hustled out a back entrance, or tarot cards being hastily swept up and hidden away.

When the door finally opened, Temple unconsciously sniffed the air for cigar smoke or incense. What her nose picked up was . . . tuna-fish casserole in the oven.

Electra's always interesting hair was wrapped in something plastic, pink and chemical-smelling.

"Temple! Sorry I can't ask you in. I'm conditioning."

"That's okay. I just wanted to know if you could go through a haunted house with me tomorrow. It's for work, so I have passes."

"Oh, dear . . . not that Hell-o-ween House?"

"Yes."

"Sorry, kid. I'm participating in a séance there Thursday night. It would be . . . inappropriate for me to go through like a regular tourist beforehand. Might upset the spirit world, you know, to mix play-haunting with the true Beyond. It's bad enough that the local psychic society agreed to sponsor this Houdini-hunting scheme under such commercial terms. I didn't vote for it."

"You? You're going to be there, too?"

"You, too? But why?"

"Van and Nicky are holding the After-the-Fall ball at the Phoenix, and they wanted me to get some insight into subterranean attractions by sitting in."

"Séances are not an event for casual sit-ins, Temple." Electra's head shook in disapproval, spraying Temple with droplets that stung. "Only true believers should be present. I can't believe someone in our club okayed your attendance. You don't fool with Mother Ectoplasm."

"Well, I *was* thinking it would be nice to know someone there."

"Sorry if I sounded cross. I've got a wedding in forty minutes and I can't do a thing with my follicles! I'm just so upset with the constant, crass commercialization of what should be a fine and private exercise between sympathetic psyches. Promise me that you'll keep your mind open."

"And my eyes shut?"

"Oh, look for whatever you can see. Just don't be surprised if you see something you shouldn't."

"You really believe in séances?"

"Listen." Electra stepped out into the dimly lit hall, closing the door behind her.

But, Temple thought, there was no one inside to overhear her, was there? No one except Temple's fictitious gentleman caller.

Electra took Temple's hand, although her own was still gloved in pink gel.

"Listen, dear. If you're going to be present, you must be sincere. You must believe that Houdini is out there, and that he badly wants to be back here."

Temple nodded meekly. Houdini would have loved to play Vegas, if only it had existed in his time.

"You must have faith in powers greater than the normal. You must be convinced of the strength of Houdini's will when he was living, and dying, and of the gathered psychics' powerful mental presence. You must realize that—this time—unsuspected powers may unite enough to wrest aside the Veil and reveal the unthinkable. You must give death a chance!"

"Ah . . . of course. I'm always open-minded. And it would be a great story—"

"It would be earth-shaking." Electra's arm suddenly saluted the pale hall sconce as she squinted at her wristwatch. "Ten minutes! Golly, I've got to wash this gook off or my hair will come out *brown!*"

Electra scurried back into her digs like the Little Pink Hen whose falling blue sky was turning brown. Temple ambled to the elevator area on dragging heels. She certainly wasn't going through a haunted house solo, and Electra's unavailability meant Temple would have to try Plan B, which normally would have been Plan A, had Temple not been a chicken of another sort on a certain issue.

She paused in a mellow aura of hall light to squint at her own watch. Manage to dawdle any longer, and Matt would be off to work. It would be too late to ask him.

Temple vacillated between taking the poky elevator down a floor, or seizing the moment to trot downstairs and right up to the door of number eleven.

She did the latter, her forefinger pinioning the button to its mechanism before her cold feet could turn around and tippy-toe away.

This door opened much too quickly, making her jump like an eavesdropper. "Oh!"

"Temple."

Unlike Electra, who often came to her door in a state of mid-grooming, Matt Devine always looked as if he had just come from the hand of his Maker perfectly composed, washed, brushed, combed and told right from wrong.

"I know you have to go to work soon," she said, "but *my* work means I have to go to a haunted house Halloween night, and I need to go through first so I don't get any surprises. If you could go on the six o'clock tour, I could drop you at work and you'd only be a few minutes late. Electra can't go."

He smiled at her machine-gun burst of nervous explanation. "Nothing makes sense, except that you need someone to hold your hand, and you don't want to look like you're asking me out. Sounds like a haunted house is more up the other fella's alley."

"I see that I have created my own monster. Just say yes, or no."

"Sure. Sounds like fun before another night of misery monologues courtesy of Sprint phone company."

"Meet you down by my car at five-thirty?"

"I was going to suggest we take the Vampire. Appropriate transportation, given the occasion."

"My car. I'll breeze you back here in time to jet to work on the Vampire."

"Five," he answered. "We can grab a drive-through something on the way."

"That's beginning to sound like a date."

"Don't tell anybody I know." He shut the door, still smiling.

Temple retreated over the dusty mauve carpeting to the elevator. True, Max Kinsella would have been a more apt escort for her excursion, though he would have exposed all the tricks and she would have had no faith left at all by the time she sat down at the séance table.

Date! Temple snorted to herself. She hated being hamstrung between two men. She hated dates. In fact, she was so disgusted with her own uneasy social situation that if Harry Houdini had the good grace to actually show up at midnight Thursday night, she'd elope with him and be done with it!

Chapter 5

If a Body Meet a Body . . .

I love these vague assignments.

It is fairly simple to sit in a posh penthouse and declaim "the sky is falling" to one and all. It is another thing to go out into the grimy streets and find out *where* the sky is falling, on whom and how fast.

Of course, here in Las Vegas the sky seldom falls in the physical sense. The desert climate keeps us all high and dry most of the time. That is okay with me. When I lived on the streets, it was nice not have to deal with much rain, sleet and snow. I am not a postman, though I have been known to carry a message now and then.

The last time the Sublime Karma word-whipped me out onto the streets of Las Vegas on errands of a dangerous nature she was just as vague. I think she knows that this gets my goat, and relies upon my instinctive nose for the nefarious to unearth some evildoing, which she then can take credit for predicting. Though there are more things in heaven and earth than most people suspect, I have seen most of them on my travels and they are fairly ordinary evils: poverty, hunger and dirt. And the meanness of one to another, no matter the breed. Oh, and maybe Free-to-be-Feline without dressing.

Like life's little pleasures, evil also most often comes in teaspoon-size servings, though I must admit that I have become hooked on Miss Temple's occasional dollop of murder most foul. There is nothing like having a mitt in righting the ultimate wrong to feel all is correct with the world.

Murder is an interesting human concept. Among my breed, there is no such thing. There is killing, of course, to eat, and humans do it too, on a grand scale, not one-on-one so much. And they have the edge of weapons and technology. I am a bare-knuckle kind of guy; I only carry the weapons Ma Nature gave me, tooth and nail, just like any predator since Adam had a little lion.

What happened to humans I cannot say, not being an anthropologist, and, given human history, I can see why these people have developed a scientific system that studies how to make apologies for the species' horrific history of mayhem and murder. I believe it is all based on overcompensation for inadequate equipment from the species' infancy.

Have you ever really examined human teeth and nails? Pretty pathetic. Obviously, these were a bunch of weed-eaters from the git-go, destined to stand and chew and watch the clawed and fanged crowd do all the dirty work.

Then they got tired of us saber-toothed tigers getting all the glory (not to mention the gory) and invented fang and claw substitutes. They are ingenious when it comes to inflicting damage, I will say that for them, as thousands of my ancestors found out during the Mid-Evil Ages, when we served as kindling for witch hunts.

That is why I shudder to be afoot and aprowl at this superstitious time in the human calendar of events. Though these are modern times, and humans keep congratulating themselves on "knowing better," they have been doing that for millenia, and apparently still have a few geological eras to go.

Even they have the good grace to fear those of their own kind who hark back to the Bad Old Days with demented fervor and are called Satanists. I got a whiff of these throwbacks when I was investigating crimes against cats at Our Lady of Guadalupe. Poor Peter, one of a pair of convent felines (his pal was called Paul, get it?) was the victim of attempted crucifixion, the same fate almost two thousand years ago of the human for which he was named, which will prove how little the species has advanced in so long a time. Sometimes I have been accused of playing with my food, but I have never resorted to such tortuous strategies.

Hey, I need to keep up my strength to battle wrongdoing and listen to Karma channel the Great Oblivion.

So anyway, I am walking along, looking like an ordinary dude, all the while musing on life, death and the eternal verities, such as what is for supper, when something blows by that stops me in my tracks.

I stare down at a crumpled newsheet of the variety that decent men keep their families from seeing, especially when they are in Las Vegas.

Besides the odious sight of a lot of bare human of both genders—and I hope no little kits are exposed to all this abnormally furless flesh; our kind does not have much to do with anything in this state but eat it, and I always close my eyes when Miss Temple switches from day- to night-wear, as I prefer her well covered—I spy another bare-faced horror: Mr. Crawford Buchanan, who appears to have had a face-lift by an earthmover.

Still, I can glimpse a smidgen of his all-too-mortal prose and a photograph of a many-gabled and -towered edifice, a veritable Frankenstein's monster of architecture; that is to say, a mansion of many parts hacked together.

I cannot say what comes over me, but I am suddenly shaken by a sense of doom and presentiment that would knock Karma off her high horse. I know where I must go, for it is the place I am least safe: among a flock of humans celebrating Halloween by subjecting themselves to a night of programmed fright, hideous semblances and deviltry. And then they have the nerve to beg for food. Eat, drink and be nasty.

Only the mind of man would create holidays to scare his kind, as well as those of us who have become unwilling symbols of the season because of our ancient history of mass victimization, which sometimes is all too modern. I have said it before and I will say it again: only humans will sentimentalize the things they kill.

Unless, of course, it is another human.

Chapter 6

Habitat for Humane Haunting

Six o'clock of an October twilight was definitely not prime time for the Hell-o-ween Haunted Homestead.

The painted façade, lit by lukewarm spotlights and an evening sun going down in a spectacular welter of violet and orange clouds, looked like a pallid watercolor by contrast.

Temple and Matt, fresh from the innocent indulgence of a fast-food hamburger franchise, were among the first thirty customers. A kiosk that resembled a Gothic outhouse now sat ten feet from the front door. Inside, a chainsaw-massacre victim was exchanging lime-green tickets for leafy-green money.

"Looks like later is better," Matt commented. "The spotlights will really show up, and the crowds should rev up then, too. Right now the potential hauntees outside probably outnumber the possible hauntors inside."

"It doesn't look . . . lively," Temple admitted.

"That's what you get for inviting an escort who works the night shift. I could call ConTact, see if they need me there first thing," he offered.

"No. The inside lighting is the same, regardless of time." A sudden thought occurred. "You're not allergic to haunted houses, are you? They're not against your religion or something?"

"Heavens, no."

"What about *The Exorcist?*"

Matt took Temple's elbow and ushered her toward the people waiting for admission. "Sounds to me like you're the one who has reservations."

"I don't have reservations, or we wouldn't have to stop at the Horror in the Ticket Kiosk. I'm paying, by the way, or, rather, the Crystal Phoenix is."

When Temple flashed a blue pass card, a huge red-smeared hand proffered a pair of slime-green tickets.

"Thanks," she told the Abomination from the Beyond, extracting the tickets without touching the loathsome rubber extremity.

"Bfkerdiouwdanuummph," the misshapen head murmured, nodding so that its dangling eyeball did a little jig against its mushy cheekbone.

"I hope the stuff inside is a little less hokey than that," Temple whispered to Matt as they queued up. "Why does everyone think that extreme gore and walking states of decay are so scary? It's what you don't see that truly terrifies."

As he bent forward to listen, the lurid spotlights highlighted his blond hair with purple and green and put his face in a sinister, upcast light.

"Ooh, counselor, you look spooky!"

"You should see what these lights do to your red hair."

"Scary?"

"More like . . . turned brown."

"Berrown, oh, no!" Temple remembered Electra's disdain for that everyday color. "Isn't there a blond light somewhere around here?"

"Too cheery. They're shuffling in ahead."

Temple bit her lip and clasped her arms.

"Did I detect a shudder?"

"It's cold," she complained in self-defense.

But, in fact, she was happy to have company. Much as she was not about to be impressed by this homegrown effort, Temple knew that special effects were state-of-the-art nowadays, and could be more realistic than she might want.

"Hang on," Matt warned as she handed their tickets to the ghoul at the door.

He took her elbow again, just in time, because an instant later the four teenagers in front of them vanished into sudden darkness.

"How bad can it get?" Temple asked the darkness. "We're just walking a programmed maze. I've been here by daylight."

Still, shrieks erupted ahead and behind, whether from happily scared paying customers or tape-recorded actors imported to raise the fear factor, Temple couldn't tell.

"Hey!" Matt laughed as a figure whooshed toward them from the dark into sudden light, a giant bloated spider spewing creepy-crawly minispiders.

Temple couldn't keep from squeaking as a few of the spider spawn tumbled into her hair. She batted them away like autumn leaves. Bats. That's another featured creature she should expect to see and hear tonight. Ick.

Because she was slightly ahead of Matt, she was the first to step off the sudden step-down. This time she screamed, because now it was so dark, and because the spider spawn kept falling off with feathery parting gestures that gloved her forearms in goosebumps.

"You better grab my hand," Matt's calm voice counseled from the darkness above her head.

Boy, if she ever needed a helpline, it would be great to dial up a voice like that.

His hand felt warm, which meant hers was icy. This was ridiculous! If a spider on a guy wire and a six-inch drop were going to unnerve her, what would happen when the real effects made an appearance?

"Eerie light ahead," Matt warned, steering her around a corner as if he could see in the dark.

Eerie indeed, a soft pulsating blue . . . and while she was straining to see, hands closed around her neck.

att— Don't scare me!"

ot breath panted on her cheekbone. Warm, gooey liquid ooled down her neck. Spit? Did public health laws permit spitng on paying customers? Or indirectly paying customers?

A villainous voice grated in her ear. "Hello, Batgirl. Time for a transfusion."

Something pricked her neck. She would have screeched again, except a strobe light flashed on to reveal waves of red-eyed bats flying right at her. . . .

Matt jerked her out of Count Dracula's custody. The vampire himself was stepping back into the stone wall, vanishing into the solid rock, blood drooling down his chin.

Dodging a screaming surf of bats, Temple swatted at her neck. Her mopping-up operation found nothing wet except for some soft, rubbery threads that dropped to the floor.

"Why did I fall for that?" she wondered aloud. "How can they see us in the dark?"

"They're used to it, while we're being unpredictably plunged from dark to light so our eyes never adjust."

"Any spiders, bats or eye of newt still caught in my brown hair?"

"Naw."

By the strobe light Temple could see Matt grin as he dusted bat droppings—tiny black rubber balls the size of poppy seed—from his own hair before he added, "We would have to pay for classy souvenirs like that. If you catch one of those spiders, save it."

"This is all such simple stuff, but I've learned one thing."

"What?"

They were walking in the dark again, waiting for the next shock to the system.

"Fright is not about sophistication, is it?"

His hand tightened on hers. "That's a rather profound observation— Watch out!"

Where? Who? What? When—now? Arghghgh . . .

Temple tripped on an unexpected sudden step *up* and found herself scooped into a passing chair. Matt grunted as he landed beside her.

They were swept away together, into the dark, a situation that might have been romantic if their stomachs hadn't been fighting *mal de mer.*

No hand-holding here. Just grabbing for anything stable to hang on to . . . the seat-side, the floor beneath their feet, a pipe . . . no, a steel bar that held them in the open car.

"This is a *ride!*" Temple announced indignantly to the dark.

The dark echoed her, adding vibrato and a bass to a first-soprano slide that made her words into a shriek.

"Nobody mentioned an echo-mike," she added, hearing those few words expand into an eerie aria for all to hear. "Must it make me sound like I'm whining?"

It did.

"Shhh," Matt counseled sensibly from the dark.

Even though he was male, he probably wasn't as fiercely adamant as she about being in control of herself. When you're a grown woman five feet zero short, you have to fight to keep both your feet on the ground. Temple felt real anxiety. Where was she? Where was she being carried away to? When would it stop? Was there a God?

This wasn't a foxhole, but it certainly wasn't what she had expected. That alone made it a successful attraction. She would have to rethink subjecting impressionable youngsters to this kind of trauma in the Jersey Joe Jackson Hidden Mine. On the other hand, only kids could take such programmed stress and bounce back giggling for more. When did they grow up and realize that they have something more to lose than their cookies? When had that happened to her?

"You okay?" Matt sounded worried.

"Apparently. You?"

"I won't order the fried onion rings before this thing next year."

"You'd come back?"

"Sure. It's a hoot."

Temple hooted in despair and had it reverberated right back.

"What do they do if they don't get an overreacter like me?" she wondered under her breath.

"They probably run a tape of Madonna backwards."

"You know about Madonna?"

"How could I not?"

‚he a hoot, too?"

‚ence. Temple wondered whether the outerwear underwear or almost-blasphemous name gave him pause.

"I think she's a troubled soul," he said, loudly enough for the mocking sound system to pick it up and repeat it until the word "soul" rocketed off the unseen walls like spraying surf.

Wails and shrieks, laughter turned to screams came rolling in like breakers, breakers of the sound barrier. Uninhibited, the sounds sobbed and crashed. Some seemed to come from other riders; other sounds—groans, moans, cries of anguish—seemed piped in, at least Temple hoped so.

Now they were climbing the dark, their small car seeming to travel upward at a right angle.

Temple tensed her body against any surface it touched, fearful of losing this last island of solidity. Matt, she knew, was engaged in the same struggle. Only sound ricocheted around them. She began to feel sub-marine, like something that floated, steering by sound, an explorer of watery spaces.

Brightness sifted into the vastness, spotlights cut through midnight Jell-O. The cries continued, but not from their car. Something bobbled in the dark distance, fuzzy and unfocused like fog, or fireflies, or Tinkerbell on LSD.

"Hang on," Matt warned just before the phantom swooped toward them, grew into motes of shimmering rainbow light, shot out ectoplasmic limbs . . . eight of them, like Shiva, goddess of death. The head was feline, panther-black in a ruby collar.

Temple felt the soft passage of boneless limbs, saw the cat face fracture into a fang-lined maw, then reel by waving eight long black fuzzy tails like a tarantula's legs.

"Ooooh!"

They were spun around, dipped quickly enough to maroon their stomachs on an upper level, then spun fast into a cavern lit by undersea green. Skeletons danced on the water, skulls floated under the water-dappled ceiling, bony hands snagged their clothes, the car sides, then pulled away and snapped into fragments while a spectral voice promised to reveal all the secrets of the dead seas.

They plunged again, and the car was streaking through water!

Splashed by liquid again, this time quite wet and wild and genuine, Temple squealed on cue. So, from the sound effects, did every other female currently enduring the attraction.

Why didn't men scream?

Matt was an unseen stoic beside her. She had her own spirit guide along. Not as spirit, but as a person unafraid of the spiritual. Of the spooky by necessity. Of the dead and the undead. Or, at least, she thought he was beside her. . . .

Temple uncurled her fist from the steel bar hot under her grip and reached into the dark beside her.

A phosphorescent snake of mist wreathed her arm, then coiled toward her torso.

She batted it away, but now it curled around the steel bar toward the only hand that still clenched it. Hers. Matt. Where was Matt?

Ghostly faces hovered and whispered. Dank, chill breath brushed her face. Other faces loomed up from underwater beneath the car, floating like lilies on the black, mottled surface.

Swoop.

Up again, where flying monsters shrieked louder than the screams of women and children, and came onward with great, stretched talons. Temple ducked, as programmed to do, hating the knee-jerk reaction.

And then something caught her attention, and held it.

A crystal ball floating in the middle distance, encompassing a room. A normal room, though glassed in all around, like a custom railroad car. And, as the car careened closer, with normal people in it.

Maybe.

For a woman in a long gown paced before the fireplace.

A man lifted a glass of brandy to his mustached lips. Music whined from an old record on an older Victrola. A child sat on the wooden bench, turning the pages of a book much too big for its tiny hands. A dog lay on the hearth rug sleeping, floppy ears fanned on the Oriental design.

So sharp, that scene, like a play when the curtain is opened and the little world of stage set and directions begins to turn and unfold. A mystery in the making.

And she, floating toward it on mental swells of a Viennese waltz. . . .

Then the woman's face turns from the firelight, and is scarred into a mere mask of humanity. The man stands to smash his glass into the hearth . . . on goat-hoof stumps protruding from his striped trousers. The child rises, upside down, and floats up to the ceiling to float there like a jellyfish just under the surface of the sea. The book flaps its pages like wings and begins beating against the window glass, again and again. The dog . . . the dog rises as a gigantic black cat, a panther bigger than the Parthenon, powerful as a bat-winged lion, and turns around and around until screams shriek to escape the tiny world growing bigger, big enough to crush, as Temple is swept past it like Dorothy in her wind-borne house on the way to Oz.

Now she can hear and feel the rattle of the rails her car rides on, now inhale the dark smells of stone and water, now sense a straight, level shot to somewhere recognizable.

"Some ride," Matt's voice declares from the dark.

Ride. Right. Over.

The light is real, constant and unbearable.

Gruesome faces hover, leaning over to help them leave the car that was their wooden shoe through Foreverland. That's how long it felt they had been gone, out of touch, in other hands, not in command of themselves.

Matt looks . . . taken aback by the friendly ghouls pulling them forward.

Next! Hurry up, please, it's time.

Standing on shaky legs, Temple tries not to totter along the dim exit corridor, Matt behind her. It feels like leaving a mansion via the cloakroom.

Outside, night in full bloom. Now the dark is lit by millions of gaudy kilowatts and mythical beasts hover above the Strip in living color, demanding tribute and attention. Trash snakes along the dry ground. The air is cold enough to demand sweaters.

Temple breathes.

"More than you expected," Matt suggested.

She nodded. "Maybe Houdini *could* come back from the dead. Maybe I shouldn't get involved in something so . . . borderline kinky. We're supposed to do the séance in . . . that room."

"The Little Big Room from Hell?"

She nodded again. "What do you think?"

"I think it's an exercise in special effects, just as your séance will be."

"The usual hokey hocus-pocus, huh?"

"Do you know what the word 'hocus-pocus' derives from?"

"Huh? A dance: do the hocus-pocus? Really, it just sounds spooky, like heebie-jeebies, right?"

"Wrong. It comes from the Latin of the mass, a key part of the transubstantiation."

"Beg your pardon?"

"When the bread and wine are transformed into the body and blood of Christ. The priest says, or used to say in Latin the world over, 'Hoc est corpus,' repeating what Jesus told his disciples at the Last Supper. 'This is my body.' "

"How did the Latin phrase get translated into a magical formula?"

"Maybe because miracles are magic, and there were a lot of wonders in both the Old and the New Testament."

"Doesn't it bother you that something sacred was garbled into a password to something so secular?"

"No, because it happened in an Age of Belief, when the sacred and secular were not opposed, but allied. Today 'hocus-pocus' means 'piffle,' means 'fraud and foolery,' means that miracles don't happen, and Lazarus stays unrisen."

"You don't have the slightest expectation that anything uncommon could happen at this séance?"

"Only if you've got a sleight-of-hand artist present to make it happen. Theater, Temple. You say you've had experience. It's just theater."

"Like The Exorcist. Doesn't this get to you at all? This extrareligious ritual drama of challenging death? The potential for touching evil by violating whatever afterlife might be?"

He shook his head. "You don't understand. True evil always looks so ordinary." His face softened with an emotion she couldn't name. "True evil doesn't give a damn about dramatics."

Chapter 7

Could This Be Louie's Lucky Number?

It is only an hour after sundown that I lurch out of the House from Hell.

I have done my duty and reconnoitered.

And I am indeed sobered beyond belief by what I have seen and heard inside the Hell-o-ween Haunted Homestead.

What a disappointment!

First of all, despite all the advertised blood and guts, I can tell you with the certainty of one to the red claw born that mass-produced substitutes masquerade as the real thing. Fee fo fi fum, what I smell is not the blood of an Englishman but the aroma of paint tubes and polyurethane.

Granted, there is a nasty puddle area the little carts splash through in the dark, but it is only standing city water perfumed with an oily ambiance from the gears and wheels churning through it.

And I do not like the dark, vast high space that houses the maze of tracks for these open vehicles that cart the gullible public around half the attraction. Imagine, if you will, a roller-coaster framework twisted into a pretzel. I am not afraid of heights, but my climbing efforts are perilous. At any time a parade of these miserable cars packed with screeching humans may whiz by, destroying my concentration, and soon I will be hanging from a support structure by one nail—mine, not its.

As for the quality of the spirit infestation, I have eavesdropped behind the scenes. Oddities of a sort do prowl the premises. Most of the so-called horrors are unemployable teenagers who should well don masks to hide their pimple-ridden pusses. When not engaged in popping out at some unsuspecting stroller, they hang about behind the scenes, their fright masks pulled half off, smoking pungent unfiltered cigarettes that seem to have come from places farther south than Tobacco Road.

And the hubba-hubba and hullabaloo! It is enough to wake the undead. As if the piercing shrieks of startled clients were not enough, the entire place is rigged with speakers that bawl forth howls, pants, gasps, whines, bays and basso growls. One would think one was at a dog fanciers' convention. I am sorry to say that I add to the chorus when some careless visitor stomps on my extremities in the dark, which is so deep at times that even my fabled night vision is useless.

Yet this same impeccable vision is called upon to witness the impossible. I glimpse in the unseen vistas above me airy spirits rushing to and fro. My first such sighting did cause me to freeze like a Labrador retriever, one foot paused in midair. I have seen dry-ice fog and I have seen the diaphanous garments on the ladies of the Las Vegas chorus. What I spy pirouetting above me resembles both of these special effects, if they were blown from the mouth of a fairy tale's giant who was smoking swamp gas.

At first I take them for UFOs, so high above me are they. Then they float down, wreathing the little cars jerking along the twisted tracks, and I see that they are larger than they appear to me on the ground. In fact they begin to swoop and swirl from high to low and back again, causing a new epidemic of shrieking. One thread of this mist falls all the way to my level where it gathers into a mass,

takes shape and stretches until it is the granddaddy of all cats, perhaps even Kitty Kong himself. (Or herself, as I understand the case
may be nowadays.)

This creature snarls, which is duly echoed by the speakers, and
springs aloft like a constellation to stalk the cowering people in their
airborne go-carts. They scream and apparently enjoy their terror.

My own is made of subtler stuff. For the Big Cat is not real, I per-
ceive, but most realistic. I actually wonder for a moment if my kind
has an elephants' graveyard where those of us free to do so with-
draw as our lives dwindle down to the ninth one's final moments.
A place where we can sit in a circle and sing at the night without
anyone hearing. A place where large and small sniff noses and
shake whiskers, where feral and tame meet and step politely
around each other, some last great Litter's End of the rainbow.

But the fact is that our wild shadows shrink in the jungles as our
fiercest species dwindle like our lives, and their only safety is in subtle cages made to look like all outdoors. So I watch the shadow cat
pounce and play among the little mouse-cars that dart along their
zigzag tracks to no avail . . . until I realize that the Great Cat is pre-
programmed too, and will threaten but not win. And I hear again
the wretched wails of my kind, somewhere near but far, and this
gives me the shivers, for this mighty imitation is silent.

This moment is truly chilling. It is one thing to sit smugly by and
listen to humans howling like dogs, and vice versa, but when the
mellifluous feline voice is presented in scalding hysterical tones, it
hits uncomfortably close to home.

Speaking of which, that brings me to the only truly terrifying moment of my entire expedition.

I am on my way out, having concluded that Karma's utter evil is
hardly likely to haunt this frightful funhouse. If I truly wish to scare
myself out of my catsuit, I can do it more efficiently trying to cross
the Strip during rush hour.

By now my trusty sense of complicated ways and dark paths
knows the place pretty well. I pussyfoot along the place where
floor and wall meet, following the deliberately twisting corridor. I nip
past the fake Count Dracula who wears Nikes under his floor-

sweeping cape, and sweetens his breath with a spearmint spray. What is he afraid of? A little garlic-breath?

I overleap the spider-ambush niche, avoiding slipping on the collected spider droppings, which reek of rubber.

I dart around the corner and come face-to-face with . . . myself. Naturally, I growl. I do not like cheap imitations.

Then I reconsider. I might have encountered a mirror, which I have seen oddly angled here and there, the better to multiply a lurid effect.

I hiss. My mirror image hisses. I narrow my green eyes. Ditto. I arch my back in the patented Halloween position (my kind has practiced this ritual martial-art position for millenia). It matches my posture perfectly.

Knowing it to be a trick with mirrors, I turn away.

It pounces and bats my departing tail.

Since when do mirrors fight back?

I whirl like a dervish and show my incisors to the gumline. It returns the favor, showing a few back teeth missing.

Then I notice that the muzzle hair surrounding the striking white whiskers is grizzled. Is this some kind of psychic picture of Dorian Gray? Am I seeing my aged self a few years hence? Is this vision sent by an evil spirit to dishearten me?

By now my soft growls are questioning both myself and my eerie doppelgänger aloud.

"Do not talk to yourself," a growling voice admonishes. "You could be taken for a toothless old duffer."

This is a recorded message I have not yet heard in the Hell-o-ween Haunted Homestead. I sit back to regard my spitting image, which now is also turning off the fireworks.

Silence holds between us while faint howls reverberate everywhere else.

"So," myself says to me, lifting a coal-black paw to his whiskers. "Long time no see. What happened in town after you and the spitfire took off?"

"What are you doing here, Three O'Clock?" I ask in turn.

"Drafted," he says, wrinkling his muzzle. "Right color, wrong place, wrong time. The old Joes offered me up as mascot to this haunted house, so I run around and give the rats a scare."

"You talking real rats," I ask with interest, "long snouts and long, naked tails, nasty teeth?"

"Naw, more like mice. Every time the tourists spot me they shriek and beg me to not walk in front of them. As if I would. I know that is not polite. I was not raised in a barn."

"Where were you raised?"

"Inland a piece. In a tract home with those cute little swinging saloon doors into the kitchen."

"No! I have only heard of such a thing."

"Well, I am here to tell you they are real. As are sandboxes."

"Sandboxes! Outdoor public facilities every block or so? Las Vegas is surrounded by a lot of sand, but nothing as civilized as that."

"Overrated, son. And you gotta wait your turn until the kids are through churning up all that good sand and burying useless things like rubber trucks and toy soldiers in it. And then they poop in their pants. Pretty crude breed, humans. Ignorant about what to do with the dirt Bast gave them. You would not like suburbia, son. I have been there."

"So how long you been doing the haunted-house routine?"

"Too long. Pretty boring. And hard on the ears."

"What about those caterwauls? They strike me as the genuine article."

The old man shrugs and boxes his ear before giving it a good washing-out. "What was that, son? Hard to hear over all this yowling. Get a little waxy buildup now and then."

"I say, it is kind of creepy to hear the cries of one's own kind. Do you know how they obtained these recordings? It might be illegal."

"Probably is. Some people treat us like animals. My old guys are pretty decent, though, and the perks at Three O'Clock Louie's are primo. Come on out again, solo, and I will treat you to some filet and shrimp."

"What about carp?"

"Aw, I do not do much fishing anymore. Had enough of that on the open sea. At my time in life, I want someone else to do the catching, carrying and cooking for me."

"There is nothing like fresh game," I say.

"At my age, everything is a little stale."

A horrendous scream shakes the rafters, if there are any. We both look up. By the time we look down again, the old man has risen.

"You better run along now, son. It will freak my old fellas out if they see you; start thinking they are losing their sight, which they have been for years. I try to keep them from any unnecessary strain."

"Understood. Humans are fragile beasts. My Miss Temple is a very dainty lady and much in need of artful surveillance, like my distant ladyfriend, the Divine Yvette. Funny, I almost thought I heard her scream among the chorus above."

"You are working too hard, son. Take some time off. Lounge by the pool; bask in the sun. This is a resort, you know."

"I know, Dad."

It is the first time I have called him that. I think I detect a slight grin, and I am a pretty good detective.

We shake paws and go our separate ways. I am sorry that my old man has been called out of retirement to work in his old age, but no doubt it gives him a sense of usefulness that is good for the soul.

Me, I am feeling pretty useless at the moment. Snookered by that uppity Karma into a pointless journey through the usual tourist attraction. I am ready for a slow amble home, with perhaps a moonlight detour via Chef Song's carp pond at the Crystal Phoenix. These tired old pads could stand a dip in cool, carp-filled water. . . .

Soon I have slithered my way out of the old homestead and stand in the open. The spotlights ring the attraction. I can see a respectable line of suckers waiting for the next show. The suckers can also see pretty well.

"Look!" someone yells. "A black cat."

"Ooh," cries a concerned female voice, "it should not be out so near Halloween. Someone demented might try to catch it. Come here, kitty."

If there are three words in the English language that will make me run like a bat out of a Hell-o-ween Haunted Homestead, they are "come here, kitty."

I head toward the dark beyond the spotlights, but by now the one good-deed doer has become a crowd. Three or four women are coming toward me, bent over like crones, crooning "come here, kitty" with empty hands outstretched, as if I could not smell that all they have to offer is sweat.

My brisk walk becomes a trot.

"Don't let it get away!" comes the cry. "There is no telling what could happen to it alone in the dark at this time of year."

Yeah, like I could be accosted by a mob of well-meaning folk who will mess up my life and curtail my freedom. I put my ears back and my tail out and make a run for the cyclone fence.

"The gate," one yells to a confederate. "Block the gate!"

They really do not think we understand a thing. I head straight for the steel fishnet of fence, and climb it like I would a nylon stocking. I am over and fading into the natural darkness of night before they can get to the fence and set up a wail.

Karma was right about one thing: I did face true danger at the haunted house. Unfortunately, it was not from the ghostly inmates, but from the ghastly visitors outside.

I suppose the Queen of Sheba would say that counts as a reliable prediction, but in Las Vegas so does losing at gambling.

Chapter 8

Lizards and Tarantulas
and Bats, Oh My

Leaving the Hell-o-ween Haunted Homestead was like walking
out of a movie theater. The outside brightness and activity were
overwhelming after the imaginative journey in the dark.

Matt and Temple came out the innocuous side entrance into a
blaze of colored spotlights.

"Whew." Matt raised an arm to shield his eyes.

Temple, blinking, probed the depths of her tote bag for her sunglasses.

"More people lined up," Matt commented. "Better business."

She clapped the dark lenses to her face and turned to view the
painted façade. "More weird-colored lights, better illlusion." She
laughed uneasily. "Speaking of illusions, I was pretty reactive to
those cheesy effects. I must be a little worn down."

"Why not?" Matt pushed his hands in his pants pockets against
the night chill. "You've been through a lot. Almost choked to death
by a dying romance-cover model, then that dank expedition to the
Goliath for the Midnight Louie shoe—"

"You were the one who got wet!"

"I wonder how Kinsella got out of there without us seeing him, and without getting wet."

"Who said he didn't get wet? Max has done underwater escapes before, you know."

"Have you seen him since?"

"No." Temple turned away from the haunted house to eye the long stretch of empty lot to the fence.

"Neither have I."

She looked up, startled. "Why should you?"

Matt shrugged. "He seemed to enjoy inflicting himself on me."

"Why did you put up with that?"

"Because . . . he claimed he could help me find out about my stepfather."

"Maybe he can, but it'll only be because that will help Max."

"Is he that selfish?"

"Selfish? No, just a survivor. And he's had more to survive than most of us, I think."

"So are we survivors?"

"You mean . . . by nature?"

"I mean, you and I. We were starting to be we, and now—" He looked off to the fence too.

Temple sighed. Max might be absent, but he had become a fence between them just as effectively as if he had turned into interwoven steel and encircled them.

"I guess we can be whatever we truly want to be, no matter what," she said.

"But how do you *know*?"

"Instinct. Experience."

"And if you don't have any?"

She saw his point. "Hey, even with those things, it's still a struggle."

"Maybe it's for the best." Matt stared off at the fence again. He was used to fences; what he wasn't used to was freedom. "Maybe we needed a . . . time-out. I've got to concentrate on settling the issue of my stepfather: is he dead or isn't he?"

"The police aren't sure?"

"The fingerprints are different. The question is, was someone masquerading as Cliff Effinger until a few years ago, or doing it more recently? Then the question is, why the masquerade?"

"Tough questions. The police will probably have to put them in the dead-case file."

"Memory has no dead-case file. I have to know, so I'll look where and when and how I can."

"I could help you."

"I know you could. But it's something I have to do on my own, without any magical assistance. Kinsella got me thinking in some new directions, I'll give him that. I'll probably see him again too; he's right about the two casino deaths being connected. That I know. By instinct."

"See, you're getting some."

"Maybe's there hope."

What there was hope for stayed unspoken.

"Just don't hesitate to ask if I can help," she said.

He turned to her, looked down, about to say something, about to move, about to follow some instinct he maybe had never had before.

A spotlight lifted from the ground and arched toward them like a falling comet. They blinked and reared back from a nova-bright light the size of a dinnerplate that burned everything around them into anonymous darkness.

"What do you think of the protesters?" a male voice demanded from the dark. "Are they interfering with your right to have a little Halloween fun?"

"What protesters?" Matt asked.

"These people who are all for bats, rats, snakes and spiders. Haven't you seen them picketing outside the fence?"

"They weren't there when we came," Temple said, "so we have nothing to say." She grabbed the sleeve of Matt's windbreaker to pull him out of the spotlight.

"Still." The reporter's voice followed them, as did the light. "You saw the haunted house. Does it give rats, bats, snakes and spiders a bad rap? Do you believe these vermin are really our friends?"

Temple stopped to confront the following camera crew. "I believe that I would know *some* vermin with my eyes closed, and it's generally human. So, Crawford, I have no comment on those other creatures."

By now they had reached the gate. As new attraction-goers trickled in, they had to pass a marching string of men and women bearing signs.

"He'll film us anyway," Temple muttered to Matt, her low voice sinking to an irritated growl. "Just to be a pest."

So they plunged into the protesters' midst, still haloed by the blazing camera lights.

"Do you want to support the exploitation of helpless creatures?" a woman in a nylon parka asked. She lifted her cupped hands to reveal something small and furry. "Bats eat hundreds of thousands of insects, protecting our plants without chemicals. They don't deserve to be portrayed as bloodsucking sidekicks to vampires."

"Large spiders like this tarantula can live for twenty years, longer than the average domestic pet." A teenage boy held up a small glass terrarium occupied by the large desert spider known for never using Nair on its legs. "Would you want Lassie to be a figure of horror and distaste like Stella here?"

The spider's formidable legs worked against the confining glass.

"Maybe she's trying to tell us Timmie is down the well again," Temple suggested as she stared at an arachnid she'd never before seen up close and personal. "I'm sure she's an upstanding citizen and a model mother. But . . ."

"We don't want to see our friends made into monsters," the boy went on, his earnest adolescent face aimed at the camera, "just because some people are afraid to see them for what they are."

Thanks to the setup, Temple and Matt were cast as the ignorant creepy-crawly-haters. Although, Temple thought, in fact she was an ignorant creepy-crawly-avoider, if nothing else.

"I couldn't kill a fly," she added in her own defense. "And I'm sure that few people take the Halloween image of these animals seriously, any more than people really think black cats are unlucky. I happen to have a black cat—"

"Do you know where your black cat is tonight?" A man had thrust his pale, intense face into the well-lit circle.

"Well, uh . . . sometimes he gets out."

"Out?" The first woman was back, more indignant. "Letting a cat roam is bad enough, but a black cat at this time of year? Are you crazy, lady? You want some Satanist to swoop him up and do something horrible?"

"No! He isn't a cat you can swoop up easily. I mean, he's big, really big."

"What about the closet sadists who like to run over animals if they can? Who's going to see a black cat on the street?"

"I'm sure he'll be at home waiting for me. He always is."

"Until the day he doesn't come home," the woman said ominously.

The boy lifted his spider house. "Someday she won't come home and all the baby spiders will die."

"It's all right to kill things that we portray as horrible and scary," the man said. "We vilify creatures that we fear because they compete with us for something, or because they have defenses against us."

"Stop persecuting rats, bats, spiders and snakes," the woman sang out. The man and boy and other protesters joined her.

Matt and Temple stood by, silent vilifiers helpless to do anything, poor misrepresented creatures caught in a media trap with a relentless Crawford Buchanan hidden behind the camera.

Tiring, the protesters huffed off to march and shout other slogans.

"Well," came Crawford's deeply insincere baritone from beyond the hot circle of light. "Have you changed your mind about these creatures?"

"Yes, indeed," said Matt blandly. "We will definitely give them up for Lent in future."

With that they ducked past the camera crew and bustled down the sidewalk into the simple racket and bright lights of the Las Vegas Strip.

"Oh, that was . . . intolerable journalism, trapping innocent bystanders between the devil behind the camera and those well-meaning protesters. Only Crawford Buchanan would pull such a stunt, and for *Hot Heads*, the sleaziest tabloid show on TV. Looks like the worm is still working for them, our bad luck."

Matt chuckled. "Worms. They forgot to include worms among the libeled victims of Halloween. We could have sworn off eating worms for Lent too."

"That was very wicked, but do you think everybody knows what Lent is?"

"Don't you?"

"Yes, but I did a lot of reporting for a while. You sort of get a . . . a catholic overview of different religious customs."

"I think they'll get the idea," he said a bit vaguely. "Temple, I didn't finish what I was going to say back there."

"Rats."

He smiled briefly, then sobered. "I may not know where I'm going yet, or what I'm about, but I do know I'm not going to accept a position of weakness again in any situation."

"You were just a kid then."

"I'm not now. So, although I can't say what I can offer . . . anyone, or in what way, and though I need time to settle some old business before I can take on any new roles or relationship, I won't bow out just because someone else comes along and says this is the way it was or is. I won't walk away from what I believe in, no matter who says I should."

She couldn't quite believe what he was saying, though she could read in his eyes that he meant it. "You mean—?"

"Don't count me out. I've got to follow the path I started, but nothing says I've got to stay on it forever. He can't scare me away."

She nodded.

Even though it was almost Halloween, nobody she knew was much in the mood to be scared.

Chapter 9

. . . Need a Body Cry?

Temple was relieved to find Midnight Louie home alone when she got there, reclining regally on her zebra-striped coverlet, not a whisker out of place.

"Louie! I'm so glad to see you. Those protesters really had me worried."

She sat on the bed beside him, kicked off her shoes and stroked his sleek fur until his purr was droning louder than the buzz on her morning alarm.

"They do have a point, though," she told him meditatively. "Maybe I should close your bathroom-window escape hatch until Halloween is over. I don't know why I have this batty idea that you can take care of yourself. You're just a lit-tle kit-ty, after all."

Temple tried to bury her face in his neck fur, but Louie flattened his ears and tried to pull away, his purr on hold. She drew back to study his narrowed green eyes and air of deep affront. Must not like too much petting. It couldn't have been something she said.

Knowing when to leave well enough alone, she changed into her fall fuzzies, a purple velour jogging suit and knitted slippers, then skated out to the kitchen on her slippery soft soles.

Time for a postsupper snack. Temple hunted her cupboards, uninspired by anything she saw. Then she remembered her resolve and skated over the smooth parquet out the other side of the kitchen to her office. Papers fanned around the computer; she wrinkled her nose at the idea of tidying up tonight. After the stress of the haunted house, she just wanted to relax, but first . . .

She darted into the bathroom, pulled down the toilet-seat lids, climbed up on the closed seat, leaned out to reach the opposite wall, got both hands on the tiny window pulls and pushed it shut. No more Louie escapades until November!

Grunting satisfaction, she pushed herself away from the wall and clambered down from the seat. Something nagged at her, something she had forgotten to do . . . a phone call? No.

Shaking her head, she sped back to the kitchen and resumed inspecting her shelves. Still nothing called to her, and she became aware that she was humming, humming something sort of familiar. Listening to herself, Temple finally found words popping into her mind . . . *that you do so well.*

That old black magic won't work so well, she thought, when Mr. Midnight tries to make a fast escape out his favorite window. Funny she had never thought to name him Magic.

Temple stared dully at an opened box of Fruity Patooti breakfast cereal. She had forgotten something important, she knew it! Something, just now, that should have made her realize . . . something due for work . . . no. She yanked open the freezer compartment of her refrigerator, staring at a carton of six-week-old frozen yogurt. It would be a rubber ice sculpture by now. Maybe if she microwaved it . . . What was she missing? Missing. Louie. Something about the cat. No. Something about the cat's escape hatch . . . or the pathway to it. Yes!

Temple felt the tight expression of consternation on her face stretch into horrified comprehension. Holy banana fudge!

At that very moment she heard a tapping, as of someone gently rapping, rapping on the glass top of her coffee table.

She sped around the kitchen corner and took her first good look at the living room since she had come home.

Max Kinsella, dressed in cat-burglar black from neck to toe, was reclining full-length—though not regally—on her living room sofa, browsing through a copy of *Entertainment* magazine.

He looked up, lifted his knuckles to the coffee table's glass top and rapped again. "I did knock, several times, but you didn't hear me."

"You were already inside!" she charged.

He shrugged and closed an article on Halloween disguises for celebrities (that he probably could have written) before sitting upright. Luckily, the reclining Max was long enough that his feet overhung the off-white sofa edge.

"You weren't home, and I make too good a target hanging around closed doors."

"You don't have a key anymore."

A duck of his head admitted the charge. "I can get in some places without keys." He smiled. "Besides, I brought you something."

She watched him bend over and lift something from the floor. A small bag with an aluminum coating.

"You've been here a while," she suggested.

"What a detective!" He rose to hand her the bag. "I suppose you can tell just how long by checking the melting factor of the contents."

Temple hefted the bag, then rolled down the top to peek. "Oooh, caramel-pecan maple-marshmallow chocolate ripple, just the thing for a frosty October night. Too bad the manufacturer couldn't get any raspberry in there somehow."

She whisked it into the kitchen, not surprised to find that Max had followed when he lifted down a nest of glass saucers she was stretching to reach.

"So how did you figure out that I was here?" He leaned against the countertop while Temple used a serving spoon to pile colorful slabs of the low-fat frozen yogurt into two dishes. "And how did you know that I'd been here a while?"

"You won't be so smug when you find out. It's not my brilliant deducing faculties; it's one of your own unmistakable little ways."

"What? I need to know these things for future reference."

"Well, it'll only give you away to people who've lived with you. How many can that be?"

"Not many, and I'm certainly not going to give you statistics when you're holding out on me. Stop teasing, Temple."

She handed him the filled dish and a tablespoon. Neither of them bothered eating ice cream with a teaspoon.

"You fell into that eternal masculine trap. The toilet seat lids were up, *both* of them. Ergo, you were here, and long enough to use the facilities. You never did get the hang of closing it."

Max made a face not produced by the tasty caramel-pecan maple-marshmallow chocolate ripple frozen low-fat yogurt he'd just sampled. "I tried, but new habits are hard to build. Why did you suddenly rush in there anyway?"

"I remembered to close Louie's exit window. He's a house cat until Halloween is over and any crazies who don't like black cats are off the streets."

He nodded. They were standing around eating in the kitchen like they used to, as easy as pie.

"What's the occasion for the treat?" Temple wondered after her third spoonful.

"I thought your throat could use something soft and cooling."

"My throat? I haven't got a sore throat, not even a sniffle."

"Maybe not inside, but outside."

Temple shut up. Her voice still sounded raspier than usual.

"Why didn't you tell me?" he asked.

"What should I have told you?"

"That you'd nearly been throttled to death by that muscleman."

"It wasn't that close a thing."

"Then I dragged you out on that shoe-scouting expedition to the Goliath, and you never said a word."

"Near-throttlings can't hold a candle to hunting magic shoes, and besides, it was your show. So how did you do it?"

"Do what?"

"Vanish from the Goliath gondola while Matt and I were gawking at the shoe."

"Are you sure it wasn't at each other?"

"Get real, Kinsella. You're a pretty effective chaperon. So, why don't you tell?"

"Professional secret."

"Matt doesn't think you just swam away. Maybe he thinks you're like Louie, and don't like to get wet."

"Maybe he's right."

Temple shook her head. "Louie sacrificed himself in my service, and took a bath in the Treasure Island's moat. Yes! He was aboard the pirate ship, even tipped open the chest so I could see inside. He was the last man overboard."

"Mine was a disappearing act," Max admitted. "There's a service vent in the ceiling near the emergency stop panel for the gondolas. It wasn't hard to slither up and out without either of you noticing. Those crystal shoes make a pretty good distraction."

"But why didn't you hang around for the applause? You deserved it for figuring out where the shoes were, and did Electra tell you I was after them?"

Max shrugged, finished his frozen yogurt and rinsed the dish in the sink. Some domestic habits had sunk in during their cohabitation.

"I didn't want to steal the thunder of your triumphal detective work."

"And you left Matt and me alone in the Tunnel of Love. I thought you were jealous."

"Not jealous, realistic. I can't be a stable factor in your life, not now, maybe not ever. Why should I be a dog in the manger?"

"Because you can growl? And why come around Matt and offer to help him?"

"Know thine enemy? He's an interesting guy. I sense I'm missing the key to his character. He's too nice for his own good, but . . . I see darkness." He glanced at Temple with Louie-green eyes. "You could give me a clue, if you wanted to."

"If I had any right to."

"And I don't have any right to press you." Max thrust himself away from the counter like someone pushing himself from a Thanksgiving table when he has no appetite. "Temple, you can't depend on me now for anything you depended on me for previously, not even just being there."

He was leaving again, and she felt the same unreasoning panic she had felt when he had seemed to be gone for good.

"I have matters to attend to, which may never be settled," he said. "I wouldn't bother you, or your new neighbor, except that you've involved yourselves in them. Please don't anymore. I know it's not fair for me to bounce in and out of your life like a Ping-Pong ball. I'm disturbed to discover you've been risking your life. I'm here to tell you such risks aren't worth it. I did it once when I was young, and I've never been able to stop running. So. I'll try to stay away from you and yours. I'll hope you stay safe and sane from now on."

He had already eased to the door, leaving all the unanswered questions behind.

"Max!" She followed, catching him halfway out the door.

He put his fingers to his lips and shut the door as if vanishing into one of his own trick boxes. When she jerked it open a half second later, the hall was empty.

"Max?"

But he was gone, and his frozen-yogurt carton was dribbling on the countertop.

Temple went back inside and put the carton in the freezer. Then she washed the dishes and cried into the soapy water in the sink. Then she picked up one of the bowls and smashed it in the sink. As the water drained, leaving a rainbow foam of suds, she stared at the shards glittering under the overhead light.

Something told her she was not alone. She turned her head to find Midnight Louie sitting on the drainboard, staring with polite feline horror at the broken glass.

Temple fished out the surviving saucer, rinsed away the lukewarm suds and filled it with a few dollops of caramel-pecan maple-marshmallow chocolate-ripple yogurt.

"Eat up, my lad," she told him. "I'm not letting you out until I know that it's safe out there for cats, 'cuz it sure isn't for people."

Chapter 10

A Monstrous Notion

"I really feel silly," Temple said, "although that's nothing new lately."

"Nonsense, dear girl. Trust me. Muumuus cover all."

Temple turned in Electra's dimly lit entry hall, checking herself out in the mirrored vertical blinds.

A five-feet-tall woman in a floor-sweeping muumuu covered with fuchsia orchids the size of dinnerplates was indeed an outré sight.

"This is Halloween," she said finally. "Maybe they'll think I'm going as the Incredible Shrinking Woman wearing her formerly fat wardrobe."

"Just who is this 'they' you get all hot and bothered about?"

"You know, Them. Everybody else who's too cool to be caught doing something silly, like looking as if they're going trick-or-treating when they're thirty years old!"

"Thirty is nothing. And if you don't want to wear my muumuu—"

"I'll wear it!"

Electra was resplendent in one of her own tropically lively muumuus, her hair sprayed a flaming red color that Temple found disconcertingly close to her own natural hue. She bent to peer at Temple's hem.

"Are you wearing your magnificent Midnight Louie high heels under there?"

"No. They're in here." Temple patted her trusty tote bag. Tonight's licorice-black patent leather model had genuine Halloween flavor. "Too nice for tramping through the haunted house; I'll put them on at the Phoenix afterward, when I take this off for the Crystal Ball."

"Ooh, this is going to be such fun! Too bad your aunt Kit isn't here; she'd love it."

Temple wasn't at all sorry Kit wasn't present; Kit was a worse influence than Electra. "Oh," she said, peeking into Electra's dim inner rooms. "What a neat cat statue. Is it new?"

"No, old as the hills, and not a cat statue."

"I could swear . . ."

Electra rattled her boxy purse. "Got to get going. One doesn't wish to keep the spirits waiting. They might start rapping their toes without us. Might get up to some mischief. Now, shoo into the hall and I'll lock the door. . . ."

Temple shooed, then waited until Electra had secured her door, still peering inward.

"If you *have* got a cat in there, you're well advised to keep it locked up until the Halloween tricksters are history. Louie is pacing and howling, but he's confined to quarters until the streets are safe again for black cats."

"What makes you think I've got a cat? Honestly, Temple. I think your grip has slipped a bit since Max came back."

"Nothing has slipped except my patience. Men are more bother than they're worth, anyway. I imagine you figured that out with your—how many?—husbands."

"I don't believe I've ever mentioned the exact number of my past spouses, dear, and I'm not about to do a body count now. I suspect that we ladies only say men are a bother when we're bothered by them, or they're not bothering us as much as we might wish." Electra pushed her half-glasses down her nose and regarded Temple quizzically. "Who's not bothering you now?"

"Everybody except creepy Crawford Buchanan! Let's go."

But Electra remained firmly planted, an appalled look on her face.

"You have . . . objections to Crawford Buchanan?"

"Doesn't everybody?"

"Well, no. He's joining our séance tonight."

"Awful Crawford? Why?"

"He represents a television program that has done some worthwhile features on spirit phenomena before—"

"*Hot Heads* do anything worthwhile? Especially if Crawford Buchanan is involved?" An even more dreadful eventuality occurred to her. "You mean I'm going to be *filmed* in this outfit? I'm going to be *seen* by somebody besides ghosties and goblins?"

"Now calm down. Mr. Buchanan has agreed to abide by a strict set of rules. Nobody will be photographed who doesn't want to be."

"Does that apply to any spirits who drop by?"

"The camera will be discreet, so as not to spook them. Some of the most respected mediums on the West Coast are participating; they wouldn't allow anything that didn't meet their standards."

"Promise me one thing," Temple said.

"Anything, dear, within reason."

"That I won't sit next to Crawford Buchanan under any circumstances. If I'm going to be hand-holding and knee-nudging somebody, it had better not be him."

"Of course. I'll sit on one side, and we'll find somebody completely trustworthy for the other. I know or have seen most of these psychics speak, and they are so wonderful! We can't have unhappy participants and discord at that table; the spirits would refuse to come."

"If the spirits have any smarts, they'll stay miles away from Crawford Buchanan. He just may jinx your séance."

"Oh, don't say that!"

"What? Jinx?"

"Not *again*! It's vital to have a completely positive attitude when attempting to reach the spirit world. The more disorder among the

gathered mortals, the more likelihood that we could raise something . . . not so nice."

"Really?"

"Indeed. I am simply an amateur at these things, but I know
that."

"What if Houdini comes back and he doesn't like what—or
who—he sees?"

"He won't come if the atmosphere isn't right."

"It won't be," Temple predicted. "If I had a chance to come
back from the dead, and the condition was that Crawford Buchanan
would be one of the first faces I'd see, I'd take the endless sleep."

"I hope you're wrong." Electra stood still, even her hair—despite
its fortified Bloody Mary–red hue—wilting slightly. "But Karma
has been unusually agitated the past few days, and that isn't a good
sign."

"What about karma?"

Electra blinked, then spoke quickly, drawing Temple down the
hall to the elevators. "I said the karma seems agitated lately. Bad
vibes. We must meditate on the way over so we are calm. Can you
drive and meditate, Temple?"

"In my sleep," she swore.

Temple was glad she'd checked out the haunted-house site ahead
of time. She knew the best place to park, not too far from the light
thrown by the attraction. She knew just where to go, and which
ghoul to wave her pass at.

The shapeless, rubbery vision of vivisection-in-progress eyeballed
her outfit, then nodded solemn approval, shaping the huge hand
into a circled thumb in the "okay" sign.

"Rhadddikkell cahstooomb, laaahhdee," it moaned as they
passed.

"What did . . . it say?" Electra wanted to know.

"An ancient Theban password to the Minotaur."

"Really? Have you considered where Houdini might have been
all these decades, waiting for the right call back? I have an idea it
could be Atlantis!"

They were forced to wait as a lump of costumed clients clogged the door.

Temple eyed Electra. "I thought you were going to finish your award-winning romance novel proposal and submit it; *Sun City Sweet Pea*, or whatever."

"*San Antonio Sunflower*. And I am."

"You sound like you've been delving more into the paranormal than the hormonal."

"Oh, pish. I've always had a psychic streak. Goes back to my uncle Titmouse."

"Uncle Titmouse?"

"That's just what we children called him. His real name was Thaddeus, and he had some major stories about the family's occult past. Besides, the paranormal romance is all the rage. I'm thinking of adding a reborn Egyptian princess to my plot."

"In San Antonio?"

"It's warm there, and they have palm trees."

"But do they have sunflowers in Egypt?"

"I don't know. Do you think it matters?"

"Obviously not. Come on, get this line moving!"

Temple's exhortation must have worked, because thirty seconds later everyone funneled into the swallowing dark.

"We're with the séance," Electra told a seven-feet-tall Franken-stein's monster just inside the door.

He lifted a four-feet-long arm and pointed to a young woman wearing a cobweb body stocking, dewed with the occasional rhine-stone and spider.

"I'll take you ladies right up," she assured them in a solicitous voice, as if they might trip on their muumuus.

Temple clumped up the stairs behind the would-be Elvira, Mis-tress of the Dark, as Electra, Mistress of the Lark, lifted her floral hem to keep from tripping.

Temple's watch dial glowed in the dark, so she brought it close to her face. Eleven forty-five. In an hour and fifteen minutes it would all be over and she could race over to the Crystal Phoenix with Electra and tell them all about it.

Chapter 11

Home Alone . . . Not!

I am sitting in my empty condominium, lashing my tail and cursing my bowl of Free-to-be-Feline, when I feel itchy all over again.

During my street days there was never any question what feeling itchy all over meant. I had fleas all over. Now that I lead the sweet life, however, there is never a reason to itch, scratch or behave in an inelegant manner in public or in private.

So I leap up, further out of temper. Not only am I left behind and locked in, but I am infested with pests.

Then I stop, sit down and think the matter over calmly.

Where would I acquire this circus of flying fleas all of a sudden? Have I not led an exemplary life of late? Am I not a polite son, patient father and gracious, protective roommate? Who would give me fleas, the Divine Yvette? Not bloody likely.

No, what I suffer from is a flea in the ear, and this allover itch is merely a barrage of psychic nagging. So I hunch over into as tight a ball as I can make, tuck my toes under my tummy and wait.

If Karma wants my attention, she will have to cook up something a bit more spectacular than spectral itching powder.

At first I notice nothing. Then a kernel of Free-to-be-Feline pops out of my banana-split dish and rolls across the kitchen tile. This allows me to meditate upon the truly unwholesome appearance of this health food, each nugget of which resembles a dried spinach spitball. *My* saliva will not be found at the scene of this culinary crime, not unless I am abandoned here for days and forced to resort to actually eating the stuff, instead of batting it off the baseboards in a game of Ping-Pong.

When a second grungy-green nugget pings like corn before hitting the floor, I sit up and take notice. I did not know that Free-to-be-Feline offered snap, crackle and pop along with nauseatingly superb nutrition. Or could the stuff be self-destructing from the pressure of so much perfect balance?

Then again, this is Halloween.

Has a gremlin possessed the unprepossessing foodstuff, pitching it to and fro to unnerve me?

It would be ironic if Miss Temple had confined me to quarters for my own protection, and ended up locking me in with some anti-cat demon.

Whatever has gotten into the Free-to-be-Feline has one thing in common with me: it wants to be out. Each kernel pops higher, until the exploding beads almost hit the ceiling. I watch with my customary vigilance, but can detect no human intervention. When I gaze up at the white ceiling, though, wondering how Miss Temple Barr will like it with polka dots of Free-to-be-Feline splattered all over it, I view an eerie phenomenon.

The old-fashioned round fluorescent tube is glowing distinctly blue, or at least two spots of it are, and as I gaze the halo of light glows so bright that I blink.

Has a UFO landed on Miss Temple Barr's ceiling?

Are little green men coming to take all the Free-to-be-Feline back to some small green planet where they have no taste buds?

By now the light has reached spotlight intensity, illuminating every nook and cranny, including a few sheltering dustballs. I feel the hair lift all over my body and arch myself into a defensive posture.

Do not be afraid.

The disembodied voice does nothing for my composure. I spit furiously.

You know me in other form, Louis. My name is Karma. I will help you.

No one has called me Louis—and lived—since my dear departed mama. Now this alien lightball is claiming to be my upstairs neighbor, who never forsakes her digs.

"I do not need help."

So say those most in need. But it is true, although you face danger, others face greater foes and you are needed to help them.

"No can do, swamp-gas. I am a prisoner. I suggest you glow on over to some other dude's pad and play with his food."

While I watch, the light dims. Maybe I hurt its feelings. But as it cools, it takes on the image of a feline face, and one of my acquaintance. I kid you not! The apparition on Miss Temple's kitchen ceiling is the face of the Sublime Karma. Aglow with a plump Buddha-like serenity, Karma almost seems to be smiling. Though her lips do not move, I now hear her dulcet tones.

Louis, you layabout! Do not send help away. You are needed elsewhere.

"I would love to be elsewhere. Confinement does not agree with me. But I am locked in."

Are you? Sometimes we ourselves are our own prisoners.

I hate this soupy pseudophilosophical guff! But it is true that I have not yet tried to break out, so I suppose I could give it the old street-side try.

Besides, this "abandoned for days" possibility begins to gnaw at my stomach. I have not had a snack in hours. So, with a last look at Her Serene Highness on the ceiling, I rise and reconnoiter.

The more familiar a terrain, even a domestic one, the more one is likely to take it for granted. I am so accustomed to easing out the open bathroom window that I have used no other means of entrance or egress for weeks.

First I sniff along the French doors. I like their easy-opening levers, but this method requires easy-giving locks, and a few trial jump-and-pulls reveal that Miss Temple has corrected laxity in this department.

I visit the obvious, the solid mahogany front door, though I have little hope here. It was always built to hold off the Mexican army. Nevertheless, I run my sensitive pads under the door, feeling for any weakness.

Next are the bedroom windows. These are the original 1950's models, metal frames and puttied panes of glass. The only way through these babies would be "beaming" elsewhere, as on the Good Ship *Enterprise* when the crew dissolved into sparkling arrays of atoms that are reassembled in some other place.

Alas, I am far too corporeal to harbor illusions of subatomic transference, although a *Star Trek* Classic episode did feature a player of my species and color, if not gender.

While at the window in my roommate's bedroom, I stare out on the twinkling lights of the Strip that warm what passes for Las Vegas skyline with a wavering neon glow similar to nuclear meltdown in certain grade-B movies.

It is clear that mere brute force will not spring me from this well-intentioned trap. I run certain scenarios through my mind. Leaping up to the counter to eyeball the Touch-Tone phone, I picture knocking the receiver off the hook. Then I could dial out for a pizza, but once the delivery dude found the door locked, he would vanish, and there would go my snack too. I think some more. I could dial Mr. Matt Devine at work. If ConTact has caller ID, he would know Miss Temple's line was calling and, alarmed by the silence on the line, race back here to investigate, breaking into the unit and thus freeing me.

Great scenario, Louie. But . . . what if a ConTact counselor who doesn't know Miss Temple is a friend of his answers? What if ConTact does not have caller ID in order to preserve its clients' privacy? There is always 911, and a snap to punch in, too, even with these big paws of mine.

They would send someone to break in, what with Miss Electra and Miss Temple both gone. My stomach growls. I am in no mood for long leaps of logic, much less lengthy bounds through solid glass.

My only hope is the long line of French doors in the living room. The French are always most accommodating when approached in the proper fashion. I jump to the floor and patrol the perimeter, trying each door with my weight. They creak but do not crack open.

I select the middle one, and sit before it, subjecting it to my secret weapon, "The Stare." Every feline knows that if one sits before a door, and stares at it long enough, with sufficient concentration, that circumstances must eventually bow to the feline will, and someone will come along, in time, and open it.

I am hoping, however, not to have to practice "The Stare" until Miss Temple returns in the very wee hours. I realize that this is a last resort, that my Stare is out of practice and that there is not one human about to answer my needs, anyway.

Still, in desperate circumstances one relies on elder lore and magical formulas. "The Stare" has served my kind well for centuries. Perhaps it will again.

That is right, Louis! You have unthinkingly touched an ancient power. Continue to concentrate and I will soon be able to, to . . . oh, it is exhausting. Keep it up! In only another moment, I shall be in the proper position to—

My concentration wavers. Karma's instructions sound alarmingly like the usual female demands that are guaranteed to send dudes of my persuasion fleeing to the high ground.

Then I see a tiny spark twinkling on the brass lever that operates every French door I ever knew. At first I think the lever is reflecting the night-lights Miss Temple thoughtfully leaves on in every room for my convenience. Then I see that the light is too bright and that it twinkles.

Yes, Louis, yes. Another moment and I will be able to move the mechanism and the door will explode open.

It is hard to concentrate with a feline Tinkerbell tweaking the door lever in front of your very eyes. I feel an overwhelming urge to blink and run before I discover that someone is filming this interlude for a blue movie. I keep "The Stare" on at full force, though, and watch the lever swivel toward the floor as if the fuzzball of light upon it weighs a ton. Come to think of it, Karma in corporeal form is a pretty solid piece of pussycat.

The lever dips to its lowest possible level and the door pops open an inch, admitting a sliver of cool night air and the distant sounds of the city.

Aaaah!

The light snuffs out, and so does the uninvited sound system. I am alone again. I hope.

I paw the door open and edge into the cool dark, my pads shrinking at first from the chill patio stones. The full moon is beaming over the silhouette of the Circle Ritz's one, rather shabby palm tree. I do not know if the midnight hour has arrived yet, but I know where I am heading.

I leap upon the rail, inhale a lungful of dry, cold air and sail onto the palm's bent old back. Then I am running under the light of the moon, down, down into the shadows that know me as well as their darkest deeds. The night is mine to make of it what I will, and that will be a mad dash to the place where my lovely roommate and her landlady play with spirits. If anything like the Sublime Karma is abroad tonight, they are in for the surprise of their lives, and I must be there.

Landmarks rush by in the wind of my passing. Evil-doers everywhere, watch out! I am free again, free! Free to be feline.

Chapter 12

Temple Doesn't Give a Rap

In theatrical circles, a green room is where performers meet before the show begins.

So Temple found it appropriate that the séance cast should meet privately before gathering in the glass room to make a spectacle of themselves.

She hadn't counted, however, on the likely location of a green room in a haunted house. This one was inappropriately painted blood-red, and it served as the haunted house's staff kitchen.

Temple tried to relax while various fiends, phantoms, ghouls and demons, not to mention overtly dead people, wandered in and out munching on slices of cold pizza and guzzling cola drinks.

To watch Walking Rot nibble on long-cold sausage and pepperoni peeping greasily from under a winding sheet of congealed mozzarella was enough to turn her stomach.

No one else seemed to notice the unappetizing juxtaposition, mainly because the gathered psychics were so uninterested in anyone else besides themselves.

"I hope the séance area isn't as tawdry as the kitchen," an imperious female voice was complaining.

"You would have thought," came another woman's petulant whisper, "that the organizers would have provided some decent refreshments for *us* as well as for the resident ghouls."

"Maybe we *are* the food for the resident ghouls," a man answered with a brusque laugh.

"Don't be gruesome, Professor Mangel," another woman chided. "Houdini is hardly a ghoul."

"But wouldn't Houdini consider us little better than a motley bunch of grave-robbers?" asked a woman whose face was hidden by a mammoth picture hat—black, with veiling of the same sober hue. "Is there one of us present that he wouldn't dismiss as a rampant fraud, were he alive? What makes any of us think he'll show up in person, instead of just showing *us* up as latter-day bawds and humbugs? In life, he often went in disguise among such gatherings to get the goods on the mediums."

"We are professionals!" the first woman—whose flowing silver-gray mane of hair rivaled any hat, however dramatic—said haughtily. "We aren't even requesting remuneration for this sitting."

"Ain't that a pity?" someone muttered.

She went on unflustered. "Houdini would be in bad faith if he showed up in disguise. Besides, we are psychics. Wouldn't we sense a ringer in our midst?"

The silence that met this question proved that several psychics present harbored secret doubts about the others' abilities and intentions.

Temple whispered uneasily to Electra, "Methinks these crystal-gazers don't see much future in each other, or this séance."

"What a prime group!" Electra's admiration was oblivious. "You are gazing upon the cream of the West Coast clairvoyants."

"They look like the cousins of the Addams family, except for that woman in the denim."

"D'Arlene Hendrix. She's often assisted the police in finding dead bodies. She says she's just a housewife who senses things."

Temple no more believed in "just a housewife" than she did in messages from dead victims. But D'Arlene Hendrix sat sipping coffee from a Styrofoam cup at the large empty wooden table. In her hand-painted T-shirt and denims, she looked as normal as apple pie, her metal-framed bifocals on a pearlized string and her serviceable watchband cutting into her plump wrist.

"That one over there is Mynah Sigmund," Electra whispered as if in church.

"The 'Woman in White' act?"

Electra's wide eyes rebuked. "She says she is a white witch and can dowse for water, read health or sickness in people's auras and commune with Indian spirits. Guess I should say 'Native American' now."

Temple reevaluated the Sigmund woman in view of Electra's advertisement. She was tall, her thick cascade of silver-gray hair as sculpted as a frozen waterfall, though she was not yet forty. She wore white as if color were a curse: long, flowing gown, probably stretch polyester. Moonstones glowed in silver jewelry, an elaborate necklace and a ring-bracelet that linked the fingers of one hand to her wrist with a web of fine silver chains. Sarah Bernhardt had commissioned René Lalique to make a similar piece with a richly enameled serpent motif. Temple had often admired photos of this mock-decadent theatrical trinket. Mynah—after the black bird that spoke; could that be an original name?—needed no blatant snake designs on her jewelry. Her entire figure and its calculated presentation spoke of sinuous manipulations of both the corporeal and spectral variety, Temple thought, bet your best albino snakeskin boots!

Maybe that was why the men in the room clustered around her. Clever, Temple thought, to play upon white instead of the dramatic black. Aimée Semple McPherson, the meteoric evangelist of Harry Houdini's time, had plyed the same cynical contrast of light and darkness with spectacular success.

"Temple, I get very negative female vibes from you." Electra frowned. "You don't like Mynah Sigmund on sight."

"I don't trust her on sight; there's a difference."

"She is considered tops in her area."

"Don't doubt it. What about the short dumpy woman with the ridiculous hat?"

"Never seen her before. Must be from L.A. But the nice-looking man is Oscar Grant, the television narrator for *Dead Zones*."

"Perfect." Temple sighed dramatically, eyeing a director's dream man for the part of "A Prominent Occultist."

Oscar Grant, somewhere vague between thirty and fifty, was engaged in brushing back his curly dark hair, which tumbled to his shoulders like midnight on a roll, a dramatic white streak zigzagging like a lightning bolt from his left temple to the very ends. He wore plain black, of course, rather in the Max mode: silky black shirt, expensive noir slacks, sleek patent-leather Italian loafers that ran about six hundred dollars. A braided leather belt circled his narrow waist and a similar braided leather neckband ended with a large silver or pewter charm of cryptic design.

He was talking intensely to the dumpy but eccentric woman, whose deeply brimmed Edward Gorey hat trailed awkward bunches of veiling and black silk flowers.

She nodded, or rather the hat did. And lucky that she wore it, for glimpses showed a late-middle-aged face that was full, frowsy and far too emphatic to be considered attractive.

"What about 'mine host'?" When Electric looked blank, Temple tried to be more descriptive and had a tough time coming up with specifics. "The guy in black polyester." Electra's mystified expression remained. "The guy who shops at Big and Tall, who led us up here."

"Oh. That's Mynah's husband."

"Oh! Really, the White Witch is married to him? What does he do?"

"Nothing interesting. Works in an office somewhere. Hangs around. Mynah doesn't seem to take him seriously."

"I consider that an interesting situation. What's his name?"

A frown temporarily closed down Electra's normally open features. "You know, I don't know. It never seemed to matter."

Temple eyed the man who stood alone. For all his size both vertical and horizontal, and he must be six feet tall and three feet wide in the middle, he was astoundingly easy to overlook: medium brown hair, thinning; ordinary features, sinking in flesh; lackluster personality, flirting with an edge of depression. Yet he was the one person present, associated with the mediums, who boasted no special psychic role of his own. No wonder he looked dull and laid-back. He was probably just normal!

He certainly was a quiet contrast to a short, balding man with thick, black-framed glasses, whose karate-chop hand gestures punctuated his intense conversation with a colleague. She was a moth of a woman who might be intimidated by such emphatic delivery, a slight, fluttering presence with a receding chin, unfortunate teeth and thinning hair, a woman in gray who seemed to be turning into evasive water as one watched. She wore shifting aqua chiffon as tremulous as she was.

"Agatha Welk." Electra, following the direction of Temple's gaze, let her voice go as dreamy and warm as melted chocolate. "A wonderful, instinctive medium, but very susceptible to spiritual influences. I've heard she's had to be hospitalized twice after successful interventions in some terribly shocking cases of haunting and possession." Electra's voice lowered. "Professor Mangel there has risked his academic career in psychology to write sympathetically on the occult world. He is an observer, like us, not a practicing medium."

Temple nodded. So far, not so startling. None of those present could know that she was the . . . ex-fiancée (*such a coy, newspaper-engagement-page expression*) . . . former lover (*now that had a way-of-the-world, hard-boiled ring to it*) . . . estranged ex-roommate (*too coy again, perhaps*) . . . of a professional magician.

And Max had been just that: professional. He had never pretended that there was anything untoward to his illusions. He would despise these artsy pretenders to psychic powers.

And then the real pretender walked in the door, trailed by a cameraman hidden behind an ostentatiously flaring light.

"God," said Temple, turning away.

Electra blinked, uncertain if Temple was announcing the next player. She squinted at the new arrival. "He's just the *Hot Heads* reporter who won the special award at the romance convention for the truly terrible takeoff."

"Right. Except that I'm sure it wasn't a takeoff."

"He couldn't have *meant* that drivel?"

"You don't know Crawford Buchanan. Drivel is his livelihood.

Remember, Electra, you swore on your mother's grave—and this is the crowd that just could resurrect her—that I would not have to brush knee or knuckle with that creep in the séance seating plan."

"My mother isn't dead yet," Electra murmured distractedly. "So that is your . . . *bête noir*. Rest assured, I will see that you are well insulated from Mr. Buchanan, if that's your wish."

"Devout wish. Gosh, look at these mediums' ESP in action. Amazing how they crowd around the cameraman hoping for their proper place in the sun."

"Not D'Arlene Hendrix," Electra pointed out. "Or that strange little woman in the enormous hat. Maybe it's really Bella Abzug . . . or Dr. Ruth. You know—"

"I know. Maybe the spirits have told those two that they're not photogenic. Oh, Great Caesar's Ghost! Crawford's coming right for us."

Temple grabbed Electra's wrist, and wrung it.

In a moment a glare of several suns transfixed them in its path.

"And here we have two quite ordinary souls," Buchanan's camera-ready baritone droned, "participants but not psychics, I believe."

"Oh, no," Electra said. "I'm not at all psychic. I claim to see no more than the nose in front of my face, if I've got my glasses on."

"And the young lady?" Buchanan's disembodied voice drooled from the anonymous safety of the darkness.

Anyone pinioned by the gigawatts of a camcorder light was a deer in the headlights, trapped with no options but flight or sudden impact. Especially when she was cloaked in her landlady's most electric muumuu.

"I'm the obligatory innocent bystander," Temple said calmly. "An impartial observer."

"You don't believe in powers greater than we know?" he asked.

"Oh, yes, but I'm afraid they more often don't believe in us."

"And do you believe that Harry Houdini was such a power, that he will return from the halls of death itself tonight, at the call of these famous psychics?"

"Houdini was at no one's call in life; I doubt he'll dance to anyone's tune in death."

"But if you see him tonight, will you admit to the existence of . . . unseen forces?"

"If I see him tonight, he won't be an unseen force anymore, will he? But if I do, I'll certainly admit it. Unless he looks like a clever fake."

"And how will you know a clever fake?"

"I'll study the stills from your film. That's a form of magic with a scientific base."

"Miss Temple Barr," Buchanan's voice named her. "A very cool head for the *Hot Heads* camera, indeed. Time will tell if she remains as cool and unconvinced."

Crawford and cameraman swooped away to focus their dazzle on the White Witch, Mynah.

"You did that very well, dear," Electra chirped in Temple's ear.

"Did what?"

"Stood up to the barrage of questions under those hot lights. Your previous interrogation experience with the Las Vegas Metropolitan Police Department has stood you in good stead. Oh, my, that's redundant, isn't it? 'Stood you in good stead'?"

"Redundancy isn't going to be our problem tonight."

"What is?"

"Keeping me from strangling Crawford Buchanan and stewing him in his own juices—that is, oil."

"Don't mention murder, Temple, not even in jest! I'm just a New Age amateur, but I've had a very shivery feeling tonight."

"Shivery?"

"I . . . sense death. Maybe it's just the death of October, do you think? This is Halloween, after all. Or . . . maybe somebody famous far away will die tonight. They usually do. I mean, die far away overnight, then we read about it in the morning papers."

"Electra—"

"Or it could be an organic death, as in gardening, you know? Maybe it's a bad night for rutabaga. An amateur like me, I could be picking up anything. A star dying in the . . . ah, Stonehenge nebula, or whatever. I just have a very, very fatal feeling, but who am I to say? I'm only an aspiring romance novelist, professional justice of the peace and real estate magnate. Most of my psychic impressions I get from my cat, so it's nothing serious."

"Your cat?"

"Oh. Well, she's not exactly my cat—"

"She?"

"Well, probably. She feels like a she. I've never had the nerve to ask."

"Electra. You can't have a cat without knowing if it's a she or a he."

"You can if it demands a very dim environment, and refuses to leave even to go to a veterinarian."

"You have such a cat?"

"No. Did I say I did?"

"You implied—"

"There you go, jumping to conclusions again. How will you ever observe a séance with an open mind if it's already made up? I've got a notion to seat you next to Mr. Buchanan anyway. Now there is a man who is ready to believe absolutely anything."

"Amen."

Everyone stopped talking, then turned to look at her, as if she had muttered a profanity.

Once Buchanan and his invisible Siamese twin, the cameraman, had stepped back out of the picture, Oscar Grant took center stage, and began with a hair-toss.

"All right. A word of warning to the tyros present."

"Somebody here is Swiss?" Electra whispered to Temple.

" 'Tyro' means 'amateur.' "

"Oh. I was thinking of the Tyroleans, I guess."

"It is important that you all," he went on, gifting each person present with the hot coals of his brunet gaze in turn, "take this enterprise seriously. The professionals among us will have no difficulty, but the media and a few onlookers are warned not to interrupt the proceedings, no matter what happens. Remain quiet, calm. Allow each of your brains to be an open bay window. Relax, and the phenomena will sweep into the dusty attic of your mundane minds like beautiful, rare birds."

"And out like bats," Temple suggested under her breath to Electra.

"Bats are very mystical creatures," came the response, "sacred to the Chinese."

"So were dragons, but we don't see too many of them around today."

"Shhh!"

Mynah, the White Witch, had stepped into their midst. She bowed her dramatically silver head that reminded Temple of hippie-girl heyday haystack hairdo: parted in the middle and flowing to the fingertips.

Mynah extended her beringed hands as if following a stage direction.

"We are here on serious business, despite the frivolous nature of the setting. We are here to raise the Master. We are here to be the One Voice that can call him back from Beyond. For seventy years he has resisted all summoners. Now we call, and he will come. The world"—her dark eyes flashed to the refrigerator corner, where Crawford Buchanan's uncharacteristically dark suit was silhouetted by stark white and the camera rode over his shoulder like some unlucky star—"the world will see and we will prove that the spirit domain is a more potent realm than any imagined here on Mother Earth."

She bowed her head even lower as a tremor began in her fingers, shaking the fine silver shackles on her right hand and then her arms up to her body, until gown and moonstones and waves of sterling hair all vibrated to a trembler of silent thunder.

"Goodness," Electra murmured.

"As Mae West pointed out in one of her films, 'goodness had nothing to do with it.' That's a stage trick, Electra. Total muscular tension results in total tremor. A plus B equals—"

"Quiet now!" Oscar Grant's black-clad arms elevated. "First, I must introduce a well-known presence among us, just flown in from Machu Picchu. Edwina Mayfair."

A polite murmur indicated the familiarity of the name, though the stubby woman seemed a poor representative of such an apparently fabled personage. Oscar Grant quirked her a smile of acknowledgment before continuing. "We now will be conducted above in silence."

He nodded to the kitchen door, in which was framed the homely figure of Mynah's husband.

"Hell-o," Electra mouthed without voice.

The man nodded to her and Temple, introducing himself in a voice cursed with a perpetual frog-in-throat sound that went oddly with his overweight.

"I am William Kohler. I will conduct you. Follow me." He jerked his shaggy head over his shoulder and began to lumber up the stairs like a Russian bear in black.

The psychics flowed after him like puppets, Temple and Electra last, reluctantly so, but Crawford & Camera had refused to precede them.

"Bats!" Temple railed to Electra as they mounted the dark, narrow back steps. "I hate leaving my tote bag behind. And I *hate* having Crawford and his damn cameraman tailing my rear in this cabbage-patch dress up these stairs."

"I'm sure that's not the kind of phenomenon they're interested in filming, my dear."

Temple was not so sanguine, knowing cameramen's propensity for capturing humanity from its absolutely worst angle in the name of cinema verité. But she kept the required silence, expressing her frustration by stomping up the stairs with green-giant emphasis, so each step sounded like the ominous knock of an unseen force.

Through the thin partitions between themselves and the action attraction that comprised the haunted house, Temple could hear shrieks and rattling rails and moans.

Great mood music.

After a half flight they went along a wooden ramp until Temple glimpsed the central scaffolding, and then it was up two and a half flights of narrow, barely lit wooden stairs. Temple, hearing the gears and groans of the adjacent ride, tried to walk more softly so as not to ruin the paying customers' special effects.

At last a door opened before them, more heard (thanks to a built-in creak) than seen, so they dutifully trooped into the dark, following Kohler's harsh whisper.

"Step right this way, folks." He led them into a dim room with darkened walls. There was just enough ambient light to show his face, perspiration-sheened by the trek up three flights of stairs.

"All right. Mr. Cameraman at the end of the line, dowse that spotlight before you get to the door. Thanks. We want you folks to get set and seated first, then we crank up the lights as if you just appeared here. So follow along, end of table's fine," he told Oscar Grant, directing him to a seat. He immediately added an apology.

"The table is oval, not quite round; we couldn't get a round one that big up those stairs. And . . . there, I guess." He nodded his imperiously waiting wife to the chair on Oscar's left. "Ah, next . . . another fella. Might as well do boy-girl, boy-girl like in the movies. Professor Mangel. And you, miss, the redhead. One of the redheads, I guess." Electra sat with an airy, settling motion of her muumuu.

"Now I guess one of you media boys—"

"No!" Temple objected in the semidark. She could see what was coming with "boy-girl, boy-girl." Crawford, then her, hand in hand.

"Okay, I guess I'll sit next. And you, miss. The other redhead."

Temple complied, surprised to discover that much as she often lamented her flaming red hair, neither did she like being "the Other Redhead."

"Now, who've we got left? Mr. Cameraman? Oh, you stand. Is that right? Well, the, Mr., uh—"

"Buchanan, Crawford Buchanan," came the deep, eloquently phony tones from behind Temple.

She visibly cringed. The sheen on William Kohler's broad, corrugated forehead became dewdrops.

"Ah, the media guy should go farther along, where you can get a good view of everything."

At an oval table, in a theater-in-the-round setting, Temple thought, that doesn't make sense, but she would endorse any excuse to keep out of range of Crawford Buchanan.

Yet Mr. Mynah might not be able to pull it off. His frown deepened even as his voice clogged more. "That means, ahem, that . . . that leaves, next to Miss Temple, ah—"

"I'm afraid we've run out of boy-girl, sonny," said a fruity yet brisk voice. "Mr. Media Guy can settle on my left, if Miss Temple doesn't mind sitting next to one of her own gender—?"

"Not at all!" Temple caroled, happy to have the Hat between

her and Crawford, and hopefully his snooping cameraman.

"Well, then," the older woman's deeply assured voice continued, "that leaves D'Arlene and Agatha to hold down the fort on Oscar's left, but we still have almost perfect segregation of the sexes so the spirits have no hanky-panky among the mediums to complain of. Let us all sit and have at it."

Temple felt the air shift as Edwina Mayfair leaned toward her to say in a confidential tone, "I'm an expert at this, young lady; don't worry about a thing." A reassuring hand pat, ending in an encouraging clasp. Temple was surprised to feel thick cotton between herself and the other woman, and glanced down at the hand gloved in black that enfolded hers.

"I'm a very powerful medium," Edwina whispered. "I try to cushion my séance partners from the worst."

Temple thanked her lucky stars that someone strongly maternal sat between her and Crawford Buchanan, though being merely one body apart didn't seem quite enough when they were dealing with the disembodied.

On Electra's right, the professor cleared his throat, purely for attention. His voice rang clear and confident. "Someone must lead. I, being a neutral party, will decide. Much as Ms. Sigmund bears the respect of this entire assembly, I feel that Houdini was a man from another era, who would respond best to a masculine summoning, and Mr. Grant is perhaps our best publicized member. Hence, I have asked Mr. Grant to do the honors."

Silence held. Temple wondered how happily the woman in white took news of her reduction to a supporting role when she was dressed to deliver the crucial aria. She certainly slid Oscar Grant a poisonous glance.

But no one raised an objection.

Temple heard feet shuffle and throats clear around her, not unlike a troupe of actors awaiting the drawing of the first-act curtain, holding their places and getting ready to shine.

Then, like dawn teasing the horizon at five in the morning, a subtle light surfaced around them. It seemed too faint to detect, much less name, yet it grew. First came the glint of glass. Unlike the others, Temple perfectly understood their situation.

They were marooned on an artificial island in a vast space. They were surrounded by busy paths of programmed chaos, the moving cars of spectators. Witnesses. They themselves, the séancers, were mobile, easing up and down three stories, so they were displayed to equally mobile viewers at different times.

These few people under a bell jar were like chessmen and women on a transparent, three-dimensional *Star Trek* board placed on an invisible elevator. Up and down they would go, and where they would stop, nobody could know.

With the rising lights—sconces placed between the panes of ghostly brocade-etched glass—they were able to distinguish each other's forms across the table's empty polished wood surface. There were some confusions: the shoulder-dusting hair of both man and woman, for instance, Temple noted. She supposed that she and Electra, dressed in matching, conflicting-patterned muumuus and with their electric hair colors both natural and unnatural, looked like Tweedledee and Tweedledum on AC/DC.

Crawford in his dark suit, as faintly reflected in the opposite window glass, looked oddly nineteenth century.

And the cameraman, the only free-floating body in the room, was a lightning bug flitting at the edges of everything, ceaselessly recording, recording.

"Hands, everybody," Oscar Grant ordered.

Temple's abandoned their polite and private clasp on her lap to lift onto the table. Two others grasped them from either side, Edwina's cotton glove warm and dry from the left, William Kohler's bare hand oddly clammy from the right.

Temple had not held hands with strangers since a childhood game of ring-around-the-rosy. She discovered she suffered from a bit of xenophobia. Only reminding herself of the ignominy, of the utter disgust of holding hands with Crawford Buchanan, encouraged her to buck up.

And these strangers' hands were supposed to be conduits of unseen powers. Not the professor's though. He was another amateur. Psychically brain-dead, like her. She couldn't speak for Electra and her possibly female phantom cat. Imagine! Electra with a cat.

Maybe. One thing was for sure, Temple was learning more about Electra tonight than she had before. Now, if this trend continued with the dead . . .

Wow! She had opened herself to the spirit world, and who could say who might drop by. Suddenly, Temple realized that she "knew" a lot more dead people than she had before. There was Chester Royal, who might drop in to admonish her for falling on his last, best suit of clothes at the ABA. Or the poor cat lady might come calling through, hunting her dispersed charges. Or the stripteasing Gold Dust Twins, manifesting themselves, still joined, in a cloud of golden motes . . . or (horrors!) a handsome cover-hunk, all that marbled muscle mere phantasm now, tossing his golden mane and threatening to "swoop" her into the Underworld.

Temple closed her eyes. That was the trouble with dying and going to heaven—or hell—you might actually encounter people you had known in life. Many of them, she never wanted to see again.

"Concentrate," Oscar Grant's slightly foreign voice intoned. "Free your thoughts. Open yourself to the empyrean. See all time, all space."

Temple peeked. Outside their lit crystal ball, she glimpsed distorted visages rushing by. Happy Halloweeners on the ride of a lifetime? Or tormented spirits wafted to and fro by the Afterlife?

She felt herself sinking, very slowly. Felt the room diminishing into a tiny glass globe on the stage of an indifferent and vast universe. Felt the hands upon hers thrum with unsuspected tension. Felt a . . . pricking of her thumbs. Something wicked this way comes—

No!

Her hands were simply going to sleep from the unaccustomed pressure. How could she tell her séance-mates that she was just a computer-age baby prone to carpal tunnel syndrome . . . ?

Tunnel.

Rabbit hole.

She was going down and down, and the late little white rabbit was a black cat in an emerald collar. The Queen of Diamonds wore swords for a crown, and the caterpillar sported a hookah pipe that blew rainbow bubbles and a hat made of cabbage roses that sang. . . .

"Don't worry," said an unfamiliar voice. "Hang on. The spirits are miffed tonight. We're going to have a bumpy ride."

And Bette Davis was the Queen of Hearts.

Chapter 13

Louie's Lucky Number Is Up

Hello. Here I am again, in my old, familiar spot.

Lucky Thirteen.

Have you ever considered that thirteen is just thirty-one spelled backwards, as in October thirty-first? That is no doubt how the association of the number thirteen with ill luck began, with All Hallows' Eve, and flying witches and furred familiars like black cats.

All a filthy lie. The only witch I have ever associated with was the stuffed one in *The Wizard of Oz* exhibit at the MGM Grand Hotel, and she was not talking (unless they turned on her recorded message). Even she was not such a bad old egg. A nose job and a wen removal would have cheered up her outlook considerably.

But now I am surrounded by witches in peaked hats, with nasty painted-on faces that would stop an hourglass in mid-dribble, some of them only three feet high. So here it is. Near midnight, and here I am on the sandy lot outside the Hell-o-ween Haunted Homestead. Inside, people are shrieking in happy terror.

This is an alien notion to me, that people would go out of their way to be scared. There is enough scary about the normal world to last a lifetime, if you ask me. I cannot imagine seeking out the paranormal to add to the toll.

Of course, to some, the extraordinary is glamorous. Some might no doubt find Karma intriguing. I find her a pain in the psyche, not to mention the keister, which is generally a site unmentionable in polite circles.

Still, I am here, and she is not, and that is one of the many advantages of the purely physical state, in which I have happily disported myself for, lo, these many years. (Although some would seem to be intent on taking away my happy disportment and replacing it with the usual boredom, responsibility and male-pattern hair loss.)

Certainly Miss Temple Barr has not assured me a stress-free life by blocking my only means of slipping out to sniff the poppies now and then. I am miffed enough that I would not trouble myself to worry about what is happening to her in the programmed chaos within, were I not such a sterling fellow.

I recall my last visit to this site in relative daylight, when I was routed by a gang of do-gooders who wished to save my soul by catching me, locking me up and no doubt practicing culturally sanctioned genital mutilations upon me, all for my own good.

But I remain free and whole, and fairly invisible if I keep out of the rainbow of spotlights targeting the grotesque façade of the Hell-o-ween Haunted Homestead. Keeping to the black side of things, I slink around to the back and wait patiently by a low-profile door. This is the service entrance, and although this is not a hotel, I know according to Feline Foundation Rules that if I wait patiently by a service door, it will eventually open to admit or release a human being who very likely carries something and will not notice me flashing by his or her legs and inside.

In due time it happens, as it always does. An open door, a jug of wine coming or going, and I am inside the House of Hard Knocks and Spectral Raps.

As you can imagine, the inhabitants are all too busy haunting or being haunted to much notice a low-lying individual like myself. I skirt what appears to be an informal kitchen, though the scent of cooling pepperoni appeals mightily to my night-chilled nose.

But duty calls, and duty rarely appears in the guise of pepperoni.

So I hoof it up the stairs, careful to tread close to the walls so my not inconsiderable weight does not add any untoward creakings to the general commotion. What a strange place this is by night, lit by the special effects! It reminds me of one of those gerbil layouts that is all interconnected tubes and erratic ups and downs. The gerbils race by in their little open cars, squealing their rodent hearts out, only they are people.

I pause to watch the fireworks beyond them, which flash on and off in the artificial night sky. I recognize some of the ugliest pugs to grace the TV screen: Frankenstein's monster, Dracula, several anonymous witches and Freddy from *A Nightmare on Elm Street*. (Now there is a guy with a mental health problem; obviously he suffers from tooth-and-nail envy, or he would not be wearing those razor-sharp gloves).

I so forget myself while I am observing the human being's quaint manner of play that I am quite startled when four talons curl into my left shoulder.

"Hssspphhht!" I say, whirling with my own shivs bared and ready for blood.

"Take it easy, boy," growls a voice I recognize in the dark. Mine papa.

"Then watch out who you surprise from behind in future, Daddio."

"Daddio. You kits nowadays have no respect. Where do you learn such terms?"

I am not about to give my own disrespectful daughter credit for my newly hip vocabulary, but I must say it is pleasant to pass the ignominy on. After all, the old man did not hang about the nursery to dote on me and my littermates, did he? As for our mama, she admitted that he had not stuck around long enough afterward to even smoke a cigarette, much less a cigar, when we wee ones arrived in a mewling six-pack a few weeks later.

I ignore his question and address more vital matters, such as territory.

"I hope you are not going to abandon your cushy retirement home on Lake Mead to crowd my action here in Vegas. We may be related, but we are not compatible."

"How could an old fellow like me give a young tom like you any competition? Unless you are falling down on the job."

"Not at all. At the moment I am following up on my roommate, who is part of the séance set somewhere upstairs."

"You do not say? I saw the superstitious ninnies trooping upstairs in a body: a sleek shaded silver rhymes-with-witch, a fancy tom with a white blaze on his head and shoulder, a fussy dude with spectacle circles around his eyes, an aging tortie-shell Easter dye-job and a petite Abysscinnamon wrapped in some sort of wallpaper. I guess there was one of those preening little blue-cream types and a no-name all-breed toting a camera. You claim any of the above?"

"What you call an Abysscinnamon. My roommate has great ginger hair, almost a flame-point. But I do not understand why she is wearing wallpaper. Usually she dresses with more regard for observers' sensibilities than that."

"Maybe she is in disguise so the spooks do not get her. Well, what are you waiting for? Better trot up the stairs about your business. I cannot leave my station here, so you are on your own, son. I am obliged to show myself and scare the spittle out of these passing people every now and then."

Three O'Clock Louie shakes his big black head. "Who ever thought I would come to making personal appearances in a spook show? But my old dudes enjoy showing me off, I guess. I am the house mascot. I even have special billing on the sign outside, along with the restaurant."

I shrug and sneak up the stairs, leaving behind my old man. I can see that I will have to face the evil Karma foresees alone.

By the time I reach the room in question, it is gone, along with the pack of psychics and Miss Temple Barr in her wallpaper wrappings.

I peer over the abyss, seeing only the black of night. The stairs end in empty space.

What a conundrum. Now that I examine my situation, it is perilous in the extreme. I am perched atop a stairway to nowhere, in the middle of a roller-coaster fretwork of careening cars filled with scared-silly people, while a light show of delusions twinkle like gruesome stars all around me.

What I do not see twinkling around me is Karma's glowing astral projection, that little piece of pussycat pixiedom I call Klinker-bell.

I am not about to slink back down and confess my impasse to my papa.

I am not about to leap into the Unknown.

I am not about to connect with the incorporeal, after all.

To quote the impudent Midnight Louise, "Bummer, pops."

Chapter 14

Whoudini Dunnit?

The glass-walled room was a true fishbowl surrounded by a dark and deep sea filled with amazing creatures who floated by to peer in.

Although the room was lit, the contrast between its own milky illumination and the dark beyond that hosted sudden flashes was very disorienting. So was the fact that the room itself wafted slowly up and down like a translucent jellyfish. Temple felt no overt movement, but could glimpse the outside flashes edging away into the unseen area above the windows. Being in the room felt a bit like sitting in a sinking cruise-ship game room, playing at spooks before everyone became one. Even the chairs aided the image: high-backed carved dark wood with scant upholstery on the arms and seats.

Mynah Sigmund spoke first, at last. "I feel a strong presence. We must reach for that. We must not be distracted by this haphazard mortal activity all around us, but only heed the deep, endless pull of a powerful soul."

"Ehrich," D'Arlene Hendrix whispered. "I hear the word Ehrich.

Is that a name? The name of someone at the table? Wait! I see him, Ehrich. A boy, a dark-haired young boy. Could that be some child on the ride outside?"

"Wonderful, D'Arlene. You are already attuned. Ehrich was Harry Houdini's true given name," Oscar Grant intoned as liturgically as a priest, and Temple ought to know, having recently attended mass. "At an early age he became captivated by magic. By sixteen he had renamed himself Houdini after the great French magician Robert-Houdin."

D'Arlene frowned, though she kept her eyes shut as if to listen better. "This boy is not French. But I do not sense the man you describe."

Temple wondered why mediums always talked without using contractions, in the overformal manner of someone who has learned English as a second language. Perhaps the dead also lost the ability to use contractions because their stiff jaws were too clumsy to articulate well.

"Death, useless death!" Mynah Sigmund said suddenly, shaking back her dramatic hair in a curling, quicksilver wave. "The cards were in confusion, the magician misled. But what willpower! He performed as usual that evening, although the pain of a bruised appendix must have been excruciating. Always the agony aimed at his center: the fist in the solar plexus, the bullet in the palm of a hand. Do you feel his pain, his will that overcame it?"

Her anguished words caused a chain reaction of hands tightening on hands around the table. Temple remained skeptical. She had hastily researched Harry Houdini via the Internet, and none of this was new to her. Everyone else present had even more pressing reasons and the luxury of much more time to do the same thing. Now they were parroting back facts of Houdini's life—and death—as if receiving them from the man himself.

Temple was tempted to put on a little act and throw some hints into the pot. Raise the ante. Mention his always-loyal wife, Bess. Maybe suggest the fatal blow was deliberate, a conspiracy by rival magicians to lay Houdini low, only it had been too successful. Murder! What a scoop for Crawford Buchanan. HOUDINI SPILLS BEANS

AT VEGAS SÉANCE! MAGICIAN DEFIES DEATH TO REVEAL HE WAS MURDERED SEVENTY YEARS AGO!

But it hadn't been anything sensational like murder. Houdini the magician often used the prowess of Houdini the athlete to confound the public and buttress his carefully built reputation as a mighty man of almost supernatural endurance. He often invited men to punch him in the stomach, relying on tensed, well-developed muscles to shield him from the blow.

Then, in 1926, a young man hesitated to strike the famous escape artist, despite the older man's encouragement. Houdini relaxed his muscles just as the challenger belatedly decided to give Houdini his best blow, after all, following up with more for good measure. The first punches caught Houdini utterly unprotected.

He managed to cover his distress, continuing to hide it during that evening's dangerous underwater escape trick. He concealed his condition so successfully and for so long that by the time his weakness was obvious and he had been rushed to the hospital, the doctors could do nothing but watch the world's most famed magician die of acute appendicitis at age fifty-four.

Men of iron will and flexible steel bodies and solid-gold egos, Temple summed up. That's what magicians were made of behind the cool, studied stage presence that these days sometimes reached Liberace extremes of showmanship, and even swish.

Agile, athletic, determined to deceive. Temple found herself contemplating the magician's personality in light of both Houdini and Kinsella. Some, like Houdini, came to believe too much in their own powers. Hubris had killed Houdini. Professionalism to the point of martyrdom. Temple wondered how much of that occupational tendency explained Max's reserve about his past and present danger. A magician was always in command . . . of the stage, the audience, the action. The ultimate control freak. Such a man wouldn't ask for help, even when he desperately needed it. Like Houdini, he would rather die than reveal feet of ordinary clay, much less calluses and corns. Would Max?

"This is fascinating," Edwina murmured, grabbing Temple's knuckles painfully tight.

Temple snapped her attention back to the séance at hand, quite literally. This was why she was here: to observe a terrific publicity stunt firsthand (ouch!) and get ideas for the Crystal Phoenix's subterranean complex.

"Not to worry, my dear." Edwina tilted head, and hat, so the trailing veil scratched Temple's wrist. A knee nudged hers, but at least Crawford Buchanan wasn't her encroaching next-door neighbor!

"Spirits are just that," the woman went on, leaning close on a husky whisper. "Mere air, no matter how they storm and shriek. Like Tinkerbell, they die if you don't believe in them."

"But, don't you—?" This was an eminent psychic, after all.

A hand patted Temple's knee. "Remember: most spirits seen at séances are the creations of under-table manipulations."

"And the remainder?"

The woman chuckled and tilted back into her own place. "We shall see. We shall all see, indeed."

Temple wanted to see soon. She wasn't used to this nerve-racking hand-holding, and her arms were tiring from extending across the table; they had to stretch farther than anyone else's. But others felt the strain as well. Temple could detect a tremor traveling along the conjoined hands, like a message vibrating along a telegraph wire, but how much of that was mental telepathy and how much mere muscle fatigue?

One thing living with Max Kinsella had taught her: magicians were an act, period.

Psychics, however . . . the jury was still out on that, in Temple's mind.

A sudden vibration shook the table. Eyes consulted eyes, then the table shuddered again as the room lifted imperceptibly. No unworldly phenomenon, that, except the giant elevator they rode reversing gears and directions. They were edging upward now, past an ever-fresh audience on rails. Temple glimpsed pale, flying faces in the dark window-glass beyond the psychics sitting opposite her.

This entire environment had been set up as a ghost-factory, she reminded herself, from the costumed attendants to the paying customers, whose amazed faces played on the mirroring glass like rapid-transit spirit forms.

The psychics were a fairly eccentric bunch, so what tricks hid in the veils of Edwina Mayfair's hat, up Oscar Grant's theatrically full sleeves or within Mynah Sigmund's supernaturally thick head of hair?

Doves did not propagate in thin air; neither did ghosts.

"Harry Houdini!" Mynah intoned. Commanded.

"Ehrich Weiss," D'Arlene's faint voice echoed.

"Come," Oscar ordered.

The lights dimmed.

A confederate on the light board, Temple thought.

The lights flared.

An ambidextrous confederate on the light board, she revised.

A smell suddenly filled the chamber. Familiar but not yet nameable.

Everybody's heads twisted as they inhaled, trying to identify the source.

Temple, who'd written radio ad copy at one time, cross-examined her sensory memory until she could label the odor. Roast duck. Canard to the French, who most often served roast duck, as far as she knew.

Roast duck?

What did that mean? That somebody was a dead duck? Ergo, it must be Houdini?

Noses around the room lifted and sniffed. The psychics resembled a convention of blind gourmands. And now an astringent but somewhat fruity odor accompanied the olfactory entrée like a glass of good wine.

"A wine smell," Oscar diagnosed, the others nodding agreement. "A Sauternes?"

"Not with venison!" Edwina Mayfair sounded affronted by any flaws in this phantom menu. "I smell a sublime, and appropriate, Bordeaux."

Temple lifted her eyebrows as the others chimed in with Champagne, port, brandy. Everybody was smelling a different wine to accompany a different dish, from soup to dessert!

"Beer," Crawford Buchanan put it. "With hot pretzels."

The others stared coldly at him for having such a proletarian nose, but Temple had no time to savor the moment or the symphony of odors.

Now, what did this confusion of scents signify? Collusion among the mediums? Or a baker's dozen of spirits present, each wafting his or her favorite cooking odor in a sort of disembodied duel?

She started to giggle.

And then the lights dimmed, from the tacky crystal chandelier swaying softly above the table to the sconces mounted on the narrow pillars of solid wall between the windows.

On cue, Temple thought. First the funky smells. Then . . . ta da! . . . the ominous dimming of the lights, prefacing a—

A *manifestation!*

A boyish form hovered at one window, looking in.

Quite a little man, in fact. Perhaps five or six, with a grave, intelligent face slightly petulant. A soft black scarf was looped around his neck. He wore a suit coat and knee-length pants, reminding Temple of the Depression era's Li'l Rascals' smarter, younger brother.

He stared in at them with an odd expression, half enchantment, half boredom, as if they were both mesmerizing marionettes, and too utterly childish to believe.

"Hologram," the woman on her left whispered without moving her mouth, nudging Temple's knee.

Perhaps, perhaps not. This image was too solid to be such an airy projection. He looked more like a Lost Boy than a ghost.

And then, like a photo negative dipped in solution, he sank back into the outer darkness.

Wait! Temple wanted to shout. *Don't go away mad, little boy.* But that was the sad part. He hadn't seemed like a little boy.

"Cigar smoke," Mynah exclaimed. "Heavenly scent."

"Hideous!" Agatha Welk wrinkled her nose.

Temple smelled . . . sulphur, like the scent left behind by expired matches. Or the Devil. Was the Devil just a spoiled little boy old beyond his years looking in at them through a window? Maybe. Maybe not.

Her feet didn't quite touch the floor, as always, and her fingertips were growing numb from compression. Maybe she was developing carpal tunnel syndrome from hitting the computer keyboard too much. Maybe this stupid séance would cripple her for real work. Maybe she was getting . . . nervous.

"I see . . ." Mynah murmured, ". . . nothing."

Had there been a grandfather clock in the room, and that was one detail the designers had left out, it would have been ticking off the seconds. It would have counted a decade to each second, so that time weighed heavier than normal.

Temple tried to squint at the large-size watchface on her left wrist, but Edwina had clasped her hand so tightly that the wrist was turned toward her, not Temple. Time remained an unreadable expansion band on the white underside of her wrist, where, she remembered from some dim, teenage devouring of a palmistry book, the "bracelet" lines of her fortune lay.

Bracelets, or scars of another, less livable life? Temple shook her head. Dark thoughts circled the room, infecting them all. The seductive scents of food had given way to a strong odor of alcohol, old alcohol at the bottom of a glass, crystallizing into a sugary haze.

"Look!" Electra was staring at a window on the opposite wall.

A man filled it as a portrait would a frame, the etched brocade of phantom wallpaper tattooing his pale hands and face, his starched white shirtfront. He wore formal dress, like a Fred Astaire blow-up doll, a big man, with a wounded, brute power to his bigness. He lifted a glass to them all, a lock of curly dark hair sagging over one eyebrow like a neglected drape on a window.

The man's figure was limned all in black and white and grainy grays, like a filmed image. Temple caught her breath. She loved the old black-and-white films, their Expressionistic rainy-day distance, their glamour, their endearing decadence. Frankenstein and Dracula and Fred all lunged, slunk and danced through the black-and-white cinematic worlds of the thirties and forties. It was a time when newspaper columnists called movie actresses "cinemactresses," and magicians "mysteriarchs." It wasn't that long ago, but it was as dead as any corpse.

Was he dead too, the dignified man peering rather puzzledly at them through a window etched with wallpaper in the stippled patterns of raindrops? Or was he only an actor hired to play a holo-gram?

He seemed tall, and carried a white-tipped cane, like Fred, though he could hardly trip the light fantastic like Fred, for he was a mammoth man, broadening from his feet up and his neck down like a Russian nesting doll, only one painted in black and white and gray, instead of the usual carnival of colors.

Familiarity cloaked this figure, as if Temple had seen a black-and-white cardboard cutout of him somewhere . . . maybe at the Debbie Reynolds Hotel and Hollywood Museum. He should be standing next to a like figure of Mae West, or Ann Miller or Rita Hayworth, but he looked like a man who had stood alone most of his life.

"I'm a believer," Electra whispered from Temple's right, leaning forward to speak past William Kohler's unmoved and unmoving bulk. "But this has got to be slide projections, right? I mean, the at-traction's usual spooky effects will run as programmed?"

Temple nodded slowly. That was true. She just wasn't sure this was the usual spooky effects.

"Some holographic program," Oscar announced with disdain.

"I see nothing seriously spiritual," Mynah seconded.

Edwina leaned forward to stare through the image as if trying to dissect it with laser light. "I sense nothing, no dominant intelligence, no moving spirit. But I see this man, his silver nitrite image, as if he had been excised from a reel of old film."

"Houdini made films," Oscar Grant put in. "Bad ones."

"Execrable ones," the professor concurred. "Exploitation films of an earlier and cruder era. Would make *Waterworld* look like the Flood according to the Bible."

"This is not Houdini," Agatha announced. "Houdini's mental self-image may have been as looming, but the man himself was diminutive."

"Still—" D'Arlene sounded troubled. "I'm picking up a word. Wisconsin. And a date: April sixth, eighteen seventy-four."

"Wisconsin." Professor Mangel whistled through his teeth, an odd, informal sound for a séance. "Houdini made out he was born there, but he was actually born in Budapest and was brought to the U.S. soon after. He wanted to be utterly of the New World, you see."

"But he was born in March!" Mynah insisted. "On March twenty-fourth. He later changed the date in his biographical material to April sixth, and never satisfactorily explained why."

"Can a ghost mix up the month of his birth?" Temple asked.

"Anyone can mix up the month of his birth, if he lives long enough," Edwina said testily.

Professor Mangel had an academic answer, which he leaned around Electra to tell Temple. "The confusion owes itself to the differences between the Gregorian and Julian calendars, which were still both in effect when Houdini was born."

Temple was duly impressed by the encyclopedic nature of the psychics' knowledge of Houdini's background. They knew it in and out, top to bottom, apparently. Pretty easy to declare a stain on the wall or a reflection on a window to be the manifestation of someone dead if you know that person's résumé like a corporate recruiter.

Yet even as they speculated aloud, the still-life figure dissolved, so slowly that Temple couldn't quite believe her eyes . . . believe that she had seen it, and was now *not* seeing it.

This was a haunting spirit, Temple mused, that teased as much in absentia as in presence.

Another scent filled the room: fusty, musty, neglected. No rich aroma of gourmet cooking, of spirits and wine, of cigars. Only the smell of absence, of abandonment.

The eyes around the table widened and stared at Temple until she felt distinctly uneasy.

Then she realized that they were gazing past her, through her, beyond her.

Without disengaging her hands from the others, she turned toward the window-wall behind her, straining to see over the high wooden chair-back.

She saw mostly an upper bust, also in dim shades of gray, and the huge, bulging-eyed head that loomed over it like the face of an apoplectic Pekingese. The hair fell gray and stringy across the broad forehead from beneath the kind of brimmed black felt hat a highwayman would have worn in an earlier century.

The face did not seem of this time, nor did the loose black silk cravat that couldn't quite conceal a stunning expanse of shirtfront. The man was a monument to immensity both personal and spiritual, the most corpulent, fleshy ghost she had ever seen, if he was indeed a ghost.

His pasty gray face was distorted with fear, and for the first time his image moved, the mouth loose and round as an operatic tenor's. He was mouthing something at them, some words beyond hearing.

Edwina Mayfair twisted fruitlessly in her chair, determined to see what had materialized directly behind her. "I can't see, I can't see," she complained in bitter agitation. "If only I could free my hands."

"No," the other psychics thundered as one.

"Hey." Crawford Buchanan's voice came in like the bassoon in *Peter and the Wolf.* "I'll let go if you want, lady, so you can get a look-see. Camera! I hope you're getting all this migrating wallpaper."

Temple bit her lip. That adorable Crawford, shouting "Camera!" as if the cameraman *was* his function, nameless unless he was doing something at Buchanan's direction. Or camerawoman. It could be a woman these days, though Temple had no chance to see the camera operator beyond the blare of bright light. Who did Crawford think he was, an old-time epic director?

Still straining to see, Temple watched the flaccid lips pantomime some word or words over and over again. Lipreading wasn't as easy as it looked on TV. The motion could have mimed a dozen sounds.

And then the face drowned in the blackness behind it. An illuminated car swerved across the brim of its hat, and as the car streaked out of sight, it erased that part of the image. Other parts melted away, until only the lips were faintly visible, still moving.

"Ugh!" Electra wrenched back to the table, jerking William's right arm with her until Temple felt the pressure pull on her right hand clasped around his left. "Loose lips sink hips, at least that's what they say in my Pound Hounders' meetings. That guy, whoever he was, could use a diet, and if he really is a spirit, all the more."

"Do not be distracted by the special effects," Oscar urged. "That is what we must battle tonight. These tacky manifestations will compete with the true call from beyond. Once our séance is over, I'll check with the management. I'm sure we'll discover that this monotone blimp is one of their effects, not ours."

"What of our effects?" Mynah demanded. "Have we got any to compete with that?"

"We will if we concentrate. Now, hands tight, eyes . . . shut. Picture Houdini, imagine Houdini, however you know him. Ask Houdini to answer our joint plea: come, tell us you are here, give us a tangible sign."

Temple waited. If they weren't satisfied with the multigenerational poster boy with a face for every window, what would keep them happy?

In a moment her nose knew.

No longer did it detect French-roasted duck, or Italian wine or English gin or even Cuban cigars. No, now she sniffed something truly out-of-this-world.

A wet smell, Temple thought, damp and chlorinated.

"Ummmph!" That was Electra's inarticulate whimper.

She was staring white-eyed away from the circle of psychics, toward the giant fireplace that dominated the room's only solid end.

In the six-foot opening, a soot-shadowed mouth of black bricks leading up into a chimney-to-nowhere, stood—not Saint Nick, wrong season—but something that had definitely not been there before!

Not a breath was taken at the oval table.

Then the darker pool of shadow, where the fireplace logs should lie stretched, poured onto the gray marble apron with the silent, liquid ease of India ink.

"A stupid cat!" Oscar hissed in disappointment.

"A black cat," the hatted lady noted significantly.

"My cat," Temple said, craning her neck. "Louie?"

He blinked, looking very pleased with himself for a critter presumed to be behind a locked bathroom window, who had just plummeted from God-knew-where for Lord-knew-how-many feet.

"Leave him," Mynah ordered. "He was meant to be here. He is an omen."

No, thought Temple rebelliously, he is an anomaly, but there's nothing mysterious about it, other than that a cat will go where he wants to, when he wants to, and leave you to guess just how and why.

Magician, her mind accused him. After all, he wore the prerequisite black.

Louie moved to the side of the hearth and began washing his paws with a hot pink tongue.

"Do not let yourselves be distracted," Oscar ordered a little desperately. "We focus on Houdini. On the boy Ehrich who became the hero Houdini. We concentrate on his life, and death, and his avowed intention to return after death, if anyone could."

"Yet he was a skeptic," Edwina put in. "He used to debunk false psychics."

"False," Mynah repeated sharply. "We have no false psychics here, unless the unknown, unvouched-for participants—"

Eyes turned to Temple and Electra. And Crawford. Temple saw the cameraman's light hovering in the black glass opposite Buchanan as he zoomed in for a close-up. Bet even C.B.'s cameraman didn't care much for him, Temple thought.

Crawford's body fidgeted in his chair, sending tension along the linked hands.

"Listen, folks. I'm only here to report the show. If you don't come up with anything cameraworthy, no airtime. I'm not about to bother messing with the stage props to produce some weird phenomena. That's not what I get paid for."

"A cat is hardly a weird phenomenon," D'Arlene noted.

"It is if it belongs to one of the people we don't know much about at the table," Mynah said.

" 'Belongs' is hardly accurate," Temple said. "I left him locked in at my apartment four miles away. Maybe he's an astral projection."

"Locked in." Agatha Welk's voice was so low it seemed a delusion. Her eyes were closed, but the lids quivered. "Don't you see? He's an . . . escape artist."

"Oh." Electra sounded awestruck. "Cats can be very . . . unsettling sometimes. I never took Louie for having a sensitive bone in his body, but it's possible—"

"He is a medium!" Mynah announced with her customary certainty. "We needed another to complete the circle, the mental circle. Now Houdini *will* come!"

"I don't think so," Temple whispered to herself.

"Why not, dear heart?" The veiled lady leaned close again.

"He's just a cat—a strong, stubborn, clever cat—but I've never seen him do the slightest thing strange. Except for . . . this."

"You see!" Mynah glowed with triumph. "I can feel Houdini's life force thrusting at the glass that encloses us. I can feel it building like heat lightning, so strong, so stubborn, so strange. Do you feel it? Do you?"

There was indeed an electric sense of suspended animation in the artificial chamber. Temple felt it, felt it along the tense, fisted hands, felt it among the many minds searching for signs and explanations.

She also felt something prowling among their common intentions and discordant personalities. She looked at the hearth. Louie was gone!

Now her own tension communicated along the line of linked hands. Agatha's eyelids trembled at a speed mimicking REM sleep. Mynah's head was thrown so far back her throat was as well articulated as a spine and her eyes showed only white. Oscar's head was lowered, lost behind his Christ-like curtain of hair. Electra was transfixed by their alarming states, only her eyes moving as she studied one psychic after the other. Beside Temple, Edwina Mayfair had turned her head away, as if listening for something very faint.

The table rapped. Thumped. Vibrated.

They all jumped, as if a strong electric current had rushed from hand to hand.

Midnight Louie had appeared upon the table's center. He stood staring raptly at the chamber's ceiling. Then he sat and patted at something—clearly nothing—on the tabletop, tilting his head to pursue the invisible prey with curious feline concentration.

Then something cylindrical rolled away from his paws.

Oscar Grant leaped up, taking his partners' hands with him, and caught it as it came within reach.

"A bullet," he announced.

"From the heart of Houdini's hand," Mynah declaimed. "He carried that bullet in his hand from some mysterious incident when

he left home as a young boy and roamed for a year. It is a sign! S-
s-something is immi-n-nent." Mynah's confident voice trembled
like Agatha's eyelids and her hands began to shake at an intensity
felt among all the participants.

Temple searched the corners and shadows of the pseudoroom for
the imminent—or was it eminent?—Something. She saw nothing.

Louie lay on the table, defrauded of his find, his tail lashing as if
to dust it, each swish making the sound as of someone gently rapping . . . rapping at their séance chamber door.

Electra had a pressing confession for no one in particular. "My
knees are shaking so much, I think they're rapping the table."

"No, it's Louie's tail," Temple said.

"But why is Louie here? Karma is the psychic one."

"Karma?"

"I mean, his karma has no psychic overtones. He has no experience in this sort of thing. Does he?"

"How should I know? He didn't come with a résumé."

"Oh."

Mynah's head was horizontal to the ceiling now, and her long,
violent sigh caught their wandering attention like a clap of hands.

Even Midnight Louie looked up.

And well he—and they—should.

Mist was creeping along the seams of the walls, oozing out of the
light sconces as if from an invisible dragon's nostrils, hovering at
the ceiling.

Mist rose between those seated at the table, from the center seam
dissecting the table. Mist encased Midnight Louie in an ethereal
aura.

Mist congealed like cumulous smoke in the high hearth, obscuring its blackness. Mist moved, a nebulous form not terribly tall.
Mist floated into a humanoid mass that reminded Temple of an ab-
ducting alien, black-hole eyes an abyss in a vague white figure.

Mist sifted at the windows like a lace curtain, concealing, revealing.

A fresh, sudden scent of chlorinated water almost seared their
nostrils.

Their heads pulled back from this sensory assault, hands nearly separating as they coughed and gasped for breath, eyes blinking against instant, caustic tears.

A woman's moan was almost orgasmic. (Mynah, Temple suspected cynically.) A man made an anguished, throat-clearing bark.

Louie's growl was long, low and as deep as the darkness in his throat, sounding black-panther formidable. Temple was too shaken to make any noise.

Someone hiccoughed. Someone else sighed, softly, slowly.

The ghost?

Eyes still tear-blurred, Temple looked around. The form in the fireplace still shimmered there, as if a photograph had been superimposed over it, a grainy photo of an almost naked man with dark eyes and hair. He seemed bent over, like a dwarf. He seemed . . . bound in metal cuffs and chains.

"Houdini!" Mynah screamed, rising yet not breaking the grip that had lasted until then. People were pulled upright in jerky motion: Electra, Crawford, D'Arlene Hendrix.

A silver slice of light flashed above them. Looking up, Temple saw something hovering over the table . . . a mace from the display of arms hanging before the window-walls. How eerie to see something that must weigh twenty or more pounds floating like a heavy-metal fairy in midair.

Another weapon fell from its place suspended before the opposite wall, smashing into the nearest lighted sconce. That light vanished in a cascade of breaking glass. In the dimmed room, other weapons were flying across the chamber, dipping low over the table, flashing with glints of fugitive light.

A battle-ax came swooping soundlessly toward the séance table like some great metal hawk.

Though the circle of clasped hands never loosened, everyone ducked by instinct, and Agatha suddenly slumped facedown on the table. D'Arlene, cowering in her own chair, reached out an arm to keep the unconscious woman from slipping to the floor. Next to them, only the white streak in Oscar Grant's dark hair was visible above the table edge while he took blatant cover. Mynah Sigmund had not only sat again, but had laid her face and arms along the tabletop, watching the dancing blades as they swept past, ready to take cover if they menaced her flowing locks.

Electra just barely had her nose and crown of red hair above the table rim. Stoic William Kohler, oddly enough, had not moved.

Temple checked Crawford Buchanan next to D'Arlene and Agatha, but not even the top of his head was to be seen. She pulled her legs in closer to the chair, just in case. She herself, being small to begin with, didn't have far to go when she shrank in her chair, and so far the flying blades hadn't frightened her. She figured they were rigged on fishline to perform at certain intervals.

Louie, too, was not about to give up his possession of the table, even if the tableware seemed to be possessed and indulging in overkill. He crouched on the smooth wood, fur roughed into battle-halo, tail lashing.

Temple, savvy magician's ex-squeeze that she was, remembered much too late where she should be looking: where the action *wasn't*.

There was one person, so to speak, who had really turned tail and run when the sword dance began.

No chain-dragging spirit still crouched in the fireplace.

Everyone had given up the ghost. Even the ghost.

Temple glanced at William Kohler again, suddenly worried about his oddly stiff posture and immobile, clammy hand still grasping hers. Could he have had some kind of attack?

In the dimness, his figure remained pressed upright against the back of the chair and his eyewhites glistened. Temple was wondering if she really had to inch her fingers up his flaccid hand to feel for a pulse, when she realized that his eyes looked her way, frozen in that extreme sideways glance of disbelieving horror. They did blink while she watched. Once.

She let her own eyes stray in the direction that William Kohler gazed.

Temple realized then that Edwina Mayfair had buried her face in her arms to protect it, and that her gloved hand had pulled away so gently that Temple hadn't even noticed it. Still the circle was unbroken, for their fingertips connected as lightly as the life-giving (and life-taking) touch of God's and Adam's forefingers on the Sistine Chapel ceiling. Above the séance table hung only the dimmed chandelier; nothing moved but a faint sparkle of fairy dust.

The weapons now hung motionless back at their posts, but before she called the all-clear, Temple wanted to rouse Edwina. The poor woman must have been terrified. Even in the dim light, Temple could see her disarray.

Edwina's gloved hands clutched together as if in prayer, and the unwieldy hat had sagged off her head, revealing . . . the pale perfect circle of a bald spot.

Beyond her slumped form, Crawford Buchanan was emerging like a mole from his hole. Following the direction of Temple's stare, he bent over Edwina, officious fingers searching for the bare wrist of the gloved hand that he had, presumably, held throughout the séance.

Temple retrieved the crumpled hat and veil . . . to reveal a downed battle-ax lying beneath it.

"Lights!" Oscar Grant called. "Dammit! Someone turn on the lights!"

Crawford stepped back from Edwina and the battle-ax cheek by jowl with her face, dusting his hands on his jacket sides.

"She's dead," he announced in his always-funereal baritone. Then he frowned. "I think so. Dead, for certain. Better film this."

Temple quickly replaced the hat and its tangle of veiling, now understanding its cosmetic purpose, as the camcorder's relentless bright light zoomed in.

Blinking again, this time from too much light, everyone studied the scene. Across the table Agatha was stirring awake with frequent sighs.

"What happened? Oh! Did Edwina faint too? Where are all the nasty knives?"

Temple's eyes were mesmerized by the battle-ax's sharp and shining blade. In the full sunlight of the camcorder, a wavering line of red rusted the metal's edge.

And something else macabre showed a steely grin for the television camera . . . the clumsy metal handcuffs that locked Edwina's black-gloved wrists together like a pair of particularly ugly vintage bracelets.

"What happened?" Agatha demanded as querulously as a child whom no adult will listen to.

"Houdini," Mynah answered absently for them all. "What happened? . . . Houdini knows."

Chapter 15

Amateur Hour

You cannot imagine how surprised I am when I only do what I do best—get inside someplace where I am not supposed to be—and the supposed coal chute I stick my nose into turns out to be a slide to stardom.

Actually, the expression "slide" is too nice. It is really a drop, a ten-foot drop straight down to a bunch of bricks. Luckily, I instinctively execute my fabled feline twist in midair, which has been scientifically proven to save lives, and manage to enter standing, looking as if I were always Santa's little helper.

While the room is cooing over my spectacular entrance, I fade into the background and try to figure out what to do next.

I do not like the fog that is snaking around the premises. The occupants of the room seem much enchanted by it, but then they are an exotic lot, I see at first glance. Even my little doll looks more exotic than usual, but that is because she is attired in a gown that makes it look like she is peeking out from behind an azalea bush.

I am surprised to recognize an old opponent of mine. Crawford

Buchanan. He is sitting at the table holding hands with some dame in a black hat that looks like it got caught on a mortuary trellis and brought most of it along for the ride. Then there is a white-hot witchy number in platinum-blond everything, a dude in black with hair Yanni might envy, a fat guy in the ever-popular black, a woman whose tail would be twitching if she had one, some bespectacled dude with no hair and the usual black, Miss Electra Lark in her usual Technicolor and a woman who looks like she should be hawking bug repellent in TV commercials.

While all present are debating my method of arrival and importance to the event under way, I sidle out of sight and look around some more.

There is something unnatural about the fog hugging the windows and ceiling and oozing all over the floor and table. It is white, like regular fog, and misty-murky, but something else bothers me. I sniff around, recognizing a scent that some of my kind go kit-crazy over, chlorine, the stuff they use to stink up swimming pools and spas, so as to keep the bacteria brigade from invading the neighborhood. If I am to sniff something sublime, it will be edible at least, or perhaps a bit of primo nip obtained through purely legal channels. This here chemical trip is not my type of transportation, however, and it leaves me untransported.

Then I figure it out. The stuff is not just seen and sniffed, like most unknown substances, it is also *heard*. I realize now what has fluffed my tail all along: the slight *hisssss* the fog makes. Reminds me of our reptile friends, who are not always lethal, but who have propensities. I believe in giving wide berth to anything with similar propensities, so I forget the fog and take to the high ground to get a better handle on what is happening here.

Well. You would think I had jumped on the middle of their beds during a private moment or something. It is not as if there is food on the table that I might take away. No, the wood surface is as bare as Mother Hubbard's cupboard, and I have been superpolite and careful to keep all my fighting equipment stowed below deck before I sailed in this direction.

I am still casing the room, so I look for alternate routes of ingress and egress, simply because I have so recently found myself out of luck on that score, and forced to accede to the assistance of a dust-ball of long-distance feline electricity.

In fact, I spot a bright light reflected in one of the dark windows and cringe by reflex. This has everyone at the table forgetting my unwanted presence and oohing and aahing about my superior psychic senses and how a Presence from Beyond must be imminent.

They turn out to be quite right, but it is the wrong Presence and it is from a Beyond that is not as far removed as they would hope.

What happens is the camera operator moves, along with the big bright light that everybody has come to take for granted, only the reflection in the window of the big bright light does not move, but remains a little bright light.

"We are not alone," the dead-white blonde announces, and she is unfortunately too correct.

I blink, and the little bright light winks back twice to my once.

As I feared, my guardian Birman is with me, or at least a little of this Tibetan Tinkerbell's stardust is. Where she was when I was plunging down the dark throat of the chimney, I cannot say. Perhaps she was out getting her twinkle adjusted. I sometimes suspect her headlights of being set on "dim." No doubt communing with unseen realms saps the IQ.

So I sit down to watch the evening's entertainment, even as the Little Light That Could hovers at the window to watch me. I am forgotten now that fresh phenomena threaten.

So it is with much bemusement that I watch the assembled physics stiffen and groan and twitch and sigh . . . and totally ignore the fascinating phenomena that show up in answer to their actions.

At first it looks like the fog has coagulated in the ceiling corner like a phantom icicle, but then I see stars glimmering through the bright white radiance and then I see a belt buckle the size of a pizza pan, and then I see a familiar, fuzzy face . . . and Elvis in his glitziest white jumpsuit slides down the corner of the wall like a fireman on a pole. Hey, the King still is as limber as ever, even if he has not lost an ounce in the Afterlife. And he gives me a big wink before lip-syncing a totally silent number. I think it is "Cat, Help! Falling in Love With You," but I am not a big lip-reader, and although I knew

Elvis was into strange things, I did not think cross-species romance was one of them.

I look to see if the gathered experts can do a better job of translating the silent song lyrics, but they are all staring elsewhere, oblivious. I look at Elvis, who gives me this shrug and his cute little sneery smile, then melts into the fog.

Meanwhile, my human companions are out to lunch, except there is not even food on their table. Talk about being twelve cards short of a full tarot deck!

So I clean my whiskers, Elvis's sideburns having reminded me that grooming is the mark of a gentleman, and while I am so engaged, I catch something else out of the corner of my eye.

This is a tall, portly old gent wearing a tweedy Norfolk jacket and a checked cap. He is adjusting one of the lighting sconces by looking at it and waggling his bushy white eyebrows. Naturally, it goes faint and bright in turn, almost like one of those semaphores they used to signal people with over long distances in olden times, but do you think the assembled sensitives would notice a laser beam on their own birthday cake? No.

They are fussing at each other about how nothing is happening, and yes, the fog is interesting but what does it do?

The old dude, who is rather pale despite the plethora of plaids in his attire, pulls out a pipe and eyes me hopefully, like I should recognize him, or light his fire or something. I do not approve of smoking, so am about to do nothing of the kind, but—what do you know—the light of my life (I am being sarcastic here)—floats through the window-glass and ends up hovering over the old guy's pipe, which gives off a ghostly contrail of smoke that merges with the ubiquitous fog.

Apparently Beyond is not big on fire hazards.

The old squire's eyes light up for a moment too, until you would swear he was alive, then he starts the disappearing act, and for just a moment I think I know who he is. The name starts with *d* as in "detective," and if he would stay just a few seconds longer, I would make the connection and be home free. But he does not, and I do not, and life is like that, and sometimes even death is like that.

It is a pretty sad room in Vegas, however, when the dead present provide more entertainment than the living present. And I include those of my acquaintance in this judgment. I am nothing if not impartial, and right now I would not declare my lot with the sad excuses for extrasensory perception gathered here tonight.

A few more prestigious personas from the past lend their presence to the gathering, unobserved by anyone but me. Mae West is looking as pneumatic as ever, and pale becomes her. It takes me a while to figure out who the lanky lady in the leather jacket is, and by the time I am ready to shout "Hey, Amelia, where on earth *did* you bow out?" she is fading away too, from lack of attention.

I tell you, it is enough to make a cat cry, to see all these newsworthy folks pass through without so much as a flicker of notice from the living. I am wondering if I can make a deal with some human with vision, and we could provide prognostications from the past, complete with the signature of the visiting ghost, when suddenly all hullabaloo breaks loose and the séance folks are looking lively.

This must be good. I look where they are looking so lively, and I see the fog has amassed in my former landing zone, the fireplace. Well, it is a lot of fog and there is a form sort of quivering on it like an out-of-focus vacation slide on a sheet posing as a screen. I can almost see a person in the vague design of light and dark, but it is nothing like the camera-ready sharp-focus of the famous folks I have been viewing in solitary splendor tonight.

In fact, the old English-squire dude comes blazing back by the wall sconce, puffing on his ectoplasmic pipe until smoke signals practically scream his presence, but no one notices. He looks happy, though, and makes fists as if to say "Yes! Yes!"

As the murmur of "Houdini" comes from the live ones around the table, I cannot help rooting for this long-dead dude myself. I always root for the underdog (only in that instance), as I always like to watch a good comeback. And if this Houdini dude came back, that would be world-class news. Not up to Amelia or Elvis, you understand, but one cannot have everything.

So I even get my ears perked up, and I am anticipating something spectacular, but instead I get more fog. This fog floats around the table like a waiter looking for a tip, giving every psychic a big charge as it nears each seat.

I think my little doll will get lines on her pert little face, she is frowning so hard during this performance. And she is right: an animated fog-sheet is not worth the price of admission. If only she were a kindred soul and could see what I see, like the old dude against the wall jumping up and down and mouthing "Houdini" right along with the chanting psychics. Doyly, that is his name. I believe that he had something to do with a British opera company called the D'Oily Carte. The British always aspire to French phrases when it comes to culture and cooking. Anyway, old Doyly is having an out-of-the-body heart attack right in front of everybody, and all they can do is stare at this circular clump of fog, which strikes me as mighty suspicious.

Then suddenly something is thrown down hard on the smooth wood tabletop.

Everybody screams, and even I jump, because the object comes rolling right for me, nothing of human construction being purely level. I jump too, because I do not know if the object will explode or something, but it is as dead as a dud dumdum, which is what it is, sort of.

Anyway, I know a bullet when I see one, and I gently pat and spin it for a 3-D examination.

At this someone waxes hysterical—I think it is the doll with the spasmodic eyelids—and the long-haired dude springs up to wrest the bullet away from me like I was playing with it or something. I hate to be underestimated. I was trying to calculate the caliber, but it is an older piece of ammunition, and hard to categorize. I would have to sleep on it (via an arms encyclopedia) to be sure.

Anyway, the fog has made the rounds back to the fireplace and is drifting away like smoke. I see that Doyly is long gone; not so Karma, unfortunately.

Now the knickknacks on the wall start flying around, but I am not too alarmed, having dodged my share of hurled objects in my time. But the séance crowd is more than somewhat shook up. Even Miss Temple Barr looks a little pale as she tries to attend to the lady on her left, who has apparently fainted during the knife-throwing act.

So I look closer and I see that "fainted" is something more fatal.

Karma's little light is buzzing like a hyperactive mosquito back at the window, and the dumdums at the table are standing and frowning.

I understand immediately that this is a job for Lieutenant Molina of the Las Vegas Metropolitan Police Department. So does my little doll, for she gets a very wan and woebegone expression on her face, seeing as she was sitting next to and holding hands with the victim.

The bright side is that Crawford Buchanan was pinching pinkies with the victim's other hand, so who is to say he is not the likeliest suspect.

The other people around the table are turning up their headlights and beginning to realize that the hat-head was done in.

And they are beginning to say that Houdini did it.

I do not know. I would not know Houdini if he dove off the Circle Ritz roof into a teacup. I can definitely say, however, that Elvis Presley, Mae West, Amelia Earhart and the English Doyly dude did not do it. Too bad I am not allowed to testify.

Chapter 16

Postmortem

"At least Lieutenant Molina didn't get the case."

Temple sat on her living room sofa at six in the morning, Midnight Louie on her lap. Or on Electra's muumuu's lap.

Electra herself sat at the sofa's other end, patting vaguely at her scarlet hair. "Days like these, I thank God I'm self-employed. You can take a nice nap, dear."

"I don't think so. Since Molina's not on the case, how am I going to find out how the poor . . . victim was killed?"

"Do you really need to know?"

"Don't you want to know if a ghost did it, or not?"

"No. I have always regarded ghosts as friendly spirits. Oh, perhaps a touch misunderstood, at their worst. I do not believe that anyone who has embraced the afterlife would wish ill on the living."

"Ever heard of demons and devils?"

Electra shook an adamant head. "No. The agency was human."

"What was all that yelling about it being Houdini for sure when that bullet hit the table?"

"The professor explained that to me while we were waiting for the police. As a boy, when he was wandering far from home for a few years, Houdini was shot somehow. He never explained, but all his life he carried the bullet in the palm of his hand."

"Why? Why not have it removed?"

"Perhaps it was safer to leave it in place."

"Perhaps. We should hold another séance and interrogate Houdini instead of gawking at him as if he were a walking White Sale advertisement."

"You don't believe that manifestation was Houdini."

Temple stroked Midnight Louie's satiny ears. He blinked contentment. "And how did Louie get out of this place, and get to the haunted house?"

"You're not suggesting that Louie—?"

"I'm not suggesting anything, except that while we searched after eternal truths we missed a lot of what happened last night."

Louie gave a burst of loud purr, then stretched to knead his front paws on Temple's thigh, still upholstered in the floral muumuu.

She shuddered in recollection as she eyed her thigh. "I never realized muumuus were so suspicious. That search by the woman officer in the haunted-house kitchen—"

"I had to do it too, dear. Everyone did. Face it, anybody participating in a séance is likely to be suspected of concealing some trickery, at least by the police."

"Were they looking for a weapon? I didn't get that impression. I don't think they know yet what killed Edwina Mayfair."

"Natural causes," Electra said with the authority of a justice of the peace. "Trust me. Wild Blue Pike and Eightball O'Rourke say that the bloody battle-ax only nicked her shoulder. I'm sure the poor thing's heart overheated at all the excitement. The police will have red faces by tomorrow morning, and you'll have missed the Crystal Ball for nothing."

"Oh, thanks for calling the Phoenix and explaining why I wasn't there while I was being . . . examined in the kitchen."

"I never did see what you were wearing. Or the Midnight Louie shoes."

"Kind of moot." Temple pulled a pair of individual shoe bags from her tote bag. "You should have seen the going-over these got from the authorities. You'd think I was smuggling Austrian crystals."

"Off with the muumuu. Let Mama see."

Temple was happy to stand and shrug out of the enveloping cotton tent for the last time. She had worn a black stretch-velvet ankle-length dress, all the better to show off the shoes.

"Very classic, but . . . well. You certainly couldn't conceal much in that dress."

"So the police intimated. At least I'm cleared of fiddling with the séance."

"I'm not sure that any of us are. This unfortunate death throws the results into question. What a pity! This was such an outstanding manifestation. It's not Houdini's fault that someone should collapse at his first big show in seventy years. This might scare him away for good."

"You really think it was Houdini in that cloud of obfuscation?"

"Oh, yes, dear. I have seen photographs of the man. The hunched posture, the nearly bare body to prove no tricks, the chains and locks. Absolutely prime-time Houdini. And then the bullet."

"I suppose he has no use for it now," Temple said slowly. "Still, that figure could have been projected."

"That's what all ghostly phenomena are, projections of the living essence of death."

"I mean photographically projected."

Electra looked hurt. "Oh, ye of little faith. How or who? Why?"

"Any one of the psychics might have wanted to boost his or her reputation. You can bet this will be the lead story on tonight's *Hot Heads*, with panting teasers run at commercial breaks all day. And then there's the local angle: the haunted-house organizers might have rigged their effects to go a bit berserk for the *Hot Heads* camera, and now that someone's dead, they're not about to admit it."

"Speaking of hotheads, that Buchanan character was pretty antsy to get out of there." Electra's eyes narrowed. "Either the nose of a newshound heading for a deadline . . . or the spur of guilt."

Temple leaned back against the sofa, scratching Louie's tummy. "Even I hadn't thought of that. What a spectacular way to be rid of Crawford Buchanan forever! Could he have killed somebody merely to raise his ratings? Yes. Did he? I'm not so sure."

Temple stood, leaving an abandoned Midnight Louie frowning on the sofa cushion.

"There's only one thing to do, Electra: get better acquainted with the psychics. They're staying on for a while, aren't they?"

"With a huge psychic fair at the Oasis running the entire weekend, I doubt any will skip town before Monday."

Temple smiled nostalgically. "I can see Lieutenant Molina now, growling that this mob of suspects who are only in town for a five-day stay are murder."

"That detective team, Watts and Sacker, seemed pretty laid-back."

"Maybe. But if whatever was fatal to Edwina Mayfair turns out to be murderous, you can bet that will change. Meanwhile, when does the psychic fair open?"

Electra checked her watch. "At noon today, Friday. It's not the thirteenth, is it?"

"Not unless the spirits have rearranged the calendar. Today is November first, All Saints' Day."

"Better take a nap; I'll get you at eleven."

"You're game?"

"Of course. Someone at the fair may have insight into who did whatever was done."

Temple saw Electra out, wondering if her landlady would still be a redhead by midday.

She grabbed a bagel on her way to the bedroom, deposited the Midnight Louie shoes in their own drawer when she got there, shrugged out of the dress, pantyhose and bra, put on her purple fuzzies and burrowed under the unmade covers.

A few moments later she felt the bed bounce. Louie was ready for a catnap too, and well he should be, after his adventures of the wee hours.

It felt strange and rather decadent to be going to sleep for the night at a time when she was normally waking up. But she fell asleep too fast to think about anything. When she woke up, the doorbell was chiming and a dream-shadow of a big black cat with emerald eyes and a ruby collar was slinking back into never-never land.

Temple reached for her glasses, saw the bedside clock read twelve-fifteen and lurched up to answer the bell.

Electra was standing there, her hair a banana-yellow, her face an ashen blank slate of sobriety.

"Temple. I just heard the noon news. Hang on to your heart-beat."

"It *was* murder!"

"No, they don't know that yet, or don't say they know yet."

"Then what's the shock?"

"It *wasn't* a lady."

"The newscaster was no lady?"

"No, the victim! Your hand-holding partner wasn't a woman."

"What was it, then?" Temple blinked, still sleepy.

"A man!"

"A man?"

"Named Gandolph."

Temple frowned and rubbed the bridge of her nose. "That name sounds familiar—"

"Of course. It's the name of the wizard in *The Lord of the Rings* fantasy trilogy. Only they spelled it wrong on the TV screen. G-a-n-d-o-l-p-h, as if he were German or something. It should be G-a-n-d-a-l-f, you know?"

"No, I don't know. I've never read this *Lord of the Rings*. Has it got something to do with matrimony?"

"You've never read *The Lord of the Rings*? But you must have; everybody has."

"Not me." Temple scratched her chin and yawned. "Even though 'Gandolph' does sound familiar. What's the rest of her . . . his name?"

"Doesn't have a rest."

"Just G-a-n-d-o-l-p-h?"

"That's right. But, say, doesn't it worry you more that you held hands for almost an hour with a phony medium? A fake? A transvestite?"

"Not at all." Temple felt her eyes screw themselves into focus.

"Wait a minute! I was all worried about Crawford Buchanan playing footsie with me, and instead I had a *strange* guy in drag nudging and patting my knee! I don't know if I'm sorry he's dead."

"Hush, dear! The recently departed can sometimes hear the harsh judgment of the living."

"Good!" Temple shouted. "What a dirty trick! And I thought the poor dead lady had a hair-loss problem. All that whispered motherly consolation was a sham, you louse! Why don't you go out and get your kicks on Route Sixty-six . . . in the middle of the road where they can run you over."

"Temple, he's already dead."

"Not enough for me! That shows you what kind of flakes these so-called psychics are."

"Please, you can't judge all by one."

"I sure can. And why did you wake me up, anyway?"

"We're going to the psychic fair, to see what we can learn there."

"Now you're talking like Nostradamus."

"I've never claimed prophetic powers," Electra demurred modestly.

"I meant the local rhyming bookie." Temple sighed. "I suppose we should see what the fortune-tellers all think about being taken in by a wolf in ewe's clothes."

"Psychics are not fortune-tellers; they would get very upset if you called them that."

Electra was pursuing Temple to the bedroom, anxiously explicating.

Temple shut the door before Electra could follow her in.

"Brew up some coffee while I'm dressing," she suggested from within. "It should put me in a better mood."

Electra's footsteps ran, not walked, over the parquet to the kitchen tile, from where shortly came a great clangor.

Temple sighed again, then rummaged in her closet for something to wear. Unfortunately, Midnight Louie had already found it, pulled it down and made it into a nest to curl up on.

She squatted down to study his cozy arrangement.

"The late lady was a lad, Louie. Imagine that. Named Gandolph. *Why* is that name familiar?"

Chapter 17

Parsley, Sage, Rosemary and Crime

The Oasis was Las Vegas's answer to the Taj Mahal.

In fact, the gazebo by the pool out back *was* the Taj Mahal.

The symbolic curbside greeters were a sculptured pair of immense palanquin-bearing elephants flashing polyurethane tusks long enough, and strong enough, to seat the Mormon Tabernacle Choir for a photo opportunity.

Inside was an exotic jungle landscape chattering with monkeys and birds, among whom the ringing of slot machines chimed like distant temple bells.

"This is Elizabeth Taylor's *Cleopatra*," Temple declared, "but our Crystal Phoenix attraction will be Spencer Tracy's Katharine Hepburn: not as big as a back lot, but what's there will be choice."

"Do Van and Nicky approve of your moonlighting as a psychic detective these days?" Electra asked.

"*I'm* not a psychic detective: I'm investigating psychics. There's a big difference. You bet they approve. I called to find out how the Crystal Ball went—a smash, boo hoo, that I couldn't bask in—but

Nicky and Van were mostly agog about the fatality at the séance. They're dying to know if the haunted house organizers are irresponsible enough to play fast and loose with their special effects, and maybe commit manslaughter. Such loose cannons wouldn't be on the Crystal Phoenix team, I can tell you. So I have carte blanche to snoop."

"Eightball did offer the opinion that these punk kids that dream up special effects nowadays are technological giants and emotional dwarves."

"When did you see Eightball?"

"I can use my telephone, too," Electra said airily, "even if it isn't a cute red spike shoe like yours. Now let's boogie."

Electra eagerly led Temple to the ballrooms, her vivid muumuu for once fading into the hothouse background.

After they had paid their stiff entry fees (apparently sister séance attendees received no discounts), they were allowed into a maharajah's pleasure dome draped with imported fabrics. Sheer silks impressed with gold designs tented every exhibitor's stand.

"Isn't this sublime?" Electra clasped chubby, beringed hands before her floral breast. "I feel like I'm in Ali Baba's bazaar."

"I feel like I'm in Ali Baba's harem," Temple remarked, watching a pair of babes in chain-mail bikinis jingle by. Or did she mean jiggle? "Or on the set of *Bay Watch*."

"Hmm? *Body Watch*? What's that, dear?"

"Nothing much," she said. "Do psychic fairs always stir up so much atmosphere?"

"Oh, my, no. They're usually rather dreary affairs at off-the-beaten-path motels that smell of disinfectant and dripping pipes. This is the pinnacle of the paranormal marketplace. The Everest of extrasensory perception, the—"

"The Mount Rainier of the mountebank," Temple finished caustically.

"What do Monte Carlo's Prince Rainier and Monty Hall have to do with it?"

"Probably as much as goodness," Temple said obscurely, privately invoking the ghost of Mae West again. "Where are our friends from last night?"

"Oh, scattered among the booths." Electra waved garnet- and amethyst-ringed fingers tipped with pale orange polish at the array. "Do you want to get a bite to eat first? They have food booths."

"Perhaps. I'm feeling an insatiable craving for a fig, at the moment."

"Oh. I doubt they have figs, not even one. More like Orangeade and Coke and nachos."

"Nachos is the native food?"

"No, but it's popular. New Age people like strong flavors, you know."

"I didn't know."

"We want to experience life in all its zest and foreign spice."

"Even death?"

"Oh, especially death. Death is so interesting! The tunnel, the light, the little people at the end of the tunnel."

"It sounds rather like a haunted house."

"What a nice analogy, dear! Yes, the House of Life is haunted by all who have gone before. We who walk through the walls of reality may glimpse the wonder beyond. I hadn't thought of it before, but a haunted house is the perfect site for a séance."

"Just show me the way to someone who might know more than we do about the death of Gandolph last night."

"Any one of these prognosticators and mysteriarchs might know that." Another wave of tangerine fingernails.

"Mysteriarchs?"

"Like Houdini. Like Max." Electra beamed at Temple with an arch expression. "You know, like a patriarch, only a master of the arts of magic."

"Have you seen Max lately?"

"Me? No. He appears to have vanished again. And you?"

"Not lately," Temple said, choosing to define "lately" as in the past twelve hours. "Oh, great. The brunet bombshell has set up his tent. Shall we go drop our bombshell on him? I doubt any of these people were gawking at the noon news if they had to put out their wares this morning."

"Temple, have you considered that the police will be mad at you for telling everybody who the dead man was?"

"It was on TV. Besides, shouldn't they all have gotten the news telepathically? Even our master of ceremonies there."

"He is pretty cute, isn't he?" Electra hustled after Temple toward the table where Oscar Grant was enchanting a mostly female audience.

"Cute" was not the word Temple would apply to Grant. He was an ingratiatingly slight man, with a slightly effeminate air, which by no means meant he was gay. Such a man would always do well with women, combining an oily masculinity with the chummy camaraderie of a massage salesman.

His long dark hair, mustache and solid-black dress gave him a foreign air that was quite probably undeserved. Temple had seen his type at the front of classrooms, in seaside art galleries, on cable TV infomercials and in front of carnival midway sideshows.

She suspected that they always sold something that sounded, tasted, smelled or felt too good to be true, and that also cost too much to be genuine.

"The tapes," he was saying now, "are only one hundred and eighty-five dollars, and of course you also get a watermelon tourmaline pendant, my video and nine hundred number in case you have any questions. Ladies?"

The watching women bubbled over with questions, as eager as high-schoolers. Temple studied their sun-creased necks and hands, their cubic-zirconia–emblazoned wrists and fingers, their freckled chests and sinewy golf-playing calves and forearms. This guy could sell Retin-A to cloistered monks, and here he had an audience already sold on his snake oil, which was half mysticism and half mumbo jumbo.

"Remember," he urged as they reluctantly moved on, "to think is to know, but to *be* is to *believe.*"

Wow. Temple stepped right up, intercepting his melting look of greeting before he recognized her and washed it right off.

"Did you know," she began without fanfare, sounding alarmingly like Lieutenant C. R. Molina to herself, "that Edwina Mayfair was really a man named Gandolph? And, if not, why not?"

Not for her the hot-fudge glance, the supple vocal tone and expressive eyebrows. "You must be joking!" he sputtered. "You were at the séance last night, some flack, I remember—"

"Flack" was a fighting word. "You set yourself up as the expert on psychics. If you're so expert, how come you were taken in by Edwina Mayfair? Didn't you know her by sight? Or foresight?"

"I have never met the lady. We work on different coasts."

"Surely an insignificant gap given the intercommunication possible on a higher, less physical plane?"

"Your attitude stinks," he said. "We're not omnipotent, simply gifted."

"Still, you admit not meeting Edwina Mayfair. What about this Gandolph?"

"Gandolph? I've heard of him. A malcontent. A failed stage magician who took insane relish in attempting to slander truer talents. A bitter old man who probably died of a suffocated heart. I can't say I'm surprised, now that I learn the dead person's real identity. Gandolph was choking on his own failures and trying to pin them on us. Bile killed him, then; an excess of bile. No doubt his rank presence drove away the only solid apparition of Houdini the world has seen since nineteen twenty-six."

"Had you ever met him?"

Oscar Grant paused to calm himself one muscle at a time. When he spoke again, it was with detached serenity.

"Houdini, or this dead charlatan? Why should I answer your questions? The police have been enough skeptics for me to deal with in twelve hours. But, no, I never met the man, although I have read about him, and have seen photographs. In none of those photographs was he wearing women's garb, so I wouldn't have recognized him. That was his intent, wasn't it? To infiltrate our gathering as apparently you have done? We are used to vilification and skepticism. We are used to enemies among us."

"Am I to take it that you are also prepared to deal with them, then?"

Oscar's sad, superior smile made his mustache crooked. "We are prepared to win them over, with the truth. That is our only object, our only weapon. Now if you will excuse me; I have acolytes to address."

Temple turned. Another clutch of tanned, desperately casual women covered in cubic zirconia and crystals was lined up behind her. She gave way gracefully, trying not to be blinded by the light.

"Oh," fretted Electra, digging in her canvas bag, "now he lumps me in with the Enemy. Can't you show a little tact and sensitivity? I was hoping to get one of his singing crystal stickpins, which he gives now and then to the odd acolyte."

"You have no place to put a stickpin. And investigators have no tact."

"Oh."

Temple took her arm. "But Grant admits to knowing who Gandolph was, and did you catch *what* he really was?"

"A crusading magician who tried to unmask psychics. Houdini was one of those himself. The magical has always attacked the mystical, yet who is the true fake? Everybody knows that magicians are nothing but a bag of tricks."

"Yes, and some of them admit it, including Houdini, from what I've read. In fact, Houdini's friendship with Sir Arthur Conan Doyle came to an abrupt end when Houdini couldn't endorse Lady Conan Doyle's psychic claims to having channeled his mother in Houdini's own presence. But although Sir Arthur insisted Houdini used dematerialization to accomplish some of his illusions, Houdini steadfastly denied it. And it would have been tempting for the age's greatest mystifier to claim supernatural powers with such a respected endorser of them behind him." Temple stopped walking and stood puzzled. "Then why is Houdini, of all people, reputed to have sworn to come back from death?"

"He never did. That line was from the scriptwriter of a cheap film he made," a voice answered behind her.

The women turned to see D'Arlene Hendrix sitting on a folding chair before a plain booth with a table covered by beige brochures.

Temple nodded approval. This setup looked like it was selling dental hygiene. She instantly trusted D'Arlene Hendrix a hundred percent more than she trusted Oscar Grant. Then she realized that the low-key approach could be just as deceptive.

"You seem to know a lot about Houdini."

"Why not? I read the books and watch the movies." D'Arlene smiled. "No, I didn't get my info on the telepathic telegraph. He was a textbook case of something: death wish, mother fixation, sexual hangups, quite literally; did an awful lot of his tricks suspended upside down, or cramped in incredibly tight spaces and swathed with chains. The mother thing is true; he worshiped her. When she died, he tormented himself that she had some last, undelivered message meant just for him."

"Then . . . he would have tried to bring *her* back, not promised to return himself." Temple waited for an explanation.

"True." D'Arlene pushed an invisible hair behind her ear. "And he did hunt sincerely for a medium who could do that. Finding only frauds, he became an antimedium crusader. And he didn't promise to return from the dead, merely made provisions that if anyone claimed he did, there was evidence around to rebut the phonies. But the public wanted Houdini back as much as he would have wanted to recall his mother. Who besides sonny wanted to see Mama Cecelia Weiss in the transparent flesh? It's Houdini who has the sex appeal. All five feet four of him, bowed legs and everything. An incredible athlete, nonetheless. Actually, Houdini's wife, Bess, started the tradition of the annual Halloween séance to make contact. After a decade, she gave up, but the Spiritualists, who would have loved to bring back the time's most notorious skeptic of post-death communication, never gave up, they just faded away."

"Are you convinced? That figure we saw last night, the chained man—"

"Looked just like Houdini in one of his most famous photographs."

"Photograph?" Electra echoed, crestfallen.

"Exactly," said Temple. "We saw nothing that couldn't have been faked."

D'Arlene smiled. "No, we never do. But I have seen things at séances that could have been faked and that could not be *proved* to have been faked."

"What about Gandolph?"

"What about him?"

"He's the one who died last night."

D'Arlene Hendrix was suddenly speechless. "I hadn't heard that it wasn't Edwina Mayfair. Gandolph the Great? In that ridiculous hat? What a way to die, dressed as a laughingstock! Poor man. Quite sincere, in his way. I understood that he was retired."

"He is now," Temple said grimly, ready to move on.

Down the aisle, under an ethereal canopy of white and silver silks, she had recognized a shining silver head. She was dying to interrogate Mynah Sigmund about the poor, dear, dead deceiver. Temple paused to hunt for her own hidden motive. All right. She was dying to find out what made this New Age Barbie Doll tick.

"Come on," she told Electra, hitching her tote bag up on her shoulder and pushing her glasses back on the bridge of her nose. "I want you to make sure that this next one doesn't pull the ectoplasm over my eyes."

"Ectoplasm over your eyes?" D'Arlene rolled hers. "You wouldn't like that. In the old days, spirit ectoplasm was often made of regurgitated luminous cheesecloth."

Temple blanched. "What a way to get your minimum daily calcium requirement!"

"I don't know much about Mynah Sigmund," Electra said between huffs and puffs that wouldn't blow a marshmallow over as she hoofed along in Temple's wake. "She's local, and she used to do a show downtown at the Gilded Calf."

"Magic?"

"No, medium. She's never done magic, that I know of. Oh, and she came here from Sedona, Arizona."

"Figures." Temple gritted her teeth as she pushed against a crowd that was all going in the opposite direction.

"And she used to be married to Oscar Grant."

"No!" That stopped Temple in her tracks, which were made by Anne Klein Kelly-green pumps. "Talk about opposites attracting. Look at who she's married to now!"

"Um, that big quiet guy, what's-his-name."

"Yeah, that big guy made about as much impression on me as a bowl of haggis too." Temple glanced at the woman's tent. It looked fashioned from lamé and Lurex, and today's long, clingy white gown looked half spandex. "Odd that a purist about the paranormal from the New Age capital of Arizona should wear so much artificial fabric."

"Oh, Temple." Electra seemed glad to stand still for a while. "These people are . . . odd to begin with."

"And yet you believe they're for real?"

"Sure. People who hear and see things other people don't are bound to get a bit . . . strange."

"Include us, then, because we seem to have seen everything everyone else did at the séance."

"Yes, and I'm so disappointed. I was hoping Aunt Min would show up just for me."

"Aunt Min? Anything like my aunt Kit?"

"Heavens, no. She was a turn-of-the-century lady; never wore a skirt shorter than her anklebone in her life. The twenties just passed her by, and so did bathtub gin and even the occasional medicinal glass of wine. But she was a great advocate of Spiritualism."

"Spiritualism was still around in the twenties? I thought Spiritualism was overstuffed late-nineteenth-century parlors, with mists forming on the bell jar and apparitions mussing the antimacassars."

"My dear young thing, Spiritualism may have started back then, but it was still roaring by the twenties. Ouija boards were really sheik."

Temple nodded. Being a post-1950's baby, she tended to forget how fast the twentieth century had changed. "Let's hit the Great White Way before the next New Age Lothario stops by."

"Mynah does seem popular for a gal who's gone gray early," Electra commented, patting her cheerful shag.

Despite the stretchy modern fabrics, at close view Mynah's tent revealed itself as an albino chapel to the ghost of Art Nouveau. This was a pale, calm oasis amid the color and hullabaloo, a moon suspended over the gaudy rainbow.

Sickle-shaped mirrors hung against the flimsy curtains. An old trunk gaped open in the middle of the booth, with an artistic tidal wave of glittering fabrics. Vintage kaleidoscopes and stereopticons peeked from between pallid folds. On the booth's long front table, glitter-dotted white cotton batting played backdrop for moonstone jewelry in sinuous silver settings.

Mynah presided over this Winter Wonderland like the Snow Queen from Hans Christian Andersen's most savagely cynical fairy tale.

"The moonstones!" was all Electra could say.

Fanned, Mynah's long fingers and nails passed over the array as if hesitating above the keys of a musical instrument. Temple could almost see the drops of lucent moonstone tremble to her not-quite-touch.

"My miniature scrying mirrors," Mynah commented. "I sell them, and you buy them to find out what can be seen in mirrors, if anything."

"There are no price tags," Temple noted.

Mynah was unperturbed. "No, I establish prices on the spot, depending on how I like the purchaser." She tilted her head. Her eyebrows were dark but unpenciled, her eyes ice-crystal blue, her makeup as subtle as snow, if she even wore any. "You like something? Want me to price it for you?"

She had the air of a lazing Big Cat, a white tiger napping before deciding to pounce. Temple didn't want to give the woman the edge of instantly evaluating *her* by setting a price too low, or too high, to be real.

"There's too much to see," Temple said. "I'd need time to pick one. They're all so exquisite. Do you make them yourself?"

"No. I only . . . touch them to activate their hidden properties, rather the way I conduct séances. The one last night was not a séance, but a show," she added with quick disdain.

"A bad show," Electra put in over Temple's shoulder. "I'd really love these earrings, how much?"

"For you?" A smile, wider than it was warm. "Forty-seven dollars."

Electra didn't wince as she pulled out her checkbook.

Mynah reminded her to present her driver's license, then wrote down the number on the check. "Remember, once I touch them, these minimirrors of mineral might show you anything."

"Just so it isn't my crow's-feet." Electra laughed earthily.

Crow's-feet, apparently, did not intrude into Mynah Sigmund's world. She answered with utter seriousness. "The moonstones do not show the present, or the superficial. They reflect deep, and delve both past and future."

Oh, goody galoshes, Temple thought, *we're back in séance mode: no contractions and portentous predictions.*

Electra pocketed her package and ebbed behind Temple, leaving her to begin a disingenuous interrogation of someone who had probably been born calculating odds and memorizing state income tax tables.

"Mynah, babe!" The man's voice came from behind Temple and Electra.

"Why, Big Mike." Mynah's face tilted so she could eye him from under her black lashes. Her pale lips produced a Mona Lisa slice of sickle moon. "There's room just for you. Go around the side curtain and come into my parlor. You can sit a spell."

From her lips, the word "spell" sounded like a sinister enchantment rather than a colloquial expression for "a while."

Temple glanced significantly at Electra. She had not seen such a blatant case of Phony Female since junior high school.

The man seemed oblivious to the invitation's artificiality. He stomped around the booth's side, bulled through the delicate fabric and plopped down on a gray folding chair next to Mynah.

"Where you been so long?" the White Witch asked in tones syrupy enough to drown pancakes.

Her eyes were only for the new arrival. Temple and Electra could have been wooden Indians, for all she cared.

Temple wasn't used to being erased from any woman's consciousness merely upon the Arrival of a Man. She checked Electra, who was also suffering a sudden case of invisibility.

The Man in Question was a big beefy guy in his forties, genus rancher. He stuck cowboy-booted feet out from the chair and hitched his thumbs in his Levi's pockets. A bolo tie with an art gallery Native American slide added a regional touch of formality to his Western-cut shirt. He returned the same knowing look-for-two that Mynah gave him.

"How's the fair doing?" His brusque manner indicated that he didn't care much one way or the other.

"Fine, now that the inane semipublic séance is done. We had

ourselves a double apparition, one of them in triplicate, did you hear? And a small death."

He was nodding and smirking. Words were unimportant. What mattered was the music playing under them, the separate and secret language of expressions that made this conversation a duel of innuendo and taunt.

"Mynah!" The next man who arrived behind Temple and Electra was tall, but as well stuffed as a teddy bear sagging at the middle. "Do you need me to cart away the empty boxes now?"

Mynah's husband, what's-his-name, was as indifferent to Temple's and Electra's presence as the other man, but behind his mock tortoiseshell eyeglass frames, Temple spied a dull resentment, a cowed fury. Ah, yes, this was the Nowhere Man pointed out last night as the Snow Queen's heavyweight husband. Then who was yon frowsy middleweight parked in the folding chair?

William Kohler, that was his name! The husband's, not the rancher's.

"I just shoved them all under the tablecloths myself." Mynah's careless wave of one white hand implied William had been derelict in his duty, so the brave little woman had done it all alone.

Sour William still needed something to fuss about. "They can't all fit under there."

"They did." Her lake-blue gaze had iced over.

Mr. Mynah was not wanted here, nor was Temple, who had not bought, nor Electra, who had.

The New Man watched with smug contempt as William tightened his lips. "All right," he muttered. "I'll check again later."

It sounded like a threat rather than a promise, but not much of either. He lumbered off, still muttering.

Mynah sighed, shifted, let herself remain the focus of all eyes. "He really is a dear."

She might just as well have said, "He really is a bear," for the emotion in her tone.

"So who have you knocked dead with your smile now?" the oaf in the chair asked.

She shrugged. "A hermaphrodite, apparently." A practiced trill masqueraded as a laugh. "A man dressed as a woman, can you believe it? Came to expose us fraudulent mediums."

"Seems like he ended up well done." The guy pulled out a Navajo pocketknife to jab at the grime beneath his nails.

Temple was repulsed beyond staying to do her duty as an inquiring mind. She turned to Electra and lifted both eyebrows.

Electra nodded.

"We'll come back after we check out the other booths," Temple announced pointedly.

Mynah's demismile widened, but she didn't look at them; her gaze was only for the guy on the chair. "Take your time, ladies," she mocked, making "ladies" sound like Victorian biddies on an expedition to buy bell jars.

By the time the two were beyond hearing distance, both were too miffed to speak.

"What a . . . phony broad," Temple finally managed to spit out. "I thought that kind of billboard-obvious man-hunting went out with Scarlett O'Hara."

"Scarlett was never that obvious. I'd forgotten about that," Electra reminisced fondly.

"About what?"

"What it felt like to become instantly invisible when a woman you were with wanted to concentrate on a man."

"You were used to that?"

Electra widened her eyes. "We all did it then. It seemed logical."

"To the men too, I bet."

"I don't know. Those were the days when they used to have to jump up like jackrabbits every few minutes to light a woman's cigarette." Electra nodded dazedly. "I guess those were the days when there were a lot more smokers."

"It all sounds like people lived as if they were in an old movie."

"We were, hon! It's called your own past. And it was a time, frankly, when a woman knew her place in a situation like that: quietly ebbing away to give the other woman a clear field."

Temple shook her head. "I don't see why that Sigmund woman is such a vamp. Like I say, it's so obviously phony."

"Men don't get much of that these days," Electra said. "Maybe they miss it. It may be phony, but it's all for their benefit, which must be rewarding."

"Well, I'll just visit the other booths, then, and get the scoop on Mynah."

"Very wise. Now you have something to ask them about."

"What?"

"Edwina Mayfair was really a man, wasn't he?"

Temple nodded.

"Maybe he was in disguise because he and Mynah were in cahoots."

"You're kidding! Why would she bother with an elderly skeptic like him when she already had a husband in tow and Pa Cartright on the side?"

"As you said, she's a phony broad. They never stop handing that stuff out, because they never have enough."

"Seems to me that the motive for killing the old guy had to have been because he planned to expose someone's trickery."

"Sure. But it doesn't have to be paranormal trickery, Temple. It could simply be old-fashioned hanky-panky."

While Temple paused in mid-aisle to weigh that idea, Electra grabbed her arm with alarming pressure. "Oh, look! Crystals to die for. Come on!"

Electra dove for a booth across a stream of people. Temple tagged along, thinking.

A feeding frenzy of excitement broke out in the aisle ahead of them. Over it all beamed a bright white camcorder light.

"Crawford!" Temple felt like she had sighted Moby Dick.

"Something's up!" Electra hallooed back. "Let's go."

They weren't the first on the scene, which was now watched by an audience of fifteen fascinated fair-goers.

Stage center were Crawford and the cameraman, Watts and Sacker and . . . D'Arlene Hendrix.

"This could have been discreet," Sacker was saying, glancing around to find the reporter that accompanied the glaring camcorder.

"But I . . . I'm innocent!" D'Arlene protested. "I didn't do anything."

"Come along," Watts urged. "This is just for questioning. We are not about to cuff you for the TV cameras or anything."

"You!" Sacker barked. "Shut that off."

The two detectives turned and pushed through the crowd, D'Arlene between them and casting anguished glances backward.

"D'Arlene Hendrix?" Temple said. "Talk about an unlikely suspect. I wouldn't have thought the Martha Stewart of the paranormal set would have the nerve to skewer an olive."

"She wouldn't." Electra tried to work her way out of the crowd to follow, but was stymied. "Oh, this is nuts. She'd never kill anyone. Temple, you have got to do something about this."

A breathless, low voice spoke at Temple's rear.

"A distraught New Age onlooker has just asked Temple Barr, crack Las Vegas lady sleuth, to prove the Halloween ghost-killing suspect innocent. Will she do it?"

A mesh fist of microphone zoomed toward Temple's mouth like a mobile metal ice-cream cone, tempting her to bite, hard. The television light engorged into nova-brightness.

"Will you?" Crawford Buchanan demanded dramatically for the camera.

"I'll . . . No comment." Temple turned her back on the camera, grabbing Electra's arm and diving into the crowd. She felt the heat of the light follow them until it veered to pursue the detectives hustling D'Arlene away.

"That was thrilling," Electra said in shaky tones. "I feel like a district attorney or something."

"How about like a victim? Crawford is the consummate grandstander! You'd think he was working for *Court TV.*"

"I can't get over D'Arlene Hendrix being arrested. Her work with families of lost children is outstanding, and has even been praised by some police detectives. They have the wrong person."

"Electra, the police are just taking her downtown for questioning; that's hardly arrest, as you know from my experience."

"But it's a scandal now that your Crawford friend has latched onto it for TV." Electra's jaw set, a new expression for her. "I don't care how corny you feel about being named a sleuth, D'Arlene's quality of life and career are at stake. You've got to do something."

Temple shook her head, a mistake, because it felt loose enough on her neck to fall off.

"What I've got to do is go home and get some sleep. And so do you. Don't say another word. Not until later when we can read about it in the morning paper."

Electra frowned. "Sherlock Holmes would never wait until he could read about it in the morning paper."

"Maybe he had ESP," Temple growled, turning on her heel to leave Crawford Buchanan, the psychic fair and her New Age Watson behind her.

Chapter 18

Maxnapping

A Friday-afternoon nap.

What a luxury.

Temple stretched as she awoke, ghosts and panthers circling in her subconscious.

Louie was an out-of-focus lump curled up on the end of her bed. At least he was safe at home. Again. How she would love to interrogate *him!*

She stretched again, blinking at the black haze on her bed.

Louie was putting on a lot of weight.

She patted the bedside table for her glasses, unfolded the earpieces and pushed them on.

Oh.

Midnight Louie had morphed into Max Kinsella, who did not have to lose weight, and who—while sitting on the end of her bed—could by no means be described as "curled up." Unless it was as in: "curled up like a steel spring" and ready to pounce.

Temple wished that she was really awake. She wished she had

not put her glasses on. She wished she was wearing Chanel No. 5 and a Victoria's Secret chemise, say in teal silk satin. She wished she was wearing a potato sack. She wished she was not here. She wished he was not here.

She smiled.

"Max! What on earth brought you back?"

He just shook his head. "Tell me about the murder."

"We don't know it was a murder."

"Too bad 'we' don't. I do."

"You do? How? Did I miss the news?"

He found the television remote control she was patting the covers to corral, then clicked on a station. A group of hundred-year-old teenagers, pierced on every visible inch of skin, except on their ears, seemed to be speaking out passionately on the benefits of purple hair.

"No news on yet this afternoon but bad news." Max clicked the talk show off. "Tell me what happened. You were holding hands with Gandolph, after all."

"I was not! I did *not* know the woman was Gandolph. I was happy to be *not* holding hands with Crawford Buchanan, unaware that I had been cruelly deceived and was actually pressing palms with an elderly, cross-dressing male magician nobody had heard of in a cat's nine lives."

"Lots of people had heard of Gandolph the Great. He was retired, true."

"Retired to transvestism."

"He was a showman," Max said. "He was . . . a Don Quixote. He was there because he had something to prove, not because he wanted to pass as female."

"How do you know?"

"Because it's an honored tradition in the séance-exposing game. Even Houdini wore wigs in disguise when he was investigating mediums. Possibly women's clothes as well. And, besides, I know Gandolph. He was . . . my friend."

"Max—" Temple was shocked. Max had never mentioned having a friend before, come to think of it. "He must have lived in Las Vegas when we moved here, but you never mentioned him."

"Yes, I did, but not often."

"Right! That's where I heard the name before . . . maybe once! If you two were such buddies, why were he and I never introduced?"

"You were last night," Max said grimly.

"Max, I'm worrying about gnats in the face of tarantulas. I'm sorry."

He didn't quite look at her. "Don't worry. I don't want to hear about Gandolph's last moments. I do need to know what happened."

"So much did, Max! I still can't sort it out. I think we all saw a ghost, only I doubt it was the ghost we were supposed to see. Louie dropped in, yes, quite literally. Down the chimney, like a sooty feline Santa. Maybe you'd like to question him?"

Max smiled, dropped the remote control on the zebra-patterned coverlet, and stood.

"I'll brew some instant espresso in the kitchen. It's almost five P.M. Why don't you slip into something . . . less comfortable."

Temple eyed her purple fuzzie jogging suit while he was gone. "Something less comfortable," really. Where was her chicest potato sack when she needed it, anyway?

She found a sort of caftan she'd forgotten about, emerald-green gauze with gilt lettuce-leaf edges, and managed to be wide awake and changed before he returned with two mugs of murky Instant Sludge.

"You mean it?" she asked after her first heady sip. "Gandolph was a friend of yours?"

Max prowled to the French doors overlooking the acute end of the triangular patio. He'd talked about putting a spa out there, but they'd never gotten around to it. It would have been nice, a miniversion of Van and Nicky's penthouse Jacuzzi.

Max's mind had been somewhere else Temple had never seen. "Maybe 'mentor' is a better word for Gandolph," he said. "I had the most contact with him at the beginning, and the end, of my career."

"Max, don't say that. Your career isn't over."

"Isn't it? I walked out on a half-dozen engagements, two for charity, without a word. I knew what I was doing. I didn't want to do it, but I had to. I'm a poor man now, Temple."

"What about all the dough you raked in when you were the toast of the Continent?"

He turned, grinning. "We're not counting the Swiss bank accounts and Cayman condominiums, are we?" She couldn't tell if he was kidding, or not. "So, you sat next to him. Tell me what happened."

Ordinarily, that wouldn't have been a big order. It was now, given the confusions of that midnight séance on the crux of Halloween and All Saints' Day, suspended between two worlds, the real and the really weird.

"I don't know, Max." Temple was glad she had ditched the glasses. This coffee was hot enough to steam up retinas. "I bought his act: this ditsy old gal in a funny hat. He must have been good at it. Only one thing struck me as unusual: 'she' kept warning me not to take anything that happened seriously. I thought that was odd behavior for a psychic at a séance."

Max was chuckling. "I'm sure he didn't know who you were, but, believe me, if Gandolph were taking advantage of you in any way, it would definitely be heterosexual."

"That old goat in granny clothing! And here I was all hot and bothered about Awful Crawford, meanwhile holding hands with the worst dirty old man in the bunch!"

"Sometimes you can run so hard to avoid something that you bump right into it."

"Yes, I noticed."

They observed a decent moment's silence while the applications of that dialogue to their current situation sunk in uncommented upon.

"Gandolph wasn't a real dirty old man," Max finally said. "He just never stopped appreciating women. So Gandolph's persona did not buy the night's special effects."

"Not at all, especially the distorted face that hung in the window behind him and mouthed untranslatable little nothings. The way the place is set up—"

"I know how it's set up. I looked it over."

"When?"

"After the . . . death."

"Max, they closed the attraction, how did you—?"

He shrugged with a boyish innocence that didn't quite wash. "I'm an illusionist." He smiled at the floor as if consulting a silent partner. "Like Midnight Louie. I have my ways."

"Don't you just!" Temple leaned over the bed's edge to see that the displaced cat had found floorside accommodations.

"Shall I demonstrate?" Max asked in a way that made Temple scoot up against her pillow and rest her elbows on her knees.

"Never mind." She blew steam off the top of her coffee before sipping gingerly. Max always used to say he liked his java "hot as hell, strong as the Devil, and black as sin."

Midnight Louie, displaced to the fuzzy white bedside rug, rolled onto his side and began licking his hind leg, perhaps preparing to point a less polite area of his anatomy in Max the Usurper's direction.

"Okay, I'm thinking," she told Max. "The face in the window behind Gandolph appeared just before the dwarf in the fireplace showed up."

"Quasimodo too. You had a busy séance."

"No, I'm told it was Houdini himself. All the psychics present recognized him. An ugly apparition, really. Hunched over, muscle-bound, and this was a short man to begin with."

"Five feet four," Max put in promptly. He was a fountain of knowledge about Houdini. Temple suspected that Houdini was a lot of boy-magicians' hero.

"These cuffs and chains weighed him down," she added. "Naked, too, sinewy beyond his stature. I mean, he must have worn something, but it was hard to see through the mist. He looked like some primitive specimen, captured and brought out for display."

"Houdini wanted to make that impression. Lone, naked man against all of civilized society's locks and chains. He may have had a repressed bondage fantasy."

" 'Gorilla in the Mist,' huh? Did they know about bondage fantasy in those days?"

"Someone did."

"What do you think about the mist?"

"Obfuscation. Piped in. Vents all over the room. Part of the 'haunted' effect during shows."

Temple nodded, not surprised. "The usual dry ice. Were we supposed to be lost in London fog, though?"

"Doubt it. The dry ice was blown into various pipes, and was on a programmable timer. Anyone who has ever left town and used a light timer could have reset the mechanism to cloud the séance. It didn't take the expertise level of someone who knows how to set the VCR. By the way, who's been setting yours since I've been gone?"

"Haven't used it," Temple confessed. "Easier not to."

Max shook his head. "What did Gandolph do during the Houdini appearance?"

"He muttered stuff about believing nothing of what you see and only half of what you hear."

Max smiled. "A cynic . . . to the last."

"Was he right?"

"Of course! The whole thing was a joke. That visitation of Houdini, for instance. You described a famous photographic pose. Did the apparition move? No, except to advance closer and retreat, which you can do with a projection. This wasn't even a state-of-the-art hoax. It was contemptuous, and contemptible. I suspect the entire charade was conceived as a cover to kill Gandolph, by someone who wanted the world to know it."

"Why?"

"Because Gandolph hated humbug. Because he couldn't resist unveiling the phony. Because he was an old man with little to do, and he poked his nose into one ugly business too many."

"And why do you have to decipher this?"

Max finished his coffee with one, long, scalding gulp, never taking his adulterated green eyes from Temple's. "I owe him. I don't like humbug myself. And . . ." He sighed. "Where do you think I was staying in Vegas, since I wasn't here? Who else could I stay with? Who do you think will look damn suspicious if the police find out, and who do you think can't afford to let them find out? I've got to solve Gandolph's murder, because he mattered to me, and, as a perk, to save my own damn skin."

Temple nodded. She had avoided speculating where Max might be staying, maybe out of guilt that she couldn't welcome him with open bedsheets, maybe out of fear that he knew another woman or two or three in town. Of course the notion of Max rooming with a cross-dressing older guy . . . ridiculous!

"Want some more coffee?"

When she nodded, he headed for the kitchen. She followed, sticking her feet into the oversize burgundy velour mukluks by the bed, which did nothing to enhance the caftan's sophistication. She was relieved to be out of the bedroom. Midnight Louie, in turn, followed her out like a feline chaperon.

Max was waiting for the microwave to *ping,* so she had a chance to compare his unguarded rear to Oscar Grant's. Not for Max the other man's styled, flowing shoulder-length locks. That's what they were: locks, not mere hair. Max's new long hair was sleeked into a ponytail that blended with his turtleneck to the point of disappearing. The black garb was the same gunfighter uniform, but the effect was less theatrical. Max was much taller, though as lean; his turtleneck and slacks had the same silky ease that cried out "expensive designer togs," but Max's fabrics suffered no touch of sheen. He wore the more effacing matte black, as if he wished to make himself into the invisible sable background curtain on a theater stage.

Matt black. He wore Matt black, Temple found herself thinking. Ex-Father Matt–black. Comparing Max Kinsella with a priest made her smile, then made her think again. Magicians onstage assumed a ceremonial, priestly role, didn't they, albeit of a priest from some exotic, alien culture? Say, some ancient Eastern culture. She wondered, out of the blue (or maybe out of the black) what it would be like to make love with a man who had long hair, and immediately censored her unconscious: yikes, she was thinking like one of those supposedly love-starved females who gawk at romance-novel cover hunks and stockpile their calendars!

The microwave oven *ping*'d politely. Shortly after, Max turned with two hot mugs of coffee and a penetrating glance. "You don't look too spooked today, despite the . . . death."

Temple took her mug before the handle got too hot for him to hold. She moved quickly into the living room to set it down on the sofa table.

"I'm not spooked. Maybe I'm jaded. But . . . Gandolph didn't die brutally. Just slipped away. One of the other women swooned, so I wasn't surprised to see 'her' slumped over after the Houdini routine. It took everyone there a while to realize he was dead."

She sat on one end of the couch, Max coming toward her. Midnight Louie jumped up to stretch out full-length on mid-couch. Max paused, then sat on the opposite end.

"I'm not much for housepets."

"Louie is not a pet."

"What is he, then?"

"An old friend who wanders in and out. He had his haunts, excuse the expression, before I ever brought him home, and he likes to visit them."

"Not the haunted house, though?"

"I don't know. He could have shown up there before."

"Does he always follow you somehow?"

"No, sometimes he asks to ride along. Other times he's there before me."

"He 'asks' to ride along?"

She sipped and nodded. "Cats ask for things, just like dogs. Only they don't bark."

"That's an advantage," Max admitted. He leaned back into the sofa. "This would feel like Sunday morning if we had the funny papers."

Temple nodded, not trusting herself to deliver the next line and afraid what it might lead to. Aw, heck, why not find out what it might lead to? They both admitted that they were still monogamous. The morality police had other crimes of the libido to pursue. . . .

The doorbell rang. Max jumped up. Louie didn't.

Max was in the bedroom before Temple could say, "Three, four, open the door."

In that many seconds, she did, still carrying her mug.

Matt stood there.

Saved by the bell and Devine intervention, Temple thought with a rueful smile.

Chapter 19

Double-talk

"You look surprisingly chipper," Matt said, meaning it and trying not to stare at the gauzy grass-green robe that underlined Temple's rusty coloring. "After hearing Electra's harrowing version of your Halloween séance in the laundry room, I thought I'd better rush up to see if you required spiritual counseling."

"I'm fine." Temple stepped back to admit him. "I'm just hung over from a reversed sleep pattern. Just got up. You know how that is."

"And Midnight Louie was there too?" Matt eyed the lounging cat with respect, but then, he always had.

"In the fur. He was the least of our apparitions."

Matt sat in the only spot on the sofa Louie left him, the corner opposite Temple. She regarded him a bit edgily, as if she saw a ghost of someone else sitting there.

"I was on my way to ConTact," he added, feeling a sudden need to justify his presence.

"Do you have time for coffee?" She lifted her own mug. Matt's glance fixed on the steaming, full mug on the coffee table right in front of his place.

"Oh!" Temple looked flustered. "I had my cup in the bedroom when you rang. I must have been so dopey I'd made another one, set it down out here and forgot about it. You like it? Its yours."

"Thanks."

He picked up the pottery handle. Still too hot to hold for long. Temple, he noticed, had quickly set down her own mug for the same reason, obviously. Why would an abandoned and forgotten extra mug still be so piping hot? Matt dismissed that line of thought. He was starting to think like a detective.

Or a jealous lover.

"Want to tell me about the séance?" he asked.

"Where to begin?"

She actually paused to gather her impressions, unlikely behavior in rush-ahead Temple. The green gown madly complemented her raucous red hair, an attractive collision of curls. Even without the light makeup she used, Temple would never give morning a bad name.

"You must be on my hours today," he remarked.

She nodded. "Without being used to them. But, back to the skulduggery at the Hell-o-ween Haunted Homestead."

"I still can't believe they named the place that."

"Indeed. In a nutshell, the woman next to me—who was really a man, but who, I'm told on good authority, was not normally a cross-dresser, or abnormally a cross-dresser—fainted after the last apparition. No one thought anything of it until we noticed her picture hat had slipped and he had a bald head."

Matt laughed at Temple's patented rat-a-tat delivery of the facts, which always sounded jumbled but also always added up to exactly what had happened. He could see why the methodical Carmen Molina had no patience with Temple's communication style.

"Still, death next door is traumatic," he said sympathetically.

"It was more traumatic to find out the motherly woman who'd been squeezing my hand all night was really a man."

"Why the disguise, if not for dysfunctional reasons?"

"Well, not everyone is sure transvestites are dysfunctional. Most are otherwise straight-arrow heterosexuals. I have found a hint, however. The dead man is . . . was . . . a retired stage magician named Gandolph."

Matt nodded.

"You don't find that name strange? Don't tell me you've read *The Lord of the Rings!*"

"Several times, why?"

"I haven't. Am I way out of the loop! Can you loan it to me?"

"Sure, in paperback. But it's really three books, three long books."

"I'm up for it. Anyway, the dead man was not named after *that* Gandalf, at least overtly. He spelled it G-a-n-do-l-p-h, as in Rudolph et cetera, and his hobby was exposing false mediums."

"Uh-oh. Then any false medium present would have motive to kill him."

"Don't you mean '*every* false medium present'?"

"I'm trying to keep an open mind, but you keep slamming the door shut on me. So the night's special effects were disappointing."

"More like puzzling, I'd say. The fellow who turned up before we actually saw an image of Houdini was more interesting. At least he went though some ghostly metamorphoses."

"Such as?"

"We first saw him as a boy, maybe six years old. Then he popped up in different windows, which were actually glass walls with wallpaper patterns etched into them, but he was older each time. Bigger. Way bigger. At the end, he was this sad, massive old man with a raging face, but we couldn't hear any of the words. Kind of reminded me of a pantomime King Lear, actually."

"The play?"

"No, the part. This guy would have been a natural, in his last incarnation, that is. Seeing him made me feel so . . . sorry. That was the only spooky part of the séance, these visions of this sad man from virtually boyhood to old-coothood. He wanted to communicate so much, but something was holding him back."

"What about Houdini?"

"Gross! Grotesque. The others say the image duplicated a photograph of him nearly naked and chained into a crouch. It gave me the creeps!"

"Better drink some hot coffee; your arms are growing a record batch of goosebumps."

She shot him a glance that was both flustered and flattered before he realized that he had been observing her too closely again, like a detective. Or like a jealous lover.

He finished the coffee and set it down. Temple nervously noticed his action, rubbing her chilled forearms, then glanced behind him. To her bedroom. She looked nervous.

In the silence, the uncertainty was catching. He became acutely aware of the bedroom. He'd been in it briefly once, to help her put on some pierced earrings before the Gridiron show. Now it loomed at the back of her mind for some reason, which he could either interpret as embarrassing or flattering.

Would-be detective or would-be lover, which part was he playing today? No matter, he was what Temple would call a "bloody amateur" in both roles. Matt stood.

"I'd better go."

She didn't argue. She didn't rush him, but she stood also. "Thanks for stopping by. When I find out more, I'll let you know."

"Not 'if'?"

"Nooo . . . I'll be stuck reading or listening to the news like everybody else. No dropped clues from Molina this time. She's not on the case."

Matt felt surprise. He'd come to think of Lieutenant Molina as the conduit through which all matters of murder in Las Vegas flowed. For some reason, he felt disappointment.

"I did have an 'in' with her," Temple went on, "by virtue of her suspicion of me, if nothing else. Watts and Sacker are perfectly professional, and they don't suspect me of being anything more than an innocent bystander, but that means they're not intrigued enough to spend time chitchatting with me."

"Poor Temple, on the outside looking in, like the spectral fat man."

They were at the door now, and she was opening it to show him out.

"That's just it, Matt." Her voice grew low, confessional-confidential. "He looked so solid for a ghost. Nobody would fake something like that so straightforwardly. That's the only thing in the evening that truly gives me the chills. I think he was— Oh, Lord, I sound like Tommy Rettig on old *Lassie* reruns—'trying to tell us something.' "

Matt recognized a troubled mind when he heard it. Impulsively, he put a hand on her icy forearm, reassured her.

"Don't blame yourself, Temple. You do, you know. You assume that if you had known that the person next to you was who he really was, you might have been able to prevent whatever happened. I haven't seen anything on the TV news or in the paper that the police are calling it murder. Why are you so sure that it was?"

Her gray-blue eyes softened with unspoken appeal. "I—I can't tell you why, Matt. I just suspect that it was on the usual groundless instincts. Thanks for listening."

She went on her toes to kiss his cheek. He caught her other arm before her stretch reversed itself and kissed her mouth, tasting strong coffee, surprise, response and reservation.

"Don't worry, Temple," he told her, not knowing why. He managed to retreat without trying to gauge her reaction.

In the hall, he felt a wave of self-disgust. He didn't need anything else to obsess about, but he was tired of her always making the first moves.

Maybe he also had a nagging feeling that he ought to stake his claim.

He went down the stairs to the rhythm of his footsteps, and headed for the shed to confront his trusty steed.

The Hesketh Vampire gave him the willies, kind of like Stephen King's murderous vintage car, Christine.

Only the fact that Electra rode it had lured him into practice sessions and ultimately a license. Only that, and the bottom line that he needed transportation and couldn't afford it.

While he might lecture Temple during martial-arts sessions that tackling new skills is vital, when it came to himself he had discovered that Matt Devine was remarkably conservative.

He unlocked the padlock shed door and stared at the Vampire, standing sleek-flanked and shining in the bar of daylight he had admitted.

He hoped it wasn't the fact that the motorcycle had been Max Kinsella's toy, his pride and joy, that bothered him, although living up to his imagined persona of Max Kinsella did.

Matt walked around the massive machine, now so startlingly passive.

His entire religious life as a priest had been disciplined and dedicated to withdrawing from the material, to not needing what most other people require as a right: good salaries, good clothes, a nice place to live, money for luxuries, for status merchandise, for marriage, kids, mortgages, speed in the sense of velocity, sex in the sense of appetite.

So, though he tried to regard the Vampire as merely the best and the cheapest available, practical transportation, considering his situation, he couldn't fool himself.

All that power unnerved him. The machine's great worth as a classic 'cycle (hey, he had used the right, hip term almost naturally) made him edgy. Its implied silver sexiness made him feel like an imposter.

It was such . . . flagrantly conspicuous consumption. It was so . . . inescapably macho. And just in running operation terms, it was so much machine that Matt sometimes thought it would fly. And it was menacing, he knew, when he rode it wearing the anonymous, shaded-visor helmet the law required.

People on the street expected something of the man who rode such a machine, and it wasn't him.

Matt opened the shed's double wooden doors that opened on the back of the Circle Ritz's parking lot. All that late-day light made the 'cycle shine like a nova star. The Vampire screamed its presence just by sitting still, its powerful engine not making a single, pulsing, impatient *vroom-vroom.*

He mounted it, turned the key, eased it as slowly as it would go out the doors, turned it to idle, pushed the kickstand down, the one he never trusted to hold up half a ton of steel and chrome.

After he shut the shed tight and locked it, he came around to the waiting Vampire.

He rode it competently, he knew, but not with ease or style. Sometimes, when in traffic, he appreciated the machine's liquid slipping past stalled cars, in and around obstacles. Sometimes he almost felt the slipstream smoothness of it, the tilt of his weight as it wove this way or that, so they were one, footloose entity.

Those moments were rare. Mostly he was worried sick about it. Worried that someone would steal it from outside ConTact despite the lock. Worried that the throttle on the handle would take on a will and life of its own and run away with him. Worried that someone might think he thought he was somebody for having such a monster. Worried. Worried. Worried.

That's what he had studied to do for all his life: worry about right and wrong, all his actions and pretensions, other people's good regard, his grades, his state of grace, the afterlife, today's small sins.

Matt detached the helmet from the rear. Electra's "Speed Queen" helmet hung on a hook inside the shed. Matt's helmet was his only investment in his motorcycle-riding career, and he didn't want anything written on it.

He smiled as he booted the kickstand aside and revved the engine simultaneously.

A Hesketh Vampire's corporate symbol was a chicken, royally crowned and prominently displayed. Only the British could get away with that kind of underplaying. Still, Matt didn't think a "Chicken"-emblazoned helmet would do his health any good.

With the one thousand cc engine growling out fair warning to any small-cylinder vehicles foolish enough to be out there, Matt revved and roared his incongruous way onto the side street.

He still caught the lurid comet tail of the Strip's evening rush hour when he headed to ConTact at six-thirty. Tonight the wind was chilly, and his nylon windbreaker offered as much protection against it as waxed paper.

Potential speed demon or not, he got caught, along with about three hundred cars, by the long red light at Sahara Avenue.

While their conjoined engines idled, growling like sleeping tigers, a stream of pedestrians filled the crosswalks. Matt shivered as he kept the big bike balanced. It was colder sitting still than pushing into the wind, oddly enough. The lined leather gloves he wore on rare visits home to Chicago were welcome. He saw why leather had become a hallmark of the biker crowd: practicality. The menace had come afterward.

Maybe it was because his mind was on idle, and growling with impatience like the surrounding cars. Or because his thoughts had hopscotched to Chicago, knee-deep snows and bitter, biting wind. Bitter, biting memories.

Or because the day was in that twilight zone, when traffic lights are just beginning to brighten in contrast to the waning natural light, when shadows seem to stretch over Las Vegas all the way from the western mountains. As if a giant hand were reaching out to squeeze the light out of life like wringing lemon juice from a rind.

Or maybe it was Temple's talk of séances and death and ghosts.

But Matt recognized a certain shamble as it moved past his day-dreaming vision. A man in the crowd: aviator sunglasses, though the daylight had given up the ghost for today; cowboy hat; jeans jacket; hunched shoulders. Sideburns.

Matt blinked.

The man was already three quarters of the way through the lengthy crosswalk, swallowed to all but the high-crowned, dingy Western hat by the people who had followed and passed him.

Still. Matt studied his position. Far right lane. Guy heading away from him to the left. Couldn't be worse, couldn't be more impossible. About as impossible as that walk, that hesitating lope that never seemed in a hurry to get anywhere, but always got there faster than you thought. The icy wind Matt felt was not external. Cold was not a consideration anymore.

How could he . . . ?

The semaphore light changed to green. Surrounding cars sprang forward, fog lights straining into the creeping shadow of night. Matt found himself making a split-second decision. Maybe the Hesketh Vampire was making it: leaning left, slipping into a slot between a dawdling Volvo and a sprinting Camaro, nipping across the path of a lumbering limo as long as the buffet line at the Goliath. Dodging front and rear fenders, coasting between the massive metal walls of Chevrolet Suburbans, only inches to spare. He felt like Charlton Heston in the chariot-race scene from *The Ten Com-*

mandments. Only Matt's rival was not Messala with a whip wanting to win at any cost, but the invisible whip of memory, which always drove to lose. . . .

By the next traffic light, Charleston Boulevard, Matt was first in line in the left turn lane, waiting, waiting for time to make the red light green. *Don't it make, don't it make, don't it make your red eyes green?* When the light finally blinked, the Hesketh Vampire whipped around the concrete island in a U-turn so tight that Matt felt momentarily horizontal to the street.

Now he was veering across lanes to the right. God, if he so much as scraped Electra's—Kinsella's—precious scooter! That Geo wasn't moving, so . . . in and out. The machine was a born accomplice to recklessness, Matt was discovering. It seemed to exult in his insane stampede across lines of traffic. Where would the walker be now? Turning left or right along the Strip? Heading straight on Sahara? Anywhere in the crowd. Matt's only edge was that battered hat.

Back at the same intersection as before, only facing south, with the light having withdrawn another three shades pale and the whole flat valley looking drenched in dusk, with darkness soon to clench its angry, hidden fist until the evening sky was squeezed of everything but stars. . . .

Which way?

No choice.

The light ahead had gone green. A pulsing, pausing metal wall leaped forward, the Vampire first again. Matt scanned the groups of people dribbling into Circus-Circus, the ones walking down the sidewalk to the Stardust or the Frontier, the Treasure Island and Mirage, or even the Luxor's far faint obelisk and pyramid.

No cowboy hats, no hats at all.

A driveway. Had to turn around, go back.

No driveway, not for a long time. The Strip was like that, long segments of hotel frontage uninterrupted by anything but panhandlers.

Where? Vanishing where, even now? Back there.

Matt was sweating despite the chill wind. Rivulets ran down the sides of his face behind the Plexiglas visor. Had to turn back.

The Vampire jumped the curb like a steeplechase steed, cruised across the sidewalk and bumped down into the next driveway, not even noticing what it led to, intersecting the long semicircle almost at the halfway point.

Matt followed it around until it hit a parking-lot road heading west. He streaked along the straightaway, swerving when a car poked its headlights out of an aisle between parked vehicles. A horn screamed annoyance, but he and the Vampire were ducking into another aisle, hunting for an exit.

They paused together at the deserted entrance to Sahara, hearts beating in concert. The engine's rumble was louder. A few people ambled along the sidewalk on either side, but the cold was too off-putting to encourage much foot traffic on this dead side of the hotel.

Matt looked right and left. Saw no cowboy hat. He lifted the amber-smoke visor to study the street again. Nothing. No one worth anything.

Finally he checked his watch, its pale green face night time bright now in the deepening dusk. Ten to seven. Time to get to ConTact.

Matt waited anyway. Maybe the man had stopped to buy a news-paper from the corner machines. Maybe he would come by, if he hadn't ducked into Circus Circus or Slots-A-Fun. Maybe he was still walking east on Sahara.

Maybe he was, but Matt had to get to work on time. He was needed there. Here, he was chasing his imagination. The wind dried the liquid on his skin into pinpricks of sleet. He gave the Vampire its head, like a horse. And it took it. It rolled out onto the asphalt of the street, purring.

At the light he watched the steady red while scanning the intersection crowds for the right cowboy hat, for any cowboy hat.

There was none. Green blossomed in the dark as he and the Vampire started forward like automatons. A LVMPD police car passed in the opposite direction. Matt held the 'cycle to a decorous speed and pattern now: stayed in place, kept to the right lane. He looked right and left, but saw nothing.

Still, he was certain of something. The man who had crossed the

Strip while he waited stalled at a red light had walked like only one man he had ever known. Cliff Effinger. The stepfather from Hell who was supposed to be dead.

Matt knew that rolling walk, as surely as he had been uncertain of the corpse lying still and chill in the coroner's viewing booth. Matt looked down again from a distance on the earthly remains of the reputed Cliff Effinger. He couldn't identify him for sure, as Lieutenant Molina had wanted. Yet the man-in-a-crosswalk's name had screamed out with every step he took.

So, was Effinger the mysterious corpse who had fallen to the Crystal Phoenix craps table a few weeks ago? Or was a dead man walking? Was he anonymously patronizing the same casinos that had drawn him to Las Vegas so many years ago? How would Matt find him, if his instinct was right?

What would he do if he did find him?

His hand twisted on the Vampire's throttle. The bike plunged forward into the valley of the green light. Matt hadn't noticed that it had changed, but somehow the motorcycle was always one heartbeat ahead of him.

Chapter 20

Second Sight

While Miss Temple Barr and Miss Electra Lark have scampered off to the psychic fair, I remain at home, trying to catch up on my cat-naps.

That late-night lalapalooza at the Hell-o-ween Haunted Homestead certainly gave me plenty to dream about. I have not seen such a stellar lineup of spooks since I accidentally stumbled into the wax museum over on Harmon.

Frankly, I cannot make head or tail of what was real and what was not that night, and I am not used to being in the dark about such matters. Perhaps I have made a mistake in not accompanying my roommate and her landlady to the Oasis, but I do my better thinking with plenty of sleep. Between these two females and the Sacred Cat of Karma upstairs, I have barely been able to slit an eye shut.

So I drowse, but by evening I awaken to a familiar assault: getting the psychic saltshaker on the tail, so to speak. I lurch groggily upright, eyeing the ceiling. I know the familiar who is pulling my plume.

"All right," I tell it. "I am not up to another scaling of the Sacred Pyramid. This time Midnight Louie does not go to the mountain; the mountain slides down to his level. Get it?"

I wait for all heaven to break loose, but the ceiling is silent and still. No disgruntled gobs of plaster come at me like spitballs, no conjured enforcers, like tarantula spiders, rain down on my rebellious head.

Something out of the ordinary does occur, though. A spark flashes in the middle of the bedroom television screen, and I have not hit the remote control, not even in rolling over to get up. No picture fills the dark space, only the original spark, which bounces around like one of my favorite toys, a Ping-Pong ball. In fact, I am about to rush the TV screen for a game of cat and mouse when a voice begins broadcasting in my head.

My first suspicion is aliens taking over the airways, but the tone of the voice convinces me it is just Karma blowing the usual hot air. Her actual words do not bear repeating (that is to say, I cannot bear repeating them to any interested parties), but the upshot of her bulletin is that a second séance will soon be in progress at the haunted house and I should attend.

This piece of intelligence perks up my ears and winds up my tail. A second séance? Will Miss Temple be angry to miss such a landmark event! Although I hate to owe Karma for anything, I tip my invisible fedora in her direction before making my way out.

How, you may ask, is Midnight Louie going to leave the Circle Ritz with the bathroom window still closed tighter than a cashier's till? Elementary. I will repeat myself and slip out the same French door that Karma's little out-of-body light beam jimmied open not long before. It never bothers me to accept the aid of a lesser light. I have proven myself to be a supreme escape artist many a time before this. No doubt that is why Houdini waited until last to show up at the previous séance. He must have become tired of always having to prove he can still do it. In fact, I am beginning to adopt that attitude myself when it comes to my love life.

Holy Havana brown, but, baby, it is cold outside! I hate these cooler Nevada nights, and immediately wish I was back on Miss Temple's bed watching a good basketball game.

But I know that the best antidote to a dose of below-the-belt temperatures is a brisk trot that really gets the old fat rolls swaying. Within half an hour, I am once again outside the disreputable façade that represents the pinnacle of the human imagination for horror. Frankly, the real horror is its pathetically low profile in the fright department. But I do not take a visit to this second séance lightly; now that certain celebrity ghosts have found a way through to the mortal world, they could make a mass comeback. Just think of all the former performers who could return to torture our airways in the future: Desi Arnaz and Vera Zorina, just to run the gamut of talent from A to Z.

Despite this awful scenario, I do my duty. I find a chink in the building façade that has been plugged by the wind-blown refuse. I two-step right over Crawford Buchanan's barely recognizable mug and an old Mystifying Max flyer to wriggle into the false floor area where cords and hoses and pipes—oh my!—make like spaghetti. Soon I am shaking dust and dirt from my outercoat and trotting up to the room that rises and sinks like an elevator. I prefer to consider it a mobile but somewhat square crystal ball, given the glass walls surrounding it.

Who will be here? I wonder, not even thinking of the spirit world yet. Who will the mediums be? Or is that the media? There will surely be multimedia here this cold autumn afternoon. I hope one of them is that dame in white. I can tell from thirty feet away that she does not care for my kind, so I could make sure to land on her snow-white lap just to make things interesting. . . . I always do love to leave my calling cards where they are not expected, and some shiny black hairs would relieve the dull monotony of her garb.

I bound up the stairs to the room's only doors, which stand slightly ajar.

But the chick et al. have flown the coop. No one is there. I see only the table and its complement of high-backed wooden chairs. No arms clench the carved oak chair arms. No feet fidget under the table. No human heads peek over the high backs.

I am about to get dramatic and draw the curse of catkind down upon Karma (there is nothing like an empty stage to bring out the Olivier in me), when I hear an odd sound and freeze, my every overcoat hair on end. (All right, I have heard an odd sound here before, but then I was not present all by my lonesome.)

The sound is mechanical, a hum from a hundred generators, yet soft and utterly without expression or variance. I remember how UFOs are always seen hovering over power lines. Has no one considered that visitations to successful séances may be aliens trying to communicate? It seems to me that there is quite a connection to be made, and several lucrative books and videotapes in it. I am surprised that Mr. Crawford Buchanan has not dreamed up a show on this for *Hot Heads:* Humming Hominids from the Hyades Haunt High Desert House not far from Hacienda Hotel for Halloween!

I am ready to execute an about-face when I hear another sound: a tiny chime that sounds odiously familiar. I search the shadows for the source of the noise. The chime tinkles again, just as I spot a form sliding bonelessly from one chair seat to the floor.

"Out, out, damn Spot," I am about to abjure, except that it is not a dog. Nor is it a frog. Nor a tarantula. Not even anything so mouse-like as a bat.

"What are you doing here?" I demand.

He sashays over to me, collar chiming like the pendant on one of those cud-chewing bossies' necks. Behind him comes the hum, even and loud, only now I recognize the source.

"I am assisting Karma tonight," Ingram says, sitting before me to polish the knuckles on his immaculate white gloves. "We need to know who you saw the last time, as we do not wish to call up legions of spirits we will simply have to return to sender. A wearying process for us all, including the returnees."

"How do you know so much about this Spiritualism stuff?" I wonder.

"My dear chap, I am a bookstore mascot. I have spent hours poring over the many tomes on the paranormal that pass through the Thrill n' Quill. Miss Maeveleen Pearl is a great fan of the supernatural."

There he sits in his tattered, tiger-striped sweater that is all

baggy at the elbows and hocks, his yellow eyes amber with satisfaction, acting as if he owned the occult.

"I am not sure," I say, "that I wish to sit in on a séance run by a
bunch of amateurs."

"Amateurs? Louie, you do not know our pedigrees." He nods
over his tacky shoulder.

Ears and whiskers pop out around the chair sides, mostly on
tuxedos and spotteds and stripes.

I snort. "And how many Blacks do you have?"

"Two, including you."

"Two?" I think of Midnight Louise and stiffen.

Instead, the face that peeps around another chair is none other
than that of my esteemed sire. I am surprised the old man would
stick around for some New Age folderol, and tell him so.

"Well, lad," he says, leaping to the floor so as to be better seen
and to project his voice further. What an old ham! "Me years on the
sea have taught me a respect for Nature in her most whimsical
ways. And just last night on this very site, I, too, witnessed a human
now dead sending back a shade of itself. It seems to me that with
our species' special psychic powers we can concoct an even more
impressive parade of ghosts, and I owe my fellows the benefit of
my wider travels and insights."

Methinks the sire has absorbed a bit of pomposity while abroad
and aboard. Nor does he mention seeing any of the other visiting
apparitions, which I find curious.

I see it is too late. I have been lured into this truly hair-brained
enterprise. So I leap upon the nearest empty chair and say no
more. In moments we assume our positions, moving atop the
séance table, facing outward and linking tails. There is nothing our
kind cannot accomplish while atop a table. Of course, in this position, the forelimbs do not know what the hindlimbs are doing, but
that is always the best stance to take in a séance, anyway.

I thrill as that communal hum begins anew. A sympathetic thrum
vibrates through the conjoined tails. This is the true purpose of
these elegant extremities, and one no human would ever guess just
from looking at us waving them back and forth like elegant inkwell
appendages.

In fact, if humans were to see us now, they would be so blind as to our true potency that they would simply shout at us to get down from the table.

Now our kind's purr is unique in the animal kingdom. We purr for many reasons: we purr in pleasure and we purr in pain. Consider the purr a variety of audible tranquilizer. So it also affects humans. My kind purrs in kittenbirth, and kits purr as they suckle. We purr when we are sleeping, we purr when we are awake. We purr by ourselves and we purr together. We purr when being petted, we purr when being played with. For a few of us, there is one more purr, a secret purr. When we combine our secret purrs, we produce the Purr of Power. And that is simply the amplified amity we feel as furred and purred beings.

In that state, on occasion, we can lure the unusual. The out of the ordinary. The out of this world. Ghosts. Apparitions. Revenants. Spooks.

That is what we see when we peer so intently into a shadowed corner. That is what we hear when we sit atop the grandfather clock and cock our heads at the ceiling. That is what we sense when we run swift and intent to a night-darkened window. The human who comes after us may see, hear, sense nothing. Or the human may see, hear, sense a mouse or a cricket. But many times, we have glimpsed the unseeable, the unsensible.

What do we do with this inestimable gift? Most often, nothing. One of the great pleasures of not being a dominant species is the right to ignore our potential.

But this is a signal occasion. This is a deliberate calling-together, aimed at a specific specter. I wonder why Karma wishes to participate in the resurrection of the escape artist known as Houdini. I wonder what vision we will raise today. For we will see something. I wonder if it will see us?

Chapter 21

Wild Black Yonder

Temple was too tired to worry about an innocent suspect that
evening, even if Electra was willing to stake her life on her acquaintance's innocence. The real hidden suspect in this case was
hardly innocent of anything in the broadest sense of the word and
had a long history of taking care of himself only too well; but Max's
relationship to Gandolph gave Temple the willies. If Molina should
find out—! She shuddered. And Max, expert mysteriarch that he
was, probably would scorn her pitiful efforts to help.

What was Temple supposed to be anyway, a gumshoe?

She contemplated that as she pulled off her clothes and tumbled
into bed, sweet bed, pausing only to rear up in the covers to turn
the shoe phone's ring control to "off." A gumshoe, come on! Evi-
dently the proverbial gumshoe was a predecessor of the rubber-soled
tennis shoe, back in the days when gum trees (and not synthetics)
provided the raw material. Gumshoe. Sneaker.

There was one shoe she would never, ever covet. So clunky. So
terribly unchic. So clichéd.

Sleep came like a sledgehammer.

So did waking. She had been dreaming—not about black panthers, and not about gumdrop trees—but about gum*shoe* trees: metal tree limbs dripping blossoms of tennis shoes in every color of the rainbow. Temple (wearing her new Midnight Louie Austrian-crystal heels) was standing under this footwear umbrella, waiting for gaudily ripe shoes to plummet into her hands.

She awoke with a sense that she had lost something, or that it had been stolen. The bedroom was utterly dark. What had wakened her was a hand around her upper arm. It remained there yet.

"Shhh," came next, then a finger against her mouth.

She bit it, hard and with feeling.

The following smothered but creatively obscene remarks revealed the identity of her intruder beyond a doubt.

"How did you get in?" she whispered back.

"Someone left one of the French doors ajar," Max said. "Is that what you learned in martial arts class?" he asked in the aggrieved tone of the recently bitten.

"No, it's what I learned wrestling with an arsonist. And I didn't leave the French door ajar either . . . though I didn't check on it tonight."

"Why not?"

"I was thinking about the psychic fair at the Oasis, where the police took D'Arlene Hendrix downtown to interrogate her about Gandolph's death. Or murder."

"They're wrong." Max was so shocked that he spoke in a normal tone. "I guess we can speak up; no one here but us, is there? I haven't checked the other side of the bed."

"Louie is not in residence," Temple said firmly. "But I can't swear to the rest of the rooms. I didn't search the place. Too tired. And you were gone when I got back from the living room. . . . Max, what are you doing here? Again? So soon? I thought you were going to knock in future."

Her eyes struggled to decipher the darkness, especially the black-clad man within it. She felt the bed shift as he rose, and could sense him moving toward the bedroom door on hush-puppy feet.

"These are not knocking times, I'm afraid. I'll make sure that

French door is locked, and that no one else is in the condo; then I'll make coffee again while you get dressed."

Temple groaned. "Max, why?"

"I want you to break into a house with me."

"Whose house is it?"

"Mine."

"Gee, Kinsella, we never did fun things like this when we were together before," Temple observed as she stumbled on a sprinkler spigot and went sprawling facedown on the thick, dead-brown Bermuda grass.

"Hurry, the moon is bright."

"And you never used to sweet-talk me like that either," she added as he jerked her upright.

Temple wasn't sure where they were, except it was a posh gated suburban development, and they had breached a remote section of stucco wall. Actually, Max had breached it; she had been hauled up after, ever the lot in life of the vertically challenged.

"Those silver tennis shoes are a liability." Max's tone verged on loathing. He had never been a footwear connoisseur, so Temple didn't defend her snazzy shoes.

She did glimpse her tennie toes winking at the moon with every step. No one had ever told her to dress for cat burglary.

The house was dead ahead—low, sprawling and black at every opening. Max, his clothes the same light-absorbing black, ran hunched over toward it like a mobile bush. He crouched beside the house wall, where a Hollywood twist thrust spiky evergreen arms at the city-lit night sky pale as dawn. Temple slunk along after.

Max was prying at a crank-out window with a fretwork design; it snapped open moments later. He clambered in first, then leaned out to lift Temple through.

She tumbled, exhausted, to the floor inside; luckily, the carpeting was thick.

"Why do you have to break into your own house?" she wondered for the third time that evening.

This time he answered. "It *used* to be mine."

Max refastened the window, then crossed the shadowy room

with the agile certainty of a wirewalker knowing that what he did
might be dangerous, but knowing it too well to worry. He switched
on a lamp that illuminated a leather-topped desk on spindly Louie-
the-someteenth legs.

"Then why did we break in?"

"I left my keys on the dresser."

"You owned other property in Las Vegas and never told me?"

"I left here six years ago. I let Gary have it then."

"Gary?"

Max sat at the chair behind the desk, running his fingers into his
hair. "Gandolph the Great, recently deceased, according to the
news. Look, I'm taking the circumstances at their word, that you're
actually good at this. I'm too close. The police didn't waste any time
going over this place, but I was hoping we . . . you . . . could find
something else."

"This is a crime scene, with tape outside and everything?"

"Technically, yes, but they were only after supporting evidence.
It wasn't the murder site."

"By being here we've crossed a taped crime scene?"

"Don't worry, every window is draped, and the drapes are all
blackout quality. I put them in myself. Well, do you have anything
to contribute?"

"Why didn't you ask me that first? I could have stayed in bed."

"Then we'll go back." He stood, switched off the light.

"As long as I'm here and my tennies are scuffed beyond re-
demption . . ."

The light snapped on again. "Where do you want to start?"

By the glow, Temple found her way to a tufted leather sofa and
sat. "At the beginning. With some background on this house, Gandolph the Great and you."

She saw his smile quirk in the upcast glare of the brass lampshade.
"I've ended where I should have begun, maybe." He rose and went
to a Chinese chest along the wall. A touch opened an inlaid door.
Max stood back (like a black curtain being drawn) to reveal the dim
twinkle of crystal. "Care for a brandy?"

Temple shook her head. After clinking crystal for a minute, Max
brought her something anyway: a whisky liqueur in a shot-glass-size

cut-crystal container. Her tongue decided that a drop of this potent stuff should last her about as long as a cough lozenge.

Max sat on the sofa, cosseting the brandy snifter until his hands had warmed it enough to drink. His hands were always active, never still. Occupational hazard.

"This is a fetching house," he said. "A bit conventional, but nice for all that."

"Like me?" she wondered.

"I'm not talking about us. Or about now, or about the recent past. You didn't ask for that. I'm talking about six years ago, and more than fifteen years before that, when I first met Gary. Gary Randolph. Magicians' last names vanish faster than their lady assistants from a cabinet. And, in Gary's heyday, magicians all used hokey, made-up stage names."

"Like Houdini."

Max paused to sip, then sighed. "Like Houdini. Gary's official performing title was Gandolph the Great."

"Was it from that darn book that everybody but me has read?"

Max shrugged. "Maybe. It doesn't matter. I know that, at least. Gandolph had a very respectable act. He just missed being part of the new generation that went on television: Doug Henning, real name; David Copperfield, unreal name. Ever notice how in the seventies all the performers were cadging stage names from literary and historical figures? David Copperfield, Tom Jones, Englebert Humperdinck, Jane Seymour."

"Temple Bar," she put in wryly.

"That's not a stage name, but it would make a good one."

"Subconscious recognition factor," Temple agreed. "The titular heroes of novels, a nineteenth-century composer, a wife of Henry the Eighth. I always toyed with 'Katharine Howard' as a fantasy stage name; she was another of Henry's head-losing spouses. Besides, it sounds so veddy, veddy British, RADA and all that."

"I auditioned for the Royal Academy of Dramatic Art in London," Max noted with a certain rueful nostalgia.

"Really? Did they admit you?"

"I was a punk kid of sixteen. Hell, no."

Ah, Temple thought, *a secondary lark during the IRA summer abroad. Someday would she dare ask him about that?*

"Did you know that there's a Temple Bar on Lake Mead?" she asked instead.

"No!" Max's somber expression lightened. "I never saw much of anything out here but the Strip. Really? How . . . piquant."

"Thanks. I haven't been called piquant since you left."

"A strange condition, piquancy." He looked around. "This house was piquant after I got done with it. Gary was planning to retire, I was due to tour, and it has four bedrooms, so I rented it to him. It has a history."

"All houses do. Even . . . our place has a history."

Max leaned forward, studied the room as if it were brandy to savor. "It belonged to Orson Welles."

Temple sat straighter on the commodious sofa, as if thinking she might be impinging on Welles's generous lap. "Him? The Napa Valley wine man?"

Max laughed. "Paul Masson wines. And do you know what blasphemy it is, sitting in this house and remembering his least achievement?"

"Maybe, but when I was a kid, the Napa wine man was pretty big stuff. Yeah, that's right; the TV commercial was for Paul Masson: 'Paul Masson will sell no wine before its time,' " she declaimed in deep, rotund tones. "That's the most famous wine line since Bela Lugosi's 'I do not drink . . . vine' in the original *Dracula* movie. I used to think Welles *was* Paul Masson. In my immature mind, 'Masson' was kissing cousin to 'massive,' and that's how Orson Welles looked."

"I saw those TV commercials too, but I knew so much about Welles before then that they hardly registered on me. You do know his history?"

"Oh, sure, I learned it later, when I dabbled in theater. Boy wonder and that Martian Invasion radio broadcast just before World War Two started, and making *Citizen Kane* and some other classic films, peaking early and never regaining lost glory."

Max blinked and sipped. "Did you know the police were called out to this house Halloween night, *before* Gary . . . Gandolph died at the séance?"

"No? How do you know?"

"Neighbors told me. I played the worried out-of-town owner reclaiming his property after a tragedy. Which I am."

"Won't the police—?"

"I asked after they'd made their neighborhood sweep this morning. In fact they did me a favor. They prepared my way by announcing the death; I merely had to step in afterward. Everybody was shocked enough to spill whatever beans they had."

"And why were the police called to come out here?"

"Voices. The neighbors heard agitated voices from the house."

"At what time?"

"Between midnight and one A.M."

"But . . . Gandolph was at the séance all that time. The house should have been empty, unless he had relatives."

Max shook his head. "Lived alone. Stored his magic equipment in the extra bedrooms, along with mine."

"Agitated voices . . . arguing?"

"Loud enough to waken or disturb the immediate neighbors. You have to understand, Temple, that people in this development are very discreet. Most of them are celebrities, or at least used to be, so their names still ring bells all over the place. They dislike publicity and attention, and they all swear none of them called the police. But a squad car did drive through and make inquiries. Perhaps your pal Molina could look up the information on the call."

"Umhmmm. She's not even on this case."

Max stroked a hair loosened by his breaking-and-entry exertions from his forehead. Under it lurked a cynically lifted eyebrow. "You must appreciate that."

"Actually, no. I now realize that I used to get tidbits of information out of Molina when we had our little verbal sparring matches. From Watts and Sacker, I get *nada*, though they're a lot more polite."

"Perhaps Molina is more susceptible to your considerable charm than you think."

"No. 'Impervious' is her middle name. And if I told you what the C in C.R. stood for—"

Max tented his long flexible fingers. "Tell me. In my position, it's always useful to have an insight into members of the local constabulary."

"You don't have a position, that's the trouble. You're just a Missing Man. And 'local constabulary,' honestly, Max. Sometimes you talk like someone from an Agatha Christie play."

"I lived abroad for a while, in my youth."

"Oh, right. Your Interpol days."

"We're not here to weasel background out of each other."

"I'll need more than I have now if I'm supposed to shed any light on Gandolph's death." Temple tasted another drop of liqueur, then let it soak into her tongue. "So it's possible someone was here while Gandolph was at the séance; more than one 'someone,' or else 'voices' wouldn't have been heard. You've looked the place over, anything moved?"

"Hard to tell; it's been a while since I saw this stuff. But . . . yes, the magical equipment appears to have been moved, considerably."

"Gandolph's? Or yours?"

"Both. You realize that a magician's equipment is his stock-in-trade and worth thousands, his professional secrets all bundled up into a few tables and trunks and boxes?"

"You think someone was searching—?" Temple sat up. "Why do you assume it was *Gandolph*'s things they were disturbing? Why not yours? Not too long ago, somebody was looking for you, hard. Why not for your equipment?"

"Do you really think those thugs who knocked you around would know what to do with a metamorphosis cabinet if they stumbled over one?"

Temple sat back. "No. And no one saw anything, thanks to your blackout draperies. Nice pattern, by the way." She nodded at the cinnabar brocade curtains embroidered with teal and gold birds of paradise.

"The house is Chinese in design. I tried to honor the original intent."

"Why did Welles leave this house, and when?"

"In nineteen eighty-five, when he died."

"He died? But not here?"

"No, in Los Angeles. You didn't know when he died?"

"I must have missed the announcements. I was in college and didn't always have access to a television set in the dorm." Temple eyed the room with new worry. "And you bought it?"

"Somewhat later. First flush of success. I'd always felt Orson Welles was a tragic figure, stymied by his own fearsome talent and others' fear of the truly innovative. He was a magician of sorts, you know."

"No, I didn't. Was he any good?"

Max shrugged. "Like all amateurs, he enjoyed the flourishes but lacked the foundation to achieve any truly original effects. And the physique was lacking too."

"You mean the physique *wasn't* lacking; too much of a good thing, or too many good things."

"He still managed some stunning effects. The Great Orson swallowed needles and flames, did the trunk substitution with Rita Hayworth as long as Harry Cohn would let him, heckled hypnotized roosters, caught a bullet between his teeth and did psychic readings."

Only one item on this eccentric list caught Temple's attention. "Psychic readings?"

"Supposedly he'd done it earlier, on the road with a touring show to make a buck. But he gave up for reasons others often do: he scared himself with his own apparent accuracy. Even Houdini tried it when he was hard up early in his career, and shied away."

"Do you think Welles was psychic?"

"Not at all. Everybody who isn't a crook and toys with doing psychic readings scares themselves silly. They have no idea of the role coincidence plays in daily life. When a few of their predictions hit home, they panic, doff their turbans and head for the hills."

"You have absolutely no belief in a life beyond death, or powers beyond the normal?"

"No," Max said without hesitation. "Anybody who tries to sell somebody else stock in those notions is a fraud."

"Most religions accept inexplicable events they call 'miracles.' Most religions posit a life after death."

"I repeat, anybody or any institution that tries to sell somebody else stock in such notions is a fraud."

"We've never discussed the topic. I always assumed magicians adore the mysterious, the unexplained."

"We do, but only in our own acts. Magicians as a class abhor the spacey side of occultism. We know the ghostly visitations and the tap-dancing tables are manipulated, and we know how such tricks are done. That's why so many magicians, irritated by watching their art used to defraud the gullible, donate their services to debunk spectral phenomena."

"How is that different from charging the public to watch you do tricks?"

"Enormously!" Max leaned forward, elbows on knees, gesturing with the now-empty brandy glass. "We magicians advertise ourselves as tricksters. We admit that we are entertainers. We don't toy with people's pasts, or their pain. We appeal to their sense of reality, we challenge them in public to catch us tricking them. Psychics and mediums pretend to superior sensitivities. They take money in private under false pretenses, in exchange for useless and deceptive information. They prolong the process for as long as the pigeon's cash holds out. They are thieves of time as well as money, pickpockets of the soul. They are . . . despicable."

"And Gandolph felt as you do?"

"More strongly."

Temple sat back. "Was that why he was in disguise at the séance? Did he plan to expose one, or all, of the psychics present?"

"I don't know. Obviously, he didn't wish to be recognized. He could have been planning a book. He had the time now. Yet it was such an obvious publicity stunt; a séance in a haunted-house attraction seems beneath his notice."

"He mentioned nothing to you of the scheme?"

Max frowned and sipped from the brandy snifter. Temple noticed it was full again, and gave him a questioning look.

Max rolled the brandy in the crystal bowl, then sipped from the second snifter in his other hand. "Quite simple. I brought two glasses over, knowing my mood and capacity, then switched to the full one when the other was empty. Being a magician, I couldn't resist doing it surreptitiously."

"Ex-magicians are like ex-actors, always on."

"That's it!" Max said. "You've hit it. Gandolph was 'always on.' He couldn't resist trying to fool the eye, even if it was with that Lady-Lavinia-at-the-séance outfit. He might have done it simply as a lark, intending to rise at the end, pull off his bonnet and reveal himself."

"Happy Halloween."

"Trick or treat, you decide."

"That's why he wouldn't have told you."

"I wasn't exactly Harry Houseguest, with slippers warming on the hearth and a nice concave dip worn in the best chair. I come . . . and go. I was here if I wanted to lie low. If I wanted something else, I was gone."

"So you really don't know much about Gandolph's movements, or even his state of mind?"

"No." Max sipped again before speaking, bitterly. "I hadn't found the time yet to catch up on his fuddy-duddy retirement projects. I had life-and-death matters of my own to consider."

"Max, he might have been killed by accident. It was dark, foggy and even teary in that séance room. I could hardly see, myself. If you're going to force me to rule out the lovely ghosts we saw that night—the serial faces in the windows and Houdini in chains—then the killer was simply human, and maybe made a human error. Perhaps Gandolph was killed by mistake."

"Then what of the voices heard near the house?"

"Sound carries. It can be deceptive. Somebody leaves a window open and a television on . . . presto, eerie voices in the night, arguing."

"Somehow, I feel we're reversing roles."

"How?"

"You're talking me out of groundless suspicions. At least we can search the rooms. You might spot something that I wouldn't think anything of."

"Because I'm ignorant of magicians' tricks?"

"No, because you have no stake in seeing murderers where there are only ghosts. And this house is doubly haunted now." Max glanced up to the dark beams under the peaked roof. "Good thing I don't believe in spooks." He bolted the brandy like a man who did.

Temple wondered what kind of "spooks" he referred to: spirits, or spies.

"Where will you stay now?" she asked, hating to open that touchy topic.

Max seemed startled by her question. His eyes widened, like Midnight Louie's when he heard a noise he didn't expect.

"Here, of course."

"Here! You can't, now."

"Why not? I own the place, under a business name, granted, but it's still mine."

"But the police have been out here searching."

"Past tense. They've got what they wanted. The best hiding place is always one that somebody's searched already." He regarded her quizzically. "Were you afraid you'd have to be a generous soul and offer me sanctuary at the Circle Ritz?"

"No! I hadn't thought of that at all. I just wondered how many hidey-holes you have in Las Vegas."

"As many as there are neon bulbs in the Strip skyline."

"I see. I'm supposed to figure things out while you continue being your usual mystifying self."

"You are the usual soul of perception." Max bowed toward her, flourishing his left hand to pluck a dinner-plate-size paper rose from thin air.

Temple laughed, as she always did, and accepted the rose. Paper roses didn't require watering, unlike relationships.

"I'll tour the premises," she conceded, getting up.

Max leaped up to conduct her.

He had been truthful: the house, while no palace, was large, spacious and crammed with magical paraphernalia. Even the spare bedroom, with its massive and priceless opium bed, was otherwise stocked with painted cabinets and boxes and tables of all description.

"You rented the place furnished?" Temple asked.

Max's sculpted face had taken on an Oriental tilt once inside this room. "If you're asking if the opium couch is mine, yes. I've even slept in it, feeling like an emperor who has very expensive dreams."

Temple eyed the cushioned structure askance: part horizontal throne, part exquisite artifact of another culture and age, part harem honeymoon suite, it was both sumptuous and decadent, but hardly romantic.

"You must have had nightmares in it."

"Not yet," Max said, with an inscrutable smile.

Temple continued down the hallway. The other two bedrooms resembled lumber rooms, they were so crammed with unused furnishings and magical appliances.

The fourth bedroom was on the opposite side of the house and uncluttered, except for a black futon on the hardwood floor, and near it a low carved cinnabar Chinese table bearing a Ming vase full of paper roses.

"It that real?" Temple asked.

"The flowers?"

"The vase."

"No comment," Max said, thereby admitting everything.

"I hope Molina doesn't get her hands on you," Temple said in mock threat. "You'd crack like Tang porcelain."

"Perhaps not." Max's smile was secret, and therefore irritating.

She paced back up the hall, struck by the fact that neither Max nor herself wore shoes that made any noise on the hardwood floors. He by habit, she by request.

She stopped again by Gandolph's bedroom door, leaning over the threshold, her fingertips clinging to the frame.

It wasn't just the fact that the bedroom's resident was dead that kept her balanced into the entrance. Something in the room's arrangement—if so much jumble could be called that—troubled her, looked out of place. But how could something look out of place in a mess?

"Where does he plug in his computer when he's using it?"

"Right there—" Max pointed, and then he really looked at the room.

He marched right in, as if no old ghosts guarded the threshold.

Temple followed, with mental "excuse me's" to both Gary and Orson.

Max was standing by the small computer desk, his hand clutching a big pale electrical plug as if he were Hamlet contemplating mortality in the skull of Yorick.

"He always left it plugged in. There, by that wall. I told him he should get a surge protector. What's it doing over here? It looks like it was simply shoved out of the way."

"Let's plug it in and find out."

Max and Temple both leaned into pushing the unit back to the wall, though Max pushed and Temple merely nudged a little.

Once Temple had replaced the prongs in the socket, she knelt in front of the computer table and booted the machine. Max leaned over her, studying the screen.

WordPerfect came up, but Temple exited it to try a file manager program. The baby-blue screen went black, and up one came, like magic, or like a genie sprung from a bottle.

"Marvelous," Max murmured. The vast miniworlds inside computers intrigued him, but he was oddly computerphobic, at least when it came to operating them. Or so he said.

Temple studied the network of directories, looking for any provocative names.

"It does look like he was working on a book. Look: a directory named 'Bio.' "

"Biology?"

"More likely 'biography.' " Temple exited the program, returned to the word processor and clicked into the bio directory.

A ribbon of files scrolled down the screen.

"Is this enough for a book?" Max asked.

"And then some." Excited, and yet feeling like a computer-age eavesdropper, Temple opened a file: bio12.occ.

No spell-checker had touched this text, and punctuation was as haphazard as hail, but the subject matter was crystal-clear.

"He was writing an exposé," Max breathed behind her. "He was documenting the foremost psychics of today. He must have spent years gathering data—and, look! At the top: 'as Edwina Mayfair.' He was using that identity. But—"

"But what about the real Edwina Mayfair?"

"What if there *wasn't* a real Edwina Mayfair?"

Max's eyes narrowed in the eerie light of the computer screen. When Max's eyes narrowed, their green intensified, and usually Temple intensified too. Now, she kept wondering if he sent for them through the mail. Blasted illusions were the worst kind. Temple was actually more interested in what he was saying this time.

"You mean, he created Edwina Mayfair from scratch?"

"He'd been in retirement for years. No legitimate psychic— Let me rephrase that: no self-defending psychic would admit a debunking magician to a session, but if the visitor was another so-called psychic . . ."

Temple had been tapping keys, changing directories, looking up hard evidence: numbers and dates. "These files go back three years, and, given his computer setup, this is an upgrade. He probably has a lot on diskette."

"It is truly mysterious to me how you do all that with those nails," Max admitted, watching her fingernails kick keys all over the board.

"Pay attention! I'm saying that these are massive files, both in number and capacity. Gandolph was writing the *War and Peace* of psychic exposés."

"With long Russian names and everything?"

"With names, dates, places and . . . photodocumentation, it says here."

"Photos."

"I suppose an infrared camera, concealed . . . in, say, a large hat—"

"Or bosom."

"—could have seen quite a bit."

"Well, there's the motive."

"Maybe." Temple eyed the room. "I don't see any new diskette boxes around. I don't see any diskette boxes around, period."

"Taken?"

"Could be. Could be that Gandolph was like a lot of other people and had blind faith in modern technology. Maybe he didn't back much up." Temple rose. "Well. I suggest you go out first thing in the morning and buy a sultan's ransom of three-and-a-half-inch one point four-four meg double-density floppy disks. Then you sit right here and back up everything on the directories before anyone else messes with this computer."

Max looked up from jotting everything down like mad. "That sounds . . . tedious."

"Did you think detective work was all second-story stuff? Black designer duds and sneaking around?"

"I'm not sure I'd find this directory again, Temple."

"I'll write down the necessary formulas for you," she offered. "When you get me back home. If I can find a pen or pencil around the place that Midnight Louie hasn't batted to the Hoover Dam and back."

For once, Max Kinsella was out of snappy comebacks.

Chapter 22

Framed Dead Center

The morning *Las Vegas Review-Journal* blared all the facts on page one with an arresting headline: PSYCHIC QUESTIONED IN HALLOWEEN SÉANCE DEATH.

Temple remembered when newspaper headline style had changed from capitalizing major headline words to using all lower case except for the initial letter of the first word. Her mind still visualized sensational headlines in the old, emphatic style and even added a yellow-journalism exclamation point: PSYCHIC ARRESTED FOR HALLOWEEN SÉANCE MURDER!

Somehow, MALE MAGICIAN DISGUISED AS FEMALE PSYCHIC did not have the same, simple ring.

So the police had not come clean about the victim's role-playing. She couldn't blame them. Why leak embarrassing facts when they were still investigating why a grown man would participate in séances in drag? That was a bigger puzzle than the murder, almost. And then, think of the forthcoming testimony about the ghosts, which the mediums present appeared to have taken as gospel.

Louie had come to lie on the newspaper sections Temple was not reading at the moment, one of his less endearing tricks. She had no patience this morning, not with the sleep she hadn't gotten in the past forty-eight hours, and pulled them all out from under him.

"You're lucky I made it home at all last night," she told the cat as he eyed her in comical amazement. "You're lucky that there wasn't someone else sleeping in your spot."

All untrue, of course. But if you couldn't lie to a dumb beast, who could you lie to? Temple had harbored no intentions of inviting Max to stay once he'd escorted her safely and surreptitiously home. And he had cherished no intentions of asking, for he'd let himself out almost immediately on arrival, mumbling about all-night computer stores.

Temple smiled. Imagine Max cooped up all day like a hermit, copying files onto diskettes. Meanwhile, she was a free agent, with her current employers encouraging her to explore the outer limits of the paranormal in the name of research. She could go where her fancy took her. Which was where . . . ?

Her doorbell rang as if in answer. She scrambled to make herself presentable and yet open it in time. Meanwhile, Midnight Louie ostentatiously reclaimed every damn section of the newspaper.

At the door, Electra was waiting with an air of pent-up excitement. "One question: will you come to the séance tonight?"

"What séance? Wasn't the first one enough?"

Electra shook today's soft, magenta-sprayed curls. "Quite the opposite. The first one demands a second, a more private affair. I'm holding it in my rooms tonight."

"Your rooms? Aren't they sacrosanct or something? I've never heard of you entertaining so much as a plumber there."

"I do like my privacy, but that's why my penthouse is such an ideal site. It has not been polluted. I can promise you that no cameraman and no Crawford Buchanan will be present. Just true believers and time-tested mediums. And, of course, you too, dear; if you're willing to come."

"Why is an exception being made for me?"

Electra glanced through her half-size magnifying glasses at the floral rug as if something large, dead and insectoid lay there. "Your preeminent experience with murder. We have decided that you have extraordinary, untapped powers in that area."

"I've been elevated to presumed psychic? Won't Lieutenant Molina be sorry she has scorned my help in the past!"

"Don't be sarcastic, Temple. It puts off the spirits."

"Why not invite Max? He's the expert on magical matters."

Electra's shudder caused the huge bird-of-paradise flowers on her muumuu to sway as if in a breeze. "Just who we do *not* want present! One of those nasty magicians who always discredit efforts to contact the spirit world. Spoilsports."

"Like Houdini," Temple pointed out.

"Exactly! Unlike the police, I am convinced that Houdini did it: the dirty deed, the murder."

"Nice of him to wait seventy years after his death to turn to homicide."

"Niceness had nothing to do with it. It was motive and opportunity," Electra added, screwing her eyes into an expression that matched Molina at her most skeptical. "Houdini hated mediums, loathed them! Here was his chance to express his innermost feelings and *escape* punishment. You see the devilishly clever psychology of it? He came back, all right, but to kill a psychic. It would be the most daring, two-edged escape of all time: first to elude the Afterworld long enough to show himself as material; then to draw another into the Beyond; a hated medium, best of all."

"But Gandolph wasn't a medium, that was the point. He was another Houdini, presumably out to reveal the artifice at the heart of this darkness. Houdini would never kill him."

"Ah, but Houdini didn't *know* his victim was Gandolph in disguise."

"If Houdini died and sat around in the Beyond twiddling his thumbscrews or handcuffs or whatever for seven decades—"

"Seven. A most significant number in mystical circles."

"Well, Houdini was almost short enough to be a dwarf, probably Grumpy. Anyway, if he comes back to commit murder after seven decades, he darn well ought to know just who was who and what was what."

"Being dead does not make one omniscient, dear. It was the sort of ironic mistake that could happen to anyone. Gandolph did make a convincing woman; one would have thought he had done the act for years. I believe even you were misled, and you sat right next to him. You even held hands with him."

"Gloves," Temple corrected. "He wore gloves, and rather wisely. That entire over-the-top persona was designed as a disguise: hat, veil, gloves, the whole works. And what about the other apparition, the poor kid looking in the candy-store window?"

"That." Electra dismissed the three faces of Everyman with a couple of finger flicks. "We feel that was a symbolic manifestation of Houdini's hatred toward mediums. Each time we saw the figure it was older and larger. You see the metaphor."

"Ever older and larger. Hmm. Sounds more like the transformation of Midnight Louie since he arrived at the Circle Ritz."

"What a quaint mind you have, dear."

"Quaint? First piquant, now quaint? Are people trying to tell me something?"

"Nine P.M.," Electra said with a forefinger-wag that threatened to dislodge her pineapple-gold–painted nail. Unlike Temple's, Electra's long nails were false. "Be there, or be sorry."

She bustled down the short neck of hallway leading to Temple's unit. Temple knew how it must feel to have Woody Woodpecker as your local neighborhood enforcer.

Of course she would go, if only to get another look at psychics in action. If an act of God or Houdini hadn't killed Gary "Gandolph" Randolph, then maybe someone else at the table had.

Then, too, she was extremely interested in seeing Electra's digs from the inside out. Temple had one of her psychic serial-killer–hunter hunches that there were hidden reasons for holding the séance in Electra's penthouse. In a way, she wished that Max could attend. If there was one area in which she was still willing to trust him implicitly, it was in knowing what was real and what was not at a séance.

Meanwhile, there was another method, less glamorous but more reliable. Why didn't she just ask the special effects whizzes?

Six semi-trailer rigs lined up in front of the Hell-o-ween Haunted Homestead when Temple parked the Storm in the huge trucks' intimidating shadows. Those iron-pumping tires were as tall as her car.

She knew that stagehands and rock-band roadies could strike sets in record time, but she hadn't expected to see the inside of the haunted house stripped of its ghosties and ghouls already.

"Are the people who designed this attraction still around?" she asked the first scurrying workman she could stop. He was a she on closer inspection, a burly woman in denim overalls with dirty blond hair pulled into what had become a unisex ponytail under an orange hard hat.

"Yeah, but you shouldn't be in here without a hard hat."

"Show me the special effects crew and I'm sidelined forever."

"The boyos in body paint." The woman pointed to a wall-hugging trio that looked like a rock band whose act was being disbanded.

Temple joined them in the tortuous hallway that she had wound through twice in recent days.

"Are the police letting you dismember the séance room too?"

"Dismember. Cool expression." The one with a tattoo of a spiderweb veiling half his face shook his head. "Nope. We never unplug that ski-lift room. It's our centerpiece. Not that the police care that much. Why do you?"

"I'm interested in your tricks and technology. I represent a Strip hotel—"

"Strip hotel?" Even the guy's spiderweb was smiling. "Hear that, Crash? Guess sudden death hasn't frozen our act yet."

Crash looked like he had been in a few, all nearly terminal. He was bearish, beefy and pierced on all visible folds of flesh. Despite the biker body armor, Temple thought she detected the sweet souls of asocial computer nerds beneath an exterior of warriors trying to escape the latest update of the arcades' most gruesome and gory game, Fatal Wombat.

"You guys designed all this, really? Holograms and everything?"

Flattery will get you information.

"Sure."

"This is nothin'."

"Want something really cutting edge? You should see our studio, man."

"Well, I'd love to, but mostly what I'd like to know now is what the moneybags at the hotel want to find out."

"Yeah?"

"Did you guys, you know, skew the séance effects just to shake things up a little, with *Hot Heads* there? I hear those nasty weapons and a few uninvited spirits were really jumpin'."

"Hey." All three shook their untidy hands. Two, she noticed, had tatooed knuckles that read "Dweeb" and "Dreck." She wondered if those were their nicknames. Crash, Dweeb and Dreck Productions, Ltd. had a certain crude appeal.

"We didn't tweak a timer," Crash said.

"In fact," Dweeb added, scratching his topiary buzz-cut with dirty fingernails, "our stuff was all screwed up. Those spirits must have been playing Ouija board with our master panels, I tell you. And that's what we told the police."

"What did the police say?"

"Nothin'." Dreck swigged from a can of . . . Gatorade? "The police think we're punks."

"We are," Dweeb said promptly.

"That doesn't mean we can't put on a bitchin' show for your hotel, lady." Crash, the ever-alert salesman, added an invitation impossible to refuse. "Come over to our studio and we'll knock your socks off, or whatever else you put on that passes for underwear."

"Where is your studio?"

"North Las Vegas."

"And you've been doing this Halloween attraction—?"

"Since we were in high school," Dreck said, still swigging.

"Which was—?"

Crash shrugged shoulders the size of a polar bear's. "Couple years ago."

"Thanks, guys. I'll definitely keep you in mind."

Temple edged out on that vague promise, slipping into a stream of grunting laborers who seemed as inclined to smash her like a bug, with the heavy equipment they were toting, as not.

As murderous riggers, Crash, Dweeb and Dreck were as likely

suspects as Grumpy, Doc and Dopey, but they were also just the types to let "art" sweep them away into malicious mischief.

Heigh ho, heigh ho, it was off to work in other suspect-mines she would go. Maybe Electra's mysterious homemade séance would prove more productive than any performance at this madhouse from Helloween.

Chapter 23

End of the Line

Matt almost hung up the phone three times, at each unanswered ring on the line's other end.

The irony of a phone counselor freezing when making his own critical calls struck home.

Behind his cubicle, the buzz of other voices lulled him. Of course the party he sought wouldn't be there at this time of night, but he had to try now, while the impulse was too intense to ignore.

At last he heard a voice, a woman's voice. Though he was calling for a woman, this wouldn't be her.

"I'm trying to reach Lieutenant Molina."

"Is this an emergency?"

"No. I have some information."

"Can you call back during working hours tomorrow?"

"Not until after noon."

"Just a minute."

She was gone, and Matt wondered if they were tracing the call. He knew it was being recorded.

"Your name."

He gave it. Gave the address, the work phone number, home phone number. When it came to what the call was about, he simply said, "Cliff Effinger."

After he hung up, he felt wrung out. He shared sudden empathy with the people who called ConTact. People pitched to the breaking point. People uncertain. People hoping for help. People lost.

His hands were clammy as he rubbed them on each other. How critical a phone call could be only a veteran of ConTact—or of calling the police department—could testify to.

"It's cold out," a voice noted over his shoulder. "Like some coffee?"

He turned. Sheila was hanging over him, looking helpful, looking hopeful. Steam rose from the mug in her hand in separate puffs like messages from an Indian blanket.

"Something's bothering you," she said, quite accurately. She was a hot-line counselor too, after all.

He recalled all the brusque denial that kind of accuracy merited over the ConTact lines. *No. I don't need anything! I just happened to call. You can't help me . . . so help me!*

"Yeah." Matt wrapped icy fingers around the hot ceramic mug. "Unseasonably cold."

"That's the trouble. It *is* seasonal. Even Las Vegas has to go through a touch of fall and winter." Her smile didn't do much for that face, that voice, and he never used to notice such disparities. Why did feminine wiles in such an unfeminine face irritate so? "It's Halloween. This time of year the temperature can drop nights."

He nodded, then jumped as the phone rang.

"You're still on break, want me to get it?"

"No. I will." Though why he thought that Lieutenant C. R. Molina was anywhere out there on her time off, just waiting to take a call from him . . . "Hello."

"Molina."

She sounded as official as if she'd just alighted from a squad car. Matt wondered where she was, what she was wearing, if her daughter was anywhere nearby.

"What about Cliff Effinger?"

He could afford to speculate at leisure; she couldn't. She zeroed in. The call, the name, the need to know. Matt could jerk her chain anytime, with just that one magical name. A dead man linked to another dead man, and both linked to a missing magician, now back from the dead. Only one dead man was linked, as yet, to an ex-Chicago-boy, ex-priest with his own need to know.

No hello, no frosting, just need to know. He could understand that, but in Molina's case, he didn't understand why.

"I think I saw him."

"At the morgue? You're convinced now it was him?"

"No. I'm less convinced than ever. I think I saw him on the street, just now."

"Now? Where?"

"Tonight. Three hours ago, crossing the Strip at Sahara."

An accusing silence. "Why did you wait so long to call?"

"I . . . wasn't sure. He looks different. But the walk. I've never seen anybody walk quite that way."

"The walk."

"I know it sounds—"

"It sounds . . . like this man, whoever he was, is long gone from the corner of Las Vegas Boulevard and Sahara. What are you calling me now for?"

"Now" was rife with accusation: I'm a single mother, it said; I'm off duty. I don't need to be given false hopes any more than one of your pathetic callers does.

"I want to know what you'd want to know, what you'd need if he were alive, and in Las Vegas."

She laughed, not a very humorous sound. Not a sound that someone who loved to sing the old blues classics would make if she'd been listening to anything with swing.

"Fingerprints. Chase the guy down and wrap his fingers around a nice clean water glass, like they do on *Murder, She Wrote.* Or fly back to Chicago and dig up some extant examples, 'cause the Motor Vehicles Department here and there don't have any, the schools don't have any, the military doesn't have any, and right now, Mr.

Devine, I'm not having any. Walks don't cut it in a court of law. Happy Halloween, but I'm even out of pennies."

She hung up.

He stared at the cup cooling between his hands. He was warm now, all over. With embarrassment, and something else. With anger. *God damn it*, and he meant the words as few do, he knew what—who—he had seen. He had hoped someone else, this detective, cared as much as he did, for her own reasons and in her own way. But she didn't.

He would have to track down this ghost on his own.

Chapter 24

Calling All Cats . . .

Temple was in a tizzy. She had to admit that, at least to herself alone, often the best person to confide in.

She hesitated in the hall outside of Electra's penthouse, wondering who besides her hostess would be inside. Certainly not the obnoxious Mynah. Perhaps poor D'Arlene Hendrix, fresh from her grilling downtown. Temple could certainly compare notes and sympathies about that!

And the professor, probably. Agatha Welk was a maybe; a little fragile for Electra's taste, Temple thought. No Oscar Grant. No Crawford Buchanan. No Max, boo hoo. But . . . maybe Matt?

Temple sighed and lowered her shoulders so she had a soldierlike posture when she rang the doorbell. This should be fascinating.

As usual, it took the requisite Ice Age for the door to open, and then it opened just to peeking width, despite the magnifying peephole the resident could rely on.

Electra peered out, her hair in a condition Temple had never seen before: obscured.

The obscuring mechanism, however, was even more brash than Electra's round of washable spray-on hair colorizers. It was a gold lamé scarf arranged like an Egyptian pharaoh's headdress.

Electra checked the usually deserted hall before admitting Temple.

"No one followed you?"

"Nope. Louie's resting comfortably on my bed downstairs."

Electra nodded solemnly.

Standing in her circular entry hall, with the mirrored vertical blinds reflecting slices of each of them, felt oddly like the hall-of-mirrors scene in some old intrigue movie, say *The Lady from Shanghai,* with Orson Welles and then-wife Rita Hayworth.

In the spirit of the evening already, Temple could hardly wait to penetrate the heart of darkness beyond, often glimpsed but never explored. Already she could see light gleaming from the huge green ball atop Electra's vintage TV set.

Electra turned and led the way into the inner sanctum.

"Does that work?" Temple couldn't help gushing the minute they were in the large room.

Electra glanced at the TV set surmounted by what resembled a huge green glass turban.

"Like a top."

"Really? You can pick up contemporary signals with no trouble?"

"Contemporary, old-time, anything your heart desires."

"Cable even?"

Electra frowned and turned halfway to the television set.

"Cable? Do you mean 'Gable'? I've never been one to try for the celebrity spirit, dear. I've been tempted, but that's kind of amateurish, if you know what I mean."

She lifted the green globe by its complicated brass base. "Clear that end table and we'll sit right down here and get to work."

Temple obediently swept away several alternative health magazines, an issue of *Modern Maturity* and . . . a Frederick's of Hollywood catalog?

Well, she was learning *some*thing, albeit nothing unworldly yet.

"Sit," Electra said, beaming, as if instructing a favorite Pekingese. Temple sat.

"Is this it, Electra? Just us? We're the only 'true believers'?"

"Almost. Our most important séance partner has not arrived yet."

"I'm breathless with suspense. Let me guess."

"No, don't! Expectations can destroy a séance. While we're waiting you can fill me in on the latest developments in your love life."

"Electra! Why would I do that?"

"I have gingersnap cookies, with icing. And raspberry zinger tea. And it does one good to unburden one's soul."

"You can't bribe me with tea and cookies."

"Besides, you might get some good advice from the spirits if you come clean."

"What spirits? You might conjure up Bluebeard. Not my idea of Ann Landers."

"Well, while we're waiting for our special link, we could at least discuss my fascinating tenants."

"Get the cookies and tea, then."

"All right!"

Electra bustled off to what must be the kitchen, allowing Temple time to give her place a long look.

Wow. The sofa she sat on was almost seven feet long, upholstered in a nubbly fabric with gilt threads here and there. The big green glass ball was not entirely smooth, but nubbly in its own right. Must be sixties glass, when wavy-everything was decoratively chic, especially in pole-lamp shades. Ooof. Speaking of pole lamps, a rather rank example held up a corner, its lights aimed hither and yon.

This place was a paradise of the Truly Tacky. Kitsch in Full Flower. As Temple looked around, she even discovered a brandy snifter filled with colored marbles, an aquarium occupied by multicolored crystal growths, a black-and-chrome institutional cigarette snuffer, a stuffed squirrel on a very inauthentic-looking tree branch (the squirrel was absolutely true-to-life) and, well, lots of unbelievable junk. The odd decorative marble lay scattered here and there. In fact, two of them glowed a desultory green from under the very sofa she sat on.

And then they moved.

Temple lifted her feet from the floor and shrieked in the lady-like manner of a vintage cartoon lady who had seen a mouse.

"What is it, dear? See something awesome in the globe?"

"I saw something sentient under the sofa. Do you have rats?"

"Oh, good. She's warming up to you."

"What is 'she'? Cleopatra's asp?"

"Silly! She's just the psychic we were waiting for. Remain calm and I'll bring your goodies out and we can begin. Just pretend you didn't see her, and she'll relax and come right on out."

"I didn't see her, except for the eerie eyes. You mean to say a grown woman can fit under this sofa? I know it's big, but—"

Electra had disappeared, leaving Temple to slip her heels off and curl her feet beneath her on the cushion. No way was that green-eyed mystery going to snap at her Achilles' heels from under the sofa.

Electra returned with a hammered aluminum tray bearing teacups, cookies and a shallow dish of dried greens that looked like very minced loose-leaf tea.

"This is a . . . condiment."

"Oh, no. It's a bribe. Just munch and sip and we'll be ready to begin in no time." Electra bent to position the dish near the sofa bottom.

Temple shrugged and ate icing off a slab of cookie. "I haven't had one of these forever."

"Sometimes store-bought is superior. Well?" Electra waggled her eyebrows at Temple.

"Well, what?"

"Have you seen Max lately?"

"Um, sort of."

"Max is not the kind of person you sort of see. He's either there, or he isn't."

"Don't I know it. Yes, we ran into each other once or twice."

"What about Matt?"

"What about him?"

"Don't you run into him more often around here? Is it really fair to see both men?"

"Electra, that's my business."

"Maybe, but I can't help feeling solicitous."

"For whom?"

"Well, Max did bring you to the Circle Ritz."

"So he's your favorite?"

"But Matt has really been here for me, and for you on some serious occasions."

"I know that."

Electra sighed, sipped her tea and leaned over to check under the sofa. "I confess, it's a good thing I'm the grandmotherly sort and a mere onlooker at life these days. I would be hard-pressed to choose between those two darling boys myself."

"Thanks, Electra," Temple said between her teeth. "You took the words right out of my mouth. Now, my cookie is eaten, my tea is drunk and I have been debriefed. Can we get on with it?"

Electra leaned way over, until her headdress almost touched the floor. "I think so. We have decided to approach the offering."

Temple leaned over to witness this signal event.

What looked like one of those beige faux-lambskin (she hoped) dust mops was edging out from under the sofa to sniff at the bowl of dried leaves.

When soft white paws appeared, Temple opened her eyes wider. When she glimpsed stunning bright blue eyes, she blinked. When dark-tipped ears perked, her own twitched in surprise. When a dark-tipped but bushy tail swished free of the sofa's shadow, she breathed a sigh of relief.

"Electra, this is a cat."

"I know. And not just any cat. A Sacred Cat of Burma. This is a Birman cat, and her name is Karma."

"You've denied having a cat for months!"

"She's shy," Electra said in melting tones. "We do not allow just anyone to know of our existence, do we? No . . . She has abilities greater than those of mortal cats."

"Oh?"

"She is a gifted psychic."

"How do you know?"

"You will see. Just watch the green globe. When Karma is present and participating, the most astounding visions appear within its murky center."

Temple had to agree about the murky center. She watched the cat, which was a beauty, no doubt. All that golden hair ending in paws gloved in dainty white, while nose, ears and tail were tipped with sable brown. And in between, the pools of limpid blue, like morning-glory hot springs in Yellowstone National Park.

Nothing murky about this lady.

"Electra, why so secretive about this cat?"

"She's so very, very sensitive. All the great psychics were that way. Too much outside influence can overwhelm her. It is a great honor that she deigns to show herself to you. Please don't make any sudden motions. Simply sit back and prepare to wonder at what the crystal will show when Karma begins her wonders to perform."

"I can hardly wait."

"If you have any urgent personal matters you wish guidance about, merely keep them in mind and watch the crystal."

Temple rolled her eyes. Maybe she was most deeply interested in guidance on her Crystal Phoenix renovation project. She doubted the crystal would have much to say about that. She kept an eye on it, wary of any sudden images that might show up.

But none did.

Although Electra clucked and crooned at the cat, the animal simply fell over on its side, as Temple had seen Midnight Louie do dozens of times, and gazed at them, blinking every now and then.

A subtle hum rose from the floor.

"Well, she's purring. She must like you," Electra said. "But I don't understand. Usually by now the crystal ball is teeming with interesting images. Karma, dear, time to tippy-toe through the empyrean."

Even this lilting reminder did not seem to rouse the cat, who laid her head on the carpet and drowsed her eyes shut.

"This is most embarrassing. Karma is such a strong medium. Her mere presence is like heat under a pot of water: everything comes to a boil. I don't know what to say. I'm totally perplexed."

There wasn't much Temple could say either. This was like being invited to the music recital of a friend's child, and then said child forgets the music.

While Temple searched for consoling words appropriate for the owner of a contrary cat, a sinister thump sounded from elsewhere in the penthouse.

"I thought you said we were the only ones coming," Temple said.

"We are." Electra was so downcast she merely stared sadly at Karma sleeping on the carpet; she didn't even react to the distant thump.

"That noise could be an intruder."

"Probably is," Electra said mournfully, regarding Karma as if the cat were on her deathbed, when she simply looked at ease.

"Electra. Matt is at work now and I don't know where your phone is if we have to dial nine-one-one."

"Yes, Matt is gone, and Max is goner. And I don't remember where my phone is. I am heartbroken. What has happened to my poor Karma?"

"She looks fine—"

"She is *not* fine! Karma lives and breathes her role as a medium. If she is present and nothing astounding is happening, she is terribly, terribly ill. What will I do?"

Temple recognized true distress and quickly shoved her native skepticism aside.

"She is obviously physically healthy, so . . . there must be some psychic interference, that's all."

"But why now?"

Why now chose that moment to walk right in.

"Electra, it's Louie!"

"What can Midnight Louie do from two floors below to a receiver of Karma's power and experience? He is just an alley cat."

"He is just an alley cat," Temple agreed, "and what he can do is get to where he wants to be. Louie is here."

Electra looked up to the shadow at the edge of the room and the two glowing embers of green. "Louie! Are you interfering with Karma?"

Midnight Louie affected his usual bored look as he stalked over.

He bent to sniff Karma's supine form when he arrived, then looked up at them, eyes narrowed.

He leaped up onto the sofa between Electra and Temple. While Temple ran her hand down his back, Electra leaned away in suspicion.

Louie sat and stared at the green globe, tilting his head most intelligently.

Temple exchanged a look with Electra.

"Don't watch me; watch the globe," Electra urged her with sudden fire.

Temple complied. She had spent many less interesting evenings watching the screen in her TV set, especially since Max had left.

Midnight Louie was as focused as herself and Electra. Karma was off in Lullaby Land.

And as Temple stared at the rippled glass, as her thoughts drifted to other matters, as her body relaxed and her mind softened, she seemed to see small beams of light darting like tiny translucent fish in the shoals of glass.

The motion, the image was soothing, in a self-hypnotic kind of way. Imagine. Electra thinking her cat could produce phenomena in a garage-sale globe . . . consider the crystal a kind of aquarium, like the Mirage's immense tanks. Consider the cats as not psychics but predators watching snail darters of the Id and Ego swirl through the empty air within the globe. Air-breathing fish of the imagination. Phantoms. Ideas. Memories in motion. Subconscious submarine spirits.

Cats would like that kind of scenario. Cats might watch it for hours, but it didn't mean that the cats evoked anything within the globe. It didn't mean that they saw anything other than motes in an emerald eye. It didn't mean that people saw anything either.

Except . . . Temple saw swirls. Saw oily patterns in the water, saw words written on waves, saw images . . . like the Luxor, that pyramid of a hotel on the Strip.

She saw a pyramid!

She saw . . . stone walls covered with images . . . glyphs. Egyptian tomb scenes. A lotus flower floating by. And cats. Cats in profile. Perk-eared cats, lean and bronze. Mummified cats, wrapped in the Egyptian equivalent of Ace bandages. Mummy cases floating in the tide inside the globe like Moses's willow basket.

Motion, motion. Waves, waves. Images darting like schools of fish. Why was she hungry? Sharply hungry. Yet, pleasantly . . . sleepy too. In the sun, the dappled sun on the water, the flicker of torches on stone, on gilded mummy cases and furniture and jewels. King Tut's tomb. She was inside King Tut's tomb, under water, under waves, but she recognized the world-renowned treasures and her eye panned a train of tomb friezes like an educational channel's camera. But she had walked here. Trotted. On all fours. And she looked up, sniffed the torch fumes. Her eye-slits narrowed in the bright light. Her whiskers twitched with recognition.

Birds. Painted in profile. Feeders. Painted in profile, with dark-rimmed almond eyes. Our Kind, painted in profile, ears erect, necks richly collared, tails curled neatly around the feet.

An entire string of the Kind, forming words and concepts. Glyphs. All bronze gods. All sacred. And there, the King himself, in profile, looking down.

One of the Kind lying, not sitting. One of the Kind sprawled like a Pharaoh himself awaiting a pat of the Royal Hand. Why shouldn't a King look at a Cat, and why shouldn't a Sacred Cat look right back at a Pharaoh? And why shouldn't this particular Pharaoh look at this particular specimen of the Kind, seeing that it was most large and unusual, handsome, gifted and wise: the only all-black one in the bunch?

Chapter 25

All the Pharaoh's Phelines

I am reclining on my bed when Miss Temple returns from her sojourn above.

Actually, Miss Temple thinks that it is her bed, as Mr. Max used to think that it was his bed, but ultimately it is *my* bed, and I am willing to share. I have learned a lot in five thousand years.

She looks a little dazed, and I understand that these are trying times, but look at all the times that I have been through, and I am the same simple accommodating soul that I always was. Which is remarkable, considering my antecedents.

"Louie," she says, looking at me like Bergman looked at Bogart at the end of *Casablanca,* a bit dazed but really appreciative at long last.

"I guess I should ask how you got out and up to Electra's place, but frankly, her so-called psychic cat was such a dud that it was a good thing you showed up. I was so tired, though, I sort of dozed off. I'm afraid that Electra has delusions of grandeur. That cat Karma of hers is a dust mop. Pretty as can be, but pretty useless too. She thinks it's sensitive, but I think it's just lazy."

I cannot say how these words thrill me.

Of course, I know that the annoying Karma has been riding herd on me so mercilessly of late, that she has worn herself to a nub of her former powers, which is why she was making like a doormat and I was able to walk right in and kick Kitty Litter in her face.

Not that I like to rub all that sand into the eyes of a noble feline descended from a hardy and once worshiped desert race, like myself.

Now the genie is out of the bottle. Midnight Louie has antecedents, after all, and they are not too tacky. I have it on unassailable authority that one of my great-great-greats many times removed, and perhaps many lives and reincarnations previous, was a palace favorite.

I am talking about that honored Temple of Karnak cat, that Pharaoh's firstborn friend, the unofficial house dick at the pyramid and environs, that Sphinx's first cousin, Louie Sr. Sr. Sr. Sr. Sr. et cetera. No wonder I am associating with a Temple even today.

As for the languid Karma, she has fallen down on the job.

Those nouveau Burmese haven't got the family tree that goes back to the real roots of our Kind.

Just wait until I tell the Divine Yvette, who is no doubt the reincarnation of one of those Queens of the Nile.

I am not just a contemporary cool-dude detective. Once, I was King Tut's bodyguard.

Chapter 26

Calling Mrs. Bates . . .

Matt sat by the phone in his Circle Ritz apartment.

The fact that he kept it in the bedroom, rather than in a more public room, was mute testimony to how seldom it rang. And he seldom called anyone himself, so no wonder that his telephone seemed more like an ugly modern sculpture than a home appliance. He wondered how different his life was from that of Cliff Effinger, who was supposed to be dead, maybe.

He thought again about the body he could not positively identify while it lay static in a morgue viewing room, his to contemplate for as long as he wished. Then he resurrected the image of the walking man he had glimpsed with such certain instinct. Matt knew he had to make the call he most wanted to avoid.

The number came to his fingers by heart, after all this time, and after infrequent use. Perhaps "dutiful use" would describe the situation better. Holiday dialing.

He checked his new-old watch that he had run across among the contents of a packed box, a gold-edged rectangular face on a black leather band, a parting gift from the parishioners of St. Rose of Lima. At the time, it had been a touch of luxury in a minimalist life. His life today, however altered, was still minimalist, but the leather watchband was worn shiny, and the watch face looked genteel and old-fashioned, as if it should belong to his great-uncle Stash.

Was Uncle Stash still living? He hadn't asked about him in over a year. Should. Matt jotted the name down on the notepad next to the phone. Like a cue. A cue for calling home.

The phone rang several times. He kept checking his watch, though he knew the time perfectly well: seven forty-five P.M. in Chicago. There should be an answer.

There was.

Her voice sounded distant. Midwestern. Flattened. He hadn't noticed that until he had left the Midwest and heard other accents.

"Hi, Mom. It's Matt."

"Matt! Are you—I didn't expect . . . is something wrong?"

She always expected the worst, his mother. In the past, she usually had been right.

She spoke again quickly. "Let me turn the news down."

The phone on the other end klunked as she laid it down. She didn't have a remote control, which had even come with the small color TV he had bought for the living room here. Not for himself, he noticed. "For the living room," as if it were a person in need of placating.

A faint bleat in the background suddenly stopped; the phone thumped again as she picked it up.

"Nothing's wrong?" she asked.

At least this time she phrased it in the negative. Matt smiled.

"No, Mom, nothing. Are things okay there too?"

"Fine."

Fine. It said nothing, and said volumes. It was his mother's period to everything. *Say no more.* It's fine. *You don't need to know.* It's fine. *None of your business.* Fine. *It's my problem.* Fine.

Of course nothing had ever been fine.

"Good," he said. His usual answer to the finality of "Fine."

"Are you still . . . in that place?"

She could have meant the Circle Ritz, which he had told her

about, with details intended to enhance its zany vintage attractions. Or she could have meant Las Vegas.

"Same city, same job."

"It seems a shame . . ."

She left it for him to fill in the blanks: with your education and training, to be just a telephone counselor, to be a low-paid layman, when he had been Somebody once. A man with a vocation, an ancient role . . . a low-paid priest, Matt added as he finished the fault-finding litany. If having a son or daughter enter the religious life is the crown of a Catholic parent's life, having that same child leave the religious life is a disappointment beyond telling.

"Have you found a Polish parish there?" she asked anxiously.

"No, Mom. Not too many Poles in Las Vegas. But"—he knew he was about to mislead, knew he shouldn't, couldn't stop himself— "ah, I've been involved with a Hispanic parish. Our Lady of Guadalupe."

"Oh. The lovely holy card. Do they still have a statue of the Virgin in church?"

"Yes, it's an old parish."

He could almost see her nodding, slowly, her face the same faded gold color as her gray-streaked hair, both coarsened by time, by . . . circumstances. She looked at least a decade older than her fifty-two years, and nothing like the only youthful photos he had seen of her, as a young girl in her parents' house on Tobias Street.

"That's wonderful," she said, no joy in her voice, only the same, resigned monotone he had heard all his life.

"Yes." He made his hands unclench on the telephone receiver. "Everything's fine here. And I met one of my old teachers, from Saint Stan's, at OLG."

"Oh?"

"Sister Seraphina from seventh grade. Do you remember her?"

"A little. That's nice. Is she all right?"

"Retired now, but fine. Still a dynamo."

"We have all lay teachers at the school now. I thought of being an assistant, but—"

"Why don't you? It'd be a great idea. And I'm sure the school can use all the help it can get."

"Oh, I'm too old to deal with all that grade-school clatter."

"You're only fifty-two, Mom. Just a kid."

She laughed, flattered despite herself. "Not when you get to be my age. I do all right, but the winter is coming on again, and everything aches."

Matt ground his teeth. He remembered Chicago winters and the bone-chilling blasts of wind that blew off the great cold lake until the city crouched around it like a bum. He also remembered other reasons his mother had to ache in every bone.

The parquet floor at his feet became use-scuffed linoleum. Cliff Effinger was laid out on it like a corpse, definitely Cliff this time, and only unconscious, not dead. Matt looked down into that slack face of memory now as he did then, amazed, thankful that he had done this, exploring a universe of what he'd like to do next. . . .

But he hadn't, and that had been seventeen years ago. His mother should have forgotten by now, moved on, joined a folk-dancing class, met new people, maybe even remarried. But she hadn't. And Cliff Effinger still lay outstretched on the kitchen floor of memory, down but not counted out. Out cold but not out of their lives. No longer strong enough to cow a sixteen-year-old boy, but still potent enough to leech the life out of a woman past fifty. . . .

"Mom, I've got to ask."

"Ask what?"

"Have you got . . . anything? A photo, a belonging, anything of Cliff left that I could have?"

"What are you asking?"

"I need . . . something concrete that was his. It's part of . . . my therapy." True enough, if truth stretched all the way from Chicago to Caesars Palace.

"He left nothing." Her voice was even duller than before, and Matt blamed himself. "He just left, after you . . . made him. Took what junk he valued and went."

"And you never heard from him again?"

The silence was long and wounded. Matt began wondering how he could backtrack, change the subject, avoid the consequences.

"A postcard a couple of times."

"Did you keep them?"

218 • Carole Nelson Douglas

"Are you crazy? Matt, I was glad when you went into the priesthood, I thought at least the boy'll be safe from now on, but you left. Why did you leave? It was sanctuary. Now you're in that horrible place, where he went."

"So the postcards were from Las Vegas?"

"I suppose. I don't pay attention to that kind of thing. Gaudy. Corrupt."

"Do you remember the pictures?"

"What do you want?"

"I need to know this. It's our past."

"It's not past."

She was right about that. Matt relaxed, let his breath ease out. "I have to understand my own past," he said.

Another silence. "A . . . tall tower. With a bulb on the top, like in Russia."

"Russia?"

"One of the postcards. That's what it showed, night. There were all those little colored lights."

"And the other one?"

"I crumpled it and threw it away the minute I saw the bright lights. I never got another one."

"What did he say?"

"On the first one? He was bragging how great it was. Saying I should come out and see the sights. You know how he could be when he felt . . . like Somebody. Las Vegas." She snorted derisively.

"He was Nobody then, and he's Nobody now, Mom. He isn't in our lives anymore."

"Isn't he?"

"Look, one last, crazy question. Just think about it. You don't happen to have anything—anything—he might have left his fingerprints on, no matter how unlikely?"

Another long, long silence. "Just me," she said.

Matt wished he had followed his vengeful sixteen-year-old instincts and killed the man when he was still certifiably living.

Temple was caught between her bedroom and the living room when the phone rang, and she didn't really feel like answering it.

She had a lot on her mind: what Max Kinsella was doing to Gandolph's computer; where Midnight Louie might be; what Matt Devine would think if he found out that she was consorting (provocative word!) with the Mystifying Max.

Temple's biggest qualm was Matt. Poor baby, he had depended upon her so much lately. Who was rattling his cage now that she was otherwise occupied? Who was providing him the feminine advice and comfort he so badly needed? Sister Seraphina? Please . . . more old nuns and Catholic cats Matt did not need.

So when the phone rang, Temple considered ignoring it.

But . . . she finally skittered across the slippery floors to the kitchen phone and swooped up the receiver.

"Temple?" The voice was female and familiar, yet out of context.

"Righto."

"You sound . . . flustered. I didn't interrupt anything?"

"Just dealing with a few loose ends." *Who was this? One of the psychics ready to confess?*

"You'll never guess who sent me a long, gossipy letter."

Temple stopped fretting about absent problems to listen to the phone, to really listen.

"Mom! Why are you calling? Is Dad okay?"

"Fine, honey. I was trying to tell you. Honestly, Temple, will you ever slow down long enough to hear what anybody is saying? I got this long letter from Ursula just the other day."

Ursula? Wasn't that a nun-name? Why would somebody at Our Lady of Guadalupe be writing this Unitarian lady in Minneapolis?

"Oh, you mean Kit. Aunt Kit."

"That's not how she signed her letter, or ever has. Anyway, she says she met you in Las Vegas."

"She did. We did. She was here for a convention, and I ran into her."

"Convention? What kind of convention would Kit be attending? Doesn't she still work for that antiquarian bookstore in New York City?"

"Maybe so, but I didn't really hear much about that. Like I said, we literally ran into each other, and she recognized me, can you believe it?"

"Yes, I can. You've changed very little from the time you were in your teens, Temple. Never even grew. Your aunt Ursula was always a keen observer."

Temple had not wanted to hear—again—that she was Tammy Teen, so cute, so clever, so immature.

"Anyway," Temple said, "we had . . . lunch and—"

"Funny. She says dinner."

"Dinner too. Later. And we hit it off. She's really kind of neat."

"For somebody who lives in New York City, I suppose so. Are you still planning to stay out there?"

"Here? In Vegas?"

"Vegas. It sounds like the name of a gas cloud, or something. Not like anywhere normal people live. I wish you'd move back home, and get a good job like you had before."

"I have a good job. In fact, I have a better job. I've just been . . . hired to supervise the repositioning of a Strip hotel."

"Repositioning? Why can't it stay where it is, and why can't you come back home where you belong? All your brothers and sisters miss you—"

"And I miss them, but I can visit."

"You haven't."

Temple was silent.

"You can't imagine," her mother went on in her pleasantly singsong Minnesota voice, "how odd it is to get more news about you from my sister that I haven't seen in twelve years, than from you, my own daughter."

"What news?"

"Well, I didn't want to ask right out . . . but Ursula never mentioned Him."

"Him?"

"You know, That Man."

"That man?"

"The magician," her mother said grudgingly. "The cradle robber."

"I was hardly in the cradle, Mother."

"Temple, you like to think you're mature, but no one really is until—"

Thirty-five, Temple filled in the blank.

"—at least thirty-five."

"You had three kids by then."

"How do you think I got so mature so fast? You don't have any kids—"

"I have a cat." Temple threw in the child substitute. "Did Aunt Ursula mention that?"

"Nothing about a cat. I hope it's . . . sanitary. You did get all the proper shots? Cat scratch fever—"

"He's fine! He's shot up from one side to the other. He's safe. Pure as the driven snow, except he's black as coal."

"Temple. You haven't been out with some fast crowd that's . . . you know, drinking?"

"I'm of legal age, Mother."

"Chronological age means nothing."

Temple rolled her eyes and ground her teeth, and thanked God and Ma Bell that TV-phones were not common yet. Every mother on Earth would have one.

"About this magician," her mother went on. "Did you happen to get rid of him?"

He got rid of me, Mother! But Temple didn't say that. It would be more evidence that her darling daughter was not capable of running her own life.

"Max is fine," Temple said, so calmly she almost looked around to make sure that it was she who had spoken.

"Um. Well, I was surprised to hear from Ursula at such length. She says the bookstore is fine, though one wonders how much money she can be making on what selling books can pay."

Oodles, Mother. If you happen to be a best-selling author named Sulah Savage, which you aren't, because your baby sister is! And your baby daughter isn't doing too badly either!

"I'm sure Aunt Ursula's doing all right, Mom. And so am I."

"Are you sure? Temple, your father and I—and all your brothers and sisters—are very worried about you. You are our baby, you know."

I know, I know!

"Thanks, Mom. But I'm fine."

Temple sighed, realizing that she wasn't fine at all. But she was surviving, which was enough for her, and ought to be enough for them.

"You sound—"

"Harried, Mom. I've got a lot on my mind."

"Working late? You shouldn't let people take advantage of you."

"I work for myself, so if anyone's taking advantage of me, it's me. Actually my main project right now is . . . an eminent magician I'm hoping to interview."

"Another magician! I hope you're not going to see him alone."

"No, I'm not. A slew of colleagues are sure to be present. And this eminent magician is very elderly."

"Oh?"—*Like a hundred and twenty-four,* Temple was tempted to reply, *and the name's Houdini*—"Who is he?"

What a web we weave when we attempt to twist the truth into an origami ostrich. Temple heard herself saying something even more unlikely. "Orson Welles. Bet you didn't know he was a magician, too."

"Orson Welles? The Napa Valley wine man who used to write science fiction movies? He *is* old. But, Temple dear, isn't he . . . didn't I hear someplace that he . . . died?"

"Not permanently, Mother. Now I really have to run. I'm late. Talk to you later. Bye."

"Bye-bye, sweetie. Make sure you cover your head now that fall is here, and wear those mittens we sent you for Christmas three years ago—"

"Yes, Mother. Thanks for calling. Say hi to everybody."

Temple heard a disconnecting click and breathed again. What had Kit said in her letter? Nothing to give away her own game, you can bet your best Minnesota muffler!

Still, she paused, rerunning the conversation. She hoped she hadn't been too abrupt. Mom was used to her frantic public relations lifestyle, but she would have been alarmed by the slightly flaky idea of reviving Houdini. Mom only meant well. It was hard to let go of the youngest, because then you were older than you wanted to be. Someday her mother wouldn't be around to call her, or to call, and then Temple would be sorry. She sighed. Guilt was a terrible thing to waste.

Hey, maybe she underestimated the Afterlife. Look at Houdini and his devotion to mama from both sides of the grave. Maybe, with a little help from her new psychic friends, including Karma and Louie, she could always dial up the Beyond for the usual dose of maternal fussing.

"Son, son," the shade called in a voice of longing, which happened to be broken English with a strong German accent.

"Mother!" The man's voice was strong, but emotion-laden.

"So long, Ehrich. And I have wish to tell you . . ."

"I've waited for a word, a single word. If I'd only been there when you passed on, Mother. You know you are the Queen of my Heart. I've told the world you are. I've wept on your grave at twelve-fifteen in the morning, the time you died. You know of my devotion, don't you? Don't you?"

"Always, my boy. Always my boy."

"But I must know, the word you meant to tell me when you died, and I an entire ocean away. I came back, sick though the waves made me. I would not let them bury you until I had come to lay my head on your heart, your life, one last time. You were silent, Mother, through no fault of your own. I was a madman. I sought mediums to find you. What were you going to tell me?"

"You are with me, Ehrich. Always."

"But the message? I have lived in torment, needing to know what word you wanted to give me. I tried to chase down Death, and he finally slowed enough that I could catch him. But even Death did not know, nor poor Bess who survived me. What would you have said to me, Mother, had I come in time?"

"A word, Ehrich. No one hears enough, that word."

"Now! Can you say it now, in this vast emptiness that still is my heart?"

"Yes, dear one. One word. 'Forgive.' "

"Forgive. I was not sure, so I could not."

"Now you can, son."

"Now . . . is not then."

"Forgive, son. Forgive."

"And then I will forget?"

"Yes."

"But will they forget Houdini?"

"Not now."

"No?"

"Not . . . yet."

Chapter 27

A Sign from Cat Heaven

Quite frankly, I do not have a superstitious bone in my body.

Then what, you could quite rightly ask, is that very body doing back in the now-closed haunted house, right in the middle of a coven of cats, adding the deep bass of my perfect-pitch purr to the general catophony in progress? (We do indeed sound like a convention of pitch pipes, all stuck on the same note.)

Some might suppose that I have allowed myself to be herded here by the out-of-body agitation of Karma. And I admit it looks like that. In fact, the Light of my Life appeared to me in a dream, demanding that I show up for this all-feline folly of a séance.

But the fact is, when Midnight Louie is seen to do something that is apparently against his better judgment, his better judgment has a better reason for doing it than is readily apparent. Got that? I hope so. I am not going to produce that sentence again.

My higher reason tells me that although the psychic powers attributed to my kind may be a lot of Huey, Dewey and Louie Duck, who am I to point it out? If I go along, I may pick up the odd admission amongst the claptrap that will lead me to some legitimate line of investigation. In other words, I am big on psychology though skeptical of the psychic, at least the kind of psychic phenomena that come when called. Such ghosties strike me as too canine to be believed. Now Jersey Joe Jackson, at least, is refreshingly arbitrary about his appearances, which makes me tend to think there may be more than ersatz ectoplasm there.

But I no more expect these earnestly humming feline hoodoo seekers to come up with something than I believe that anything genuine manifested itself at the Halloween séance, other than the cameo appearances of Amelia Airheart, Elvis Presley, et al. Certainly the so-called Houdini in the chimney was a humdinger. I had been down that chimney in person not many minutes before, and I can testify that more than cobwebs lined its length. My unsheathed razors twanged a few taut fishlines as I shimmied down, and may have messed up the appearance, for all I know.

What psychic powers I do attribute to my own breed include supernaturally sharp sets of ears and a knack for knowing the human bent for evil. So these cats sitting here in a circle on the empty séance table may look like a bunch of tail-twitching half-wits, but I believe that they know more than they think they do. I am here to eavesdrop on any meaningful tidbits among the trivia.

Also, the presence of at least two cats of midnight color is required for a proper feline séance, and I feel I must honor my heritage and participate in the folderol, if only to uphold tradition. Especially now that I know Midnight Louise has not been invited, to my great relief, although she would claim that her exclusion is a matter of gender bias. I can assure everyone that only male cats were invited because they just happened to be the nearest, bravest, smartest and strongest, see? No prejudice allowed here. What you see here is what you need. (If a séance were what it is supposed to be, which it is not.)

Now that the who, how and why are clear, the *what* should unfold in its own sweet time.

And that time is turning pretty sour, to my mind. I soon tire of hearing the first note of "Melancholy Mewser" held ad infinitum. I break ranks (or the rank hum) long enough to tell Ingram so and am told, "Shhhh."

So we go on making like a one-note organ on eternal hold. I begin to wonder when we will attract some unwanted attention of a purely temporal nature.

And sure enough, the pinprick of light that is Karma flashes over to one glassy wall. The dark beyond us is indeed lightening. I watch the growing haze broaden as it nears. The hums around me grow louder and more fervent, and the tail-twitch is practically electric. I twitch my personal extremity out of the hysterical circle. Have not these ninnies heard of night watchmen, with flashlights? And guns?

I check for my old man down the circle, hoping he has seen the light and drawn the same life-saving conclusions as I. But, no, he is thrumming along with a deep basso purr, his eyes half-shut, lost in the rare joy of a community sing.

I always preferred solo gigs. Maybe that is why I am a city cat and he is a seaside cat. Or why he works at a restaurant and I work at the big, year-round buffet of bad behavior that is my beat. Las Vegas at its best is always at its worst.

It also may be why I look out for Number One (that is, my first life) as if it were my last. So, as I edge outside, the circle closes upon me, its participants so transported that none notices my absence, nor mourn it.

Their loss. I leap down to the floor, where I can observe unnoticed. If any shooting starts, I can at least knock some sense into my old man. Which I will do by leaping up to drag him down before the lead flies and finds any convenient holes to fill in the heads here gathered (in which there are quite a few holes, by my count).

I watch the light near, wary of any sudden changes. I know that if I were the shade of something from Beyond, manifesting myself as a warm, glowing light, I would be ready to cream the creators of the current dissonant, monotonous hubbub. Why any lost spirit would head straight for such a clamor is beyond me.

I am right. The light does not head straight into our happy humming midst. Instead it pauses at the window. I flatten my ears, so they should not get notched by any stray bullets, which also has the happy effect of somewhat deadening the humming. Perhaps "deadening" was the wrong word to have in mind.

For, lo! What image breaks in yon window but that of a deathly pale human with haunted, drawn features and thin, elongated hands. In fact, this personage looks as if it has been drawn on a balloon that is inflating, for soon the faint outlines stretch into thin air and vanish.

A pathetic mew of triumph underlines the humming above, which has the table legs practically vibrating. But Midnight Louie knows that what others see and accept as paranormal is merely some cheap trick built into the Hell-o-ween Haunted Homestead's séance chamber. The light is still there, hanging in air (another old trick). It is still outside the window, a dead giveaway, if you ask me. What self-respecting spirit would ignore getting a few easy horrified gasps by doing something so simple as gliding through glass?

Apparently the bearer of the flashlight agrees, for the light slowly dies, as if ashamed.

Now we will see the night watchman.

But all is dark, and remains so.

The feline hum increases in intensity. Poor desperate fools, trying to lure danger and death in all too human guise!

And . . . and there he is! The watchman.

I can see his form quite clearly now. Dark. Portly. Garbed in a brimmed hat and cape. Cape? Who does this bozo think he is? An escapee from that famous Rembrandt painting of night watchmen? I have seen a Work of Art or two in my day, when Miss Temple's television set was accidentally turned to an educational channel. Of course, this is a haunted-house attraction. It only stands to reason that the night watchman should dress the part. I wait anxiously to see if the face appears from the shadow of the hat brim, and if it is green. Or has fangs. Or fallen eyeballs to match the fallen arches this heavyset house dick must have.

More is coming into focus. Ah! By the hair of his chinny, chin, chin, this antique figure has a beard under that hat. A disguise? A beard and broad cheeks (naturally; he probably spends most of his time guarding the kitchen, not that I would do any differently). And eyes. Merry, twinkling eyes under ungroomed brows. Is Saint Nick working a night job until he gets busy in a couple of months? Then on with the red suit and off with the reindeer?

The would-be apparition's face leans close to the glass. (Here is where he will give himself away; if his nose or chin should touch glass they will pool against it, proving a corporeal presence.) The man grins and looks right at me. That is correct, at me and at no one, nothing else. He puts a chubby finger to his lips, just like jolly old so-and-so. Except his expression is not jolly now. It is pleading. It is conspiratorial. It is urgent.

I stare. I am being enjoined to silence, when I am the only silent one in this room.

Above me, the faithful humming continues unshushed. I stick my head out from under the table and eye my compatriots. All stare vacantly forward, some gazing directly at my night watchman. None see anything but their own faint reflections in the glass.

I look back to the panel the night watchman waits behind. His finger has left his lips. His hands are clasped before the darkness of his cape, clasped in supplication, in urgent supplication. Even as I stare, he suddenly sweeps open his cloak. I see a room lined with bookshelves. I see a lamp upon a table . . . no, it is a bright spot upon a table, a pale, square bright spot, like an open luminous book, no, like the face of the machine Miss Temple uses to write upon and that I amuse myself with now and again by running over the keys. Without noise, books begin tumbling from shelves, and the old night watchman is laughing silently behind his beard and under the shadow of his broad-brimmed hat. Then the lighted screen dims, as it always does when it is turned off, but more slowly now, dimming like a day dims, when a whole sun must sink somewhere to make it happen . . . and the night watchman is sad, downcast, so despondent that he dims with it. The cloak falls closed, the darkness outside is mere darkness, the lit screen is a memory as distant as the first fire.

And still the ninnies on the table hum their tuneless formula. Still they seek a phenomenon from Beyond.

I sit, pondering. Obviously, they did not see what I saw. Then again, I am beginning to think that I am as superior at seeing what is not there as I used to be at seeing what was there. In other words, I am better than they are, even at nothing.

Now the foolish felines begin to moan between their purrs. They sound like a 1973 Volkswagen starting, or thinking about it. Urrrr-rummmm. Urrrr-rummm. Uuuuur-eeee. Uuuur-eee.

Hurry?

Ouuuu-eeee. Ouuuu-eee.

Hurry Ouie?

A spark snaps in the fireplace. I turn to look, not wanting my only escape hatch to go up in flames. But I spy only an old flame of mine, after all: Karma, the kibitzing ember. The spark dodges into the room and dances around yours truly, shedding no heat, but much static. My hair is soon whipped into enough peaks to pose as a Baked Alaska dessert, and I am forced to retreat to the high ground of the tabletop.

Once there, the demonic Karma buzzes me with shocks until I am herded back into place in the circle.

"Quick!" Ingram hisses at me through his fangs. "You are the focus of the invading spirit."

Oh, goody. First I am the "focus" of the electric eel of the Circle Ritz, that dominatrix of the light, Karma. Now I am soon to be zapped by some invading spirit. No, thanks.

Before I can shake my coat into shape again and make a break for the chimney, I am stopped cold by the clear sound of a spectral voice amidst the humming.

"Ooo-eee," it moans. Hollowly.

If you accept that "oooo-eee" is ghost talk for "Lou-ie," then I am one marked dude.

If, however, you are of my turn of mind that "ooooo-eeee" could mean absolutely nothing, then I have no reason to remain.

Before my paws can dig into the tabletop for a sudden dash, though, another light beams in the dark.

I wish that I could say that this was Karma's mean little spur of spark, or even my night watchman's spectral TV. But it is not. It is a huge green eye of the feline kind, slit up the middle, and it is looking right at me.

Chapter 28

Cameraman

On a cool early November Monday morning, Temple Barr called the offices of the *Las Vegas Scoop* to make an appointment with one of its employees.

She once swore that it would be a cold day in Hell before she'd need anything from anyone at what she privately called the *Las Vegas Pooper Scooper*, but pride goeth before a frigid fall in temperature. And Gandolph the late Great's death was growing very cold, very fast.

When Temple reached the office, she was almost disappointed to find her quarry not only on the job, but reasonably ready and willing to receive her.

She had donned her most washable clothes and expendable shoes. She had confined makeup and nail polish to funereal pales. She would have worn sackcloth and dumped ashes in her flagrant hair, if she'd had them. Unfortunately, in this secular age, sackcloth and ashes weren't the staples of life they once were.

Despite the seasonal cold snap, Las Vegas refused to wallow in an autumnal funk. The desert sky was Lake Mead–blue with scattered clouds afloat on its surface like icebergs. On a more down-to-earth level, hardy flowers still blossomed among the greenery.

Temple parked the Storm at the weekly paper's strip-shopping-center offices, its front wheels on preflattened front pages saturated with oil-pan drip.

Temple entered through a glass door so smudged with fingerprints that it looked opaque. Why were fingerprints always so obvious when it didn't matter?

Inside was instant chaos—the click and clatter of computer keyboards, and the chatter of people scurrying to pull another Gutenberg miracle out of their heads, hands and hats.

Newsroom noise always made Temple nostalgic for her WCOL–TV days, but the receptionist was never like this.

"Help you?" he asked, sweeping a mailing list aside and showing off a nail polish job far less subtle than Temple's. His spaniel-blond hair was all one length to the tops of his ears, then shaved to the skin below. He wore one tasteful aurora borealis crystal stud in his right ear, and eyeliner on both eyes.

Temple asked for the man she wanted, or rather, the man she didn't want, but needed to see.

The receptionist tossed his hair toward the large room's far wall. "Photo desk. Over there."

Temple headed in the direction indicated. Like all foot soldiers dispatched by duty to foreign turf, she hoped that it would soon be over over there. She kept an edgy eye out for another *Scoop* employee, whom she was even less eager to encounter.

The photo desk was presided over by a squat, graying man who looked more like Ed Asner with a hangover than Asner himself ever could.

"I've got an appointment with Wayne Tracey," she told him.

"Aren't we fancy now? Appointments and everything. Wayne!" he bawled over his shoulder.

A revolving door only big enough for one customer at a time, with opaque black dividers, slowly thumped around until it disgorged a harried guy of thirty in rolled-up shirtsleeves.

"Come on in," he said. "I'm souping some stuff and can't stop now."

Cranky at the desk nodded brusque encouragement, so Temple jumped for the revolving door's next empty compartment. She shuffled along in complete darkness, like someone in a small, circular haunted house, until she found the only way out on the other side: the eerie, dim, infrared atmosphere of a development chamber.

She edged up to the only man inside, who was submerging paper in solution until an image appeared. This was not unlike being at a séance, Temple realized, though in the past she had taken photo studios and their processes for granted.

Yet, when you came to think of it, there was something spooky about the entire process. First you caught people's essences—their frozen images—in reverse light-and-dark. Then you projected them on paper. And finally, you let those encoded vestiges stew in a strong chemical soup until the person begins to peer out from the developing pan like a shy spirit. Instant ectoplasm.

"Yeah?" the photographer asked without looking up.

"Wayne Tracey?"

"Right."

"You must remember me from the haunted-house séance you shot the other night."

He glanced at her, surprised. "Why should I? I shoot a few dozen photos a day, and when I'm videotaping for out-of-town media, I shoot thousands of feet. I don't pay much attention to exactly who's in front of my lens, just as long as the reporter gets the names and faces right, and clues me in on what's happening so I know where to point."

"Oh. Well, I *was* there. I wondered if any of the spooky effects showed up on your live footage."

He tonged a dripping wet photo of a mangled van surrounded by even more mangled passengers into another chemical bath.

"What was to show up? Fog. No different from when it shows up outside along the road, though we don't get much fog out here. Not wet enough."

"Did the police see your film?"

"First thing. Confiscated it. Only let me have a copy of my own stuff, period. And for what? The film just shows these shifting patches of fog, and the people sitting around the séance table look like wooden Indians playing ring-around-the-rosy."

"Not a lot of activity to warrant a live camera," Temple agreed sympathetically. "We were instructed to be still and concentrate. But didn't you catch the action when the person keeled over? You, know, the man who died?"

"So someone faints. An Oscar it ain't. And it's a guy under that wig and Hedda Hopper hat, yet, can you figure it? He reminded me of our work-in-progress receptionist. These psychics are ultraweird, man, and I see plenty of weirdos every day in this job."

"If you're an expert, maybe you could say whether this seemed like a normal séance."

"A normal séance? Hey, they're no fun unless everything's abnormal." He shook his head. "Nope, nothing out of the ordinary but the usual hazy theatrics."

"You mean the knife dance and the woman fainting, then Gandolph keeling over?"

"And the chimneyful of fog-bound ectoplasm."

"So you did see something in the fireplace."

"Smoke, probably. That's what the police concluded too. Excuse me."

He brushed past Temple, a photo dripping solution between his fingers, and hung the print on a drying line.

"What about the face that appeared on the various windows?"

Wayne stopped what he was doing to frown at Temple.

"Face? No face. Except maybe some uneasy rider outside slipping past in a programmed car. Or a reflection of my light. That glass all around is murder to shoot in. No wonder the freaks fantasized seeing someone's face there."

"But you . . . didn't."

"Nope. Just saw what my film showed. A lot of nothin'."

"And there's nothing odd or unexplained on the film?"

"Only the psychics, like I told you, and the police. They can play with it all they want; what they see now is what they'll have later."

"Then what killed Gandolph?

"Boredom?" he asked pointedly.

"Sorry, and thanks. I won't keep you." Temple turned to feel her way out, then paused. "You work with Crawford Buchanan much?"

"Just lately, now that he's got this national TV stringer job. It's a good deal for me, great for the résumé, you know? Never hurts to look big-time nowadays. That's what I love about Las Vegas, opportunity comes to you here."

"So you're new to town?"

"Been here a couple of months."

"Think you'll stay?"

"Maybe, but not at the *Scoop* for long."

"And with Crawford and *Hot Heads*?"

"As long as I have to in order to make a name for myself. That Buchanan guy is a pain in the butt. Thinks he's the cat's pajamas and its cream and sugar too."

"I know." Temple sighed. "Did the police ask you anything special when they interviewed you?"

"Only said not to leave town without telling them. I hope to God there's nothing on my film they give a piss about. I hate testifying at trials. I'm a shooter, not a talker."

"Got the message. I'm through, anyway. Aren't you curious why I want to know about the shoot, though?"

He shook his head. "Everybody wants to know. That's why rags like this exist. That's what pays my rent. Everybody's got to know the gruesome details about everything. And I'm the guy who'll give it to them in Technicolor."

He lifted a close-up print of a mutilated body to the line, clipped it, and left it there to drip-dry . . . developing solution oozed off the limp paper like body fluids.

Outside the revolving door, Temple stood still for a moment while her eyes adjusted to the overhead lights. That moment of disorientation was her mistake: she wasn't a moving target anymore, just a target.

"There she is," a voice rumbled too nearby to dodge.

Cold fingers clasped her forearm. "What brings the star of the local newspaper Gridiron Show to our humble doorstep, T.B.?"

Crawford Buchanan was looking suspiciously cheery. Maybe it was the orange tie. Even his usual smirk turned up at the corners as if auditioning to be a grin.

"Just checking into a few things."

"Check on," he said, his smirk now a full-fledged expression of extreme self-satisfaction. "If you're trying to get the spotlight by solving another murder case, though, you should have read your horoscope this morning. You are out of luck."

"Why?"

"See it on *Hot Heads* tonight, and weep. Will you be surprised! This time I've got the scoop, and you're out of the loop, my little amateur snoop."

"Watch your adjectives, Crawford. 'My' and 'little' could be actionable." Temple jerked her arm out of his custody, but he remained perfectly smug. "I can't believe anything you've got to say about the séance murder could be news to anyone."

"Just keep on burying your perky little red head in the sand, T.B.; there's plenty of it around here."

"There's plenty of nerve around here too, and you're a fine one to sling the word 'little' around."

Crawford adjusted the lapels of his double-breasted navy blazer that made him look annoyingly officious, like a cruise-ship captain, or something.

"Keep on fooling yourself. This time I was at the death scene too, with a cameraman, and my report tonight is going to make you look like yesterday's warmed-over squash." He edged nearer and lowered his voice. "We could meet in the Crystal Phoenix bar at six-thirty to watch the show together. I'll even buy you a drink. You'll need it."

"I would if I was dumb enough to meet you anywhere."

Temple headed for the safety of the newsroom, but Buchanan caught hold of her tote-bag strap.

"You're so cute when you're mad, T.B. And you will be tonight. Don't forget to turn on the TV and tune in."

"Drop out!" she suggested, digging her high heels into the cigarette-burned vinyl tile.

He released the tote-bag strap just as she shrugged away, so she hit the floor running and took several steps to slow down to normal speed.

Meanwhile, heads all over the room looked up to see Temple lurching toward the door.

Crawford Buchanan was gifted, she had to admit, gifted at making everyone around him look almost as bad as he did.

She was so infuriated by the encounter that she fussed aloud at the Storm all the way home.

"Creep! He's just pretending to know something I don't. The cameraman said the film canister was bare, so to speak. *Nada*. The Big *Nada*, like C.B. himself. Or . . . why should the cameraman tell me if his footage has a hot image on it? It could be his ticket to the top. He admitted he came to Vegas to 'make it.' Damn Crawford Buchanan! I knew when I heard he was on the séance list that he'd be trouble. What does that make me, huh? A fortune-teller?"

Temple slammed on the brakes before the Storm bruised its nose on the oleander bush at the end of her parking space, and came out of the car slamming the door shut as well.

She stormed into the Circle Ritz and ran up the two flights of stairs to her condominium. After she let herself in, she bolted for the living room VCR to ravish the instruction book until she was sweating bullets and to push buttons until she was fairly sure that the machine was set to record every annoying second of that night's *Hot Heads* telecast.

When she rose after her struggle with button sequences, she took her spleen out on the lifeless television and recorder.

"He probably won't even get on tonight. He'll end up on the cutting-room floor with the rest of the second-stringers. He'll probably lose out to a Rush Limbaugh feature."

That notion was so pleasant that Temple headed for the kitchen to grab a bite. She ended up taking a carton of nonfat yogurt in the car with her. This time when she put the Storm into gear, it backed out as smooth as vanilla-raspberry yogurt.

"You know," she speculated aloud, "Crawford could have done something himself to create a story, to get him the notoriety he so desperately wants."

An interesting theory. Maybe even collusion between Buchanan and the ambitious cameraman. Temple nodded. Who was the one person who was almost as effacing as a ghost during the entire séance? Wayne Tracey. Everyone in these media-conscious days—and spirit mediums in particular—knows what to do when there's a videocamera in the room. Ignore it, act natural, maybe get your face on national TV. The last person anybody in that room was looking at Thursday night was Wayne Tracey.

She clicked on the radio and nodded along to the country music as the car headed toward her next stop, where she would meet another man she wouldn't trust as far as she could throw him. And even with Matt's martial arts lessons, she'd never been about to throw the Mystifying Max.

It took Temple ten minutes of driving around the housing development to find the front of the house she and Max had broken into the night before.

Then it took Max three minutes to answer her knock, even though he should have expected her.

"Hi," he said, immediately moving away and leaving her to secure the door.

Temple followed him. Such indifference was not Max's usual mode. She found him in the first of the two bedrooms, hunched before the computer screen. A half-ream of paper lay uncollected in the printer well, and another sheet was scraping across this pile as it struggled to print out.

Temple swooped up the paper and disciplined it into an even-edged pile on a nearby table littered with floppy disks and cold pizza slices.

Max, his face not turning from the screen, reached out a hand for something.

Temple filled it with a sloppy slice of congealed hamburger/pepperoni/anchovies. Ugh!

Max held the pizza slice poised for a moment, in front of the disk port, then lifted it to his face and chewed. And chewed. And swallowed. Double ugh!

"A mess, huh?" Temple said soothingly. "You haven't had much experience with computers, obviously—"

The hand with the pizza (now a mere triangle of crust and anchovies) pointed to the table.

"This is incredible. Take a look at those pages. I printed out whatever seemed intriguing. Gary had been writing up a storm."

Temple fanned through the sheaf. Words jumped out at her: illusion, show, St. Louis, Missouri . . . somebody's "Aunt Velda," housing doves, Houdini, *Citizen Kane*, mention of cemeteries . . . some dialogue, as if from an interview or a . . . a novel.

"This is a jumble of everything. It doesn't make sense."

"Except that it's a jumble," Max agreed.

He leaned his elbows on the padded wrist rest. The supernaturally smooth hair at his temples was roughened, as if gophers had been burrowing into it.

"Maybe you'd like me to run the computer—"

"No, I'm doing fine. It's just that there's so much, and Gary used some cryptic naming and filing system that would baffle anyone else. I don't think he really meant for me to unlock this stuff, only he couldn't hide it from me. It's all done like stage magic, with the assumption that the abnormal pertains, and I'm used to thinking like that. . . ."

After another minute or two, when the only sound was the clatter of the computer keyboard now and again as Max moved through directories and files, Temple pulled a chair over to the pizza table and tried to install order among the abused diskettes.

Like men not used to typing and computer keyboards, Max punched each key with his forefingers. But otherwise he seemed to be navigating the screen just fine.

"This is incredible, Temple."

She nodded, unnoticed, behind him. Max, mesmerized by something other than magic. And it wasn't her. It was whatever had been on Gandolph's apparently overworked hard drive.

"It'd take months," he went on, "to decipher and untangle this stuff. Everything's misdirection. Two files in a naming sequence match, and the third is totally unrelated."

When she didn't answer the silence, Max actually turned from the screen to look at her. "Sorry. Rapture of the Deep. This is something I'd never imagine Gary doing."

"This is something I'd never imagine you doing. You gave my home computers about as much attention as a dust mote."

"I had to learn a bit about them during my . . . leave of absence. Some of them have too much information about me for comfort, and some of them have information I need. I can't just whisper in Molina's ear when I want an inside track."

"Stop grinning like the Microsoft mouse that ate a conglomerate. Your keyboard technique may be strictly Rocky Marciano, but you obviously are no longer a stranger in the land of Cyberspace, where the local gods are Byte and Megabyte."

"Have some pizza," he suggested in an absently placating tone. "There's some . . . something to drink somewhere."

"This cold . . . slab of cholesterol and sodium on cardboard? You want me to eat it? I might as well chew on one of these not-so-floppy disks."

"No, don't fool with the disks!"

But when he looked up, he saw she was stacking disks, and not into a Dagwood sandwich.

"Max, computer nerding does not become you. Get off-line for a minute and tell me what you've found so I can see what I can find."

"Okay." He uncoiled from Gandolph's big leather desk chair, then winced as he realized what several hours hunching over a hot computer screen will do to muscles and joints.

"Grab those papers," he told Temple. "Let's go into the kitchen where we can get some good light, and maybe something warm to eat or drink. Or both."

"Thank you," Temple said devoutly, casting her eyes to the ceiling. "Thank you, gods of the Computer Kind."

"Somebody out there scuff your shoes?" Max asked curiously as he led her into the house's large and . . . wow! . . . superbly equipped kitchen.

"You did say that Orson Welles lived here, didn't you, and he was quite a gourmet."

"I think the exact word is 'gourmand,' but words are your business."

"No, you're right. 'Gourmand' it is." Temple opened a stainless-steel door and found an upright freezer filled with catering-firm entrées. "Gandolph apparently was no slouch in the food department either."

"No, that's why he was so ideal for the house. I felt secure leaving it in his care."

Max probed the various clear plastic boxes, tubs and containers. "So what went wrong today?"

"Nothing. It's what might go wrong tonight."

"How so?"

"Oh, Crawford Buchanan is boasting that his spot on *Hot Heads* will have startling information about what he calls the 'Halloween Havoc.' "

"Awful Crawford is on *Hot Heads* now?"

"Oh, yeah. And he really pulled a dirty trick at the Gridiron Show, getting me to write a bunch of skits just so he could have the pleasure of *not* using them."

Max leaned against the marble-topped counter and folded his arms. "Old C.B. sounds like he's taking over the world."

"Not the world, only my part of it. I just had a run-in with him at the *Las Vegas Scoop*. He is so scummy. Half the time he acts like he's coming on to me, and half the time he acts like he wants to stomp me flat; either mode is equally unwelcome."

Max smiled tolerantly. "You *have* been dealing with elevated media. Temple, Buchanan thrives on riling you. Just regard him as a kid in sixth grade who figures the way to tell a girl he thinks she's cute is to put garter snakes into her lunch bag."

"It's not so harmless when that kid grows up still feeling he has to put down women to feel superior enough to hit on them. And I don't want him thinking I'm cute!"

Max shook his head. "Oh, he's a sleazebag, but not worth worrying about. Concentrate on something crucial: what do you want for dinner?"

He unfolded one arm and then the other to reveal two of Temple's favorite cold-weather comfort foods, genuine Kraft macaroni and cheese (lots and lots of cheese) and linguini Alfredo (lots and lots of Alfredo.)

"I haven't had macaroni and cheese in ages. I don't know! Choosing between two equally tempting dishes is not my strongest point."

"I hope you don't mean that." Max's most piercing look always thrilled 'em in the twelfth row. Up close it was a lot less enjoyable.

She realized she had blindly walked right into his allusion. Maybe she could talk her way right out of it.

"The linguini needs reheating. The macaroni has to be boiled from scratch, sort of, as convenience food goes, but . . . oh, heck, the macaroni."

"Ah, yes." Max turned for the pots hanging high on a rack. "The unassuming, all-American staple, not some pretentious, somewhat pricey item with antecedents abroad. Good choice."

"Just get the damn pot down, and I'll start the water boiling. What's for dessert?"

Max was opening another series of cupboards. He produced a brown glass bottle.

"Gary was getting down to the luxuries. Bailey's all right?"

"Macaroni and cheese and Bailey's Irish Cream. You do know how to set a table, Kinsella."

"We should have a vegetable, to be virtuous. I'll see what I can do."

While Max foraged for what promised to be a truly original repast, Temple frowned at the copper-bottomed pot on the expensive smooth-surface ceramic cooktop. (As opposed to the stainless-steel stove on the other wall that grilled, barbecued, seared, fricasseed, took credit cards and gave change.)

Watching water come to a boil was a thankless occupation, but it gave her time to reflect how oddly ordinary it felt to be rummaging around a kitchen with Max, hunting up an impromptu meal. Never mind that the kitchen was equipped to coddle the five-star chefs of Europe, or that the man who had used to live here had died holding Temple's hand only four nights before. Or that Max actually owned this house crammed with fancy food and magical apparatus. Or was that apparati? Apparatuses?

Any port in an emotional storm.

Speaking of port, Max apparently had also found the wine cellar, no great feat for a former owner.

"For Madame's entrée." He bowed like a sommelier and extended a bottle with the usual flourish. "An uppity Médoc."

"I think beer is the liquor of choice for macaroni and cheese, but wine is fine, and no doubt Orson Welles would approve."

"I don't think Orson Welles approved of much," Max said, working the cork out the way any old mortal would, with a corkscrew he found in a drawer. "Especially himself. He always had film projects under way, you know. He didn't just drop out, as many people thought. But he couldn't find the backing and the finances, and so many of them vanished into thin air."

"Thin air," Temple repeated. "Was that why he ate so much, all his dreams were immaterial, so he became totally material?"

"I doubt it," Max said, sitting opposite her at the breakfast table. "I think he ate because he truly enjoyed it. He probably inherited his tendency to overweight, and age simply ensured that heredity took over. The camera is as cruel to heavy men as it is to women."

"Yes, the camera is an equal-opportunity offender, but people aren't. Overweight women are more despised than overweight men."

"And overweight Beautiful People are despised more than anybody. Media idols aren't supposed to have our same feet of clay."

Temple gazed down at her mound of pasta tubes and bright yellow cheese sauce, steam rising from its surface like mountain mist.

"Now I feel guilty about eating this. Think of all the starving Beautiful People in the world who would give anything to exchange their diet of Kitty Litter and purified water for this!"

"Eat, drink and be merry while you may," Max suggested, lifting his glass.

"Good advice, but since I'm the legwoman of this outfit, I'm planning to do some extensive running around tomorrow . . . and tomorrow. Not much time to eat."

"What's going to keep you in constant transit?"

"My . . . unconventional personal life. I'm afraid things have come to such a pass that I'm going to have to consult some psychics."

Temple couldn't tell whether Max took her statement as a promise or a threat.

Chapter 29

Behind Door
Number One

Mynah Sigmund, wouldn't you know (Temple told herself), was a native talent and a local act.

She lived in an older area of residential homes, not nearly as nice as the one Max owned (Temple also told herself). During the psychic fair, she was available at home for one precious hour a day, and Temple had brazenly booked it. For some people, five of an afternoon was the cocktail hour. For Mynah (rhymes with Car-o-lin-a), it was the withdrawing hour.

"Be there at five," she had instructed Temple. Her eyes—blue, clear and cold—had wordlessly emphasized the importance of obeying directions to the letter. "I always meditate at three P.M. for an hour, then . . . collect myself. You may let yourself in."

"I'm not to knock?"

"Knock? No. Rapping is a phenomenon I neither stimulate, nor tolerate, in my vicinity. You'll see."

Mynah smiled then, a Mona Lisa pristine-madonna smile probably intended to drive men mad. Most women would describe it as supercilious big-sister smug. But Temple had noticed that men usually fell for what most women disdained, and vice versa. It was too bad that the sexes didn't develop an anonymous cross-gender warning service.

Now Temple parked her Storm in the semicircular driveway that aped the semicircular poured-concrete fence comprising the front of Mynah's address. Other neighborhood houses lay exposed, crowded by Joshua trees and various tall, spiky and pale desert growths. Mynah's establishment was ringed by this contradictory and virginal wall, both fluid and rounded in form, like a wave of supernaturally white sand, yet discouragingly solid and opaque. It was a wall that begged for breaking.

Against this soft/hard cold/hot white wall, and the bleached stones that covered the ground, and the uncompromisingly spotless cocaine-bright concrete that formed the driveway, the Storm's soft aqua silhouette looked strangely apropos. A blob of Southwest paint, perhaps, torn from the sky, dropped on a blank canvas and about to be smeared into an approximation of the native precious stone, turquoise.

That was the trouble with the whiteness of Mynah. Like the whiteness of the whale Moby Dick, it was unnatural, despite the naturalness of its environment. It existed to set off the color of everything else, and everything else usually suffered by comparison. Oh, the Storm looked its ordinary spirited self: blue and white are the eternal partners of peace. But Temple's red hair; now that would be an intrusion here.

Also her color-blocked linen pants suit, chosen perhaps unconsciously as a gauntlet to throw down before the anemic Mynah. And her purple, orange and Kelly-green high-heeled J. Renee pumps.

On the other hand, five was also the Sunset Hour in some parts of the country, world and time zone. Temple straightened her gaudy padded shoulders and prepared to ring the bell, since knocking was prohibited.

But the gateway (a double-doored expanse of milk-stained mesquite) was merely arched doors split by the obvious line of separation. No knocker to drop. No practical, round period of a built-in bell to ring.

Beyond the wall and the gate, water fell in a talkative turquoise lament upon pale stones. Village women weeping and washing in this vale of tears.

What women? What village? This was a one-time tract house, for God's sake, Temple reminded herself. She hated spells of any kind, unless they were uttered by grandmotherly women with wands, who could bring forth dazzlingly different shoes with every wave.

Glass would not be welcome in this place of stones, which were the raw material of unfired glass. Here was cool earthen removal. Withdrawal. Here was Western asceticism. Here was high-toned hokum incarnate.

While Temple searched for some implement with which to announce her arrival—a car horn, perhaps, rudely tapping out "Happy Days Are Here Again"? A single stick, scratching on the untouched-by-human-hands-except-to-buff-it wood? The sound of one foot kicking . . . ?—the gate split into two sections and silently swung inward.

Temple searched for the Cyclopean eye of a security camera, but found none.

A bell rang. A single bell. One of those tony Sonoran desert bells designed by a monkish architect building a modern City of Cíbola in the Land of the Peyote Sun, Temple just knew. One of those bells that just one of cost a fortune through the very best (the most quiet, discreet, verbose) catalogs: *Found at a Spanish Mission forgotten since Frey Junipero Serra first boogied down the Baha . . .*

Temple's travel-brochure meanderings never grew so thick as when she was feeling on foreign ground, so she cut the mental chatter and stepped onto the (get this!) clear glass paving stones set into pure-white cement.

The fountain she had heard suffered postnasal drip in a corner of the courtyard. One lugubrious drop of water after another fell from endless levels of copper-leaf ladders to vanish among the wan blades of bloodless plants massed at the fountain's bottom.

The single ponderous bell, now curiously mute, still trembled from its recent attempt at sound.

Beyond the fountain and the white stone garden and the copper-

and-verdigris-colored leaves hung a curtain of glass beads, winking back the white, with no visible split in its surface.

Temple waited, knowing by now that some effect was forthcoming, that petal by bloodless petal the portal would part, and Mynah would choose to show herself lurking at its pale heart.

But the wall did not part, because it was not glass. It was running water. The waterfall sheet broke into individual drops as fat as glass beads, then thinned to harpstrings and finally dispersed to a mist that vanished except for an occasional drip in counterpoint to the fountain's steady tympanum beat.

Mynah stood beyond the absent barrier, dressed in a white gi. Her belt was black, and its dramatic charcoal slash matched her aggressive eyebrows.

"Come through," she suggested, "unless an occasional drop of rain frightens you."

Water, Temple recalled, could make vivid colors run. She clicked like a beetle over the glass flagstones dewed with moisture.

Once inside the room sound fell in tinkling sheets of digitally recorded New Age music, as random as rain and not nearly as refreshing. Mynah had not moved, but the window of water was in smooth place again, falling so perfectly it seemed plate glass, albeit a little wavy.

"Reminds me of the séance room," Temple commented.

"Séance room? In that . . . joke of a haunted house? Please, you're talking about a cartoon."

"A cartoon didn't kill Edwina Mayfair."

"Edwina Mayfair. Such an obvious pseudonym."

"Obvious?"

Mynah cocked her wiry eyebrows and sank onto an arrangement of cotton-covered pillows. " 'Edwina.' A feminized version of a man's name. Check the man's birth certificate and you'll probably find 'Edwin' is his middle name, or his father's name. And 'Mayfair.' A pun on 'Playfair,' do you think? No doubt he felt that true psychics didn't 'play fair' because they achieved their successes by intangible means. A master of the Tangible, our Gandolph the Great."

"Our?"

"I speak of the situation. He perished at our séance, cheesy and insincere as it was; therefore his death is 'ours.' "

"You take credit?"

"Credit . . . no! My dear Miss Barr, you have been severely affected by this . . . melodrama, haven't you?" Blue eyes piercing through the rain of everyday appearances. "Don't! It was foreordained. Who was there, when or where it was held, is immaterial. He was doomed to die. Somewhere. With somebody."

"By murderous means?"

"Murderous means? Well, we don't know that, do we? I think . . . heart trouble is a suitably sentimental diagnosis for such occasions, don't you? Poor Edwina. Poor Gareth, the kitchen boy. Such Arthurian names, so Pre-Raphaelite! So Victorian! We are modern, to our cores!" She pounded her fists, knuckles white as baroque pearls, upon the harp-bones of her chest. A gi can gap open or shut, depending on its wearer's bent. Again Mynah eyed Temple as if her vision were a threat, or an instrument. "Is that why you are troubled, why you seek psychic healing? You obsess about death?"

It was as good an excuse as any. Temple looked down, trying to get up the nerve to feign nerves. Her very indecision did the trick.

"You poor girl!" Mynah's clasped fist uncurled, stretched out to Temple. "I read your confusion. You are torn between two—convictions."

"Yes!" Temple said, relief at Mynah's benign conclusion sounding overemphatic.

"What are they? You must tell me."

When Temple hesitated, Mynah pulled a small unbleached-muslin bag from one turned-back cuff. Six or seven tiny colored stones poured into her palm.

"Pick one. Only one. Quick! You must choose with your reflexes, like a master of martial arts, not with your head."

Temple never chose unthinkingly; that was all the fun. Not amethyst or garnet or pearl, they meant something common, she remembered. Something uncommon, to confuse the seeress in her lair. Temple snatched at a facet of light bright as a lizard's eye.

"Peridot," Mynah pronounced. "How unusual." The cold blue

eyes flicked to Temple's hair. "Perhaps not for one of your coloring and temperament.

"You are . . . impulsive." *Ridiculous*, Temple answered internally. "High-tempered." *Stable*. "With buried psychic talents." *Rubbish*. Mynah leaned nearer, across the gulf of white marble floor tiles. "Passionate." *Weeeeell, about the truth.* "Imaginative, to a fault." *Tell that to the nightly news.* "You worry too much," she added soothingly. *Bingo! Like, what am I doing visiting a manipulative, lying snake like this?* "Nothing is wrong, my poor, impulsive, imaginative, frightened girl!"

She took Temple's hand and began to uncurl her fingers from around the semiprecious peridot. Temple considered resisting, but didn't want to blow her worried-girl cover.

"See how you secretly desire to reveal all the secrets at your core. . . ."

Temple gazed into her bared palm, seeing only the peridot—a truly insignificant chip of peridot, really, hardly big enough for one tiny ear stud. Ralph Fontana would spit upon this piece of measly peridot! It wasn't big enough to reveal the hidden heart of a Thumbellina! Hardly worthwhile for an ant to tote it back to the anthill. . . .

"You are making mountains out of anthills," Mynah went on, "murder out of mere natural causes. Trust me. I read more than crystals and sand paintings, you know."

Temple didn't even know about the crystals and sand paintings; why didn't she get to see the main event? What did she have to do, cross Mynah's palms with peridot? She did so, turning her hand edgeways to let the nile-green chip drop into her hostess's hand.

"Generous." Mynah's smile indicated that she was back to enumerating a litany of Temple's virtues and vices.

"Does your husband practice any psychic powers?" Temple asked.

"My husband?" Mynah's big blue eyes blinked vacantly. It was as if her attention had been rudely shifted to the inhabitant of another planet. "Why would you even mention him, when you are seeing me?"

"Well, you are married—"

"And how does that concern you?"

"Not at all. I just thought he might be . . . around." Temple glanced nervously toward the hovering plant forms.

"William is a dabbler," Mynah said shortly. "He is quite separate from my work."

"Where might I find him?" Temple persisted.

"At his day job." Mynah's white-frosted lip curled.

"At—?"

She tossed her head as if being forced to reveal the mundane facts were physically restraining. "An . . . office building. I don't keep track of such places, such pursuits. You'll have to ask someone else who does."

Temple nodded, slowly. A wife who couldn't be bothered to remember where her husband works? Granted, modern married couples often went their own ways, but they usually at least knew the path to their spouse's workplace. Yet Temple sensed that Mynah wasn't keeping something from her; she simply hadn't bothered to know these things.

"Why do you want to see William?" the woman in white demanded, a tiny pout puckering the lipstick rime at the corners of her mouth.

"I'm new to all this. I'm trying to get a rounded viewpoint."

"No!"

Temple politely raised her eyebrows. Mynah's dark brows were drawing together as if a stitch had been taken between them.

"You are . . . generous, as the peridot says, but also have another side of the peridot in your character, a flawed side."

Temple waited. A recitation of her supposed virtues had gotten boring; perhaps the flaws would be more insightful.

"You are envious. Unmarried, you seek after my husband." Temple would have protested this extreme conclusion, but Mynah was in full pronouncement. "But you are also envious of the powers of others, such as myself. Oh, you pretend to be seeking enlightenment, but your purpose is very different. Keep the small cyst of green poison—" She dropped the grain back into Temple's palm before she could draw back, and rolled her fingers shut on the sharp stone.

"I see everything, you know. You came here hoping to learn my powers, to find powers of your own, and you have learned only of your own limitations."

"What do you mean?" Temple felt honestly indignant. Information, yes; but a "powers" thief she was not.

Mynah stood. "Don't you know I can read every ignoble thought? You seek my secret."

"Secret? I haven't even asked to see the sand paintings."

Mynah tossed her Loving Care #88 sterling silver mane over her shoulders. "You envy my power over men. You, who are ignored by men. Who live alone, like an old maid with her cat—"

"What about my cat?" Had Midnight Louie been in the neighborhood? What had he done now?

"See how defensive, how pathetic you are? And you admit you have a cat. This meeting, an excuse! Deny it if you can."

Temple couldn't.

"You care for nothing but the adoration you see me turning away. You are consumed by the flames of jealousy. You covet paranormal powers only for base and futile reasons. Go, college girl! Dream your feeble dreams. Show your true colors. The simple purity of true ability will never be yours."

That "college girl" did it! Did this dame think she was dealing with some raw amateur? Temple (impulsively) considered unleashing (with high temper) a few apt observations of her own, which were far more on target than this mumbo-jumbo attack.

But that would be blowing her cover, wouldn't it? Temple reflected (generously). Her buried psychic powers revealed that it was better to let a suspect stew in misconceptions than to set her straight (passionately) and ruin the interview.

No, she was better off continuing with her psychic interrogations, then reporting the results to Max, or Matt, whichever one of her psychological or magical experts was better suited to restore her battered self-esteem, especially when she repeated the charge about having nothing better to share her life with than Midnight Louie! Come to think of it, Louie would be most solicitous himself at news of this rank slander.

Envious, hah!

Temple left without waiting for the water-curtain to be drawn.

She emerged, somewhat wet, into the tranquil courtyard and a dusky, cool evening not suited to running through walls of water. Walking on water, maybe, with her hidden powers, but not running through . . .

Shivering, Temple scooted into the Storm, pushing the heat level to the max. Onward, she told the car as the engine stuttered in sympathetic cold. She dropped the peridot into her glove compartment.

But before she showed the house of Mynah Sigmund the smoke from her tailpipe, she drove around it once more for good measure. That was when she spotted the glossy black rear fender of a Viper protruding from a plumy stand of pampas grass.

Either a Fontana brother was calling on Mynah while her husband was off working who-knows-where, or somebody else who drove a flashy car was. Darn, too bad Temple was such a wimp of a vamp; otherwise she could sweet-talk Watts and Sacker into running a license check for her.

Temple sat up in her seat. She didn't want to drip on the vinyl. Maybe the detectives wouldn't check on a dog license for her, but what had Max been doing all day? Sitting safe at home, cracking into computers. He was a quick learner; maybe he could track down the right Viper, in a manner of speaking.

Temple kicked her feet out of soggy (sigh) shoes (cursed be Mynah and all her waterworks!), then gunned it hose-footed to her next appointment. Maybe Mynah had murdered Gandolph the Great for providing too much competition with the hat. A long black veil will outdraw bridal illusion every time.

From the sublimely ridiculous to the ridiculously substandard: all in a day's work for the unsanctioned investigator. Temple's next appointment was at the Hi-Lo-Motel.

"Sorry," she told the Storm, as she wriggled out and left it in its humble parking space. "We sleuth types must go where even Vipers dare not leave tread marks."

Las Vegas had always offered its visitors a full buffet of entertainment options, from bargain basement to penthouse pizzazz.

And that was exactly how to tell low-rent district from high-rent district: height. The cheapest motels were one-story high; less cheap ones were two or three stories; moderate places hit ten or twelve stories, and the really, really ritzy outfits lit up the sky as well as their patrons' credit-card balances.

Temple personally had always resented that low was a sign of lesser luxe in this town.

D'Arlene Hendrix occupied room 223, which meant a climb with her luggage, but less access from street-level intruders. The place was well lit and clean, but frills had been given the cold shoulder. Temple mounted the concrete exterior stairs to the second floor, then cruised the gallery until she reached the right room.

A knock brought the TV-buzz within to a sudden halt. D'Arlene Hendrix opened the door on its security chain to check Temple out, then closed the door to release the chain and admit her.

She wore blue jeans, scuffed tennis shoes and a T-shirt that advertised a Lexington, Kentucky, landscaper. Her bifocal spectacles on their pearl safety chain bounced against a lofty elm tree on the T-shirt.

"Nice of you to see me," Temple began.

"I never did understand why you were present at the séance." She gestured to the plainly upholstered desk chair opposite the bed, then sat on the paisley spread.

"As a sightseer. I'm working for the Crystal Phoenix hotel and casino. We plan a similar attraction, and I was there to see what was what."

"You certainly didn't do that." D'Arlene shot the silent television screen dead with one punch of a remote-control button.

Remote control, Temple thought. The Hi-Lo-Motel wasn't totally no-frill.

"Have you been to Las Vegas before?" she asked.

D'Arlene's grizzled permanent remained unruffled as her head shook a firm "no."

"If I'd have realized what a charade this so-called séance was, I'd have never come."

"What do you mean 'charade'?"

"I guess I was lured by the promise of Oscar Grant's participation."

"Really?" Temple didn't peg D'Arlene Hendrix as the kind of woman who would find Oscar Grant promising in any respect.

D'Arlene laughed ruefully. "I hear you, Miss Barr, even if I haven't the slightest idea who you are. You don't see me as an Oscar Grant groupie. I'm not, but I do recognize the large viewership of his program, and I always hope that something I do will raise the respect level authentic psychics need if we're to help with this horrendous crime problem, especially against children."

"So you weren't interested in Houdini at all; only in drawing attention to your work?"

"Houdini, it strikes me, was well able to take care of himself. The cases I'm asked to assist with usually involve the most helpless persons in society: innocent children snatched from the streets or even their very own houses; grieving families who feel that the hunt-and-peck of police work is not enough."

"So they seek the hunt-and-peck of psychic work."

"I can't argue with you." D'Arlene Hendrix picked a cellophane bag of dried apricots from the plain-Jane bedside table and offered some to Temple. "My . . . intuitions hit like bolt lightning. Here. There. Close to the ground. Up in the air." She chewed meditatively on an apricot skin. "I've learned to accept the ambiguous nature of my gift. The police want predictability. Programming. Some, though, do recognize my flashes of insight, if they don't respect them."

"You sound like a latter-day Joan of Arc."

She shook her head and rolled up the apricot bag. "I'm no crusader, but my families are."

"Your families?"

"A perquisite of my often unsung work. My clients become foster families. Usually they bring me in at their own expense, much against local law enforcement preferences. I'm always unwanted. And when I do find the missing one's body, my 'success' is proof of everlasting sorrow to those who begged to have me on the case. By then I often feel it as much as they."

Temple nodded slowly. "How does your . . . intuition work?"

"Like a car that was the biggest lemon you ever owned."

Temple smiled.

"It's true. All fits and starts. It's like I eavesdrop on one of those early telephone party lines. I'll just get snatches of this and that: a place or person I see; a voice I hear; a gut feeling when I look at a map, or a mother's face."

"Do you have any children of your own?"

D'Arlene's face saddened. "No. Couldn't. I sometimes think that's why I get intuitions about missing children."

"Do you ever find them alive?"

"Yes. Yes, I do. Twice in almost eighteen years. Then the press . . . oh, yeah, everyone's ready to admit the possibility of more than we know out there. After the fanfare fades, the cases come and go, the dead are buried and I'm forgotten. Until the next time."

"You sound like a burnt-out cop."

D'Arlene tilted her head toward Temple like a curious squirrel. "You must have a few 'instincts' of your own. Yes, I'm really kicking myself for coming along for this. First the police decide I'm the one person worth questioning in Gandolph's death—"

"Why?"

"Who knows? Maybe someone pointed them in my direction. But you'll notice they threw me back. Then I had booked myself into this modest motel because I'm so used to them. I never could see charging families for fancy accommodations when they're under the kind of stress that brings us together. But the show is paying my way, and I realize now I was dumb not to have taken advantage of an entertainment hotel like the Camelot. At least there I could wander the casino or the shopping arcades or the Strip. But, no, D'Arlene the Tightfisted has to stay on in Las Vegas at police say-so in the equivalent of a Nowhere, Kansas, motel. Want some wine?"

The final sentence's abrupt change of subject made Temple blink, but she nodded, more curious to see what D'Arlene Hendrix was swigging in her motel room than anything else.

Out from the bathroom sink came a screw-top brand that must match the room rate of a Hi-Lo-Motel. Certainly Temple had never laid eyes on Olde Grapevine wine before.

"Plastic glass offend you?" D'Arlene asked.

"Not at all. I do some of my best work on plastic . . . plastic keyboard, plastic credit cards—"

D'Arlene laughed and propped herself up against the standard-size bed's headboard. "You didn't come here to hear about the frustrations of my job."

"Actually, I did. The frustrations of every profession or job are pretty much the same: standoffish co-workers, associates who don't recognize your talent and bosses who give you no respect. What's interesting about your gripes is the offbeat job you do. What about that séance? I'm green, but I . . . sensed something going on."

"Don't get me wrong. I said it was a phony mess, but I never said something wasn't going on. There was a lot of pain in that room." She shook her head and sipped some red. "A lot."

"Psychic pain?"

"Psychic pain, mental pain, emotional pain; that's the only kind I pick up. At least I'm not tuning in every hammer-hit fingernail."

"And this was before Gandolph died?"

"Oh, my, yes." D'Arlene set her plastic glass on the nightstand and gazed up at the opposite wall as if screening a movie there. "Maybe that's why I'm so depressed. Maybe it's not just that poor man's death, and in such a silly getup too. That séance was a Palace of Pain. My skin . . . ached just from being there."

"And your feelings were genuine?"

"You can't fake thin skin, honey, even when it's psychic skin."

Olde Grapevine had really relaxed D'Arlene Hendrix. Even her tight permanent wave seemed to be coming unsprung. Temple felt like an uneasy neighbor at a coffee klatch where the hostess was suddenly spiking the Postum with Kahlúa.

"So where was all the pain coming from?"

"My 'impressions' don't wear name tags. I sensed a terrific anger. And will, incredible will. All these violent emotions snapped from person to person, like electricity. Didn't you feel it?"

"I felt more than I expected, that's for sure. And I saw—"

"The wildman in the chimney?"

"Sure, I saw that; I guess anyone who's read a book about Houdini has probably seen that photograph."

D'Arlene nodded and retrieved her plastic wine glass in a limp-fingered hand.

"So you don't believe that was Houdini either?" Temple pressed.

"Houdini wouldn't come back bare like that. Any spirits I've ever heard of that have a ghost of a chance of being genuine are always quite decently clothed. Unlike my poor victims."

Temple blanched at the reference, but blundered on.

"I didn't know about that then, ghosts preferring to appear fully dressed. But I did see another . . . person. A little boy and later an old man I thought was the same boy grown up and old."

A nod. "Terrible pain, terrible rage."

"You saw those figures too?"

This time her head shook. "No. The only thing I 'see' are death sites, and nobody had died in that bizarre room . . . yet. I felt the emotions, like other people hear music. A whole symphony was playing that night."

"Who played what instrument?"

D'Arlene nodded, prodded by Temple's analogy. "Each person had his or her own tone. The bassoon, that was hard to place; I never quite did. But the cello was Gandolph, deeply dark music, quite sad."

"Who else?"

"There was a whistle. A melancholy low whistle. The other man, I think, besides Oscar Grant, an obvious, and the professor."

"William Kohler."

"The women were a pilgrim's chorus, all wanting something lost quite desperately."

"Who, though, broadcast the kind of pain you were talking about?"

D'Arlene's eyes were quite unfocused now. Her whole face had deadened. Temple realized she was watching someone strip-mine her psychic senses, peel back the outer layers one by one until she dug deeper and deeper into her own protective emotional epidermis.

"You did, for one."

"Me? I'm not in pain."

D'Arlene's slack lips tried to smile. Her eyes were slits as she peered through the veil of her lashes.

"Painful confusion at least. I can still hear that agitated flute trying to calm its pulse."

"I was working, that's all, and thinking about reality and illusion."

"Illusion. Much illusion that night. Gandolph's. Yours, I think . . . you are working an illusion now, you are no more simply what you say or seem, as Gandolph was not that night. And That Creature. Oh, my God. Born to give the occult a bad name, as if it weren't maligned enough without posing witches on the wing. And around you all, this slipstream of Will. Pure Will. And Anger, white-hot anger. Oscar Grant was the bassoon perhaps, though he sounded more like a tenor sax. Slippery. Tenor sex. *She* didn't sing, that one."

"Who?"

"Your link with the Technicolor aura. Electricity. Strange reverberations. And quite wonderfully serene, like a . . . harp."

"I'm a hysterical flute and Electra's this elegant harp?"

D'Arlene's lazy eyes flicked slightly open. "It was your analogy to begin with, Miss Barr. And quite productive too. I've never had such clear psychic recall. Your gift is not always to see, but to lead others to see."

"I see."

D'Arlene laughed. "You think that is a little gift, and you loathe the little, the little in yourself, the little in other people, which is a much more serious flaw. Little people. But who is the bassoon? Such power, such waste. Such rage, such fear. And the mute rabbit, who only screams in desperation, what instrument does she play? A violin scraping out of tune. And then one last, hysterical high note, quite impressive, quite final."

The woman shook her head, still not causing a flutter among her greige curls. She sat up, putting her feet on the floor as if restoring herself to solid earth.

"I feel better. I hadn't wanted to see that séance again, but I could bear to hear it. I think you got what you wanted, Miss Barr. I think you are a satisfied client, even if you won't know it until later."

"This . . . has been fascinating."

D'Arlene Hendrix didn't look at her. She sat hunched over, regarding the wall-to-wall carpet so unworthy of viewing. "It would have been, if it were faked. But it wasn't. Therefore, it's not fascinating, but sad, and you'll find that out later too."

Temple stood, set her empty glass atop the TV and went to the door. D'Arlene seemed too leaden to move, perhaps ever again.

"Oh," she said, like a dreamer remembering one last detail. "I sensed many unseen lives, some not human, but that kind of static is often present in the face of true phenomena. And one thing you must bear in mind, Miss Barr, above all others. I can swear to the veracity of the emotions I channeled, but not to their origin or any action they might have generated. It's the same as on my cases.

"I never quite know whether I'm picking my impressions up from the victim . . . or the killer."

Chapter 30

Two, Three . . .
Open the Door

By the next day, Temple was beginning to feel like Miss Scarlet from the game of Clue. With each change of locale, she met another of the suspect characters in the larger game of Murder. Maybe.

She found Professor Mangel under a spreading cottonwood tree on the University of Nevada at Las Vegas campus, where he was addressing two dozen blue-jeaned and jacketed undergraduates Socrates-style: outdoors.

Temple turned up the collar on her linen blazer and stuffed her hands into pockets meant to be stitched shut (for a better line) until the day they departed for the Goodwill with the rest of the jacket. Not that the daytime temperatures were that cold yet, but the idea was in the air.

So were loftier ideas.

"Psychic, medium, fortune-teller, tea-leaf reader," Mangel was enumerating with dramatic precision. "Actor, arranger, artist. None of these names directly figures in the deck." He held up a fanned fistful of oversize cards whose beautifully illustrated backs made Temple edge nearer, all the better to see them.

"But the one card that covers them all is . . . can anyone guess?"

Students buzzed among themselves, but none ventured a suggestion.

Mangel snapped over one card to reveal its face: not some numerical arrangement of diamonds, clubs, hearts or spades, but another elaborate illustration: a robed man of imposing mien.

"The Emperor!" a man's voice sang out.

Mangel smiled and shook his head.

"The Devil!" a tremulous female voice called.

Smiling, Professor Mangel shook his shiny bald head. "Seeing visions is not evil, only exceptional, though all too often in this world the exceptional is mistaken for the evil. Any other guesses?"

His challenge drew a flurry of answers.

"The High Priest" was first.

"No," he chided. "I said this figure encompasses that of the priest."

"Strength," came the next stab in the dark.

Mangel laughed, enjoying himself, enjoying their attempts at an answer.

"The Hanged Man," a long-haired biker-dude at the back yelled out.

"Spoken like a true pessimist," Mangel slung back. "But is the Hanged Man hanging, or are we just looking at him upside down?" Another cryptic smile.

Temple recognized a rare soul: one who loved to teach. Had she been a class member, she would have contributed. In fact, she couldn't help herself; she knew a few major arcana cards of the tarot. "The Fool!"

"Not bad." Mangel pointed to her, pale eyes sparkling behind the crude glitter of impossibly thick lenses. "And a more versatile and potent card than it is usually accounted. For what is the Fool but youthful possibility? And that is always both promising . . . and dangerous, as you young people know very well. Well—?"

"Death," suggested a dark male voice that was impossible to trace to its owner.

Temple shivered as she scanned the group, wondering, but the professor laughed like a college-production Falstaff. "Gloomy youth, who can afford to dwell on decay, since it is so far off. So you *think*. No. Valiantly suggested, but if I let you continue, you'd name the entire arcana. No." He moved his thumb aside, letting them see the name of the card.

"The Magician," came a thin chorus, with a mutual groan in their voices.

"The Magician," Mangel repeated, well satisfied. He even beamed at the immobile face of the figure fronting the card. "And what is a magician? Don't worry! I won't tax your ingenuity any longer this morning. I will do my job and tell you what you need to know. In fact, I will be an esteemed educator and let someone *else* tell you what you need to know. Edmund Wilson. You have heard that name, children?"

The silence said otherwise.

Mangel gave one sad "tsk." "An American, after all, ladies and gentlemen. An American pundit, novelist, commentator, only dead a couple of decades . . . no bells to be rung, eh? Only sad songs to be sung. Ah, well. Here is what this nobody Wilson said about the function of this very figure, the Magician: 'He has characteristics in common with those of the criminal, of the actor and of the priest' "—Mangel paused, lifting his eyebrows over the thick black line of his glasses frames to ensure that his audience was paying attention—" 'and he enjoys special advantages impossible for these professions. Unlike the criminal, he has nothing to fear from the police; unlike the actor, he can always have the stage to himself; unlike the priest, he need not trouble about questions of faith. . . .' "

"Are there," a girl in the front row asked, "no women magicians?"

"Few." With a dramatic clap of his hands, Professor Mangel compressed the fanned Tarot cards into one solid deck. The Magician under discussion vanished into the mass. "However, in the practice of the psychic arts the female of the species has always had an edge. A special ear, as it were, for the less seen, the less heard, the less regarded. The less-often believed. Houdini may be regarded as the epitome of the male magician, reenacting symbolic escapes from castration and death. We must also remember that the greatest influence in his life—and death—was his mama. He was tied to her . . . heartstrings, so that he did not survive her by very long. Perhaps his lifelong quest of the ultramasculine was a flight from the feminine within himself. He was not so much a magician as an escape artist, and his legend still strives to escape the one trick that does in us all. So we have inducted into the annual Halloween Academy of Attractions the usual Recall of Houdini Séance, even here in Las Vegas, where there are many more pertinent ghosts to recall, such as—?"

Suggestions erupted now like the Mirage's volcano. "Elvis!" "Marilyn Monroe!" "Frank Sinatra!" "Hey, he's not dead!" "Yet—" "Bugsy Siegel!" "Jersey Joe Jackson!" someone contributed. Not Temple. Who had called out *his* name? she wondered. Jersey Joe Jackson was ancient history in this town.

"On a note of dead celebrity, we will end this inquiry into the mantic arts," the professor said, checking his watch. "Thank you for coming."

Temple studied the dispersing undergraduates while waiting for Mangel to disengage from a couple who had run up to speak to him afterward. She was not that long removed from their ranks, but they seemed so young as they bustled by, their small talk studded with expressions only hip among the teenage set.

"Nice to meet you close up, Miss Barr." Professor Mangel was standing beside her, smiling at her eye to eye, glasses frame to glasses frame. "Your interjection of the Fool enlivened the forlorn slate of guesses just when I desperately needed some sign of invention. Pity you were not one of my students."

"I was for a few minutes. And I enjoyed it."

He grinned. "At least my subject matter can compete with *Geraldo* and *Close Encounters* and *Sightings*. Television shows! Who would have thought transistors would replace the groves of Academe?" He gestured to the low-profile panorama of the desert campus. "Shall we walk while we talk?"

They did, while Temple tried to calculate the last time she had heard the verb "shall." Despite his academic speech, Mangel was younger than his bald head implied; his walk, his talk, his mental agility added up to a dynamic masculine energy that made being short, shortsighted and prematurely bald immaterial. Temple would bet that many a female freshman had developed a crush on him.

He settled his papers and Tarot cards into a soft black leather case as they walked. "I like to do these guest seminars on local campuses when I travel, though my study of paranormal matters is considered 'popular' education. So you're interested in information on mediums and the immaterial world for a hotel theme park?"

" 'Theme park' is a pretty grand term for what I have in mind. It would be part of a Jersey Joe Jackson attraction at the Crystal Phoenix."

"The Crystal Phoenix I've heard of. Jersey Joe Jackson, no. I take it back: let's sit and chat. I may want to take notes."

"Me too." She pulled a stenographer's notebook from her tote bag as they settled onto a low stone bench in an area devoted to landscaping. "That's a beautiful tarot deck you had."

"Isn't it, though?" Mangel pulled a black velvet pouch from his case, then slipped out the cards. "The Tarot of the Cat People by Karen Kuykendall."

"That's what the design on the back was! Cats—but with blue- and green-striped bodies! Rather Cheshire Cat–looking. Can I see the Magician close up? And how did you draw it blind?"

"Magician's trick, of course. You've got to perform to keep the modern student's attention. Psychology professors are a lot less intriguing than web browsers and computer games these days."

He handed her the correct card, face up. The Magician was an exotic figure, his full robe patterned with a rainbow of bubbles, his hair an enormous black Egyptian wig surmounted by the jeweled figure of a spotted cat. Levitated before him were a pentagram, a chalice and a sword.

Temple studied the card. "Something about the figure reminds me of Beardsley's drawing of Salome with the head of Saint John the Baptist."

"Grisly analogy," he said, taking the card back again to view it. "But I see what you mean. Perhaps it's the central figure's intense concentration."

"You mean that magicians and murderers must both be obsessed?"

Mangel's watery hazel eyes, so light they were almost alley-cat-yellow, sharpened with interest. "Another intriguing analogy, but apt. No one is more obsessive than a magician."

Temple pointed to the floating objects in the picture. "I see the chalice of the priest, and I suppose the sword could represent the criminal, but the pentagram is a poor symbol for an actor."

"I don't know; it takes magic to command a stage. David Copperfield considers the magician first and foremost a performer, and that conviction has made him enormously rich."

"What about mediums and psychics? Are they magicians? Criminals? Priests and priestesses?"

"Assuredly, Temple, if I may call you that?"

"Assuredly, if you'll tell me if professors have first names."

His laughter was abrupt and brief. "Yes, I am always 'the' professor, seldom 'Jefferson.' "

"And never 'Jeff'?"

"Never! It doesn't go with my PhD."

"So, Jeff, what about psychics and mediums, fortune-tellers and tea-leaf readers? Are they for real, or frauds?"

He carefully tucked the tarot deck into its pouch, even more carefully selected his next words. "I sense that you are seeking more than some lurid details for a hotel attraction. So I'll tell you what I wouldn't tell pompous academics: yes, most of these people are frauds, many are self-delusional frauds and a few, a precious few are . . . ambiguous at best."

"I thought you were a gung-ho advocate—"

"That's the popular assumption. No, I'm a gung-ho hunter of the rare real thing."

"As the late Gandolph was a gung-ho hunter of the unreal thing?"

"Poor man. Do you realize that he became what he abhorred to track it down? The Edwina Mayfair persona was decently well known, even respected, in psychic circles. Everyone wondered, when Gandolph came out with one of his sudden exposés of a particular practitioner, how he had gathered the goods. Nobody dreamed he had done his groundwork undercover, and under such potentially comic cover too." Jeff's face sobered. "Of course it wasn't comic when he died in character."

"No one suspected Edwina Mayfair of being anything other than she was? Isn't that a little hard to believe?"

"The psychic field is filled with extreme personalities who pursue extreme positions. There were never any rumors that Edwina was anything other than she seemed to be."

"Given the theatricality many mediums seem to cultivate, how can anyone seriously believe in any of them, or their effects?"

"You mean, how can I? Simple." He rummaged in his case and drew out a vending-machine packet of peanut-butter-filled cheese-flavored crackers. After he pulled the red opening strip of the cellophane package, he offered Temple one of the crackers as nonchalantly as if he were extending a cigarette. She would have preferred a cigarette to the salt, flavoring and dye-laden cracker before her, and shook her head.

"You see," he went on, happily munching and strewing orange cracker crumbs on his jeans, "I'm not that different from Houdini." He caught her expression, which had gone from being appalled by his snack to being appalled by his statement. "Oh, I'm not confessing to being an unreformed mama's boy or even a magician. And you've got to remember that Houdini spent the most impressionable half of his life in the nineteenth century, when mother-worship was sentimentalized. It's just that when it comes to the notion of contacting the dead, I'm a hopeless optimist while remaining about as skeptical as a rattlesnake."

"Houdini was as skeptical as a rattlesnake? Then why did he even entertain a hope of anyone returning from the dead?"

"That old obsessive personality. Mama. He desperately wanted to see Mama again. She had died while he was out of the country, and at a time in the family drama when he was about to disown his brother Leopold for marrying his brother Nathan's ex-wife. See, they had dysfunctional families even then, but they labeled it "sin" instead of "sickness." If Houdini's mother had asked him to accept the new couple to avoid a family chasm, he would have. He had hoped to be there when she died, and had hoped that her last word to him would have been 'Forgive.' "

"Did he forgive Leopold?"

"No. Houdini had been the family patriarch since his father's death when he was seventeen. His mother was the only person who could persuade him to accept what he perceived as a family betrayal. But she died without speaking to him, so he banned his brother's body from the family plot and even cut his photo out of the family pictures."

"No!"

"Houdini was never one to do things by halves, and he had a disturbing history of turning on those nearest him, especially on those he had once idolized. Eventually, he became his only idol, the only one he strove to outdo, and he died trying to do just that, a competitive personality to the last. That's what gave him his almost legendary reputation. Many people of his time thought that Houdini had paranormal powers, you know. Even Sir Arthur Conan Doyle insisted—to Houdini himself—that he must unconsciously draw on dematerialization powers to accomplish some of his feats."

"I had read that. Still, it's hard to believe of the creator of Sherlock Holmes."

"Don't look so disappointed. Toward the end of his life, Conan Doyle became a thoroughgoing Spiritualist, and sincerely believed several things that people today consider crackpot." Jeff Mangel smiled and crunched the last cracker to crumbs. " 'Course, you've got to remember I believe in postdeath presences myself, or at least surviving energy."

Temple shook her head as if to clear it. Like all decent academics, as opposed to insufferably smug ones, Jeff Mangel relished contradictions. She could see the precocious twelve-year-old squinting through glasses almost as thick as today's at the lurid, tall-tale pages of *True* magazine, in which he kept his place with a report card bearing straight A's.

"Okay," she conceded, "but do you believe in *mediums*?"

"A more germane question. And more specific. You mean do I believe in *the* mediums at the séance?" He peered at her as intently as she imagined his preteen self perusing *True* magazine. "I get the distinct impression that your interest in my opinion has more to do with the recently dead Ms. Mayfair/Mr. Gandolph than the long-dead Mr. Houdini. Oh, well, in my profession I take what female attention I can muster. It's like this, if you want to boil down what I believe, it's a thick stew of murky probabilities: Agatha Welk, a likely Self-delusional; D'Arlene Hendrix, a real Probable. Oscar Grant, a possible ... Emmy winner for unconvincing reality-programming emcee." Temple couldn't help thinking that Grant's flashy looks influenced that summation. Mangel had another thing in common with Houdini, uncommonly short stature, though she'd never met a man less affected by it.

"What about Mynah Sigmund?"

Something flashed in the eyes miniaturized by the lenses that allowed them to see better, but to *be seen* less. "Did I forget her? How unforgivable. A definite Maybe."

"Really?"

"I understand your skepticism, especially being a female. Remember that in the paranormal world, normal is a disguise."

"As in Las Vegas, loud clothes are a better disguise than outright nudity."

Mangel nodded until he had to anchor the bridge of his glasses against his nose. "Exactly right, and well put!"

Temple could hardly credit the Mystifying Max.

"But, heck." Mangel grinned again. "I may be wrong about the White Widow. I would have rated Edwina Mayfair a very strong Possible. She/he was good." His firm hand held out a card between two fingers. "If you want me for an opening lecture when your supernatural attraction debuts, just give me a call. I love doing unacademic things publicly. It wouldn't hurt to have some mediums on hand, or even a good magician. Good luck with the ghosties and goblins."

She shook his hand and then he was up, striding across campus, innocent energy and insouciance and inquiring mind personified. Temple remembered Jeff Mangel's own advice about his field: the normal was suspect. So: was the peanutty professor act a diversion? A lot about Professor Mangel seemed a diversion, mostly for himself.

And how could any man have "overlooked" Mynah Sigmund? she wondered. Of course, Max had often pointed out that most women tend to deal with a vixen in the henhouse by blaming the roosters for their gullibility. And why did Mangel call her the White Widow? Did it refer to the fact that she was not very faithfully married?

Temple pulled out her trusty reporter's notebook and studied the next suspects—oops; candidates—on the list. The most "normal" medium, and therefore the most suspicious, according to Mangel, would be refreshing herself from a hard day at the psychic fair at her hotel: Agatha Welk was staying at the Debbie Reynolds.

Only Oscar Grant remained, and he had suggested six o'clock cocktails at the Mirage. Temple eyed the large, accusing face of her wristwatch. Would she have time to go home and change before meeting the suave Mr. Grant, or should she use any spare time to check in on Max back at the Welles house? Time, she decided, would tell.

Chapter 31

... And Ladies
of the Séance

Temple tap-danced into the Debbie Reynolds' Hotel and Hollywood Museum, ready to do a Fred Astaire glide right into the registration desk. The light and airy lobby sparkled under its trio of
chandeliers on high, as long and elegant as the pale-powdered and
bejeweled ladies' hairdos from the Marie Antoinette era.

The hotel's air of nostalgic, slightly used elegance would suit a
sensitive woman like Agatha Welk, Temple decided. Agatha struck
her as someone who would suffer from the Specter Mountain High
atmosphere most Strip hotel-casinos cultivated, where a rock-band-
intensity noise level and an amphetamine-overdose action level
were models to be envied.

Here the chink/clink of slot machines was discreet, and if the
Chairman of the Board eyed the action over the lobby balcony, Ol'
Blue Eyes was both blind and deaf, being a mannequin togged out
in a vintage Sinatra suit.

Agatha's room was on the fourth floor, and when Temple arrived, Agatha was in it, with a room-service tea table laid out on

white linen like *The Streets of Laredo*'s deceased cowboy.

"I travel with my own teas," she explained when Temple stopped dead to eye the elaborate array. "They rarely serve herbal brews anywhere, and of course, never loose-leaf."

Temple sat and shook out a white napkin as big as a chessboard. "This is so nice of you—"

"I always relax with tea after a day out of town, whether it's for a psychic fair, of which I do very few, or a . . . private consultation. Green or gray?"

"Gray will be fine," said Temple, whose legal addiction of choice was coffee.

Agatha Welk pushed back the trailing ruffles on her three-quarter-length sleeves and filled a stainless-steel tea ball with dried leaves that resembled tobacco. "Redheads always prefer gray to green tea. Perhaps they feel their coloring requires subduing at teatime."

"Not me. I've heard of Earl Gray tea, but I'm ignorant of any other kind."

"What a pity." Though not an Englishwoman, Miss Welk was the refined sort of old-school woman who would use the word "pity," and who, one felt, really ought to be one.

While her hostess did civilized things with the tea paraphernalia, Temple noticed a beige horn bangle pushed up above one elbow, from which trailed a green chiffon scarf. Though the fluttery accessory suited its wearer, Temple had never seen such a style. She checked out the hotel room (not a personal effect in sight, darn!) and her hostess for further eccentricities.

Agatha Welk was the quintessential old maid, a breed Temple, in her brash youthful confidence, had thought extinct. Her aunt Kit, for instance, was certainly an old maid by age and marital status (sixtyish and none, ever). She herself was perhaps a candidate-in-training for this ancient title, though she supposed no one could suggest that until she had reached forty. She had never seen marriage as a goal, but she had always regarded it as a likely eventuality; now she had begun to wonder. She was as curious about Miss Welk as a freshman might be about a senior at a brand-new college.

The woman's antique air did not seem feigned, but Professor Mangel had warned her about that. Agatha Welk reminded Temple of the first silent-film actresses, those tiny, big-eyed waifs who were always tucking their chins into their chests and dropping their eyelids in shy reaction. Lucky thing, too, they had such gestures; like Miss Welk, their chins were both short and receding, a fact that enhanced large wounded-doe eyes and an air of girlish reticence.

Although Temple had seen women whose dress and appearance perpetuated the styles of their youth, it was usually 1970's Flower Child, which even in extremis was a youthful model; Agatha Welk's image seemed mired in the 1930's. Even if she was a well-preserved seventy, the thirties wouldn't have quite been her heyday. Yet she wore the period's drooping crepes and chiffons, wan florals dragged down by limp ruffles; shapeless, flour-sack styles with nary a pad anywhere to keep the wearer from looking round-shouldered and flat-chested, beaten by life into a paper doll of her own image. Even spirits would seem too robust company for such a personality.

"Not my kind of china," Agatha Welk said dryly, handing Temple the thick restaurant-ware cup.

Temple saw the steam rising like a curtain, and set the cup on its heavy cream ceramic saucer. The tea had been brewed molasses-dark, and the cup was filled almost to the brim.

"If you like," the medium added, "I can read your leaves when we're done."

Oh, no! Temple thought. *I'll have to slog down all this strong tea to find my future!* Not that she believed in tea-leaf reading. Jeff Mangel had listed it last, as the least significant mantic art. And what would a cut-rate reading be worth anyway?

"I get my most amazing results through the leaves. Tea is ingestible, you see. It becomes part of us, it touches our innermost being."

Creepy, when you thought of it that way, like swallowing one of those high-tech medical cameras. Temple lifted her heavy cup and sipped, trying not to make a face when the bitter tea scalded her taste buds.

Agatha Welk laughed, a bell-like sound, some nineteenth-century novelist would have put it. "Really! Strong medicine is good for the soul, and strong tea is good for the psyche. Drink up;

I'm sure you've ingested far more bitter brews in the name of imported beer, my dear."

"True." Temple set her cup back down. "But I don't like dark beer." Max, of course, had. Did.

"It's an acquired taste."

"Have you acquired it?"

"Only on trips abroad."

Max, of course, had been abroad, and then some, from the evidence of his past.

Why was she thinking about Max! Temple admonished herself.

"Tell me about your ghost attraction," Agatha suggested, only a faint disapproval showing at linking the words "ghost" and "attraction."

"It's inspired by Jersey Joe Jackson. Have you ever heard of him?"

Agatha shook her head, highlights making her gray hair look blue. She sipped slightly but steadily from the rim of her clumsy cup.

"Local character," Temple explained. "Built up a pretty good fiefdom here back in the forties, then lost his grip. Died, oh, twenty-some years ago in a suite at the hotel I represent. The Crystal Phoenix."

"Oh, yes! That lovely fountain of neon I can see from my window each night. I took it for the late Duchess of Windsor's famous flamingo pin."

"There's no Iron Duchess hotel here, just the Crystal Phoenix."

"Actually," Agatha said with a slow, reminiscent smile that made her absence of a chin moot, "I first took the neon sign for some kind of tree. I suppose the tail feathers fanned like a tree, only . . . this was no full, apple-orchard tree, but a stubby, few-limbed specimen. To my imagination. Perhaps some of the lights were out that first night here."

"Actually," Temple answered, "few lights are allowed to dim in Las Vegas, and the Crystal Phoenix used to be called the Joshua Tree hotel. You ever seen a Joshua tree?"

"Not in Philadelphia."

"Well, it's a stubby, little-limbed desert plant that resembles a tree, sort of."

"Really?" Agatha Welk ducked her gray head to sip gray tea from a white cup.

"Anyway," Temple went on, unsettled as well as interrupted, "Jersey Joe apparently lost most of his wealth and died in his last home, a two-room suite at the Joshua Tree. Except he's rumored to have stashed lots of treasure all over old Las Vegas, and into the desert beyond."

"Local characters often are rumored to have done that. So you want to revive the Jersey Joe Jackson heyday in some sort of museum?"

"More of a live-action ride, a subterranean Jersey Joe Jackson mine ride, with different sights along the way. I thought a ghostly vignette of old Las Vegas, including Jersey Joe's forebears and contemporaries might be fun—and educational."

"Let us always be educational. Part of the new appeal to the family trade, isn't it?"

"I thought you lived in Philadelphia."

"Don't look so surprised. We read in Philadelphia too. But what gave you the ghost idea?"

"Supposedly old J.J.'s ghost haunts the Crystal Phoenix."

"Have you seen it?"

"Not I. Although my cat acts like he has, but he's a black cat and they have a spooky reputation to keep up."

"All cats act like they have a reputation to keep up. You should put your cat in the attraction."

"He'd love it; fancies himself some sort of freelance operator."

"As do all cats, again. So how can I help you?"

Temple sipped some tea, so eager to address her investigation that she took a big gulp of tea she barely tasted. "It's about the Halloween séance. How much of that was real, and how much staged?"

The woman's sweet, unassuming smile froze as a harder expression took over inch by descending inch, as if she were channeling Eric the Red or somebody.

"That was a dire occasion. I'd prefer not to talk about it. A spirit was quenched that night. Besides, the entire event was manipulated in the extreme. There is fakery, and there is bald fakery."

"But you were there—?"

She looked down at her jacket, then fingered one of many small, fabric-covered buttons marching down the flaccid placket. "I am . . . overoptimistic. I have a rather foolish ambition. I am convinced that I alone can draw Houdini's energy from the prison of the final trap he built for himself. If you only knew how tormented he was to be truly locked up! How his whole life was an escape from that eventuality. How cruel it is that his last wish to elude the immaterial gate between the living and dead and astound us all one last time has not yet been honored.

"Once or twice in his life, someone boxed up Houdini as a joke, in a place and at a time when he was not prepared to escape. He nearly went mad with frustration. I think of that man, that spirit, fluttering at the doors to life like a moth seeking light for seventy years. I was born the year Houdini died, so that period of imprisonment is *all* of my lifetime. I have had some . . . unsettling encounters with spirits in the past. I hoped I could be the path to Houdini's brief moment of freedom before sinking into the inevitable incarceration of death. I was proud, foolish and so misled."

"Then you don't accept the figure in the chimney as Houdini?"

"Houdini dropping down the chimney, like Santa Claus? Please, Miss Barr. You may be a mere commercial exploiter of the paranormal, but even you could hardly be taken in by that cheap projected image—"

"As a matter of fact, I wasn't," Temple said hastily. "I just wanted to know what you thought of it."

"I hardly saw it. I did make contact with . . . Another who wished to break free, whose will—or whose ego—was strong enough to almost accomplish that feat for a few moments."

"Was that the little boy who became an old man?"

Agatha Welk set her teacup down so swiftly it almost broke against the saucer. "You? You saw . . . something?"

"Didn't everybody?"

"No." She put her right hand to the center of her forehead, as if reversing or turning on some mental movie camera. "No. They all said they had seen nothing but that laughable Houdini, although not all agreed the Houdini sighting was laughable."

"When you say 'all,' who do you mean?"

"Oscar. D'Arlene. That Mynah woman. Jeff. I never had a chance to ask Edwina."

"But you didn't ask Electra, or myself?"

"You were amateurs, mere observers! You couldn't possibly have—" She stared at Temple, those limpid gray eyes widening until they seemed to match the two, dark, bitter wells of filled teacups hiding fortunes in their tepid depths. "But you say you did. You saw the boy? The old man?"

"I assumed that everybody did."

"What about this Electra?"

"I never asked her."

"Do so. At the first opportunity."

Nothing wavery about Agatha Welk now, Temple noticed as she mulled that snapped directive. She tapped her own recall in the ordinary way, by thinking back and visualizing.

"The Other Apparition. He appeared in different windows, so not everybody might have seen if the angle was wrong."

"Angles! Those are the concerns of magicians, not mediums. Viewing angles had nothing to do with it. You and I were opposite each other, don't you remember? I saw the boy in the window behind you."

"He was in the window behind *you*!"

"No doubt, to your view. And the old man—?"

"Was behind Gandolph."

Agatha nodded, picking up her cup again for a good, long bracing swallow.

"What about the man in midlife?" Temple asked.

Agatha regarded her with icy suspicion. "I never saw him."

"But I did. He was . . . over to the left, between the boy and the old man. But they never appeared together."

"I saw no adult male but the old man, and the ridiculous projection of Houdini bound for one of his escape challenges. You know how he arranged those?"

Temple shook her head.

"Well, he was first a master of self-promotion. Frankly, a better promoter than he was an accomplished stage magician, though no one could top him for 'escapeology.' He was desperate earlier in his career, I suppose. Fixated on escaping, but no one found the notion of a magician getting out of handcuffs compelling; obviously the cuffs were phonies, or a key was concealed on the magician. But Houdini was a former locksmith obsessed with breaking bonds by apparently mystical means. He needed an audience that would share and even applaud his obsession. So he went to policemen in the various cities in which he was booked. He challenged them to lock and bind him however they could, and he would escape. Then he proceeded to do it, so successfully that policemen felt this was a bad example. They strived to produce truly escape-proof chains, cuffs, crates, cells—every manner of confinement. Houdini once even had himself sewn into the washed-up partial carcass of a whale."

"Ooooh!" Temple wrinkled her nose and every other feature that could crinkle in disgust. "Dead meat."

"Exactly. Houdini almost became your 'dead meat' as well. Some scientists had preserved the carcass with chemicals: formaldehyde; the closed atmosphere inside was so toxic that he couldn't remain conscious long enough to escape."

"But he got out?"

"His associates realized something was wrong and pulled him out, much to Houdini's humiliation. Another of those cases where he bit off more than he could chew."

"Or would want to chew!" Temple sipped tea to remove the bad taste imagination had put in her mouth, glad she hadn't chosen *green* tea, rot-green tea. . . . "That stunt was gross."

"Grossly egocentric. That's why Houdini's death is so pitiful. Felled by a moment's inattention, then denying it by ignoring all danger signals and pain until it was too late and the infected appendix—a tiny entity scarce the size of his little finger—destroyed him slowly."

"He died on Halloween."

"But only after fighting death for several days. Such a personality, such an ego, would find extinction particularly galling. That's why, if any psychic shard of himself exists, in any form, anywhere, he would be the one to return. He even left a strongbox with coded ritual words that his wife would recognize; except that after his death they were revealed in various autobiographies, so they became worthless."

"How would you know any phenomenon was Houdini, then?"

"My instinct. I have raised remnants before."

Remnants. To Temple, that expression was redolent of animated strips of rotting whale flesh, pieces of dead bodies: Wanda the Whale-stripper singing "Don't Get Around Much Any More" while Houdini's marvelous talking appendix pops out from a split seam to huckster a new tell-all book: *How I Did In the Master.* Or maybe the revived remnant would come in purely auditory form, like a few last words from Thomas Edison, recorded in *The Twilight Zone* with Rod Serling singing backup.

"This is more gruesome than the actual séance," Temple noted.

"A proper séance shouldn't be gruesome; it should be effective. Honestly effective. But I still can't imagine why you would see what I saw, and no one else."

"Perhaps the others just didn't admit to it."

"Why would they deny it?"

"Whoever that was, he wasn't on the guest list. So the others are prepared to accept Houdini on the half shell."

"Houdini on the half shell—? Whatever does that mean?"

"Like Venus on the half shell, he sure wasn't wearing much."

"My dear, no one cares if a ghost is naked, although the vast majority of ghosts sighted are indeed clothed."

"Makes you wonder who the couturier in Beyond is."

"I don't wonder any such thing. Once you accept that the soul's energy can survive, you understand how that energy can preserve the image of the dead person as it was in life. Very few . . . decayed ghosts are reported also."

"Thank heaven this Houdini didn't decide to do his Jonah routine right this time and materialize *inside* the rotting blubber!"

"You do have a way of putting things in their most sensational form. No wonder you're a publicist."

"At least I'm not going around swearing that Houdini is back."

"Are any of the others?"

"Not . . . yet. But they're busy with the fair."

Agatha sat forward, extending a bony forearm to tip up Temple's teacup. "Are you done yet?"

Regrettably no. She chugalugged the last of the now-cold tea, then surrendered her cup.

"No. You must swirl the dregs three times, then upend the cup on your saucer and tap three times."

Temple followed these instructions while her tongue worked large leaf flakes from her teeth. This kind of tea-drinking was as messy as smoking. She refrained from tapping her heels together three times and hoping for Kansas.

"No one brews the proper large-leaf tea anymore," Agatha said. "The art of geomancy is a dying one. Such a reading has become a rarity."

Silently thanking her good luck, Temple hoped that the tea would not lead to the good fortune of an emergency-room stomach-pumping. In fact, here she was interviewing possible murderers . . . and she had just consumed a beverage so strong-tasting that it could mask Liquid Plumr. Did she feel a bit . . . light-headed? Mildly anxious? Somewhat sweaty? What had she done?

Miss Welk had pulled a jeweler's loupe from one of her jacket pockets and now bent over the cup. Temple wondered what jewels of misinformation the medium would find among the damp tea leaves.

"This is fascinating," the woman murmured. "Absolutely fascinating."

"What?"

"Apparently you are a very brash young lady. I see you menaced on all sides by danger. No wonder a spirit would appear to you. Someone needs to warn you!"

"Any particular kind of danger?"

"Well, I see several men, all of them capable of bringing you much misery and woe."

"No kidding."

"But you have a secret ally!"

"Really?"

"I don't pick up much about him: a short fellow with dark hair."

"Anybody we know?"

"One of the men at the séance, you mean? Well, Professor Mangel is short, and his hair *was* dark, when he had most of it, but no . . . I sense prior acquaintance. Still, at least you have a champion, and he was at the séance, yes! Though not in the usual sense."

"Could this be Houdini?"

"He fits the description, but we had agreed that the pitiful display put on can only be cardboard and trick lighting . . . no, this is someone you are not used to turning to for emotional support, but he is there, never fear."

Short. Dark. At the séance and not a medium or a medium-booster. *Oh, no! Crawford Buchanan. Say it ain't so, leaves!*

"Usually the hero is a tall, dark stranger," Temple pointed out.

"Sorry, no strangers in your fortune at the moment. And I may be old enough to be your grandmother, but I am not your mother. Still, I think you should reconsider dating the Hell's Angel."

"Hell's Angel?"

"You may be able to fool your nearest and dearest, but not the leaves," Agatha Welk chided. "I see a motorcycle."

Temple was flummoxed, until she remembered the recent loan of the Hesketh Vampire and its new, uneasy rider.

"Amazing!" She tried not to smile. "You're quite right; I do know someone who rides a 'cycle." She supposed that Matt on a motorcycle was a sort of "hell's angel," after all. Amazing how you could skew your life to fit a fortune-telling.

"Examine your so-called friends and their lifestyles well. Things are often not what they seem."

Indeed, Temple said silently. *And such a pity too. And they often are not exactly what the tea leaves say either.*

"I see another dark man, or perhaps the first one in another role. A romantic role." Agatha's voice lilted with satisfaction on the last two words, as if expecting Temple to rise up and sing with joy.

Instead, Temple felt wary. Bad enough that the gray tea wanted to cast Crawford Buchanan as an ally; now who did it want her to cozy up to?

Agatha's voice grew wavery with optimism. "I see a nightclub, a tête-a-tête, a man with something vital on his mind, and you the focus of it."

"What does he look like?"

"My dear, the leaves are not a scrying glass. I only pick up vibrations. You seem to know a good many dark-haired men."

"A few. No light-haired men in my future?"

"Ummm, possibly. I sense trouble with a tax return next year. You may be meeting a blond auditor."

"Oh, great!"

"Listen, these are merely indications. It could be I'm reading everything wrong today. I am . . . upset."

"Why is that?"

"Need you ask?" Agatha looked indignant. "The real and false manifestations at the séance. I hate to be manipulated like that, by the living or the dead. The passing of Edwina Mayfair. Most distressing to have some man die, and then to know he was a notorious debunker of psychic phenomena . . . well, it makes one wonder why he died just then and there."

"Because he knew some fakery was going on?"

Agatha's gray pupils widened until they floated like overpoached egg yolks in the watery whites of her eyes. "Because he may have *caused* some fakery to have something to debunk! These crusaders will stop at nothing, and their activities verge on persecuting some poor medium. We are not claiming our visions are exact or our predictions certain. But we do, many of us, receive honest signals, even if we may misread them. We only try to pass on the word, and for that we are often humiliated and hunted. That this man, this . . . failed magician should go to such lengths to try to trap us is most upsetting. I had heard of Edwina Mayfair for years! How could he continue such an unnatural masquerade? Honestly, if I had known of his presence and his purpose, I only wish Houdini *had* come back to confound him. Perhaps he did, and frightened the pathetic soul to death."

Temple forgot about her harem of dark-haired men. It seemed to her that blue-haired Miss Welk could possibly be even more lethal to anyone who naysayed her dangerous visions.

"That's all," Agatha said, handing Temple back the cup with the soggy dark leaf residue coating its bottom third.

This was the end of an audience, so Temple took up her cup, wrapped it in a napkin and stowed it in her tote bag.

Miss Welk raised wispy eyebrows but said nothing. Temple wondered if she had seen in the leaves that Temple would have it studied by an expert, wait to see if she developed any sudden stomach cramps and then wash it and return it—anonymously—to the hotel.

Probably not, she decided, turning over her shoulder to say farewell and surprising a look of concentrated venom on the old dear's face.

Chapter 32

On to the Oscar's!

Temple had found time to go home to change—and wasn't sure what to wear.

According to Agatha Welk with her phalanx of lurking short and medium-tall dark men, chain mail wouldn't be enough protection. On the other hand, romance as well as danger could strike with the suddenness of a shot in the dark. What did the daring young up-and-coming entrepreneur wear to a combination execution-escapade?

Temple seldom wore slacks because they made her look like a lost Girl Scout rather than like a Femme Fatale ready for love or death on the run. She decided, though, that a toreador appearance would allow for quick escapes if not escapades, so she slithered into a pair of shiny stirrup tights (size small) she had found on sale for $3.98, strappy black patent heels, a red knit cummerbund and a snappy red knit "Bolero" bolero with official-looking brass buttons.

The Mirage's moving sidewalk was teeming with tourists and she was soon skimming past the teeming fish tanks to one of the hotel's many eateries and drinkeries.

At the entrance to the Black Spot bar she hesitated, studying a dim landscape of tables populated with unfamiliar faces. It was like trying to tell one sergeant-major fish from another. Actually, now that she peered at the clientele, a lot of them did look a little fishy.

One, however, waved a fin . . . that is, a hand, and she sped to where it still waved, hoping she hadn't been taken for a cocktail waitress in this getup, which might be a bit much, but, hey, either love or murder was waiting in her tea leaves and now was no time to dress drably.

She came to such a screeching halt at Oscar Grant's table that when she slung her red patent-leather tote bag around to put it on the floor she nearly decked him as he rose to pull out a chair.

Temple scooted into the chair and slang the bag (was that the proper tense?) on the long-unoccupied chair at the table. Why was she always almost-late to these crucial love-and-death affairs? She smiled at Oscar Grant like a cruising lady shark.

"Sorry I'm late. I thought I'd never get away from Agatha Welk. She was reading my tea leaves."

His mustache curled with unspoken scorn for the person under discussion, a nice trick that only Geraldo Rivera had also mastered.

"Agatha!" He laughed. "Always lagging behind the times. Tea leaves are passé."

"I don't doubt it. Reading cigarette ashes would make so much more sense nowadays, except that smokers are a vanishing breed too. Oh, you smoke, I see." Temple followed the sinuous updraft of blue haze trailing from a brass tray. "My, that is a most revealing ash—"

Oscar Grant swiftly took care of revealing ashes by grinding the cigarette out in its own excrement, so to speak.

"I hope you won't believe anything Agatha tells you," he said. "She really is in another world."

"I thought that was the idea?"

"For Agatha, it's not simply a world Beyond. It's a world Beyond Belief."

"Aren't you the organizer, though? Why invite her, then?"

"She was available on short notice, and lives nearby. Now. Let's talk about the real world."

He smiled, slid the ashtray toward the unoccupied seat and fixed very dark, very liquid, very undecaffeinated eyes on her. "How did your medium hunt go?"

"Sighted psychics, sank same. All I learned was that everyone is different. Why do you include Professor Mangel, though?"

"His eternal, dry-as-mummy-dust academic papers on the subject lend a certain legitimacy in the eyes of the media. But I wouldn't listen to much he had to say on the subject, any subject, if I were you. He's much too involved to be objective."

"And you're not?"

"Of course I'm not. I'm a journalist. I believe that you were one too."

"Oh? How do you know that?"

Oscar smiled and took her hand, turning it over to study the palm, or maybe the absence of rings. "Not by reading palms or tea leaves, that's for sure. I asked your friend Electra when everyone was setting up the psychic fair last Thursday morning."

"About me? I'm impressed."

He shook his head. "Don't be. I'm afraid it's my job to know who's booking space at a *Dead Zones* taping."

"You taped the séance for your TV show?"

Oscar nodded, a sleek, smiling Cheshire cat with a mustache painted on his muzzle. A very smug mustache. Temple wondered if Max would grow a mustache next in the interests of disguise.

Oscar's forefinger traced her . . . lifeline . . . loveline? When she got home, she would have to get a book from the library to find out. Seduction tickled, which was probably the idea. His, not hers. But then again, if the tea leaves decreed . . . A shame she had neglected to estimate his height when he had stood up to greet her. Maybe he was the short dark man who would aid her out of the blue Beyond rather than the medium-tall dark man who would sweep her off her feet. Suspecting the future was worse than suspecting murder. At least you never expected to see murder suspects again.

"What else did you discover about our circle of psychics?" he was asking a little too casually.

Who wanted to interrogate whom here? "Mynah is . . . interesting; at least she has created a fascinating environment."

"Oh, you visited her at home! Good. Quite the place. I did a half-show feature on Mynah and her way-out wonderland last season. Yes, every detail is to Mynah's specification. A fascinating woman."

Hold my hand and praise a New Age bimbo; I think not! Especially when you're not admitting having been married to her. If he wasn't Mr. Right, then Oscar Grant was definitely a candidate for Mr. Very Wrong.

Temple extracted her hand from his custody by the simple stratagem of picking up the tabletop plastic easel containing a lush color advertisement for the Drink of the Day. "An Under the Volcano. Clever."

"That ersatz volcano outside is a terrific trademark," he agreed, seeming to survive the withdrawal of her dainty extremity. "Mediums could learn a lot from Las Vegas. You need the proper ambience before you can expect anything outstanding to happen. It's as true of séances as of gambling casinos."

"A novel attitude. And how do you grade the ambience of our séance?"

Oscar shifted unconsciously to work a pack of cigarettes from his side pocket. "Not as good as I had hoped when I set it up. The activity outside seemed to upset some of the more delicate psychics, like Agatha. She insisted Houdini was a shadow of himself, quite literally. But the old boy looks pretty impressive on tape."

"How did you tape the session? Only the cameraman/photographer from the *Scoop* was there—Oh!" She had caught his apologetic smirk as he lit the long, thin spike of cigarette with a long, thin gold lighter. "He was a double agent, filming for Crawford's *Hot Heads* segment, and yours."

"Very good."

Temple hated people who rewarded correct deductions with "good dog" type comments. Oscar must be a villain in disguise. He nodded, as if agreeing with her thoughts, when he was only confirming her guess. "*Hot Heads*—dreadful name—only needs a few sound bites. I can drop in some real segments. It'll help Wayne's career to get a credit for my show."

"But what's to show? I hear Crawford's vaunted 'scoop' the other night was fakey photographs on fog. And I agree with you about the name *Hot Heads*. I think they meant to imply hot headlines about 'hot' talking heads in the entertainment industry. Instead it sounds like it's about blow-dryers plugged in too long."

Grant's laugh was flatteringly hearty and went on a tad too long.

"What a sharp cookie you are, Temple. If you want to move to the ghost beat, just let me know. I bet you look cute as a cupcake on camera."

"Sharp as a gingersnap and jolly as a jellybean," she answered, smiling.

He took her hand again. "So what did you think of our psychics?"

"Professor Mangel seemed sincere, but he's hardly a psychic. I got the impression he's hoping to be there when one of them hits pay dirt."

"A hanger-on, but useful."

"And D'Arlene Hendrix is so normal she could run for mayor."

He shook his head.

"No?"

"No. That lady is a human bloodhound when it comes to finding murder victims. They may be half there, but she's never been wrong about where they were. Says she 'hears' them calling to her. They direct her. If so, she's in touch with the most terrifying of afterdeath phenomena: spirits who have made no peace with their disembodied state. What did she say about the séance?"

"She was . . . reticent. Said she saw something, but won't say what. Won't even indicate if it was tangible or, you know . . . doo-doo doodah." Temple hummed the ancient *Twilight Zone* theme music.

"That's why *Dead Zones* doesn't use any gimmicky theme music. Just a quick montage of past pieces and a quick cut to me as the reporter. I do come off pretty 'documentary,' don't I?"

"Oh, Geraldo couldn't do it better."

"Thanks." He looked down to flick a half-inch of ash into the banished tray. The coat sleeve on the smoking hand had pulled up, and Temple glimpsed a tattoo of . . . She peered. He noticed. He chose to mistake curiosity for personal interest.

"You like my bracelet?"

The bracelet, which Temple had *not* noticed, was a suitably mas-culine (whatever that was) gold-chain affair worth a cool couple grand from a discount jeweler, but it obscured the tattoo. Not enough, however, to have hidden a ragged, two-color homemade look that didn't go with anything else on Oscar Grant's body. Oh, if only Molina were on this case! Temple could have dangled that tattoo in front of her until she became so irritated she growled back an explanation. Temple's own scenario was not particularly ro-mantic: prison or gang days. She detected a lot of unsanded edges behind Oscar Grant's Gillette-smooth exterior.

"Very nice," she said finally, not sure whether she referred to the bracelet and was lying, or referred to the tattoo and was thinking how nice it was to have spotted it. Agatha Welk had mentioned nothing about a tattoo, not even on the "Hell's Angel" Temple was supposedly dating. The next idea (Matt Devine with a tattoo) was so ludicrous that she couldn't help smiling.

"What is it?" Oscar shook her hand playfully, thinking she was smiling with the pure joy of his company, or perhaps that of his fancy gold bracelet.

If only he knew! She could picture Matt with a huge red outline of a heart over his heart: instead of reading "mom" it said "Mother Superior." Her smile struggled to become a grin. Or . . . "Born to Raise Relief Funds." Or . . . better yet, "Born to Bless."

Oscar leaned forward to tease an answer out of her and his right cuff pulled up even higher. "Deathreats" read the letters upside down, which Temple had learned to do when serving as a high school intern on her local weekly shopper, which had still been set in hot lead then. An elderly printer had been kind enough to teach her the trick. Death threats, or Death rats? Either way, it was an ugly sentiment to engrave into your epidermis.

"Well? Are you going to tell me?" Grant was still smiling behind the Black Bart mustache.

"Oh, it's something one of the psychics said. Nonsense, no doubt."

He shook her hand again and smiled.

Temple shook back and smiled more. "It's silly . . . one claims that the Houdini we saw was a fake, but that there was another, real apparition—"

"A fake!" He dropped her hand like it was a dead cigarette. "That's nuts. I've got prime footage on that appearance. What loose cannon is making those kinds of charges? My show on this séance will make the November sweeps, you just watch. You do watch *Dead Zones?*"

"I will now," Temple confessed, shyly tucking her chin into her chest like a good silent-screen star.

Oscar bought the act the way she had almost bought Houdini. "And what 'real' apparition? These flakes, always embroidering on a good scheme. Hams on Wonder bread. They should keep their eyes and mouths on what they came to see, to evoke. Houdini in the flesh, or at least the phantasm. He looked real to you, didn't he?"

"He looked real odd. Did he truly ask to be put in all those irons?"

"Absolutely. He was the first Iron Man athlete. Loved to be locked up. Loved it almost as much as Mama. Kind of makes you wonder about his childhood, doesn't it?"

Temple nodded, all eyes and smiles. Thanks to her appreciative act, Grant's cynicism was finally shining through like a piece of unadulterated aluminum foil in a recycling bin. She knew he was too good to be true to Agatha's tea leaves. Now she decided to show him that she was being too good to be true too, by telling him what she really thought.

"Kind of makes you wonder," she said, "who doctored the photo and arranged for it to be projected onto the dry-ice mist in the chimney. If it wasn't a cover for Gandolph the Great's murder, what was it?"

Oscar, struck silent by contradiction, stared at Temple as if she had suddenly turned into a cobra. She would have thought he'd be used to the effect from associating with Mynah.

When he finally spoke, he was furious, and his attraction to her hand had turned into a clamp on the wrist. "It was a damn good show theme, that's what! And keep your mouth shut about any theories—"

He got no further.

A tall—well, mostly medium-tall—dark man had materialized at Temple's right.

"Watch yer langwidge around a lady," a Fontana brother intoned in singsong John Wayne–style.

"Yeah," said another medium-tall, dark man who had appeared on Temple's left. "Unhand that dame."

Oscar's grip relaxed, then his hand crept back, but not before the man behind him slammed a stiletto into the tabletop right between the webbing of skin separating his first and second fingers.

A truly classic cinematic moment, Temple thought. Count on the Fontana brothers to bring a sort of hokey brio to all their works.

"Hey, sorry, *hombre.* Just doing my nails and the razor slipped. But I didn't finish reading your wrist." Ralph (he had a matching minirazor swinging from his left earlobe) Fontana grabbed Grant's wrist and held it to the light: the light being the candle that had flamed behind a glass funnel on the cocktail table. Now the funnel was off and the candle dripped hot wax on the tender inside of Grant's wrist.

Poor Oscar writhed, but not before Ralph pronounced: "Deathreaters. That was the punk L.A. outfit a dozen years ago. All needles and no nuts. S'cuse," he tossed to Temple before slamming Oscar's wrist, now bare of its gold chain, back to the table.

"Nice," the Fontana at Temple's left shoulder told the glowering man, "that you've started leaving such classy tips for the help around here. These waitresses work their tails off for peanuts." He turned to Temple. "Now what are you doing here in such low company when you're in high demand elsewhere? Come along, miss. I am sure that we can find some honest work for you at the mission."

She was hustled away, leaving Oscar to nurse his naked, but still tattooed wrist.

"What're you doin' at a place like this?" Ralph asked in aggrieved tones from behind them as Temple left flanked by brothers twain.

"Interviews. And the Mirage is top of the heap."

"Yeah, but look at the class of the heap. That guy's a phony."

"I know! That's why I wanted to interview him."

"But he was slobbering all over your manicure," another brother (she thought Aldo) told her.

"Manicures can be touched up. Information is hard to come by."

"Well, we didn't like what we saw."

"I gather. How did you figure on the tattoo?"

"He had that L.A. look. Besides, we were keeping a very close watch on you." Ralph pointed up to the ceiling.

"Eye in the sky? You were watching us on the security camera?"

Ralph basked in the fact that she appreciated the feat.

"We know a few folks in this town; big folks, not-so-big folks. And who knows a Fontana, owes a Fontana."

"Well, I owe you a great big thank-you for jumping in when I smashed Mr. Grant's bubble; he was turning a trifle physical."

"I thought this guy was supposed to be a physic," Aldo complained, turning to frown back at Grant, who was vanishing behind a smog of smoke. "You need an escort anywhere?"

"Pepe's Pizza?"

"Aw, Miss Temple, that ain't real pizza pie. You should stay away from those slick franchise joints. Where's your car?"

"In the lot."

"We'll see you to it. It's dark."

"Boys, it's often dark in Las Vegas and I'm often out in it all by myself."

"Not when we're around." Ralph opened a set of double exit doors so his brothers wouldn't have to squeench their well-padded shoulders to accompany her through, and stepped back.

"Luckily for you," she said, "I was almost done."

"Hey, lucky for us we ran into you."

Eduardo (she thought) took her car key when she dug it out and opened the Storm. Aldo brushed off the seat before she sat. Ralph finished cleaning his nails while he bent to make sure her headlights were working.

"Now lock yourself in." Eduardo gave a finger waggle that spotlighted his Roman glass ring.

They stood in a line like French Legionnaires and waved as she put the car into gear and headed out.

Temple waved back. They were fairly tall, dark and plural. Definitely in the running for romance. Was it possible that fate would cut one out of the herd just for her? She couldn't ask for a better escort service.

No way. She shook her head and headed for the take-out pizza place, still dreaming up fantasy tattoos for Matt Devine.

"Born to Raise Hallelujah" seemed to be the best yet.

Chapter 33

That's Amore

The Fontana brothers' "dark" had descended like a black velvet curtain when Temple parked the Storm in front of Orson's/Gandolph's/Max's house.

Not a beam, a seam, a sliver, a scintilla of light cracked the uninhabited façade. Could light be measured in scintillas? Probably not.

The real trick here was how she was going to mosey up the walk to the house, concealing a Pepe's Pizza Giant Everything Double-Crust Extravaganza box. The carton would make a good area rug.

Her neighborhood "cover" as absent-owner's real estate agent would hardly excuse her if a neighbor saw her bearing the fast-food equivalent of a UFO into the supposedly empty house.

Luckily, this neighborhood was expensive enough that children played indoors, cars were kept behind garage door openers and no one ambled out on a front porch to watch the neighbors come and go.

Temple was all the way through the courtyard and at the front door before she realized that she had no key to get in with, and even if she had, it took two hands (and on her, both arms) to handle a whopper.

Not to worry.

The wide wooden door swung silently open on the dark within. Max—or someone—apparently knew she was coming.

Creepy.

She edged inside, bearing her hot cardboard box before her.

Gandolph? Or even . . . Orson?

The door hushed shut behind her, and only when it had whooshed closed—heavy-duty, light-blocking, sound-deadening rubber weather-stripping no doubt—did a light arise. This light came on softly, on the turn of a rheostat.

"Supper, I take it." Max nodded at the box.

"You *can* take it." She handed it over, smiling. She liked the word "supper," so Midwestern, so unassuming, so cozy. Uh-oh. "Thanks," she added as she followed him into the house's still-dark and twisted bowels.

Few lights were on in the front rooms, but a faint one led them to the kitchen.

"Pepe's," Max read aloud from the box's garish top. "You remembered."

Temple shrugged. Pepe's had been their favorite take-out pizza place. Some things don't change.

"Can we let it cool for a minim?" he asked. "The big oven will reheat it in a flash."

"It could cool for a millennium and still be roof-of-the-mouth-scalding hot," Temple answered.

Minim. British for "minute." She'd always thought Max's use of the odd foreign expression reflected his magicianly travels. Now it reminded her of his mysterious past. "What's up?"

"First tell me what you've learned of those who commune with the incommunicado."

Temple duly reported her adventures in psychic land to Kinsella, who leaned against Gandolph the Great's travertine kitchen countertops and tented his daddy-longlegs fingers. Bad romance novels usually featured heroes "without an ounce of fat" upon their entire bodies. Max didn't have an ounce of fat on his fingers, which Temple found infinitely sexier.

"While you've been communing with psychics, I've been getting around some myself," he said when she was through. "I want to show you something. Wine?"

He opened one of the many tall, built-in doors of stainless steel facing the kitchen. A small wine cellar, bottles resting on wrought-iron cradles, lurked behind this one.

"Wine's fine, as long as you don't wall me up in your cellar and try to decide if you can get me to reappear on the cooktop."

"You got the usual?" he asked over his shoulder.

"Everything on it."

"So a slightly nutty but refined white would honor the veal sausage, but a boisterous country red would wed with the pepperoni. Then again, an ambitious but ambidextrous rosé would complement Everything."

"Max, you know that I don't care about wine pedigrees."

"Then the full-bodied red it is," he said, flourishing a bottle and grinning at her a bit too personally over his shoulder.

Yes, much too tall to be the dark, dangerous, romantic man from Agatha's tea leaves. Absolutely. Temple would stake her Midnight Louie shoes upon it.

Temple was also perfectly happy letting him worry the cork out. Some things in life men were truly better equipped to accomplish. She was perfectly happy to let him pour, especially since the wine glasses were in a narrow, under-ceiling cupboard above the range hood that only a second-story man could reach.

The glasses were oversize and handblown with a faintly iridescent glaze that made her feel she was holding a soap bubble. Magician's glasses. A soap bubble filled with blood-red wine. A dead magician's glasses, maybe. Maybe even a murdered magician's glasses.

"I rented the house furnished," Max said from a distance.

The distance was hers. She'd been staring into the bowl of the glass as if into a crystal ball, and he'd read her mind as if her head were just as transparent. Then she wondered if he had *bought* the house furnished, and the glass was an artifact from the late Orson Welles.

Temple managed a smile, then followed him down the dim hall, supporting the glass with a hand under its foot.

All the light in the house was concentrated in one room: the office. Yet only the peripheral lamps were lit, on low, for the central light was not the overhead fixture, but the muted glow of the computer screen. Bright tropical fish schooling in a screen-saving program made her think of the Mirage tanks. No sharks here, though; she hoped.

Max had stepped back like a showman after entering the room; indeed, it had changed remarkably since she'd left it last. Not for the better.

Books were piled everywhere, and papers spewed from the printer lay on the desk, on chairs, on the floor.

A phone now perched on a chair seat pulled up to the office chair. Alongside the desk sat a tower of trade paperbacks with garish yellow and black covers.

Temple bent to read their spines, which were all in the same style and bore variations on the same title. "Modesty becomes you," she commented, straightening.

He refused to let her needle him, but waited behind her with an air of . . . what? Kid showing off his first magic trick? Santa holding Christmas two months early? Someone knowing she was about to stumble upon the Midnight Louie shoes at any minute?

"Have a seat." He indicated the chairman-of-the-board-size leather chair before the cluttered desktop. "Let me put down your wine. . . ." Indeed. "Here." He had found the one relatively bare spot just big enough for the silver-dollar-size foot of the glass.

All right. If Pepe's pizza could cool in the kitchen, Temple could take her time here and find out what was going on. She bent to peer at the tower of books again. *Windows 95 for Dummies. The Internet for Dummies. Object-moving for Dummies.* Were these computer books, or magic books? Or *were* computer books this age's magic books?

"I don't get it," Temple admitted. The only sure way to weasel information from a magician was to profess bewilderment.

"What about this?" Max leaned over her right shoulder to tap some keys on the board with his long arms.

The screen-saver image winked away; instead of fish there were rows of typed words taking their place, with a graphic loading into the empty rectangle above them. Nothing artistic about this image. Some kind of . . . form. An employment form, maybe. Date. Name. Age. Occupation—

The image was filling top to bottom, black and white. A photograph.

"Well?" Max was still hanging over her shoulder, his face next to hers; when he moved she felt a slight sandpaper brush and looked at him. He hadn't shaved, and Max was always preternaturally groomed, without her having seen the process, she recalled a bit bitterly, which was why she had never seen his blue eyes made green.

Max had eyes only for the screen; he never noticed her perusal, her abrupt retreat into hurt memory.

"Well?" he asked, narrowing his eyes at the image as if the most stupefying magic act in the world were going on right in front of them. . . .

Temple looked back to the screen, a good move considering the slight sting in her eyes. It took her a moment to focus through her own despair. The photo was filled out now, not nearly as sharp as a good portrait, but pretty focused for a computer screen.

"Well?" Max repeated.

And then she finally saw . . . "Oh, my God! It's . . . one of them."

He nodded, not noticing that they were practically cheek to cheek and that his cheek was scratching hers. *Men!* she wanted to exclaim, in her smart single-woman exasperation with the species; they always rub you the wrong way. But the usual single-female ham-on-wry wasn't ringing true for her anymore. It wasn't *Men!* and that they'd forgotten to shave or walked out of her life. It was that she didn't have any skin left anymore. *Mea culpa. Mea maxima culpa.* For the first time, she really understood something religious that Matt had said.

"What do you think?" Max asked with an oblivious pertinence most unlike Max.

"How—? I mean, that's one of the guys I identified." Before she could say more, Max tapped a few more buttons.

The vision of a demon vanished, to be replaced with another

dossier, and another slowly assembling photograph.

Temple averted her face. At least she wouldn't have to worry about getting scratched.

"Temple? You're not . . . crying?"

"I just—"

His arm was around her shoulder as if to hold her together. "I should have realized it would be a shock. I'm sorry . . . I guess that's why all the Dummy books are here."

It was easier to let him think the mug shots had upset her. "I'm fine, just had a ragged day among the seers. One of them did my tea leaves and saw danger."

His hand tightened on her shoulder, shook her slightly. "You don't believe that mumbo jumbo, do you?"

"No, but they seem to believe in it so much, it wears you down to resist sometimes."

"That's how they get clients," Max said grimly. "That's why Gandolph dedicated his retirement to ferreting out them and all their works."

"But, Max—" She was ready to turn back to the screen, to him, to the inescapable light the screen reflected on her face. "Where did you get this? It can't be on the Internet, although there's probably some sort of police network—"

He was silent, suspiciously silent.

She was afraid she knew why. "This *is* the police network."

"Don't sound so worried." He braced her shoulder again. Apparently the posture was semipermanent. "It's not the police network."

"What is it, then?"

"I downloaded it, so it's . . . ours."

"Where did you download it from?"

Now he had to pause. "The police computer."

"Which police computer?"

"Ours."

"Here? In Las Vegas? You can't! They have security systems . . . firewalls, they're called. They'll be out here with the SWAT team any minute."

"No they won't. I got the stuff this morning."

"How? You're not a hacker. Sure, you used to noodle a little on my computers after I showed you how to get in and out, but this—! Picking up secured information like it was a toy in one of those arcade game machines . . ."

"Hey, even that's not so simple, or those machines wouldn't be so profitable. But this—" Max gestured at the second ugly mug now dominating the screen. "This is small stuff. Hardly top secret. It's meant to be circulated, in a sense."

Temple had been looking around the altered room with new eyes. This time she spotted a new hardback book on a dim corner of the desk. "*Take Down?* That's the book about how they found that guy who crashed the international computer-security expert's files."

"You can learn more from bad magicians than good ones."

"This isn't magic, Max! This is . . . computer crime."

He gestured to the screen. "The crime is that these guys can do what they did to you, and still be out there. Don't you see? If I have information about them, they don't control us; we control them."

She stared at him dumbfounded. She had never seen Max like this. Now that she looked, really looked, she could see that he not only hadn't shaved, he hadn't slept in at least twenty-four hours, hadn't eaten probably. His newfound enthusiasm for the high of computer hacking seemed genuine enough, but she wondered if he hadn't already been far more proficient than he let on when they lived together. Max needed to keep secrets about himself the way some other people bled personal data like information-age hemophiliacs. Still, even if Max had acquired his computer magic by a bargain with the devil, it was too tempting to scorn. Temple thoughtfully tapped a front tooth.

"Can you get in again, to something else?"

"Can a second-story man climb? What do you want?"

"Motor-vehicle registration."

"Easy as cruise control. What do you want to look up, license number, model and make of car, year?"

"I'm foggy on year and never got the license number."

"This could be a very long list. How many weeks you got?"

"Maybe not such a lengthy listing. I'm looking for a Viper."

"Most women settle for a man."

She made a face. "Don't be an asp."

"Who do you know who owns a Viper?"

"So far, only the Fontana Brothers."

"All of them?"

"I think so. And it's black, like the one I'm looking for. Could they even afford nine Vipers a-vrooming?"

"Can't say. Okay, here are your local black Vipers all in a row."

"Ooooh." Temple squinted at the thick-as-thieves letters as Max scrolled slowly down the screen. "I had no idea there were so many of these budget-busters locally."

"This is Las Vegas, Temple. Lots of big money and even bigger ways of showing it."

"Aha! A Fontana in the flock. Who's that car registered to?"

"Macho Mario Fontana. The uncle from Hell you don't want to mess with."

"Interesting. Any other names we recognize?"

"Wayne Newton?"

Temple shook her head. "It wouldn't be him . . . at least I hope it wouldn't be him."

"What does this Viper mean to you?"

"I'm hoping that it was out of place and trying not to be seen . . . wait! Was that last name—? Go back six lines or so."

"Hmm." Temple stared at the static screen once Max had stopped scrolling. "Oscar Grant. Of course! He lives in Vegas."

"That phony from *Dead Zones.*" Max snorted. "Figures."

"Let he who is without expensive, excessively fast status wheels cast the first gravel."

"I gave mine up," he said as Temple jotted down the pertinent entry's information. "Did I do good? Save a life? Win a perky smile?"

"Okay. At least that settles whose car was lurking discreetly behind Mynah Sigmund's place."

"And?"

"Oscar Grant."

"That prime-time snake-oil salesman! I'm not surprised."

"That he might drive a Viper?"

"That he might consort with the White Widow. What do you suppose she drives. A Whale?"

"Then you're not a particular fan?"

"You should see Gary's file on her." Max had bowed out of the fancy-car file and was clicking his way far afield. "This machine isn't just good for tracking down lurking Vipers. Look." His face was lit by the screen again and he had the farsighted look of someone cruising cyberspace. "This is not only useful; it can be fun."

He glanced at her. "I hope this won't upset you, but I was able to engineer a wee cosmetic change. Want to see?"

Of course she was intrigued. What else had Max mastered while she had been gone for a day? He hit keys, the board chattered, the screen changed, all too fast for her to follow the entire sequence.

Another dossier. Another list of attributes and offenses with another rectangle of felon filling in pixel by pixel. She watched the face and shoulders assemble, knowing them both, at least in retrospect. Molina hadn't let her glance linger on this card when she'd confronted Temple with it. So Temple was steeled now; she knew what to expect. She didn't bat an eyelash as Young Max came into view.

When he was all filled in, she protested. "So you got into Interpol. Who do *they* send out to get on-line intruders? The French Foreign Legion? And what good does it do you? They've still got the file on you in the main computer."

"Yeah." Max smiled tenderly at his record. "But I made a little change. Not in the photo. The statistics."

Temple looked closely. Max Kinsella, seventeen, U.S. citizenship. Six feet two, eyes of blue. No, not anymore . . . eyes of green.

Green. Like Midnight Louie's. Like the green eyes smiling into hers right now by the light of the cathode ray tube. *When Irish eyes are smilin', sure, 'tis like a morn in spring . . . you can't hide lying eyes . . .* But Max Kinsella could.

She almost lost it right then; she almost cried her a Caspian Sea. Except that the silly, optimistic, devious audacity of it made her laugh instead of cry. *In the lilt of Irish laughter, you can hear the angels sing . . .* And you can see the Devil polish his monocle on a bit of brimstone. . . .

She buried her face in her hands and shook her head. He was so right: naked wasn't the best disguise, loud was.

Max wasn't too sure what Kinsella hath wrought. He waited for her to surface again. When she did, she had every right to openly swipe away a few tears.

"You are a lunatic! Still, you didn't get into Interpol in one day. You may be good, but you're not that good."

He shrugged, ready to be modest now that he had amazed. "I had a little help from some long-distance friends. They talked me past the books. They sent me some fairly volatile how-to stuff you can't get in bookstores."

He nodded at the piles of printouts.

"It sounds dangerous, Max." She was fully sober again.

He nodded. "But it was pretty dangerous out already. Don't you see? It's incredible what's out there. Information is power. I know everybody's said that, but now it means something to me, personally. Temple, I can find things out without having to risk *going* out. I was ready to break into police headquarters downtown to get the dope on those thugs, but now I don't have to risk it. I don't have to risk making some sort of deal with Molina, I don't have to expose myself."

"Molina? You mean 'that bozo' who didn't believe me when I said I didn't know where you were? You were planning to deal with Molina?"

He shrugged, looked away. "It was an idea. But more than that, Temple." He'd forgotten about the screen and its secret flow of information at last. He was looking at her now, convincing her, selling her. "Maybe, maybe I can unravel this business that's been dogging me for half my life. Maybe I can do it without having to vanish and run."

He wanted her to believe him, as she had once done. As it might be so easy to do again.

She sighed as she smiled. "It's your life, Max. I can tell you what

I think, but I can't tell you what to do, or where to go, or not to go."

"I want you to tell me what you feel."

Oh, so many things, none of them quite entirely trustworthy yet, just like Max Kinsella, computer whiz kid.

"Hungry," she said.

Chapter 34

Tripping the Light
Fantastic

This is not an easy climb but I make it in forty seconds flat, even though it is the dark of night. I have been keeping a low profile for the past couple of days, for good reason.

It is not every day that a fellow learns he is the likely object of an assassination attempt. It is even unlikelier that said fellow learns of this conspiracy from the mouth of a dead cat. Actually, I prefer to think that the shade of the late Maurice was really an animated former life, say one through eight, rather than the actual corpus.

I mean, I would not like to be hauled out of my own Endless Sleep to make forced personal appearances before unwilling observers dressed in the same tacky old fur I had taken to the grave with me. I am told that human ghosts almost invariably appear clothed. I think such decency could extend to feline ghosts in death, if not in life. What would one wear? I assume anything is possible. I myself would look dashing in a Cavalier outfit, á la Puss of the fancy footwear fame, i.e., Boots. Miss Temple Barr is not the only one who can obsess over elaborate accessories. A scarlet lining for my swashbucklers would contrast nicely with my coat color and symbolize my long career as a famed hunter and detective. I can forego the floppy hat (I saw entirely enough floppy hats at the last séance to last me at least three lifetimes), but a crimson ostrich plume would be nice. Especially if the ostrich went with it, yum yum. (I understand that ostrich is a delicate, chicken-like dish with a commendably low fat content. On the other hand, I do not know if low-fat cuisine counts for much on the Other Side, where hopefully we can all cavort, indulging in everything that is bad for us and the planet without limitation. That is my idea of cat heaven.)

Right now I am climbing up hard and fast to get into Cat Hell.

I am over the last barrier in a flash. Still panting, I tackle the door. After one swipe of my powerful mitt, the latch cries for mercy and throws the door into my path. It is open only an inch, but an inch is always enough for a second-story man of my skill. I paw that door open and crash through into the dark beyond. I do not care who hears me. I am tired of the psychic, the subtle and the disembodied. I am mortal yet and I do not mind who knows it.

My quarry is cringing under the sofa, but I reach right in and make a lethal swipe, nails cocked.

I am rewarded by a startled growl from the dark underworld beyond the sofa fringe.

This changes into a glowing green scowl of two anger-slanted eyes. I snag said swaying fringe—a Fifties-vintage twine of cocoa and gilt—with one shiv and rip.

"No!" comes a horrified shriek. "Madame Electra adores every twisted strand on that fringe."

"I am not interested in Madame Electra's twisted strands. Come out here and face me like a physical being, or I will unstring this fringe from here to Hoover Dam. I will wrap the Circle Ritz up in it like a Christmas present. I will pull out all these gilt threads and give them to the flamingos at the zoo for nesting material—"

But my threats have worked. Karma slithers out from under the sofa, not a graceful move since she is too big-boned for such narrow spaces.

"I was napping," she sniffs, "and Madame Electra is sleeping, as every person of good will is at this time of night. What are you doing, barging into my temple at this hour?"

"Temple!" I snort. "I live *with* a Temple and that is all decent, law-abiding cats need. And I am not a person of good will at the moment. I am an injured party."

"You look unhurt to me."

"You above all ought to know that there are more than mortal wounds. You sent me off into a pretty pickle. Not only did I have to encounter a full program of human spooks, but when I was a good sport and went back to the haunted house for a private feline séance, what am I confronted with but a vengeful spirit of the feline kind."

"Oh. Perhaps your sins have come home to roost, Louie. That is what we of a more spiritual bent call karma. With a small 'k.' "

"Lose that smug smirk, sister! This was Karma with a capital 'K,' but not yours. Mine! The vengeful dude has no grudge against me, but he does expect me to make his killer pay. This puts me in the middle. I feel like that poor Danish dude, Hamlet, about to become somebody's scrambled-eggs-and-ham omelet. But I do not intend to let some woebegone wraith who is not even a relative spook me! I will not worry myself into a frazzle, lose myself in amateur theatrics and then end up in a mass duel of death. And given my upcoming contract for a television commercial and my rivalry with the reputed murderer of Maurice I, his body double, Maurice II, the scenario is looking awfully similar."

By now Karma has recovered her aplomb, particularly in the tail area, which she is grooming into a creamy plume that would look well upon the end of a quill pen. "I doubt that anyone would mistake you for Hamlet, Louie, or that this murderous Maurice II will get the better of you."

"He got the better of Maurice I, let me tell you. A sorrier dude I have never seen. I just want to know what was the big idea? Why did you have to whip me out on Halloween to all these eerie events. I have been subjected to seeing a whole slew of hangers-on from Elvis to Amelia Airheart. Now I have been commissioned by the dead of my own kind to confront a murderer. I am not a vigilante, but neither am I playing the patsy for anybody, not Maurice II and not you!"

"Louie, Louie, Louie. Calm down. Obviously you have psychic sensitivities well beyond the ken of mortal men, and even immortal ones. Elvis, you said? An actual sighting? Did you get an autograph?"

"No . . . although that would not have been a bad idea—"

"And Miss Earhart, now there is a coup. Did she say anything?"

"I did not ask anything."

"For shame! Opportunities to gather information from Beyond are rare. You must not be intimidated by the famous phantom."

"I am intimidated by nobody! I am just mad."

"Mad is not useful in these matters. You must have a plan. Frankly, from what I see, my advice for you to go forth and confront the psychic world proved very profitable. Were you not on the scene of a mysterious human death?"

"Yes, but nobody listened to me, not even when I tried to catch their attention about Elvis."

"Have you not been warned from Beyond about a sinister associate who may wish you harm?"

"Yes . . . but warning does not do much good, as I am not about to commit feline felony merely to forestall a possible attack on my person."

"Still, it is better to know where the stone may fall than not to see the stone at all."

"Stones have nothing to do with this, lady. A fat TV spokescat contract is what is at the bottom of murder past and possibly future. As for the dead dude/dame at the Halloween séance, I will let Miss Temple tend to her kind; I have troubles enough with my own. I will tell you what I am tired of seeing, and it is not stones. It is your glowing little astral-projected self pushing me from pillar to post and most likely from moderate to major risk of my life and sanity.

"Midnight Louie is not your errand boy anymore, get it? You can flash your emergency lights all you like, but I am not Pavlov's Puss. This cat is tuned to Here and Now. I have had it. Keep your pure-white Sacred Cat of Burma mitts out of my life, and out of my mind. Get it? Good."

With that I shake myself all over so I look a third bigger than usual and stalk out of the room. From the bedroom I hear Miss Electra Lark stir and then call, "Karma, are you having a bad vision, sweetie?"

I am the Bad Vision in question, sweetie. I must admit that it is nice to be the nightmare in somebody else's life for a change. Maurice II had better watch his Free-to-be-Feline.

Chapter 35

Piece-a-Pie

The pizza had cooled enough to require oven-warming.

Max went around opening cupboards until he found some heavy pottery plates, and a couple forks.

"No dried red peppers," he announced, spinning a spice rack.

"This is an awesome kitchen. It's as big as most people's living rooms. Whatever possessed you to buy a house with a kitchen like this?"

He stopped playing host long enough to stand still and consider it. "I never really asked myself that. Welles, of course, was a gourmand. Not a mere gourmet, a true gourmand. He ate well."

"And often."

Max nodded. "And it showed. Like a lot of creative people he was at odds with himself. He adored the filmed image, but loved his food too well to keep his image svelte on film. As for me, I suppose . . . I suppose, with the vagabond life I had to lead, a kitchen says stability. A big kitchen says you're there to stay."

"And a small dollhouse kitchen in the Circle Ritz says?"

"You've found a girl just like the girl who married dear old dad; she hates to cook."

"Really? Your mother hated to cook too?" Temple *was* pleased—not only to hear that he was used to noncooking females, but because she'd never heard Max talk about his family and hadn't known she'd missed that until now.

"You don't hate to cook; you just haven't done it with someone who likes to." He came over to her, which, in that kitchen, was a fairly big commitment. "This house was leased when we arrived in Las Vegas. If I'd been alone, I'd have stayed with Gary."

"So you bought another place you didn't need?"

"Such Midwestern indignation," he said, teasing. "You wanted to have the fun of looking, and the Ritz is a jewel. You still like living there, don't you?"

"Love it."

He seemed about to add something, then stopped himself, glancing at the countertop instead. "You've hardly touched your wine and it's almost as expensive as some of your shoes."

"You know I get most of those on sale."

"Extravagance in specialized areas is permitted. Though . . ." He looked down at her legs like Crawford Buchanan, but with interest sans leer. "That's a very attractive outfit."

"My tea-leaf reader said I might have a dangerous romantic encounter, so I dressed for it."

"Really?"

"Actually, she said I'd have a dangerous encounter and a romantic encounter, but I thought it would be more economical to combine them."

"The ever-practical Temple. I don't know how you stand on those heels on hard floors like this, though."

"You get used to it. Like one gets used to rocketing around on an overpowered eggbeater."

"Extravagance in specialized areas is permitted. So is sitting."

He lifted her atop the central island, a forbidding travertine-topped stainless-steel-sheathed block that screamed "human sacrifice" in very high style.

All the countertops were above normal height to relieve back strain. That meant that Temple perching and Max standing put them on a very similar level. She remembered sitting on the Storm fender with Matt on their desert "Prom Night." This was not Matt and this was not Prom Night. Temple swung a foot against the block.

"I feel like an Island virgin."

"You haven't touched your wine," he said again, reaching over for the glass and bringing it to her lips.

His hand was at the back of her head as she tilted her chin to take a sip, and when the glass was gone his mouth was there instead.

This was not Prom Night.

It could have been one kiss and it could have been sixteen; whatever, it was just an introduction. A reintroduction. Max ended it and spun her around so she sat facing the island's long way, then lifted her legs up and laid her down and that could have been the start of something that had to finish . . .

Only he stepped back and leaned down near her head and rested his chin on his crooked elbow.

"I've been thinking," he said, smiling into her face, "while I was away. I've never worked with a lady assistant, but if I made a comeback, and if I was to do so, you are perfect for the job."

She raised an eyebrow, that being about all she could manage when under the erotic spell of a master magician.

He straightened and spun her around on the smooth marble as if they were on a stage and he was explicating an illusion for an audience. Temple was also part of that audience.

He stepped back from the kitchen island to address that invisible audience who was Temple. "I could, for instance, work a variation on the lady-sawed-in-half illusion. Always a tacky thing to do to a perfectly lovely lady, don't you think? I could put that tradition in less lethal terms, and you are the ideal size for all sorts of illusions."

Temple rolled onto her side and braced her head on her elbow. "I've experienced an illusion or two in my time."

"Ah, but those were hasty, improvised affairs. I'm talking an entire act here, from conception to climax." He leaned down again, laying his elbows along the travertine, so they were face-to-face. He still wore his suave magician's mask, but his eyes were dancing. "Houdini worked for many years with his wife, did you know?"

Temple didn't know, and didn't know what to say. What was Max saying? He didn't have to propose marriage to make love to her. And her deep-down female-nesting hope for stability never had any strings on it.

Before any more could come of this intriguing idea, the stage manager stepped in to jerk them both offstage. The oven buzzer shrilled, making them jump. Temple sat upright, heart pounding, Max flew to the scene of the crime to turn the bloody thing off, and the moment was not about to be warmed up by any amount of extra oven-time.

Max turned ruefully from the stove, bearing the steaming pizza on its slightly singed cardboard circle. "Still hungry?"

Temple nodded and jumped down to the quarry tile. "Very."

They spent the night at the computer.

Exquisite wine in iridescent glasses had given way to cans of Classic Coke.

Forbidden files had segued into Gandolph's files, for his investigation, for his book.

Apache dances on kitchen islands had been replaced by weary sparring sessions with a computer keyboard.

"I found a file," Max began, hunting two-fingered over the keys.

"You really need a touch-typing course."

"Later. Anyway, this was not intended for the book, but for himself. It was a diary he began keeping fifteen years ago. Rather sad."

"A diary."

"About his mother. Explains everything, in a way . . . there it is. I'll print it out for you."

Temple leaned into the screen to read the beginning. "He must have been into computers early."

"Yep. Before he retired. The other magicians thought he was cracked, but I can certainly see the attraction now. Poor Gary. He never discussed this with me, and we were pretty good friends."

"I'll read it on-screen. I couldn't focus on typed pages now to save my soul."

"And a very pretty little sole it is too." Max leaned back to eye her bare feet under the desk.

"Thank you, Mephistopheles, but I'm keeping mine for a while." She scrolled down a few pages, reading, then frowned. "I see why you think this might be important. Gandolph's mother was addicted to psychics, it sounds like."

"And you haven't seen the financial records. Apparently, Gary hadn't either. He found out just how much when his mother died. Thousands."

Temple questioned him mutely.

"It wasn't the money she spent on them that enraged Gary. He had sufficient unto his needs. It was the idea of her vulnerabilities being used to bilk her."

"She lost a child at an early age."

"There's nothing worse, they tell me," Max said, his voice bleak.

Temple eyed him sharply, but he was rising to retrieve the print-out. He'd spent most of the night crouched beside her, showing her the way through Gandolph's labyrinth of files.

"This book of his would have really blown things open, wouldn't it?" she asked Max when he came back to drop a fat pile of print-outs onto her lap.

He nodded. "In the paranormal community, yes. And it will still do it. There's nothing here I can't finish."

"Writers do have a reputation for being reclusive."

"It's something I can do that Gary would want. I have to admire him as both man and magician. To pull off this long-running impersonation of Edwina Mayfair, in drag yet! If you had known the man, you'd appreciate that he was as straight as General Eisenhower. No one could have imagined him doing this, which was why his investigation was so effective. He must have been fanatically determined to unmask them; as he writes, he did it not simply for the sake of his mother, but for all the people whose grief over lost loved ones has been exploited."

"I've been jumping ahead to skim the mother file. Max, she apparently skimped on her simplest needs, even her prescribed medications, to finance her quest among the psychics."

He nodded. "I never took that ghost-hunting stuff seriously. I used to consider us all brothers and sisters under the skin, players in a wonderful show. After reading Gary's story, and about the other bilked poor souls he found and championed, I understand him a lot better. I appreciate him more. If he was killed, Temple, it was part of a very dirty and secret war. We've got to expose his killer."

"How?"

"I don't know yet. Maybe when you read all your homework, you'll put the key clue into focus, and I'll trap the killer by some clever illusion. Then we'll let Lieutenant Molina nab the perp and all the credit."

"She's not on this case."

There was a silence. She glanced suddenly at Max. He was looking at her, and it was no glance.

"You didn't tell me Molina was a woman," he said.

"I guess it didn't seem important."

"Perhaps it wasn't." He rapped the printouts on the desktop with one sharp blow so that they were neat-edged as a fresh ream, and cleared his throat. He wasn't looking at her anymore but his voice was as smooth as when he was introducing his next illusion. "Well, I know now, so I can desist in my fantasies of punching out the flatfoot's lights for doubting you."

"Did you harbor such violent fantasies?"

"It's a bit late for discussing fantasies of any nature." Max checked his watch, grinned at her, then sat back on the floor. "God, I've got to get some sleep."

"I've got to get home and feed Louie breakfast."

"And here I said you couldn't cook."

They staggered upright much too soon, then shuffled through the silent house.

"What will the neighbors think?" Temple wondered when the broad front door cracked open to admit a thin trickle of dawn light.

"That the real estate lady is a bit weird for sleeping over in empty houses. Thanks for supper," Max added, catching her and kissing her good-bye like a drunken man, which he was by now.

Temple lurched out into the cool daylight, her tote bag packed with papers, her eyes blinking.

She turned back to the door, still open a crack.

"When you wake up again, Max, don't forget to shave. You could give a cactus razor burn."

She tottered off to the car, managing to start it and zoom away before any neighbor poked nose out of house to get the morning newspaper.

Someday soon, one of those newspapers would read: MAGICIAN'S MURDERER CAUGHT.

Chapter 36

Reincarnation

"So where have *you* been?"

Electra Lark, pink plastic rollers in her silver hair looking as natural as tofu, asked that question in the lobby of the Circle Ritz like a dorm mother forbidding access to the elevators until the answer was given.

"Don't get overwrought," Temple said. "You're not my den mother."

"It's almost seven o'clock in the morning and you're just getting home, wearing the same clothes you left in last night."

"At least I'm wearing them. Fret not, I was busy researching the séance murder."

"And I know how too. After you left last evening, Agatha Welk called me up to warn me about your alarming tea-leaf reading and mentioned that you were on your way *to a drink* with the *Count Dracula* of the séance set: that smarmy Oscar Grant."

"All true, but contrary to Agatha's tea leaves, I was just fine."

"Oscar was a gentleman?"

"No, but the Fontana brothers rescued me."

"How many Fontana brothers?"

"Only three."

"Dear, I consider myself broad-minded, and Lord knows I have a few ex-husbands, and the Fontana brothers are rather adorable, but drowning your current frustrations in late nights and wild sex is no answer."

"Electra, my personal life is not a proper subject for your speculation, especially when your speculation veers in such improper directions. I assure you I was not with any number of Fontana brothers all this time. Now will you step aside and let me get an elevator so I can get to my condo in time for brunch, if not breakfast?"

Electra folded her arms, crushing the printed parrots on her muumuu. She did not budge from the elevator doors.

"You were somewhere all this time, and there has to be a man in it somewhere."

"How about a dead man? I was doing some heavy reading-up on Gandolph the Great."

"The library was open all night?"

"This is Las Vegas, Electra. Everything's open all night. Get with it."

Temple brushed past her, amazed that Electra had been stopped cold in questioning her whereabouts. Maybe the libraries really were open all night. She'd have to check that out when she had time, for future reference.

"I'm sorry, dear." Electra followed her into the elevator compartment. "I've been frantic since Agatha called. She's known for accuracy, and this 'dark, dangerous man' prediction is disturbing."

"Electra, all predictions are disturbing, or else why bother predicting anything?"

"Maybe." Electra watched the brass hand above the door jerk toward the number 2. "Perhaps I'm skittish because of the new séance tonight."

"What new séance?"

"It's Professor Mangel's idea. All the mediums are meeting again in the haunted house. This time they're going to concentrate on raising the ghost of Gandolph the Great."

"Great." Temple leaned against the elevator's varnished mahogany walls.

"Can you come? Professor Mangel says everything must be as it was before."

"Oh, I can come, if I get my beauty sleep between now and then. Otherwise I'd be mistaken for a ravaged revenant. Note that I said 'ravaged,' not 'ravished,' Electra. But has Professor Mangel considered that re-creating the circumstances of the first séance could set the scene for another death?"

"Another death? Why?"

The elevator door slid open. Temple managed to pause dramatically on the threshold before anything snapped shut on her.

"Because no one knows the reason for the first one yet."

Electra disappeared as the elevator door closed, her face slack with shocked contemplation.

Temple trudged down the hall, feeling the effects of a night lost in computer contemplation. Or maybe just the effects of a night lost. She yawned as she headed down her entry cul-de-sac, which was dusk-dim in the wan light from the doorside sconce.

Matt Devine looked pretty wan too, sitting in the corner under that tepid night-light, his legs folded like a yogi's.

Temple almost dropped her forty-pound tote bag when she saw him. Darn, if she would have thought of it, she could have waved her sixteen tons of printout at Electra to prove her night out had been spent in virtuous academic toil.

"Matt—?"

His limbs unfolded as he jumped up at her approach.

"Matt, what are you doing here?"

"Waiting, obviously. Electra called me at four this morning."

"Why?"

He hesitated. "She wondered if you were at my place."

"Electra—!"

"Don't get mad at her. By the time she called me she was frantic." Matt rubbed the back of his neck. "Apparently our dear landlady takes this fortune-telling stuff seriously. She was sure you had fallen into the hands of this dark, dangerous man."

"Dark, dangerous *short* man," Temple corrected, more for Matt's sake than Electra's. "It's a good thing she overlooked that last adjective, or the police would have been rousting Crawford Buchanan out of bed, instead of her bothering you. Have you been waiting here since four?"

"Once we discovered that you were still out, she was in an even bigger tizzy, so I promised to wait here and let her know as soon as you showed up." He checked his wristwatch. "Seven-forty. I'd better tell her."

Temple put a hand up to stop him. "Don't bother. She descended on me in the lobby. She must have been watching from her balcony for my car to arrive, so a lot of good you did playing night watchman on my doorstep. You better come in for some decaffeinated coffee. I know I need some."

He reached to take her tote bag.

"Thanks, but watch out," she warned.

"What have you got in here, a dead body?"

"Just Louie. And just kidding. Research. I found a source with access to all the computer files on Gandolph the Great's unpublished book."

"That's the guy who died, right?"

"Right." Temple threatened the aging tumbler with her key until it rolled over and played open. "Now my own lock doesn't recognize my facile touch. I guess I've been up a while too long. Just set the tote on the kitchen floor by the wall, will you, please? I've skimmed the stuff and don't want to see it again until I've had a nap and can focus."

Matt followed instructions while Temple tottered into the kitchen and dragged a couple mugs down from a cupboard. The decaffeinated coffee was in retreat in a lower cupboard, pushed way to the back behind every instant product her shelves possessed. While she was digging her way back, hoping to encounter no survivors from her insect version of the Bates Motel, something fell from an upper cupboard. An ungodly loud thump on the countertop was followed by something big flashing past her to land on the floor like a sack of solid-lead potatoes.

Temple shrieked a little, her nerves being somewhat ragged from lack of sleep and for other reasons also often related to lack of sleep but far more interesting.

Matt was right there like a lifeguard, but not fast enough for Midnight Louie, who stretched his forelegs up the open cupboard door, his weight shutting it on Temple barely before she could whisk her fingers out of the way.

"Merooowwwl." Louie gave the demanding plaint she knew well.

"He must want to know where you've been all night too," Matt commented, not entirely in jest.

Temple sighed. Vary from routine one teeny, tiny bit and everyone you knew was an interrogator.

"You obviously don't know cats," she answered Matt. "He wants to know where I've been, all right, but only because he didn't get his dinner."

"There's plenty of green pellets in this bowl here."

"That's not dinner, that's . . . bowl-dressing. Do you mind?" Her last comment was addressed to Midnight Louie as she opened the cupboard again to pull out a couple of small, low cans.

She glanced up at Matt, hoping she looked appealing at this hour of the morning, begging on jackknifed knees that were about to simply snap from this permanent squat position.

"Do you mind," she asked a lot more nicely, "opening these cans and smearing the contents over all those green pellets for Louie?"

"Nope." He vanished, Louie on his heels like a bloodhound. "Pretty pungent stuff," Matt noted shortly after the "pop" of lids. "And he gets both cans? Okay, Louie, get ready to chow down."

Temple got what felt like the right jar by the throat and pulled it into the light of day. Creaking in the knees, she dragged herself up in time to watch Louie make his morning obeisance to his bowl of Free-to-be-Feline. Usually the level of F-t-b-F didn't decline much, but the gravy atop it did.

"Smoked oysters? Baby shrimp in clam sauce?" Matt sounded unsure. "Isn't that a bit rich for him?"

"Oh, probably. But I can't get him to eat anything else. I've tried everything."

"Let him wait until he's hungry enough."

"If he's hungry enough, he just won't come home, but he will move on down the line to the nearest Dumpster, and the menu in there will be even worse for him."

"Maybe he shouldn't be out on the streets."

"No, none of us should, but Louie's a street cat, and if I pen him up he'll go nuts. Freedom is vital to some of us."

Matt shook his head but didn't comment; freedom had never been much of a factor in his life.

Temple had finally wrenched open the Postum jar (purchased a year ago when she had prematurely decided to quit drinking coffee for a day) and now had rooted a table knife from a drawer to repeatedly stab the rock-hard, granular mess the contents had become.

"Let me," Matt suggested, taking the jar, closing it and shaking loose the dried powder by rapping the bottom hard on the countertop.

Temple nearly jumped out of her skin.

He eyed her curiously. "Go sit down. I'll fix this."

"But you've been sitting up all night. I'm so sorry, Matt; Electra shouldn't have involved you."

"I actually got some sleep. I'm used to crises. I haven't been sleeping that well the last couple nights anyway."

Temple was afraid to inquire into the cause, so wordlessly foot-dragged her way past the oyster-gobbling Louie into the living room. There she fell onto the sofa, kicked off her high heels and tucked her feet under her rear.

Séance tonight. That meant she had to arrange going to the site with Electra before she squeezed in some sleep and read through the Gandolph material.

Matt brought the steaming mugs to the coffee table and stood there waiting.

"What?"

"Coasters."

"Are *you* domesticated; definite headwaiter material! There are some water-absorbing stone ones decorated in Native American motifs, but I'm too tired to remember where they are. If the mugs steam up the glass tabletop, so be it. Steam evaporates."

On the other hand, maybe it doesn't always, Temple thought, recalling certain moments from last night's research.

"Domesticated? Trained by parish housekeepers, anyway." Matt sat, almost as heavily as she had, and sipped the brew. "Pretty bad. I don't know the proportions."

"If it's hot, passes for coffee but won't keep me awake, I'll love it." She leaned forward for the mug and brought it to her lips. Just the steam curling up into her nose acted like an inhalation room, both energizing and relaxing her. "Ummmm."

"So. Did you learn who might have killed the magician?"

"Not yet. Or even if he was killed by somebody. Somebody living, anyway. He was writing a hell of a book, though. Documented exposé on mediums who cheat confused people of their money and dignity. Guess it was a crusade for him; his mother was bilked like that."

Matt nodded. "You don't like to see your mother taken for a ride."

"Mine wouldn't go. She's much too cautious. She wouldn't let me cross a street alone until I was almost eight or something."

Her comment made some troubling emotion flicker in Matt's eyes. He was so dangerously readable unless he was playing counselor. He'd never learned to hide his reactions except for somebody else's sake.

Temple felt an internal conflict simmering. Max was like a volcano, unpredictable and exciting, but Matt made her feel so utterly secure it was . . . divine. Max was caffeine, Matt was . . . chamomile tea. Max was edgy nerves, Matt was nirvana. She could have gone on for hours in this vein, she was that punchy, but stone-cold predictable Matt was showing signs of an imminent trembler.

"Temple, I shouldn't bother you with this at a time like now—"

"Bother," she ordered, being in the happy position of someone with her feet up, finally, and her hair down.

He hunkered over his steaming mug as if it were a wall he wanted to hide behind, or a fire he needed to warm himself at. His honey-brown eyes darkened with question. "I . . . think I saw Cliff Effinger this weekend."

"Your stepfather? Are you sure?"

"Absolutely not sure. The guy didn't *look* anything like Effinger, didn't *dress* anything like Effinger. He was crossing the Strip, though, and he *walked* like Effinger. Funny, I never noticed Effinger's walk when I knew him, but I saw it then."

"What did you do?"

"Tried to follow him, but I was on that damn motorcycle, and in the wrong lane to boot."

"Oooh, and on the Strip too. Not easy to move over and turn around."

"Easier with a motorcycle than a car. I doubled back but he was gone. If it was him, he sure had changed. Cowboy hat. Jeans and boots. Denim vest. All Western-duded up. Pretty ludicrous. Like a late-life makeover."

"Or he was in disguise."

"Disguise?"

"Naked isn't the best disguise in Las Vegas, loud is. Seems to me this Novo-West guy who walked like Effinger is such a hundred-and-eighty-degree turn on the sleazily suited Midwestern man you used to know that the difference might be deliberate."

"But, then . . . Effinger would know he was wanted for questioning. He'd be dodging the police, pretending to be dead."

Temple nodded, almost nodding off into her cup as well. "My point exactly, Dr. Watson."

"I *have* been stupid about this! Maybe the dead man at the Crystal Phoenix was supposed to make people think Effinger was dead. That means Effinger himself didn't want to leave Las Vegas, but couldn't stay here without seeming to have gone, one way or another. Why?"

"I don't know, but I'm sure you'll think of something. Lots of somethings." Temple yawned.

"I'm sorry. You need to sleep."

She nodded. Her eyes had closed and she didn't want to open them ever again. Thank goodness she had never been able to wear contact lenses.

Someone leaned near and took the cup from her fingers. "You want me to show you the way to San José?" a nicely deep, masculine voice asked.

Umhmmm.

She was pulled up, pointed and guided in some direction.

The best part was arriving where she could sit down on something soft and certifiably comfortable, her very own bed.

"You need anything?"

Just ten thousand years of deep, dreamless sleep. Oh, no . . . can't. "Set the alarm," she mumbled.

"What time?"

"Three." Sounded good.

"I'll let Electra know she can call you after three."

Umhmmm.

"Here's the morning paper, in case you wake up later and want to escape to the real world."

"Thanks."

"Anything else?"

Just go 'way. But first . . .

She reached out into the gray nothing, found his arms, pulled, found his face, kissed him. "Thanks."

Then she slipped back, down, out cold, feeling warm anyway.

Something floated down over her like a cloud, like a spirit. She heard faint sounds that faded. Later, she felt another heavy plop beside her. *Plop, plop, fizz fizz, oh, what a relief it is . . .*

Temple awoke in that drowsy, daytime-nap state of utter but strangely serene disorientation. She was wonderfully warm, thanks to the comforter from the other side being pulled over her and thanks to Midnight Louie warming one hip like a hirsute heating pad.

The drawn miniblinds let in tiny split-seams of daylight, striping the room's dim atmosphere. Sleep never felt so good as after being awake too long. Waking up never felt so luxurious as in mid-afternoon. Temple squinted the clock's red-hot letters into temporary focus. Two thirty-five. Three o'clock alarm, right, but she didn't have to worry about disarming it for a while yet.

Temple stretched and yawned. Midnight Louie protested the stretch and added his own yawn. Three O'Clock Louie. Another séance. Was she ready for this? Knew a lot more now; knew the mediums a lot better. Maybe Houdini would surprise them and slip into town a few days later. Maybe a murderer would surprise them and try again. But she could handle it. She plucked her glasses off the bedside table, turned her head Midnight Louie's way and wrinkled her nose at the solemn cat face so close and so closemouthed . . . now.

Yawning, she pulled over the newspaper, scanning the front page. The headline was so small that only the word "séance" caught her drowsy attention. SÉANCE DEATH RULED NATURAL CAUSES. Wow! Temple squinted at the tiny body type. Body type, how appropriate. The medical examiner had decreed: Gandolph had died of a heart attack. Heart attack? In that getup, among those people, in that freaked-out haunted house? Temple should have been relieved. Max was off the hook; so was she, for that matter. Just a garden variety heart attack. Gandolph certainly was under pressure, given his masquerade, his book.

No. Maybe somebody had frightened Gandolph into the fatal heart attack. The new séance was more vital than ever. It was now or never. Prove a psychic had meddled with Gandolph's mental health and even if the case never came to court, all present would know who had been responsible for his passing. Max would never swallow a "natural causes" verdict, and neither would she.

"It's up to us, Louie," she told him, including him purely as a courtesy. "I won't believe that someone didn't kill Gandolph, somehow. And tonight I'll find out."

The cat's green eyes blinked and blinked again, almost like a cool feline variety of alarm.

Chapter 37

Ghost-talker

Wayward papers still blew across the empty lot surrounding the haunted house, but the sign was gone and the exterior spotlights were turned off.

That made the scene look truly deserted.

The gate leading to the parking lot was chained shut, so Temple left the Storm on a graveled patch off the side street, fender to fender with a provocative sprinkle of vehicles.

One of them was a jet-black Viper.

"Oooh, you'd think *that* owner would be afraid to leave its black beauty out here all alone in the dark," Electra said. "One of the boys isn't coming unannounced?"

"No Fontanas, just the original cast of the first supernatural farce."

"I wonder who drives the red Miata."

"Let me guess." Temple had an ugly thought. "A short, dark, dangerous man named Crawford Buchanan."

"Oh, that's right! And his cameraman will have to be here too."

"I bet he owns the lime-green VW bug. Photographers make almost as little money as freelance PR people."

"And the Astro van?"

"Must be . . . D'Arlene Hendrix. She's so suburban you can practically see 'Car Pool' tattooed on her forehead."

"This is fun. We'll have to watch when everybody leaves if they get into the vehicles we guessed. And the older Oldsmobile?"

"Must be Agatha Welk; that car looks elderly enough to have belonged to Lawrence."

"Lawrence?"

"The late Lawrence Welk. A joke, Electra."

"I don't know how you can joke at a time like this."

"Another obvious owner." Temple pointed to a white Camaro convertible.

Electra nodded. "Mynah Sigmund. If white's her thing, why is her first name so dark? Mynah birds are black."

"Perhaps a not-too-subtle hint that she's a whited sepulcher."

"Just because she's a self-dramatizing man-eater doesn't mean she's a murderer."

"No, but it would be so satisfying if she were, not to mention how well it would play on a TV Movie of the Week. Tons of actresses would kill for a role like that."

"You do have murder on your mind. I hope you're wrong in thinking that death could make a return engagement tonight."

"Death always makes return engagements, just like taxes."

"What about the professor?"

"He makes return engagements?"

"I don't know about that, but what brought him here?"

"I'd bet the rent-a-car Sentra."

"Well, your little aqua Storm is the cutest."

"Please, cut out the 'cute.' The car's getting a little old in the wheel wells, I suppose, but I don't need a psychic to tell me a new one's not in my future."

"You never know," Electra answered mysteriously.

"When it comes to major purchases, I sure do know. By the time you pay off a car loan, you're yearning for a new one, which is exactly the trap they want you to fall into, so you can sign up for debt again. Not me. That car's a lot cuter now than it was new, because it's paid for."

"I meant, one's fortunes or circumstances can take a sudden turn."

"Maybe. But rarely for the better."

"My, we are pessimistic lately."

"No, just realistic." Temple stopped to gaze up at the former Hell-o-ween Haunted Homestead's dark exterior. "Funny, you're more scared of what might happen inside a carnival ride, and I'm more worried what is happening in the real world outside."

"When you get to my age, the immaterial seems a lot closer."

"Just what is your age?"

"Ladies of my generation are always coy about that; I think I'll keep up the tradition. Senior solidarity, you know."

"Then you're at least sixty-five, no?"

"Not necessarily. You can join the American Association of Retired Persons at age fifty. So I could be only fifty and still a senior citizen."

"Fifty! That's in . . . twenty years. In twenty years I could be officially *old?*"

"What an outmoded attitude. You're not old until you think so nowadays."

"Then why hide your age?"

Electra thought about it. "Maybe I go for younger men."

"Like Eightball O'Rourke."

"Nonsense."

"You said the same thing when I asked if you kept a cat. I'm beginning to think you have something to hide on every front."

"Makes a woman fascinating, my dear, at any age. And a man, for that matter. If we can't have a few secrets after living all this while, what are we early-middle-aged folks to do?"

"Attend séances and try to find out other people's secrets."

"Good idea." Electra grinned. "Let's go."

They approached the forbidding façade, which was actually spookier unlit.

Temple was thinking about the fact that most of the séance attendees had driven themselves to Las Vegas. Mobility always made murder more feasible. Someone with a car could have easily come out here ahead of time to rig the special effects, including the murder. Max had certainly come and gone at will. And that brought a truly unwelcome thought: Max could have done the murder. Wasn't that exactly what Molina suspected him of? Murder? Just who was she feeding pizzas and disks anyway?

But in general terms, if Max were right, and she had no reason to think he wasn't, even "genuine" mediums were well aware of the traditional ways to fake manifestations. Where was Max now? Temple wondered more fondly than she would have liked. Also more nervously. Sleeping, she hoped, as he well deserved after his marathon computer sleuthing session. She had read some printouts before coming. They were virtual tip sheets on how to rig séances, so she was a far more critical participant now than she had ever been. And Max was right. Gandolph's book was certainly publishable, especially when tied into his spectacular deception and death. Especially if that death were foul play. Nothing sold books like misfortune and murder.

The world was mean, and man uncouth, but at least there was always an honest buck in it.

"Do we knock?" Electra stared at the huge, snarling gargoyle-face knocker.

"I don't know how Oscar Grant arranged this, or who owns the place, but . . . let's see if it's open first."

Temple nudged the fake distressed wood, pushing just below an artistically crude imprint of a bloody hand.

The big door swung inward, without the interminable prerecorded creaking noise of Halloween night.

Bare bulbs lit the long narrow hall ahead of them. Torn spray-on cobwebs fluttered like ragged fish fins as Temple and Electra passed. The lurking monsters' empty niches showcased lurid painted backgrounds: cracked stone blocks, Day-Glo paint and fake grouting.

Once Temple and Electra reached the main open part, the layout had lost its earlier eeriness. Now it was simply a vast Hollywood soundstage-size space into which someone had pretzeled a not particularly spectacular roller coaster. Dodging a forest of support structures, they angled for the isolated island of the séance room atop its stalagmite of motorized scaffolding.

"This is weirder than the actual event," Electra commented, echoing Temple's mental evaluation. "We were really sitting up there in the middle of all those circling tracks? I hate to say it, but we were fish in a bowl. It wouldn't be easy for anything to get in there or out of there without being seen by somebody on the ride or in the haunted house proper. It had to be one of us who killed Gandolph. But how, when we were all holding hands?"

"Oldest trick in the business. Fake hand."

"Fake hand?"

Temple nodded. "It worked in the old days, before the Hollywood techmeisters dreamed up stunning artificial limbs. Someone connected to a television show like *Dead Zones*—"

"Someone like Oscar Grant!"

"—could probably get a state-of-the-art moving hand with warm flesh and everything."

"Ick! That is gross, Temple. Professor Mangel was on my right. Such a firm, warm grip. I'm sure it was his."

"Who was on your left?"

"William Kohler. I think."

"Exactly. You think. Even Gandolph could have been up to something when the lights dimmed. The old-time mediums were busy as one-man or -woman bands when their audiences were in the dark. They used knees, feet, toes, chests, heads, anything to make tambourines chatter and trumpets speak and tables dance. And Gandolph asked especially to sit next to me, remember? Maybe he thought he could fool a greenhorn with a faux limb, especially a gloved one. Now I remember someone patting my knee, *after* all our hands were linked! I certainly can't swear that I was squeezing pinkies with a real hand. Too much else was going on for me to pay strict attention to assumed stimuli, which is the idea behind séance phenomena."

"And all this is in Mr. Gandolph's book?"

Temple nodded. "Mr. Randolph's. That was his real last name."

"Say, should be a best-seller."

"Yeah." Temple smiled. "Maybe it'll solve its ghostwriter's financial problems."

"Gandolph had a ghostwriter?"

"He does now. Look! Movement up yonder. Shall we climb the stairs for our appointment with the Handcuff King?"

"Sounds like something kinky on cable TV, dear." That did not appear to faze Electra, but something else did. "Those stairs don't look OSHA-approved."

The complicated structure ahead had effectively distracted Electra from speculating on the identity of Gandolph's ghostwriter, which is what Temple had wanted. Not only fraudulent mediums had the ability to mislead.

The pair climbed the rickety wooden stairs, which creaked quite authentically. Spotlights placed here and there high above glared down on them like a constellation formed entirely of blazing, fixed pole stars.

"I just realized something." Electra stopped halfway up the stairs.

"What?"

"The séance isn't supposed to start until midnight, and we're plenty early, yet everybody else's vehicle is here already."

"Yeah, I noticed that. I wonder who arrived when, because the early birds could certainly have tampered with the worm."

"Indeed!"

"Luckily, I arranged for some even earlier birds to stake out the premises."

"*You* arranged? Who? Watts and Sacker?"

"I could hardly bother the police about something as borderline flaky as a second séance held to find a killer even the police aren't looking for. No, it's just Eightball O'Rourke and Wild Blue Pike and some other Glory Hole Gang guys. They know the layout, and they know spook attractions, so I figured we've got expert witnesses waiting in the wings."

Electra examined those three-story wings rather apprehensively. "Why didn't you tell me?" She patted her quiet, pewter-colored hair. "I would have dressed for company."

"Does it matter in the dark?" Temple nodded to the shadowy reaches of everywhere.

"My dear, at my age it especially matters in the dark."

They resumed their climb, Temple holding herself to Electra's pace, although after a couple flights she was glad to have an excuse to slow down. This was much more taxing than entering the portable room when it was parked on the first or second floor. But Electra was right, how could anyone manipulate outside effects inside a mobile chamber?

"At least," Temple said, "I don't have Crawford Buchanan and his nosy camera on my backside all the way up the stairs. Perhaps that will make seeing him at the top of the stairs more palatable."

Electra stopped. "You know, he could have done it."

"Crawford? Much as I like to think he's capable of anything, what would he have against Gandolph?"

"Nothing against him, but he did sit next to Gandolph, and you did say Mr. Buchanan was ambitious, and this *Hot Head* show must be his big chance."

"It's *Hot Heads*, plural. You mean, Crawford could have killed someone to up the ratings on his segment?"

Electra shrugged persuasively.

"Oh, great. Everyone up there's a potential murderer, except that the police can't make a case because the bottom line is that Gandolph died from natural causes, according to the newspaper."

"Are there any natural causes at a séance?" Electra asked cryptically. "I still think the spirit world punished him for disbelief."

"Then spirits are nothing more than jealous, paranoid small-minded gods, like the Greek pantheon. Why would anyone want to contact such closed-minded tyrants?"

"Nobody's perfect. I'm only saying that even spirits can get tired of being snubbed. Oof." Electra took the last step and stopped. "You open the door, dear; I'm too tired to lift a pinkie."

Temple, resisting an urge to knock, turned the cold brass knob. A screamingly theatrical screech announced their entrance.

She was startled to see the bloodied battle-ax (now wiped clean) hanging in place near the window dead ahead. The other pikes, maces and whatalls were still installed, and the broken sconce light and shade had been replaced.

Everyone sat in his or her designated seat in customary guise:

Oscar in black, Mynah on his left in white, Jeff Mangel in academic black and blue (for jeans), a space for Electra, then the charcoal-black figure of William Kohler, a space for Temple, and another space . . .

Not another empty place! An occupied space for Edwina Mayfair/Gandolph.

Temple turned to Electra. "Who—?"

"It's . . . Sophie! One of my soft-sculpture people from the wedding chapel. She does look a lot like Edwina, down to the veiled hat and gloves."

"How?"

Electra shrugged. "An out-of-body experience? Don't ask me. Maybe one of the Glory Hole boys thought we needed a stand-in. Whew. I bet she gave everybody a start when they came in."

"I imagine that was the idea." Temple ignored her pounding heartbeat to cross the threshold, where she suspected that ordinary expectations would not hold for long.

Crawford, in the seat next to the ersatz Edwina (who had, in fact, been ersatz from first to last) turned to watch their entrance. On his left was D'Arlene Hendrix and beyond her the ashen, frail features of Agatha Welk.

Nobody looked particularly perky, Temple noticed as she took her seat and nodded politely all round, even at the ersatz Edwina.

"Did you resuscitate the transvestite, T.B.?" Crawford asked. "I remember you putting those stuffed cats in the ABA booth after the real ones were kidnapped. This was a pretty dirty trick."

"I didn't do it. Was it here when everyone arrived?"

Nods and no comment.

"Who arrived first?"

They exchanged looks. "Not I." "You were here when I came." "I wasn't first."

Temple saw that this was not going to be a cooperative evening. Then why had they agreed to meet again?

"Whose idea was this, anyway?"

"Mine," said a surprising voice.

She turned back to Crawford. "And why was that, C.B.?"

He pointed to the cameraman leaning against one of the few solid shafts of wall. "Good media op. Nice follow-up piece. Actually, I suppose with this lump of old pantyhose in place we can call this a 'recreation.' If everybody mortal is here, we might as well begin. Grab a stuffed mitt, T.B., and hold on. If we have any luck, this is going to be a bumpy evening."

Temple stared at Crawford, struck by his paraphrasing the same line from the same old Bette Davis movie that had crossed her mind at the previous séance. Was Bette out there urging them on? When her mind and Crawford's showed signs of parallel thought, even almost a week apart, she began to fear for her sanity, not to mention her integrity.

Temple sat and reached for Sophie's stuffed hand in its vintage fifties opera-length satin glove. The gesture felt a bit macabre and even disrespectful. She knew more of Gandolph the Great now than she had when he had so effacingly died beside her. And the fact that he had been Max's friend . . . she almost couldn't do it, couldn't connect with this obscene substitution for the living person. An awful thought came, surprising only because she wasn't a spiritualist, she didn't believe in ghosts, she didn't expect contact.

Gandolph was a spirit now. Like Houdini he was an unbeliever who had crossed over. (Exactly *what* he had crossed over, Temple was not sure. Perhaps it was the river Styx, perhaps the river Jordan, or the Las Vegas Strip, or even perhaps the fine line between Beyond and bullfeathers.)

Gandolph, presumably, could return, now that he was dead. Ooh! And he had a reason to return here, where he had died, where a murderer might sit who had not only killed him, but had gotten away with it. Temple held her breath. (*I don't believe in ghosts, I don't believe in ghosts, I don't even believe in Tinkerbell. . . .*) But the psychics weren't so far out in their objective of the evening. If any spirit was liable to manifest itself here and now, it was Gandolph the Great.

"We begin," Mynah announced coldly.

Behind them a light flashed on. The camera was ready.

Temple glanced at William Kohler. Despite the chill touching the vast, unoccupied space, sweat sheened his face, the betraying protest of an overweight frame. Or a guilty mind.

Oscar held hands with Mynah and Agatha, but kept nervously jerking his head to shake back his dramatically silver forelock of hair, which had fallen against his face like an English judge's wig.

Agatha's eyes were closed, no way to see spirits, and D'Arlene glanced from one to the other participant as if hunting for the thoughts of the maybe-murderer among them. Electra looked determined, focusing on Agatha directly across the table, her hand in the professor's warm grip, which looked more desperate than firm to Temple. Jeff Mangel caught her eye and bit his bottom lip.

Only Crawford and William Kohler seemed unmoved.

"We begin," Mynah went on, "where we have always begun, with the spirit and will of Harry Houdini, who died beforetimes. He was not a friend to mediums, but only mediums remember him well enough to meet and call for his return year after year, Halloween after Halloween for seventy years. Now a man like him has died: an unbeliever. A skeptic. A medium-hunter. Has Gandolph the Great, too, learned the Afterlife's reality? Has he repented? Does he wish to come back to us in his new ephemeral form? Does he wish to tell us something? That he and Houdini occupy the same Beyond? That the notion of an Afterlife is humbug? Come, Houdini. Come, Gandolph, only you can manifest the truth, and you can do that only by showing yourselves. Show yourselves, I command you! Show yourselves, I beseech you! For all of those who have believed in you, show us the conviction that lies beyond death. Now! It is now or never."

During Mynah's declamation, the surrounding lights had almost imperceptibly dimmed. Temple noticed, because she was watching for it. Not only the in-room sconces had dimmed, but the spotlights high above. Who ran the lightboard, she wondered cynically, Gandolph or Houdini? Or maybe Mrs. Houdini, Bess his wife, who'd always played the page girl in his act. Temple recalled playing the page girl in Max's kitchen performance last night and found herself momentarily distracted.

In that moment, the mist had begun rising, for it was suddenly seeping in everywhere again in hissing serpent-fingers of cloud.

"The temperature," Agatha Welk said hoarsely, never opening her eyes.

And it had plunged. Temple felt icy air wafting up from under the table, slithering down the back of her neck. This was a new effect. Effect, this was an effect, not an act of nature, but an effect.

Hands tightened on each other around the table, in reaction to cold, to fear.

A muffled sound came from the chimney, and all eyes flashed there.

Something dark filled the empty, fire-scorched interior of the hearth. A screaming, snarling yowl announced it: a black cat. No gate-crashing Midnight Louie alleycat, but a long, sinuous feline force. The panther wore a collar studded with nickel-size ruby-red stones, the even larger emeralds of its light-refracting eyes shone like the coals of a perverse icy green hell in its powerful face.

Temple tried to mistake it for Midnight Louie, somehow blown up large. But she couldn't. Midnight Louie (sorry, fella) was not only *not* the size of a mastiff, but he was nowhere near this svelte, muscular and carnivorous, not even during his fiercest temper tantrum with a delinquent rubber band.

The Big Cat leaped forward. Hands along the table drew back and almost broke their grip.

The panther's mouth opened to showcase an entire Himalaya range of ice-sharp white teeth. Another wildcat cry pierced the fog as the animal's thin, sleek tail lashed like a possessed bullwhip.

Then . . . it was gone, all that feral energy, and behind it came a vacuum, a loss, a little death.

They breathed again, but tightened fingers didn't loosen on each other. Poor Sophie! Between Temple and Crawford's unconscious tug-of-war, her arms had been twisted . . . to the breaking point had they been flesh and bone instead of cotton and fiberfill.

"The panther is Houdini," Mynah's husky séance voice decided. "Wiry, muscular energy. Supreme ego and showmanship. A devouring obsessiveness."

They waited, watching the fireplace's inky mouth as they might a black stage curtain, anticipating the next act, the next appearance.

"Oh."

Agatha Welk's quaver roused them from their own obsession.

Her eyes were still shut, the lids quivering. "Who is that?"

"Where?" Temple asked.

Agatha's head dreamily nodded across the room from herself. They looked in the direction she indicated, the people on Temple's side of the table having to twist in their Gothic chairs.

They saw only the dark outer vastness at the heart of the empty building. Temple, tired of craning her neck, caught a reflection in the window opposite her, *behind* Agatha Welk.

"Someone is out there," she said.

"Oh, really, T.B.," Crawford objected. " 'Someone is out there.' It's *'the truth* is out there,' if you're trying to use that *X-Files* catch-phrase. Tired stuff, T.B., derivative and—"

"Shut up, Crawford, and look for yourself. Is that 'someone out there' or not? Then tell me I'm seeing things. At least it isn't you."

"I see some sort of black blob in a bit of light. Of course you re-alize anything out there would be suspended in sheer space."

"The panther," Oscar suggested.

"It's a seated person," Jeff Mangel interjected. "All in black. Can't you all see the big floppy hat, the slope of the shoulders, the long cloak to the ground?"

Temple nodded. He saw what she saw.

"That's Edwina, then!" Mynah sounded truly excited.

"Gandolph," Oscar reminded her.

"Do we all see it?" Electra wanted to know.

"I see it," Agatha said, still facing in the opposite direction, still with her eyes closed.

"William?" Mynah demanded, seeking a second.

"I see something," he mumbled.

"Well, I don't," complained a voice until now silent, which Temple recognized. "I gotta move and focus in. Can you all just settle down for a bit?"

They had forgotten him. Wayne the cameraman. So they waited silently while he stomped to the other side of the room and aimed his light into the glass.

"Damn hard to shoot," he muttered. "All reflection."

"What do you think it is?" D'Arlene asked abruptly.

"Got me, lady. A lump of dark coal. Maybe a hat, maybe a shadow. Maybe nothing."

When he drew back, the image was still there, still vague, still fairly shapeless.

"So?" Crawford demanded. "What is this? I could point to clouds that look more like a person. I could say I have seen Nixon's nose in a Nevada sunset. This is it? This is all that's gonna show itself after all we've gone through? Come on, people, get with it."

"Mediums are sensitive instruments," Oscar said pompously. "They don't perform on command, only as the spirits move them."

Temple considered it notable that a guy with a gang tattoo had learned to be pompous in the intervening years.

"Well, these spirits better get on the move, or we're outa here and there goes your slot on *Hot Heads.*"

"The spirits do not manifest in the face of crassness," Agatha said, never opening her eyes to regard the face of crassness, which was clearly Crawford.

Temple had to admire her technique.

Still, she squinted her eyes at the lonely figure visible yet through—or on—the window. Yes, it reminded her of Gandolph as Edwina Mayfair, and he was dead, so it was logical to presume that his spirit haunted the outer darkness and would be visible to all. Indivisible to all.

But. But Temple remembered the last séance, and the boy/man/elder she had seen, along with Agatha. The others seemed to have seen him less clearly and had dismissed him as a holographic effect programmed by the haunted-house operators. But hologram or hoodoo, in his last form he had worn the brigand's swashbuckling hat and cape. So although this vision might be Gandolph/Edwina, it might also be this other man, who had appeared before Gandolph had died. A projection of the dead magician's spirit? Or . . .

No! Temple would not consider that eventuality. It was too far-out. Too "out there." Yet goosebumps lifted on her arms as she recalled the neighbors who had heard "voices" at Gandolph's house on Halloween night, at the very hour that first séance was taking place. Goosebumps remained as she remembered the three stages of man she had glimpsed in the ambiguous dark mirrors of the séance room windows. She remembered the frantic old man, mouthing syllables into the dark behind Gandolph's hatted head, the mouth moving, moving even as its owner vanished, until, like the Cheshire cat's grin, it was the very last thing seen, pantomiming a word, a word Temple could visualize, could imagine her own mouth making and could almost put a name to. . . .

"That smell!" Electra was taken aback. "It's not like before, not food or wine."

"Not chlorine," pronounced the professor.

"Roses," Agatha said with a smile in her voice. "The most delicious scent of roses. A kind spirit comes."

Roses, yes. Temple shut her eyes like Agatha, the better to let that heavenly scent roll over her, as tangible as the mist that clung to the room's square corners. Sweet beyond description, that perfume. Piped in probably, she reminded herself, but by a true romantic. It was to swoon for . . . and then, awash in scent, it came to her, the word, the key word to the entire business . . . the name of the rose, which was . . . Rose.

"Rose," she said aloud as a charm against the overwhelming tide of scent.

That is what the lips in her vision had striven to say. She saw the lips now, behind their barrier of beard, as if she had her fingers on them and read them like one deaf, and blind. *Rose.*

But there was a second syllable.

"Rose . . . Rosa . . . Rose-beh—"

"Oh, my God!" Professor Mangel sounded like he'd gone to the moon and back in the past three seconds. "Temple is picking it up. The key to Houdini's code that he left to his wife Bess. She can't have known it; she knew nothing about Houdini when this began."

"Yes!" Mynah sounded transported.

"R-R-Rose . . . Rosa . . . beh—" Temple almost had it, but not quite. The word. The one word to unbind them all.

Agatha Welk could not wait.

"*Rosabelle!*"

"We all know it," Mynah said. "Every devotee of Houdini for seventy years has hoped to hear it spoken genuinely at a Halloween séance. We all thought we would never hear it: the title of the song Houdini's wife sang in Vaudeville with her sister when Houdini met her. It was engraved inside Bess's wedding ring; it was in the safety-deposit box in which Houdini left the code verifying his return, an acrostic beginning with the letters R-O-S-A-B-E-L-L-E; the key to his cipher that would identify his return. If this . . . amateur has received it, then Houdini has sent it. We have broken through at last!"

Agatha's eyes had finally opened. They were filled with tears. She stared directly at Temple.

"After seventy years of silence, Houdini speaks. Through her!"

Chapter 38

Ghoststalker

"Oh, please, no close-ups." Temple blinked into the Cyclops face of Wayne's camera under its blazing coronet of light. "I was just . . . thinking out loud."

"Through you, Houdini speaks to us," Mynah said reverently. "I pave your path with peridot."

No one else understood the reference. *I don't want your miserable peridot,* Temple wanted to scream. *I don't want to be Houdini's conduit. I don't want to have seen what I saw, which apparently not everybody did. And, most of all, I don't want these two thousand megawatts of light in my face!*

Luckily, Wayne backed off to register everyone else's surprise. Temple sighed and loosened her grip on Sophie, who cared not, and on poor William Kohler, who sat like a lump of stuffed séance-potato beside her, offering her his fleshy hand to be wrung dry, which it desperately needed.

Temple gauged the people around her. They watched her with the wary awe of those who were convinced she had done something

346 • Carole Nelson Douglas

remarkable. This was the reaction Houdini had lived—and died—for? That Max was hooked on?

Temple hated it. She felt more like Matt. She felt like a fraud among frauds. She felt unworthy. Why had the little boy/old man made her the recipient of his undelivered message? Why did she have to see something others didn't? She wasn't psychic, just in the wrong place at the wrong time.

"And now he's come in person!"

Oscar Grant could only point with his eyes, but their dark stare focused on the chimney.

Temple joined the others in looking there, glad to have the spotlight, and Wayne's camera, directed elsewhere.

She didn't feel right about what had just happened. Something was missing. Looking to the window behind Agatha, she saw that the Edwina-figure was gone. Vanished. Disappeared.

The fireplace, however, was jumping.

Inside its smoky frame again stood the bound, stooped and chained figure of last week, the intense eyes staring out at them as boldly as the panther's.

Except now it moved.

A sharp clink sounded as a massive handcuff dropped to the hearth floor. The man in chains twisted, writhed. His naked muscles knotted with terrible effort. Hollow groans filled the room, the sounds echoing in the vast distances beyond the chamber.

The sight, the sounds were truly appalling. Temple watched with a wince; her cynical debunking eye was history.

A length of chain swagged across his chest fell loose, and then the arm and chest muscles bulged again and a two-inch-wide manacle snapped open with the ease of a cigarette case.

Now the figure crouched like a caveman to worry at the ankle manacles. Misty as the figure appeared, with every loosened bond it seemed to solidify. Breaking free was causing it to materialize. Houdini, suspected of dematerialization in life, was now guilty of materialization after death.

"He's coming for us!" Agatha crooned.

And at that moment dark swelling images crashed like bats against the windows. Images of a bat-man in black, with a floppy, veiled hat and shapeless cloak, Dracula beating at the glass for old blood, Gandolph clawing for breath and vengeance. . . .

Then the wall-mounted weapons began sweeping from wall to wall, and beyond. They crashed through the windows one after another, until the hand-clasps broke as one. The women lifted their arms against presumed flying glass, the men clutched the arms of their chairs as if hoping to wrest them off as weapons.

Only the battle-ax ranged through the room now, swooping as low as some demonic metal bat. The women screamed and protected their heads. Temple the cynical observer was too shocked to scream, but as unnerved as anybody. It was as if the mild phenomena of the first séance had returned, berserk and lusting for human blood.

And erratically flashing at the fringes was the headlight on Wayne Tracey's camera.

"Are you satisfied," he was shouting. "I'm shooting you. I've got footage of everything, you bastard. How does it feel to be dead, huh? You can't get me."

The chandelier above them bloomed with bright light. When they looked up, afraid, blood was dripping off its crystal teardrops, falling to the center of the table.

The battle-ax swung low and suddenly impaled itself dead center in the table, amid the dewdrops of blood.

And then the table elevated, shook, rattled and rolled, as if caught in a California earthquake.

Agatha closed her eyes, started screaming and didn't stop.

Through the jagged-edged broken windows came a mad, shrill screeching sound.

Everyone looked up and outward. The Gandolph images had vanished with the window glass, but the outer dark was still there, and it was moving.

Moving inward like a screaming black whirlpool.

"Watch out!" someone shouted. "Duck under the table."

Under this eighty-pound Mexican jumping bean? Temple wondered.

Then she saw the wave of flying bats catch the light of the chandelier.

She dove under the table, looking to see Electra in mid-duck too. Shrieks and flaps and crashes and clinks reverberated all around them.

"I did it!" Wayne Tracey was shouting over the pandemonium.

Temple saw him aiming his camera at the bats like a weapon, and cringed as she heard the creatures crash into the perimeters to avoid the light.

The table had descended to its proper place and now stood stolid where it was supposed to stand. Temple poked her head over its rim, to find other heads cautiously emerging. Only Agatha in her blind trance and William Kohler, glued to his Gothic chair like a straw man, had remained seated in place.

The camera's wild light careened around the room. Wayne zoomed in close on the effigy of Edwina Mayfair and began to interview it.

"What do you say now, Gandolph the Great? Now that you've been exposed for what you are. What do you say now? What do you say to all this? Spirits are real. They've shaken this room and everybody in it with their power. You didn't have to destroy Wanda Wayne Tracey. You fooled everybody with your disguise, but not me. Have you seen my mother there, in the Beyond? Has seeing her and seeing the Afterlife made you sorry you hurt and humiliated her? Has she forgiven you? She would, you know. But I won't. I didn't. I made you see that the spirits are real. Come back, so I can film you and show all the people you debunked what a fraud you were, in your disguise and your purpose. I'm not afraid of you, just because you're a spirit. We'll all be spirits someday, and you'll face me again."

"Sit down." D'Arlene Hendrix had come to stand behind Wayne Tracey as he hunched over the slumped soft sculpture form, his camera pushed against the featureless face under the veiled hat.

D'Arlene guided Wayne away, back to her empty chair, pushed him down in it.

"You don't need your camera on now. You've recorded everything," she said in a soothing voice.

When the light snapped off, everyone breathed a sigh of mutual relief. Slowly, they resumed their seats around the table, waiting.

"This young man," D'Arlene said, "has had a terrible burden of vengeance."

"He knew about Gandolph's disguise?" Temple asked.

"Apparently, from what we just heard. Apparently Gandolph had debunked his mother. Was she a medium, Wayne?"

Wayne nodded, staring at the battle-ax embedded in the table.

"I didn't mean to kill him. I wanted to expose him, scare him. I didn't want him to escape into the Afterlife. I wanted him to face consequences, like my mother did! The articles, the TV shows, the digs, the laughter. He went on television with hidden videotapes of her séances. He made the circuit . . . The *Tonight* Show when Johnny Carson was still doing it. Tom Snyder, on his first TV show. And after she'd been humiliated half to death, he and they went on to other victims. When she died last year, I knew I had to take action. I wanted you all to know what he was!" He looked around the table. "You can't blame me."

"I can," Crawford Buchanan put in. "You'll never work again in this town."

That seemed to stir some life in Wayne Tracey. He looked up and grinned. "Thanks. I needed that."

"What exactly did you do?" Temple asked carefully.

Wayne looked at her, but he didn't seem to recognize her. He was still walking through past emotions and present guilt. "I came in early to 'check lighting.' Nobody notices a cameraman, especially Crawford Buchanan's cameraman. The blades were already rigged to zip around on their almost-invisible lines, and I was supposed to stand on the sidelines. Once everyone was seated, I lengthened the line on the battle-ax, thinking it ought to come close enough to scare Gandolph. I didn't think it would cut him."

"It did, but it didn't kill him."

"Were you responsible for the fog?" Jeff Mangel asked. "That confused us."

Wayne shook his head.

"I—" Oscar Grant cleared his throat. "I came in hours early and rigged that. I needed effective footage for my show. I figured the murkier the better. I mean, the effects were here, why not use them?"

"And the chlorine?" Jeff Mangel sounded angry. "That made us all teary-eyed and confused."

"It was a screen." William Kohler's weak voice hit everyone like a clap of thunder, for he'd never spoken before in this room. "Mynah had me set up the projection of Houdini, and she didn't want anyone to see it too well."

"Shut up, you goddamn lump!" Mynah was not in the mood for confidences. Her face was the mask of a peeved Medusa and her silver hair fanned around that ugly expression as if it had been struck by heat lightning. "Can't you do anything right? Keep your mouth shut at least!"

"What about this latest Houdini tonight?" Temple asked William.

He suddenly grinned, his heavy face lightening. "Same photo, much better effects. I had nothing to do with it, and Mynah couldn't even thread a sewing machine to save her soul. I designed her whole setup at the house and made it work. Maybe poor old Gandolph had a hand in it. He was right; mediums are a bunch of lying fakes."

"Not all of them," D'Arlene Hendrix said from across the table where she held Agatha's hand on one side and kept her other hand on Wayne's forearm.

The gesture reminded Temple of something. "What about the handcuffs: Someone, or something, had to put Gandolph in irons and it had to be when he was already unconscious."

"A brilliant touch," Oscar conceded, "but not mine, alas. You were holding hands with the guy. Gal."

"True, and the cutlery flying around was distracting enough that I didn't notice Gandolph's hand slip from mine." She sighed.

Another silence.

"I thought she had just fainted," came a low, confessing voice.

"I should have known!" Temple turned on Crawford Buchanan like a watchdog. "Why did you even have the handcuffs with you? Planning a little S & M expedition after the séance, C.B.?"

"Don't excite yourself; we might have another untimely death to explain. No, they were a good prop. Television shows need visuals. I'd planned to throw 'em out on the table, so to speak, but when the old dame next to me keeled over I got the idea of cuffing her so it would look like Houdini had issued a challenge. Unfortunately she—he—was dead and it ruined the effect."

"Did you throw out the bullet Louie found too?"

Crawford shook his gel-slick black-haired head as soberly as the chief mourner at a mob funeral. "No, never thought of that. A bullet isn't big enough to show up well on camera."

"Then who contributed the bullet to the show-and-tell?" Temple asked the table at large.

No one 'fessed up to that particular red herring, and Midnight Louie certainly wasn't going to say where he found it.

Electra looked around like a lively white-haired robin. "Maybe the real Houdini was trying to take a shot at a lousy medium, and missed. So as far as phenomenon go, that only leaves the strange man we saw outside the windows unexplained."

"And the other smells," Jeff Mangel added. "The food, the wine—"

"The roses," Temple finished.

"Were you in on this?" Mynah suddenly demanded. "I always thought you were a treacherous bitch."

"No." D'Arlene answered for Temple with something very like righteous anger. "She honestly understood something the rest of us couldn't see, which makes her the only honorable medium in the room besides Agatha. You're projecting again, Mynah; you're trying to pass off your own dishonesty on someone else. It won't work anymore. Not after tonight. Word will get out. Here and Beyond. They don't call you the White Witch for nothing."

"I was going to say," Temple added, "that I've been called worse, but I don't think I have been. And it's true, I did think I saw someone outside the windows. I didn't get that word you all recognized from the likeness of Houdini, but from him, a tired old man, a kind of King Lear in a hat and cape."

"Maybe it was a prescient vision of Gandolph's spirit," Agatha said timidly. "I saw him too, and he looked much more like Gandolph than Houdini."

352 • Carole Nelson Douglas

"So we've failed." Oscar Grant's voice was heavy. "I suppose tonight's footage was useless."

"I'll take custody of that." Crawford stood and picked up Wayne's camera.

He almost dropped it again, being unaccustomed to the weight.

"What are you going to say about us, show about us on TV?" Mynah asked hysterically. "You can't believe a thing this so-called husband of mine says. Oscar is an utter fraud and Mangel's an academic fool and Agatha a neurotic and D'Arlene has pretensions of being some sort of head dorm-mother for helpless humanity—"

"You'll see. I may have something to sell to *America's Most Wanted*."

Crawford headed for the door, camcorder clutched like a babe to his chest.

Oscar stood up to shout at his departing back. "But nobody killed Gandolph, can't you see? He just died. Maybe his heart was bad; maybe he was allergic to chlorine, maybe he got blood poisoning from the ax? There's no crime here."

Crawford was gone, only the pounding of his footsteps down the stairs echoing up. Temple listened hard, hoping maybe she'd hear a crash.

"Well," Electra said. "Oscar is right. I don't see what we could report to the police . . . if any of us felt we ought to report to the police. But I must say that I am disappointed in many of you. I can't help thinking that the spirit world is too, and showed its disappointment in what we saw tonight. Temple, I think we should leave. It's been a very trying séance."

Temple stood, glad that her knees still supported her. Clearly, although Gandolph had died, no one had directly killed him, or had really meant to. She had arrived at the same conclusion as the police, much later, and after much more personal turmoil.

With all she had heard, there was something she couldn't get out of her mind. She had a confession to make too, about her part in the evening's events, but this was not the audience for it. Maybe the only audience for it was, as she had said before, not truly meaning it, "out there."

She meant that now.

Chapter 39

Ghostwriter in the Sky

Max's voice on the phone reverberates as from an echo chamber; it sounds like a communication from a ghost. Temple hasn't heard him on the phone for months. He sounds like a stranger again.

"You never did get to wear your prize shoes at the Crystal Ball at the Phoenix after the Halloween séance," he begins.

"No," she agrees. "But who told—?"

Max is a man less worried by who than by what. "Why don't you dig them out"—[he knows her closet]—"and we'll go out for dinner tonight?"

"But—"

"I can make out-of-the-way personal appearances, and I assume you're not a wanted woman . . . yet."

"Where can I wear such elaborate shoes?"

"Wherever you want to. You didn't worry about that before."

"I didn't have these shoes before. Max, I need to know where we're going so I know what else to wear."

"A classy little out-of-the-way place. Wear whatever goes with the shoes. I'll come by at seven."

Temple listens to the lull of the dial tone until the telephone wrangles at her to hang up. Max is even more mysterious than before. She used to love his spur-of-the-moment social style. It seemed spontaneous, fun. Now she understands that his sudden whimsical turns were dictated by grave considerations she never saw. Still, Max found the shoes; he deserves to celebrate his feat. Her feet. The Midnight Louie shoes.

Temple is ready by six-thirty and discovers that she can't sit down because Midnight Louie has left fine black hairs on every horizontal surface. She's wearing the ankle-length, stretch-velvet dress that never saw the lights of the Crystal Ball, and it's black anyway, but she doesn't want it to be furry too. Max isn't used to cat hair.

Tonight she's pinned a black enamel panther-head pin with emerald-green eyes a couple inches below the dress's soft turtleneck. Except for the Shoes, that's her only jewelry. She should be appropriately dressed for anything from Caesars Palace Court Continental restaurant to Three O'Clock Louie's at Temple Bar. She used to get so excited wondering where mysterious Max Kinsella would take her; now she's just worried. Should he be doing this? Is it safe? For him? For her?

He rings the doorbell, like a good lad.

She realizes she's never opened the door for him in this place. It does feel a little like prom night, only any flowers she'd get from Max would be paper.

He's wearing a matching black turtleneck, not velvet, and black blazer, slacks, shoes.

She can't help smiling. "We look like we're going to a mime's funeral."

"Except for your shoes." He looks down and she turns, the flared skirt swinging out. "Spectacular, but I hope you don't think the real Midnight Louie should have a night out too."

"No. He's resting comfortably in the bedroom."

Max wanders in, looks toward the room under discussion. "I suppose he regards it as his territory now."

Temple thinks, and decides to leave that unanswered.

Max turns. "Ready?"

For what? "Sure."

She picks up her only evening bag, a silver minaudière on a black satin string.

"Coat?"

"How cold can it get?" She holds out her arms in their wrist-length sleeves.

"You'll be all right."

She hopes so.

Locking the door behind her seems ostentatious, especially when she drops her key-heavy chain into the shallow black mouth of the tiny purse.

On the way down in the elevator Max leans against the polished wood. Temple wonders what kind of wheels he uses now.

It's cooler and darker outside than she had expected. In the parking lot, her aqua Storm is parked next to Electra's pink Probe; together they look like an ad for a *Miami Vice* rerun. Next to them sits a new Taurus that looks . . . black.

Max opens the passenger door. "Gandolph's."

"Can you just use it?"

"I'm his heir," Max mentions after he gets in and pulls on the seat belt.

"Won't that be awkward? Won't you have to show up in court eventually?"

"No." Max doesn't explain further, and his voice, his profile don't encourage Temple to probe.

She stares ahead, thinking that the evening feels all wrong, that the Taurus isn't Max and it isn't her, it's a dead man's hearse. It's a dead relationship's hearse. The little purse sits on her lap like a dead thing, heavy and still. She curls her hands around it, not being used to carrying small purses, or sitting in a well-upholstered sedan with velour upholstery, or feeling like she's in a magazine ad for something.

Only when the car makes several turns does she look at Max.

"Ah, is this place we're going to on the west side?"

He nods. She'll have to get used to that ponytail in profile. It doesn't look bad, just different. Like the car. Temple is terribly afraid that they are heading in the wrong direction, but doesn't know how to say so, so she says nothing, not even when the Taurus turns into the parking lot of the Blue Dahlia.

Disastrous! Temple is speechless. Sick. Shocked. Does not dare say anything. Then she glances cautiously at Max, and suddenly suspects that he knows exactly—*exactly*—what he is doing. He grins at her like Sean Connery as James Bond, insouciantly pleased with himself, with her.

"I just discovered this place. Quite unusual."

Temple nods in a daze, trying not to notice the place in the lot where she and Matt collapsed with laughter at the idea of Molina the singing policewoman.

This is getting interesting. Just how much does Max know about the Blue Dahlia, and who sings there sometimes, and when Temple might have been there and with who? Whom? Whoever.

She is demure as he lets her out like a large little gentleman.

They are like two coiled springs trying to guess when the other will make like a Slinky and flip . . . right for the stairs and a hasty exit.

They enter the restaurant, are shown to a table for two lit by the small coral-shaded lamp she remembers from last time.

"This is darling," she remarks, as she probably did last time.

"It's fairly new. Since my . . . sabbatical."

"Is that what you're calling it?"

He settles into the chair, which he has to push back from the table to accommodate his legs, as usual. "It's as good a term as any. Do you like it?"

He means the restaurant, of course. Temple looks around. The small dance floor is empty, but a few musicians are shaking out their arms and their instruments under the spotlit stage area. A lone stool sits at the side, unoccupied.

Temple strokes the cold metal purse on the white tablecloth. She should probably tell Max they have to leave now, that Molina could come in at any moment, but when she looks at him he seems so at ease, so in control, so sure of himself that she can't quite warn him.

Besides, then he'd ask her how she knew Molina sang here and she'd have to explain she'd been here before, which would ruin the "surprise" aspect of the evening, always a big thing with Max. And then he'd ask with who—whom?—not out of jealousy but because he always wants to know everything about everything; that's what makes him a master magician, always knowing every situation inside out.

And she'd have to say it was just a dinner out with Matt, hating that "just," because that seemed to put Matt down and he didn't deserve it.

Better to let Molina nab Max and let him break himself out of jail afterward, Temple decides morosely, than to ruin the present with an autopsy of the recent past.

"You seem more serious than usual," Max says.

"Just worried."

"About what?"

"Our being out in public like this. *Your* being out like this."

"Let me worry about me; I've been doing it for a while." Max's smile could cut through fog. "Come on, you want to show off those shoes, don't you?"

He takes her hand to draw her up and onto the tiny parquet dance floor.

No one else is there, but Max is used to solo numbers in the spotlights. The musicians have indeed got it together by now and are playing something familiar and forties and vaguely Brazilian (fascinatin' rhythm).

Max can dance and, as he's proving tonight, has even mastered some ballroom moves. Temple thinks that she is doing the samba or something similar, but it doesn't matter what she thinks she's doing, because Max's lead is so smooth and so strong that she is doing just the right thing no matter what. She had forgotten how easy it was to dance with Max, because she is so small and he isn't. He's right; they'd be great on stage together if she could stand to be locked in cramped cabinets and wear fishnet hose. Well, maybe she wouldn't have to wear fishnet hose. . . .

Max can slow-dance too, and Temple is swung out and drawn in, whatever the music and moment dictates, until she stops worrying and looking out of the corner of her eye to see if the stool is occupied yet or if any yellow-haired ghosts are watching from the sidelines.

They are of course making a spectacle of themselves, exactly what Max shouldn't be doing for his own good, but then her shoes might be drawing a tad of attention away from him. Midnight Louie would like that.

"You're finally smiling," Max says when the music has them swaying together cheek to shoulder again.

"I haven't danced like this in a while."

"Me neither."

When the fourth number starts and they leave the floor, a smattering of applause accompanies them.

"Honestly." Temple unfolds her napkin with one mighty wrist shake and arranges it carefully on her delicate velvet lap. "What an exhibitionist. You couldn't remain undercover in a dust storm."

While Temple is taking her worry out on the table linen, Max has folded his napkin into an intricate star-shape, which he presents to her like a bouquet. In the center is one breathlessly perfect, perfectly pink fresh rosebud.

She stares at him with the proper amazement, not so much for the trick and the posy, but for the underlying meaning. And suddenly the night is not a dream, but the opening act for just what she needed, distance and a sudden snap back to reality, time for a discussion:

"For your sterling performance among the mediums the other night," Max said. *"Magnifique."*

"You . . . you were there?"

"Who do you think stage-managed the entire thing?"

"Max, you couldn't have."

"Of course I could have. It's what I do."

"But you were home, asleep."

"I should have been," he agreed as the cocktail waitress sashayed into place, flouncing her abbreviated ruffles into his shoulder.

"Temple?" he asked.

She waved her hand. "Surprise me."

Max took the waitress's order pad and wrote something on it. She dipped with a wink and vanished.

"How did you even know about the second séance?"

"I didn't, until I called Electra that morning to see if you'd gotten home safely."

"Max, you didn't!"

"She told me you were resting for the séance that night. She seemed particularly pleased to hear from me."

"I bet she did."

"Asked if I'd been spending a lot of time at the library lately, and what I'd been looking up."

"Grrrr."

"Do you have any idea what that was about?"

"Electra's unquenchable curiosity. Okay, so you then hie over to the haunted house and set up. Didn't the Glory Hole boys get in your way?"

"So you're responsible for that added complication! We were working at cross-purposes, apparently, but it came out all right in the end. The old guys didn't come along until after ten o'clock, so I was mostly set. I just had to make sure they didn't see my illusions in motion and blow the whistle."

"What did you hope to accomplish?"

"I don't know. I only know that magic has always worked for me when I most desperately need it. I hoped, I guess, to flush out the conscience of a killer."

"And succeeded beyond your wildest dreams, as always."

"Not always. I still have some wild dreams left."

Temple toyed with the cut rose at her place. "What effects exactly did you produce?"

He looked as if he didn't know where to start. "The panther."

"Where did you get a panther? You're not working with one now."

"No, but a lot of magicians do. Nice size cat, very dramatic, easier to handle than a lion or tiger. Kahlúa was on loan for the night."

"Then . . . the fireplace was lined with mirror . . . or you had installed a false back."

Max shrugged modestly.

"But, Max, you were the walking dead when I left you at Gandolph's house."

"And after I talked to Electra I'd had, oh, four hours' sleep, so I walked right over to the haunted house and started setting up. You know how much intense effort is involved installing a magic show; same thing. I'm used to working under pressure."

"But how could you know that the psychics would react to the phenomena?"

"Modesty is not one of my weaknesses, of which there are many." Temple rolled her eyes.

"I guess you know that from experience," Max added modestly. "I happen to believe that any competent magician—and I am far, far more than competent—can outdo any fraudulent medium. I figured if I put their tawdry tricks to shame, they'd be so unnerved they'd begin to believe they had conjured something real. Even fake mediums hope for genuine success. They wouldn't be in the spook business if they didn't half believe."

"Well, it worked like a charm, Kinsella. I'd have you take a bow, but you're a wanted man."

"Wanted here right now, I hope."

Temple glanced toward the stage. "I hope not."

"She's not coming."

"What?"

"I love it when you're surprised silly and trying not to show it. You do such a good job, but not quite good enough. Molina isn't singing tonight."

"You know about her performing here?"

Max nodded. "She's on a case; not a chance in homicide that she'll turn up."

"And you brought me here, with me thinking you were walking into the lion's mouth? Why?"

"It's a fun place. It's where I wanted to be with you, sans the songstress, of course. Why should I let a detail like Molina stop me? All I had to do was check the duty roster—"

"In the police computer!"

"Right. It's never magic, Temple. It's just damn good planning."

Like magic, a drink in a footed glass appeared in front of Temple. Foamy, pink. A Pink Lady. The waitress dipped to position a matching green drink in front of Max. A Grasshopper. Together, the two drinks looked a lot like Electra's Probe and Temple's Storm: *Miami Vice* colors.

"I think you got it wrong this time, Kinsella." Temple sipped her drink through the straw. "Dessert first, substance later."

"The mediums and son of medium nicely confessed, didn't they?"

"To harassing Gandolph to death. None of them necessarily killed him, or even meant to. No arrests, no trial, no case closed. No vengeance either."

"The book will be vengeance. I'm hoping you can help me with it."

"With the writing?"

"Nope. Oh, maybe some light editing. No, I need a front woman."

"A flack to hype it?"

Max shook his head. "A ghostwriter to take credit. I don't care to be in the limelight. You'll do nicely. Of course it will be a co-author credit with Gandolph the Great."

"Max, it's a pity you can't do it; you'd be much more promotable as co-author."

"Can't. Anyway, I won't be able to finish it for a year or so. Gary had lots of research and notes to cull through. At least the project will keep me off the public streets."

Temple picked up the rose she'd laid by her water glass to inhale the indescribably wonderful scent again.

"Aha! What about the bats, the hundreds and hundreds of bats?"

"They did scare the goblins right off the rafters and tangled my many lines of illusion. I assume they were imported to have at the happy haunted-house patrons. Or has Houdini adopted a familiar?"

"Not a genuine bat in sight when I did my tour of duty at the Hell-o-ween Haunted Homestead, and nothing to do with Houdini, or Welles. Some protesters were picketing the Halloween attraction for vilifying spiders and snakes and rats and bats. I bet the zealots salted the empty premises with a brood of bats once the attraction had closed to make a point how peaceful the critters are."

"As you have made a point." Max bowed his head in her direction. "I'm delighted that I didn't suffer the slings of bat guano for some more sinister reason."

"So you created everything: the panther, Houdini's second appearance, the flying martial arts weapons, the fog, the figure in space."

"Or amplified what was already there. What figure in space?"

"The Gandolph-like figure in the Edwina hat and cloak that everybody saw floating in the darkness and the distance."

"Mass hysterical delusion." Max dismissed the phenomenon. "Didn't hurt the impact of my effects, though."

"I think there was something there."

"Of course. There's always something there when people see things. Reflections, or just an expectant state of mind."

"No. That figure was real. I saw it at the previous séance, in three stages: boy, man and elder prophet. So did Agatha Welk. The others saw something then too, but they took it for a hologram programmed by the haunted-house operators. They never saw it with the detail I did, especially when it appeared last behind Gandolph, before he was dead, the mouth saying something—"

"Temple, you've had a trying time. Sit back, relax, drink your drink."

"You're sounding complacent, Max, and I find that annoying."

"I know better than to annoy a redhead, unless she wants me to."

"Well, you're rubbing me the wrong way now. I know what I saw. I mean it! I finally know what I saw, and it wasn't Houdini and it certainly wasn't phantoms from the ingenious mind of Max Kinsella."

He was silent.

Temple picked up the rose. "This is lovely. Thanks. But . . .you gave it to me for the wrong reason."

"How so?"

"You remember when I was trying to come up with the word?"

"Wonderfully ingenious. I had no idea you had researched Houdini enough to know the whole Rosabelle routine. Worked perfectly with my illusions to unhinge the mediums. That's what finally did the trick and loosened their tongues. When you came up with 'Rosabelle.' "

"That's just it, Max. I didn't come up with 'Rosabelle.' "

"But . . . you said it."

"No, I started to say something like it, and the mediums jumped on it. We've all been looking for the wrong ghost. It's like you always say. People see what they expect to see. People hear what they expect to hear. Even Max Kinsella. Sometimes."

He was listening now, his face serious, sober.

"I was trying desperately to remember the one true thing I saw at the other séance: the figure through the window. And the last time I saw him, the last thing I saw was his lips forming a word over and over. A last voiceless word. He stood right behind Gandolph, and I think he was trying to warn him of danger."

"Why would any ghost want to warn Gandolph . . . unless it was his dead mother—?"

Temple shook her head. "This ghost has a lot in common with Houdini and Gandolph. And you. 'Ghost' isn't an adequate word. 'Spirit' is better. This was a spirit that would not be quenched in life, despite many reasons. A man who was born in Wisconsin on a date very near Houdini's amended birth date. A man who was deeply attached to his mother, though she died when he was still a child. A magician with an intimate connection to Gandolph, and even to you.

"And I didn't realize that until I searched for the word. I work with words. I write them. I used to say them in front of a camera. I can't lip-read, but I have a certain instinct. So I was trying to sound out that unspoken two-syllable word."

"Not 'Rosabelle'?" Max looked bewildered, but like a believer.

Temple shook her head.

"I was *just* getting it when they interrupted me and declared it to be 'Rosabelle.' But it wasn't."

"What was it, then?"

"One word, a last word, from long ago."

"Temple, don't tease me."

She took a deep breath and inhaled the rose's scent first. And last.

"Rosebud."

Max and Temple were back on the dance floor, stunned in the spotlight.

After a long time, Max spoke.

364 • Carole Nelson Douglas

"The arguing voices the neighbors heard Halloween night."

"Yes?"

"I have an idea, but we'll have to go back to the house."

"Fine."

"Can you wait until after dinner?"

"No."

"Too bad we're not talking about something else."

"First things first."

"I still can't believe it."

"I don't expect you to."

"It changes everything."

"Not everything, but a lot. We'd better go."

Max pulled her closer and rested his chin on the top of her head. "One more number; it helps me think."

"That's a new one."

"The music. Cryptographers use music to get themselves in a de-coding mood. Very mathematical and inspiring, music."

Temple smiled. After what she'd told Max, she felt like being held, because the implications were very scary. Being held on a dance floor was both stimulating and safe. Max seemed to think so, too, as they swayed together.

"Oooh! What was that?" Temple asked after a dramatic move.

"A dip. I understand that they're all the rage."

"Where'd you learn to do a dip?"

"Danny Dove isn't a bad example."

"You were all over the romance convention too?"

"Maybe I needed to learn a thing or two."

"I don't think so."

They spun in a tight circle as the music shifted into the intro for another instrumental.

Words were running through Temple's mind. Rosebud. Halloween. Ghosts. Midnight Louie. Black magic. Spells. *That old black magic* . . .

Those last words weren't thought, or merely mouthed without sound, or even spoken. They were sung! Temple looked up, appalled, at Max.

He was staring over her head, appalled. "Damn! She's supposed to be investigating a transient murder on the north side."

Instead, Molina's contralto was crooning softly over the microphone.

Max backed them out of the light and off the dance floor. They slunk along the sidelines to the door, where Max thrust some bills at the headwaiter.

"Emergency. Got to leave. For that table over there. Waitress in the ruffly thing."

"Max, they're all in ruffly things," Temple whispered as they tiptoed out, much good as discretion did now. "Did she see us? I couldn't bear to look."

"She's onstage. The lights are in her eyes. She wasn't expecting us."

"And vice versa. So she couldn't see us."

"Probably did." Max sounded resigned.

"My purse!" Temple stopped dead in the parking lot.

Max reached into his jacket and produced it.

"Oh, thank God."

She stopped again. "My rose!"

He reached into his pocket, came up with a ten-dollar bill folded into a rose. "I'll have to make you another one."

Temple shook her head. "If she's seen you?"

"What can she do?"

"Arrest you."

"Find me first." He let her in the car and went around. "Sorry about dinner."

"At least we hadn't ordered yet."

"I've still got the linguini Alfredo."

"Done."

The drive back to the house wasn't as self-conscious as the earlier drive.

"I'm almost afraid to go in," Temple commented when they stood in the garage before the connecting door to the house.

"It's not haunted."

The kitchen was so big and impressive it was impossible to be scared once Max had turned on all the under- and over-counter lights.

He rummaged in the cabinets, then turned to consult her. "Do you want to eat here or on the opium bed?"

"You don't *eat* on that priceless bed?" Temple envisioned cracker crumbs in the fretwork.

"Ah, no," Max admitted. "I thought we could eat . . . after."

"I think we better talk . . . first."

"First wine, then." He ducked through the glass door to emerge with another rare bottle of something. "At least we can drink on the opium bed."

"You seem a little fixated."

"It's comfortable. Besides, all Gary's furniture is huge and clubby. It's my turn to confide a few home truths; let me choose the confessional, at least."

Glasses and wine bottle accompanied them to the bedroom where the opium bed provided the exotic centerpiece.

Temple had to step out of the Midnight Louie shoes like a good little geisha girl before climbing onto the embroidered satin coverlet. The bed was built like a latticed house, even a sort of gazebo, with open roof and sides. It was as cozy as a children's playhouse on a rainy day, despite the inlaid cinnabar and mother-of-pearl. Temple could see why Max liked lounging there; it was vast enough to accommodate his length both ways. He installed the wine bottle on a table behind the bed's low back, then settled into a pillow-piled corner.

Temple sat cross-legged beside him, sipping her wine.

"What's your theory?" he asked.

"I think that Orson Welles's . . . spirit felt protective toward Gandolph. It also was drawn to Houdini."

"Welles called himself 'The Great Orson' when he performed magic. And he was born, forty-one years after Houdini, a month later, to the day: May sixth, nineteen-fifteen."

"And of course Halloween is a key date for him, too."

"The Martian-landing radio broadcast on Halloween in nineteen thirty-nine that half the country took for real. It was the first time he shocked the world, but not the last."

"The 'noises' heard here on Halloween night, that could have been a spectral radio replay! And Welles, like Houdini and Gandolph, was devoted to his mother. Didn't he live mostly with her as a child?"

"Yes. She was a superb singer, a very cultured woman."

"So, given these similarities and Houdini's death on Halloween and his tremendous will, I think Orson Welles's spirit drew somehow on this conjunction of forces and learned that Gandolph could be in danger."

"Then he appeared to warn him. But he didn't save him."

"How do we know he didn't? The battle-ax might have killed him otherwise. What no one—and maybe not even a spirit—could know was Gandolph's cardiac vulnerability. He had no history of heart disease, but I think the stress of the séance killed him."

"Hmm." Max nodded and poured more wine in his glass.

"There's something you're not telling me."

"For one thing, I've had the advantage of poking through Gary's files on mediums. He had all your séance partners on disk."

"And—?"

"They all did have motives for killing him. Obviously, Wayne Tracey might have had much more lethal feelings than he confessed to, but Oscar Grant was not simply the respected host of a rather unrespected television show, he—"

"Had a gang history in L.A. Maybe drugs. Maybe still drugs today."

Max let his eyebrows lift in tribute. "Very good. Very true. And of course the treacherous bitch—"

Temple interrupted him again. "How did you know about that?"

"You think I would rig the room and neglect a microphone and tape recorder? Anyway, the lovely Mynah's extramarital affairs were legion, including a revived encounter with her own exhusband, Oscar. I wouldn't be surprised if she was getting it on with the spirits in between more fleshly engagements. Exposure would not have helped her, and besides it could have endangered her marriage."

"Why would she care?"

"Because William Kohler made all the money. He financed her New Age retreat."

"No! That . . . slouch potato? Where'd he get the money?"

"He's a stockbroker, and not a very ethical one, according to Gary's investigation. He also operates a lucrative financial newsletter. A scandal about Mynah and her New Age psychic and physical escapades would undercut his creditability."

"And the others?"

"Well, D'Arlene Hendrix seems to have done some good on the psychic front, but the reason the police took her in for questioning is that they discovered that Gandolph had been questioning police departments she worked with about her methods. That sort of thing makes the police suspicious, and his inquiries certainly weren't helping her reputation with law enforcement. Her work is her life, so . . ."

"So Gandolph was a real threat to her, simply by investigating. But surely Agatha and the professor—"

"Oh, tried and true, each in their own field; but Mangel is up for a prestigious chair and now soft-pedaling his approval of psychic phenomena, which made any possibility of appearing in a Gandolph investigation troublesome. In fact, he hasn't participated in a séance for two years, which makes one wonder why he would come to Las Vegas for such a public stunt just now—"

"Unless he knew Gandolph was living here and expected him to find the Houdini Halloween séance irresistible. Is anyone really that serpentine?"

"Tem-ple," Max rebuked her with great green cat-eyes.

"And Agatha? I'm afraid to ask."

"Simply put: quite crackers. She tried to poison some tea-reading subjects, under the assumption that they would make good contacts in the spirit world if she had sent them there herself. She was ultimately released from the mental hospital, but you know how overcrowding permits premature release of all sorts of people."

Temple sat bolt upright, clutching at her throat.

"Temple?"

"Poison in the tea? Max, I *drank* her tea, when she did her reading and warned me about a short dark man who was a secret ally. Hey, maybe she meant 'male,' not man. That could have been Midnight Louie!"

"Like all objects of predictions, you're finding ways to justify them. How long ago did you drink tea with Agatha?"

"Two days ago, but—ahh! I feel as if I'd swallowed a bug, or at least a marijuana joint; either way it's a roach."

Max patted her on the shoulders. "Two days? Drink your wine, then, and bless your lucky stars that dear Agatha didn't consider you good spirit fodder."

"Well, they all could have killed Gandolph, then."

Max topped off her glass, and then refilled his own empty one.

"Aren't you hitting that a little heavy?"

"Yes. Yes, I am. You see, there's another means and motive that could have killed Gary. I still suspect human intervention, only I can't prove it, and I doubt any trace will be found. But to explain my theory I can't research dead magicians' lives or their computer files. I can't rely on the spirit world showing me the way. I have to exhume some rather painful parts of my own life."

Max smiled a bit crookedly at Temple. "Want to help me turn over some of the auld sod?"

She just nodded.

Max stared past her, into the opium bed's farthest corner. Temple wondered what ghosts might haunt an artifact like this, what dreams, what nightmares. Maybe that was why Max liked it; it took his mind off his own dreams and nightmares.

"What you call my 'Interpol summer,' when I was sixteen-going-on-seventeen: our families sent my cousin Sean and me to Ireland our senior summer before college. You know my full roster of given names. Michael Aloysius Xavier. Sean got Patrick Donnell too. Our families were fourth-generation American, but their hearts were still in the homeland.

"Sean and I were best buddies. The summer was to be a last lark before hitting the books for real. I was going to major in communications and earn money on the side with magic shows. Sean was going to become a history professor. Our families' blessings and a list of a few hundred cousins all over the auld sod accompanied us on our first big trip away from home."

"It must have been a fabulous opportunity."

"It was. Except two teenagers loose in a foreign land will try anything: passing for overage in pubs, dating every colleen that clog-dances, talking passionate politics. . . . We were appalled at the op-pression in Northern Ireland. Most American sympathies are with the Irish, because so many of us fled here during the Famine.

"It's a long, sad story, so let me boil it down for you. We got to hanging around with the wrong elements; we got caught up in the uncivil war over there. It was all so involving, so eye-opening, so exotic. We didn't know how to walk the thin line between orange and green, we didn't even see it. Sean was blown up in an IRA hit."

"No!"

"I would have been there to be blown up too, except . . . there was a girl we both met, both flirted with. She was a bit older in years, and decades in experience. I was off with her when Sean died. We'd had a real fight about it, bloody knuckles and everything. Sean stormed off, went to the wrong pub, and that was that."

"Max, that's awful. But how did you end up suspected of being part of the IRA?"

Max swigged the expensive wine as if it were beer. "I joined the IRA, determined to find the ones who had killed Sean. Then I would turn them in."

"What? But you sympathized with the IRA."

"Not then."

"There's a name for that."

"Counterespionage. I doubt I could have spelled it then. It was a guilt-offering. I'd gone home for the funeral. Of course we'd each written home all summer, and Sean had written of our romantic tri-angle. I discovered he'd always taken it more seriously than me. If I'd have known I'd have bowed out, but it seemed like a game, a friendly competition. Anyway, at the funeral it was obvious that Sean's parents blamed me. My folks, of course, were fiercely parti-san on my behalf. So the war came back to Wisconsin. My family didn't want me to go back to Ireland, but our two families had al-ways been close. I couldn't stand the carnage, so I left."

"And became a teenage spy."

"There are no teenagers in Ireland, north and south, Temple. At least not in those days, and not for centuries before. Children fight that guerrilla war, and pay for it and die for it. I was in way over my head, but I did finally trace the cadre of men who had bombed that particular pub. All my magic practice proved to be quite useful, after all. Then I turned them over to the British."

Temple propped her elbows on her thighs and put her face in her hands.

"I know. For the fantasy of avenging Sean and purging myself of guilt I put my entire life into a meat-grinder. I didn't even understand yet that the particular bombers didn't matter, that it was a conflict that had been bigger than anybody in it, including me, for centuries."

"How did you survive?"

"I didn't. I ran, to the Continent, and that wasn't far enough. In some circles what I did was considered an accomplishment, because I was finally found and offered a 'scholarship' by . . . another organization."

"What do you mean?"

"I can't say much more. There are those who oppose terrorism in any cause, in any place. Nations, commercial concerns, individuals. They offered me sanctuary; they offered me an education all over Europe, a chance to become a real magician; they offered me a family, and a more positive career in global espionage. Gary was allied with them. One of my first tutors. He could have been killed for that past, and there would be no trace."

"But he was retired, even from his magician career, wasn't he?"

"There is no retirement. I tried, and you saw what happened."

Temple nodded slowly. "I was your retirement."

He reached for her hand. "You weren't very retiring, though. That's why Gandolph has to have a book out; not just because the subject was dear to his heart, and he deserved a life after his many years of service and risk, but some . . . elements might fear what he would write. If this rather innocuous book on mediums is published, that will lull their suspicions. They will think that was all that was in his mind and his computer files."

"This is insane! You have to go through the rigmarole of publishing an entire book just to mislead someone?"

"Not for Gary's sake. It's too late. For mine. The more normal I can make the life around me, the more chance I've got of escaping the old life."

"But you were a public person, a performer before."

"And that was tolerated as long as they knew where I was and what I was doing. I wasn't a danger to anyone. You're only dangerous when you drop out. I might have tried for a new identity ultimately. That's why I was so unfair to involve you, but I was tired of life on the run, of being aloof from anybody human, from love. I guess I reverted to being a stupid teenager again when I met you, Temple, and that was that."

"No one has ever told me that it takes a stupid teenager to get involved with me."

"You know what I mean. I have no business being with you now. So if you have something . . . compelling going on in your life, just tell me, and you'll never hear from me again."

"Oh, fabulous. It's either all or nothing with you. And this noble renunciation doesn't ring very true when you seem fairly obsessed with us getting back to where we used to be . . . in bed together."

"Oh, absolutely," he admitted. "In a New Delhi minute. No lies or obfuscations there. I just don't know if I can be there tomorrow, or the next day, or if it's safe for you. I'm tired of other people paying for knowing me."

"And in a way you like it: popping in and out of people's lives like a stage magician, mystifying them, confusing everyone, your friends as well as your enemies."

"Maybe you're right." Max finished his second glass of wine. "We'll find out."

"How?"

"I'm staying this time, Temple. I'm not running again. I may have to lie low. I may have to work some not-so-legal magic, but I'm going to get to the bottom of everything that's worked against me in the past. Do you have any problems with that?"

There was only one possible answer.

"We'll find out," she said.

Chapter 40

The Mother of All
Hauntings

I am by no means a fancier of the occult.

I do not wish to see what is not there, and even what is there if it is not readily apparent to the average individual.

I have never been subsumed into the belly of an extraterrestrial vehicle. The only missing time I suffer is when I am snoozing.

I have never walked through walls unless a door or window of some kind had gotten there before me. And I have never walked on water except occasionally in the pursuit of carp, and then only for the tiniest nanosecond.

So I am not enthralled by my recent encounters with things that go bump in the night, apparently having grown myopic in the Afterlife.

Most of all, I am sorry to have been visited by the spirit of the original Maurice. I was really happier not knowing that Maurice is—was—a decent dude I might even have liked in life, with no particular interest in the Divine Yvette, had certain appalling events not come to pass. How am I better off knowing that the yellow-striped dude who struts his stuff on the Yummy Tum-tum-tummy commercials today is a homocidal huckster who has dusted the true spokescat. We are talking a body double with a triple helping of chutzpah.

So, given my distaste for spirit emanations, you will understand that only my great loyalty to Miss Temple Barr could have lured me back to the Hell-o-ween Haunted Homestead on the occasion of the second séance. In television circles this is called a rerun, plain and simple.

However, I got more than I bargained for, least among them the hysterical bats bouncing their high-pitched little screeches off my cranium.

Of course the actual goings-on of that event are hardly known to the human participants, who, as usual, missed the main events.

I arrived before the first of the so-called psychics, ready to scout the territory for any unauthorized spooks. My attention was first drawn to someone big in a black catsuit. At first I took it for my esteemed sire, Three O'Clock Louie, but no such luck. Once the little shop of Halloween horrors was closed for the season, the organizers did not need local color any more. Three O'Clock was returned to his retirement home on Lake Mead. Besides, this new cat is a more impressive dude than my old man, being kept in a cage . . . except that an introductory sniff reveals that this is no dude! Her name, I discover after a few gingerly inquiries, is Kahlúa and she does a nightly disappearing act at the Oasis.

"So, who's paying the freight on your ruby collars tonight?"

"Colleague of my boss's," Kahlúa answers with a quite unnecessary preliminary snarl. (I think she just likes the sound of her own voice.) Like the coffee-flavored liqueur she is named for, Kahlúa is strong, dark and heady. Her big green eyes flash toward the catwalk under the roof. "He is a long, narrow cat all in black, fast as a mongoose and smooth as a velvet glove. I would go anywhere to work with him."

Naturally, I had spotted the Mystifying Max right away, so I never had any delusions about who was pulling strings in the dark wings above the séance chamber. (I feel the word "chamber" adds a nice touch of the classy macabre to the scene below.)

"So what is on your program tonight?" I ask the lady, who is obviously a prima donna of in-the-body prestidigitation, unlike Karma, who just projects her meddling ditzy little aura into situations that are none of her business.

"Cameo role." Kahlúa touches up her manicure. "Nothing to break a nail over. I do my usual appearing act in a fireplace, look gorgeous, exotic and lethal, then bug out as usual. I could do it in my sleep."

"You might not want to," I warn her. "I did a sudden entrance down that same chimney and it is rigged with enough fishline to bag a barracuda."

"Thanks for the tip, but Mr. Max would never let me go into a situation he had not checked out from top to bottom," Kahlúa tells me with a yawn that reveals a maw the size of a pink-velvet cave lined with elephant tusks for teeth.

Well, Midnight Louie does not have a devoted frontman to do his dirty work for him, but I am not about to point this out to Kahlúa when she is showing her dentures. Those fangs are probably all capped or bonded or bleached. Show biz!

Bidding this she-panther a distant farewell, I explore the rest of the area. That is when I discover an even bigger population explosion at the fringes of the séance chamber. Eightball, Wild Blue and Spuds of the Glory Hole Gang are posted as guards on all three levels, at Miss Temple's behest, I suspect. I am relieved to know that reinforcements are at hand should revelations during the séance prove too dramatic for a guilty party's nerves.

It is while I wander—small (relatively speaking), silent and the same color as the vast darkness that surrounds the séance chamber—that I become aware of disquieting influences.

For there are again Uninvited Guests. I am still seeing much more than I should be. Not a glimpse of Elvis and Amelia and Mae, sadly (to them I could sell tickets), but faint flickers of the phantoms seen before, like photo stills from old black-and-white films. The boy in the Little Lord Flauntleroy suit dangles from a rollercoaster scaffold. The fat old man in black sits in empty air, hunched under a bandit's hat and over a cane—or is that what's left of Edwina Mayfair, animated by the spirit of Gandolph the Great? Even Old Doyly, the hearty-looking (for a ghost) chap with pipe who seemed to be urging on Houdini's apparition flickers in and out of view near the baronial fireplace in the séance chamber. As for the reputed Houdini himself, what a fizzle! I do not see even a mote of his previous image, crouched in his seine of chains, a bare pale gray blot on the darkness. Why do all these ghost guys turn up in shades of gray? I wonder. They are a sober-sided lot, unlike Elvis. It is nice to know the King is having a blast even in the Beyond. I hope that when my lives have run their course, I will have as much *joie de vivre* in the Afterlife too.

I finally find a concealed niche where I can get an overview of the action below without coming into the purview of the Mystifying Max or the Glory Hole Boys. With my natural advantages of coat and color, I am part of the scenery at this scene of the crime . . . or crime to be confessed.

And I like the setup: the séance chamber has no roof, which makes sleight-of-hand easy to perform, and easy to oversee. I am not deceived for one moment by the stuffed figure that looks like it escaped from a taxidermist's shop; I have seen soft-sculpture people, and animals, before, and much prefer them to the real things. One by one the dramatis personae arrive. My little doll and Karma's Madame Electra are the last to assemble.

Above me, I can see the Mystifying Max moving like some giant spider to set strands of his hidden web in motion. So I am not distracted by the usual spooky effects below. Neither fog nor knives nor sniff of chlorine will deter Midnight Louie from his appointed duty: to seek out the wrong elements of the bigger picture. I do not know what I expect to spy from my cozy point of view. Another murder attempt, perhaps? A guilty party reacting to the evening's entertainment? Alas, all of the Mystifying Max's wonders—and they are much more chilling than the previous tricks—do not smoke out the lurking menace we all search for. Kahlúa, her throaty voice a symphony of danger and disdain, makes a much more prepossessing apparition in the hearth than yours truly, I fear. The Houdini image actually moves. The dancing cutlery whirls like ninja wheels. And the gathered attendees regard the effects with a certain nervous stoicism that does not bode well for an instant confession.

Then my sharp eyes notice something. Miss Temple Barr and and Mr. Crawford Buchanan have gamely joined hands with the dummy in their midst. Call her Edwina Sophie Gandolph. I see her head nodding under its large veiled hat and cannot blame even a stuffed lump for losing interest at this point.

Then I see the figure jerk. Perhaps in the heat of the séance Miss Temple (or more likely Mr. Crawford Buchanan, the cowardly weasel) is wringing the gloved hand. No one notices the dummy dance, however, and no one notices when the slumped figures straightens and the head turns slightly from right to left, as if by itself.

Oh, come on! We are talking a literal sit-in here. So much fiberfill and fabric.

Still . . . I hear a disembodied voice drift through the chamber and then up to my perch.

"Son," it breathes, whispers, sighs.

Son. Okay. Midnight Louie is bursting with theories to explain the inexplicable. Maybe Gandolph's late mother, the bilked patroness of spirit mediums, has finally been rewarded with a genuine manifestation from the Afterlife: herself. Or maybe Houdini's mater familias has found an empty body into which to pour her frustration with the many failed attempts to reach her darling boy. Or— hey!—maybe this animated piece of stocking stuffing is really Mrs. Bates of *Psycho* fame. Maybe our gathered psychics are more psycho than anyone thought.

Only now do the Others start agitating.

What Others, you ask? I wish I did not have an answer, but I cannot deny the testimony of my own eyes.

For the seated figure draped in cloak and hat, who might be Orson Welles late in life, or Gandolph in his Edwina disguise or something entirely different, sweeps closer to the chamber, like a slide that is brought into nearer focus. And Doyly has crowded near one of the etched windows to watch the Houdini image shed his chains, each muscle straining to shrug off the bonds link by link.

"Yes," Doyly says, taking the pipe from his mustached mouth. "I knew you were doomed, poor fellow. Predicted it, but I always knew you possessed powers you never admitted to. I always said that you were the greatest publicity agent that ever lived. Now prove that you are the greatest publicity agent that ever died. Come back."

Poor Ghost. He is so sincere that I feel a twinge of regret. Too bad that the Houdini we both watch is an image manipulated by the Mystifying Max on the haunted house's holographic system. It is, in fact, the Mystifying Max with Houdini's face superimposed. The real magic here is how a man of six-feet-three can so convincingly mimic a man of five-feet-four. The cramped and chained position aids the illusion to the point of fooling a ghost, no mean achievement, Mr. Mystifying Max! Someone said that there is a fool born every minute, but you can quote Midnight Louie: it also figures that there is a fool dying every minute, too, and the Afterlife must in time get a bit crowded with as much foolishness as can be found on earth.

Meanwhile the draped black figure hovers on the periphery like a mute member of a Greek chorus. At least some people at the séance seem to see him. What a relief! I do not like to think that I am alone in the Twilight Zone.

And now I think I know who Doyly might really be. His full name has something to do with a barbarian warrior and a desert king; at least I picture a camel lot. But even Doyly is fading now as the image of Houdini turns into smoke and mirrors.

"Son," the animated dummy calls again, in vain. "I try so hard to reach you, for so long. Forgive—"

Poor Mrs. Houdini! Her boy is the only fellow who has not deigned to show up here.

And then the flying mice come pouring down out of the rafters like, well, bats out of hell.

Hell! I would love to snag a few on the wing, but I do not snack on the job. There must be a couple hundred of the furry little gliders, but they seem like two thousand as they swoop down into the roofless chamber and bounce off the windows screeching like bad brakes.

We are talking chaos now, and I notice that the cameraman has gone a little batty, swinging his powerful light into the oncoming bats, at the still air-borne weapons. I expect we will soon have minced bat pie, but the Mystifying Max hastens to anchor the edged weapons so the bats are flopping around solo. Their built-in sonar soon guides them out of the nest of humans and things less-than. As I watch the distant figure of the hatted man comes closer to the chamber, hanging on every word Wayne says and nodding. As I watch I wonder if Gandolph knew that his Edwina Mayfair costume so resembled the huge, dignified, black-draped figure of Orson Welles late in life, or if Gandolph ever knew that he shared his house with a ghost who felt a protective urge for his successor.

And I also wonder something else, as I—and I alone—see the fabric figure of Edwina Sophie Gandolph deflate like an exhausted balloon with every word Wayne Tracey spits out.

A son was asked to forgive. Perhaps others were implicitly asked to forgive a son.

It occurs to me that there might be one other candidate for the brief possession of Sophie the soft-sculpture's passive body: Wayne Tracey's dead mother, the debunked medium, both taking revenge upon the now-dead Gandolph by taking control of the figure that represents him and encouraging her son to purge himself of the hatred that infects the living.

The dead, it strikes me from what I have seen of them here and that is more than enough for me, have had enough of hatred.

Midnight Louie Encounters Pharaoh Moans

Although I have often had to put up with insults to my decedent antecedents, like many peace-loving individuals I have never had a good answer to the yahoos who bring up my crooked family tree.

Now I do.

I can now direct these low-lives to bow down and take a good look at my roots.

Not everybody is directly descended from foreign royalty, but my recent experiences amongst the ESP set have made it plain that royal blood pumps through my veins. I will not let it go to my head, though—the fact that I am Somebody, that is. I will definitely let the royal blood keep rushing right to my head, where it belongs, in my brain. There is no brain-drain in Midnight Louie.

I must admit that I have not been totally candid about the manifestations at the last séance. It seems that I have forgotten an important fact. With Kahlúa on the premises with me, we have the requisite two blacks to form a feline power nexus. And Kahlúa and I add up to a formidable pair of blacks.

laws, he might actually draw on some sort of cumulative psychic skill.

In the end, Houdini's skepticism won out over his emotional needs. Despite his extreme desire to remain connected in death to the mother he had literally adored in life, he left behind the means to debunk any who would falsely claim Houdini had been drawn back from death to perform at various séances. Such claims were often made and never proven.

The magician's personality is even more intriguing than the feats he performs. (And may explain why so few are women.) As Edmund Wilson pointed out, the mythic role of magician combines function of the criminal, the actor and the priest. I would add to that roste the role of detective, for the magician concocts tricks and alway has the means to explain them to the larger community. Few la bare their own machinations, but many have turned investigato like Gandolph, to reveal the shoddy hoaxes of spiritualists wh want to defraud as well as to deceive.

Criminal, actor, detective, priest. Which of these four roles w prove the key to the Mystifying Max's character? Only time (a perhaps Temple) will tell.

As the human spirits fade, I retreat to Kahlúa's cage to congratulate her on a fine performance. The lady sits upright in her container, still as a statue, her satin coat raised against the grain as if by static electricity.

Her green eyes outglow the blood-rubies on her collar, and she hisses like a fire hose when she sees me.

"You have erred, Midnight Louie," she announces in a hollow voice.

"Ditch the spook act," I tell her. "You're offstage now and I am not impressionable."

"You have seen truly, but you have concluded falsely. She Who Lays Before Pharaoh is indeed a forebear—"

"What are you talking about? The only Pharaoh I know hangs out at the Oasis."

"You have been allowed to see the ancient past of our Kind, but you will not be suffered to misinterpret it: I repeat, your forebear was female. You descend from the Kind by the maternal, not the paternal line. As you would bear the blessing of Bastet, remember this."

Bast! I gulp, watching the emerald fire fade in Kahlúa's eyes.

She blinks and yawns engagingly. "I must have catnapped. Did I miss any fireworks?"

"Not a thing," I tell her, taking the scaffolding down as fast as I can.

I have heard it on good authority. My great-great-great et cetera grandmother was King Tut's bodyguard. I wonder if she wore a small ceremonial beard on the job? I do not wonder if I will ever pass on this genealogical tidbit to Midnight Louise. She already has too high an opinion of herself.

As for myself, I have always lived by a strict moral code, and now also will follow the statutes of Bast, which were written down about the time that Hammurabi was entering law school. There are several of these statutes, but I have not had time to memorize every one.

I believe that they go something like this:

Be kind to animals.

Be kind to humans.

Never leave a whisker unlicked (or a leaving unburied).

Walk softly and carry a big tail.

Do not walk in the rain if you can help it.

Share your favorite resting spots (i.e., every soft, high or warm place in a human domicile) with the human residents thereof on occasion.

Show evil-doers no mercy.

Know how to keep a secret.

Of course, it is not easy to abide by this aristocratic noblesse oblige. I have always done it instinctively, and now that I know my antecedents, I will work harder than ever to become worthy of their precedence.

Besides, the Divine Yvette will be really impressed when she finds out.

P.S. If you're not planning any psychic journeys to ancient Egypt, you can reach Midnight Louie at the other end of the spectrum (in Cyberspace) at his (and my) homepage:

http://www.catwriter.com/cdouglas

—CND

Carole Nelson Douglas Mulls Black Magic

Now that Midnight Louie has discovered that his ancestors have held such exalted positions as Pharaoh's footstool, he'll be even harder to put in his proper place. Perhaps I can convince him that *author*'s footstool is the modern equivalent of the ancient role, but I doubt it. It's pretty hard to pull any wool over a cat's eyes, yet those beautiful features—particularly the vertical irises—have also been the source of much cruel superstition about cats.

Superstition surrounds spiritualism, too, and people are as easily misinformed and misled. Arthur Conan Doyle, a doctor by training and the creator of the world's most prominent scientific detective in Sherlock Holmes, later in life became a stout believer communication with the dead. He was fascinated by Harry Hdini both as the ultimate self-promoter and as a magician, insis that Houdini's astounding feats of escapism had to rely on d terialization. Houdini roundly resisted attributions of paran powers. In a superstitious corner of his magician's heart, th he sometimes wondered if, by repeatedly defying apparent p